AVENGER

BOUDICA'S LEGACY

Book 2

BY

ALLAN FOX

ISBN-13:978-1539897095
ISBN-10:1539897095

DEDICATION

To my grandchildren; Jessica, Samuel, Robert, Natalie and Lily.

CONTENTS

ACKNOWLEDGMENTS

As with my first book, many family members and friends have given me constant support, encouragement and advice. I wish to make particular mention of the following:

John Ward, Bourne Robinson (map design), Liz & Roy Friendship-Taylor, Helen Davison, Hannah Fox, Kate Robinson, Carole Fox, David Fernley, John Turner, Judith Turner, James Fox, Alex Fox, Anthony Davison, Phaea Cope, Mavis Bailey, Rafiq Rahim, Jane Keeley, Sandra Hall, James Cope, David Mitchell, David Keeley and last but definitely not least Derek Bailey.

LIST OF MAIN CHARACTERS

PROLOGUE

Agrippina *   Wife of Claudius
Claudius *   Emperor
Nero *   Emperor/son of Agrippina

PART 1

Burrus *   Commander of the Praetorian Guard
Cailan/Flavia   Daughter of Boudica
Camillus Pecius   Senior Tribune/ Legate
Cerialis (Petillius) *   Legate/ Governor of Britannia 71 AD
Decianus (Catus) *   Imperial Procurator, Britannia 60 AD
Julius Agricola *   Tribune/General/Senator
Linona/Lucia   Daughter of Boudica
Olsar   Iceni warrior/slave of Julius
Paulinus (Suetonius) *   Governor of Britannia 60 AD
Poppaea *   2nd wife of Nero
Seneca *   Senator/Adviser to Nero
Septimus   Father of Decianus
Titus Vespasianus *   Tribune/son of Vespasian

PART 2 (additional characters)

Alexus   Son of Julius Agricola
Domitia *   Wife of Julius Agricola

Faenius *	Commander of Praetorian Guard
Fausto	Estate manager for Lucius Agricola
Livia	Daughter of Julius Agricola
Lucius Agricola	Father of Julius
Octavia *	Nero's first wife
Piso *	Senator
Procilla	Julius's mother
Quintus Tiberius Saturninus	Lucia and Flavia's father
Sabinus *	Second-in-command Praetorian Guard
Sarah	Olsa's daughter
Selima	Daughter of Procilla/Lucius/ Wife of Olsar
Vespasian *	Emperor

PART 3 (additional characters)

Antonius Primus *	Legate/Commander in Vespasian Army
Bolanus (Vettius) *	Governor of Britannia 70 AD
Domitian *	Younger son of Vespasian
Josephus *	Judaean rebel leader/Historian
Miriam	Selima's older sister
Mucianus *	General/Governor of Syria/supporter of Vespasian
Vitellius *	Emperor opposing Vespasian

PART 4 (additional characters)

Alcimus Leonius	Decianus's false name
Caris	Lucia's companion
Cartimandua *	Deposed Queen of the Brigantes

Felix Pontius	Trader/horse dealer/chariot team owner
Livius	Staff officer to Julius in Britannia
Lucia	Linona's adopted Roman name
Marcus	Son of Linona/Lucia
Paulus Marellus	Nephew of Tullius Marellus
Tullius Marellus	Trader/land owner Londinium 70 AD
Venutius *	Husband of Cartimandua/leader of Brigantes revolt

* Historical characters

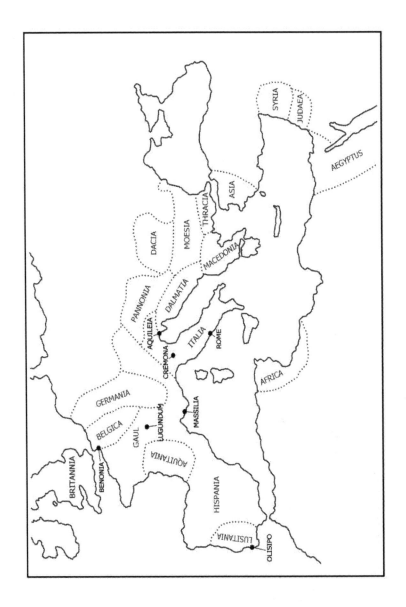

Roman Provinces 1ˢᵗ Century AD

PROLOGUE

ROME, 54 AD

"They are going to do what?"

"It's true, Claudius," said Agrippina, his wife. "The Senate have decided that when you die they will make a pronouncement that you have become a God, to be worshipped throughout the Empire."

"That's absolutely ridiculous. For most of my life I was ridiculed by them because of my slight stutter and my limp, both of which I've had since birth. Those Senators had considered me some sort of fool because of that. Now they think I'm perfect enough to be considered a God. Do they think the m-m-mighty Jupiter, King of the Gods, and Mars our glorious God of war were once mere mortals like me? Are you saying those immortals will welcome me with open arms to sit amongst them?"

"It's not what I'm saying. They are adamant that it will be done whether you're in favour or not. So, don't be an ass. Just accept that it's going to happen."

"Why are they even contemplating such a folly?"

"You forget what you've achieved as Emperor. You brought back the stability and authority of Augustus after the terrible years of Tiberius and especially Caligula, my own mad brother. You've also added four new Provinces to the Empire including conquering one of them yourself, Britannia."

"That was a big fraud. You and they know it. I only went there for a f-f-few weeks when it was virtually all over and considered safe for me to go to get all the glory. I just sat around letting the Legions finish things off for me."

"That may be so. But it's what the Senate want. They know it will be popular throughout the Empire. People will have a God they can relate to."

"If only they really knew me. Anyway, I won't give those Senators the opportunity for some years yet. Hopefully they will have forgotten about it by then."

"Nero and I won't let them forget."

"Enough of this silliness. However, since you've mentioned your son, there's something else I want to talk about. Let's be quick about it, though. I need a bath. I stink."

"That suits me fine. What is it?"

"You've brought up the matter of my d-d-death in one sense. I've been thinking about it in another. I'm having second thoughts about who will succeed me."

"What! You've already made a public declaration that it will be my Nero. I accept he's only your adopted son, but he's 16 years old, that's three years older than your own son Britannicus. You agreed when we married that as the elder he qualified to be your heir. Remember, he's the grandson of Augustus. You can't just change your mind on a whim."

"I can if I want to. But it wouldn't be a whim."

"What's possessed you then? Has it finally become a preference for your own son rather than an adopted one? That's something you said would never happen."

"Not at all. If that had been the case I wouldn't have chosen Nero in the first place."

"Then, is it because you've been listening to those Senators and other noblemen who hate Nero and myself because I'm Caligula's sister? You know they still yearn for revenge against my brother, even if it would be through me."

"Of course not. Stop panicking and guessing. Calm down and let me explain."

"What is it then?"

"I've been studying Nero more closely lately. His behaviour has been causing me growing concern."

"What do you mean?"

"Nero and Britannicus have always been friends and played well together despite their age difference. However, once Nero realised he was to become Emperor on my death, his attitude towards Britannicus changed. He began to treat him as his inferior. Lately, that has turned into physical and mental bullying."

"Britannicus has been running to you with these lies. He wants to succeed you. Nero says that he taunts him saying that he has the better claim, being the true son."

"I very much doubt that last bit, and he hasn't said a word to me about any mistreatment. The acts of bullying are what I've witnessed."

"You've been mistaken. That's not like my Nero."

"On the contrary, he is very prone to that sort of behaviour. And I fear worse."

"What do you mean by that?"

"I've seen characteristics in him that I saw and suffered with Caligula when he was a youth. If only someone had stopped him becoming Emperor then. He was Nero's uncle and, please forgive me, I see his character flaws coming out in him. If I'm right, he could be a disaster as Emperor, as your brother was."

"I can't accept your decision."

"I haven't made one yet. I'm still thinking about it."

"Have you discussed this with anybody else? Which Senators have you spoken to?"

"I haven't said a word to anybody and won't do until and if I decide to change things. It is my decision alone. I'm not in any rush. I assure you I will tell you first."

"Go and have your bath. You do stink!"

*

"We have to act quickly."

"About what exactly, Mother?" asked Nero.

"That old fool is about to make Britannicus his heir instead of you."

"He can't! He mustn't! You have to stop him, Mother. Please!" Nero began to stomp around the room in a mixture of panic and rage. "I'll kill that little swine, Britannicus. He's always hated me and looked down on me."

"Calm yourself. I have to think."

"Please, Mother. You have to stop it," pleaded Nero. He grabbed hold of her loose gown in desperation and began to cry. She contemptuously knocked his hand free.

"I said control yourself. You're behaving like a little girl."

"If you don't do anything the answer will be simple. I will just kill Britannicus."

"And everybody will be convinced it was with my help, especially Claudius after what he has just told me. You and I wouldn't last a day. Claudius loves that boy. He would have us both crucified."

"What then? I can't stand this. I think I'm going to faint."

"Shut up, and less of the drama. Save that for your performances in the theatre. Just keep quiet and prepare to become Emperor very soon."

*

"What happened?" a concerned Agrippina asked the surgeons surrounding Claudius's bed. He lay unconscious, his arms folded across his chest.

"As you know, I've been away all day visiting friends. I arrive back this evening to find my husband unwell. What are you doing for him?"

"He's more than unwell. He's fading fast. There's nothing we can do."

Looking shocked, she grabbed the senior surgeon's arm.

"What! That can't be."

"I'm afraid it is. He won't last the night."

Agrippina moved close to the surgeon, fixing him with a cold stare.

"What's caused this to happen so suddenly?"

"We've all agreed on that. He's quite old. It must be his heart. It appears to be failing very rapidly."

"If what you say is true, then there's no need for you to remain. Please leave me alone with him."

The room emptied rapidly.

"So, you old fool. You thought you would deny my son what is rightfully ours. After all these years of waiting to take over from you, did you think I would allow you to thwart me? You're a bigger fool than I believed."

She leant close and whispered in his ear.

"I could just take this pillow and end it now. But, no. I prefer to let you suffer a few more hours for wishing to betray me. Goodnight, my love. That's the last time I shall have to say that, thank goodness. By the way, I hope you enjoyed your last meal."

She walked with a light step the short distance to her son's room.

"It's done, Emperor Nero! Your loving father is dead, give or take a few hours."

"The Gods have blessed us," an astonished but ecstatic Nero cried.

"The Gods with a little help from me, of course."

"Why, what have you done?"

"There's no need for you to know that."

"What do we do now, Mother? You've said before that there are those who would see me dead before I became Emperor rather than Britannicus."

He began to tremble at the possibility of what might happen.

"They would have to get through me first. Besides, we are going to the Senate first thing in the morning to instruct them to declare you Emperor, in accordance with the wishes of the soon to be created God."

They both had a little snigger at that last comment.

"But what is to happen with Britannicus?" asked Nero. "He and his supporters could still be a problem in the future."

"Don't you worry yourself about him. I suspect he may be suffering from the same heart defect as his father only much earlier in his life."

"I owe you so much, Mother."

"And don't you forget it. We shall rule together as joint Emperors, in fact if not in name. Together we'll rule the Empire with the strength that it needs. It's been lacking for years while that idiot ruled."

"You have my word on it, Mother."

"Indeed I do. Now I must go to the kitchen. There's a particular female slave in charge of food preparation who I need to deal with. She's been causing me some concern all day while I've been away."

PART I

TIME OF RECKONING

60 AD

Chapter 1

The light shone into Catus Decianus's eyes with a bright fierceness. He was reminded that the strength of the sun and the almost unbearable heat it produced was something that he'd rarely if ever experienced during all his time in Britannia. No wonder the Brits were a sullen, miserable people, he thought, forever complaining about the weather and how difficult it made their task of growing crops and raising animals.

He thanked the Gods that he'd managed to escape from the disaster which Boudica and her Iceni tribe were bringing to that Province. Even at this moment Governor Suetonius Paulinus and his army had probably been annihilated by her vast horde. Emperor Nero must be told of how this disaster had occurred, but not without including an explanation of his own part in trying to prevent it.

However, before he did so, he'd decided to make a slight detour on his seemingly endless journey to Rome. His father's estate lay in the lush farming lands through which the main broad road made its unerring way from the north to the mighty, ever-growing city. It was less than half a day's ride to his journey's end. It would give him time to rest, seek his father's advice and reflect on what he would say in his report. His future, even his life, would be determined by how carefully he told of the events in that accursed land.

His father, Septimus, had been for many years the tutor of the young Nero, before he became Emperor. Afterwards he continued to be valued by him and became for a time one of his closest advisers before his fairly recent retirement to his estate. As a result, a strong bond had grown between them. Decianus was hoping that this still remained and that his father was still one of the few men that the increasingly erratic and unstable Nero trusted and respected.

His own imminent meeting with Nero would be fraught with danger. If things turned out as he expected, and at best that would be a loss of some Legions and a major part of the territory of Britannia, then scapegoats would be sought. He was determined not to be one of them. This day, talking it over with the wily old fox that was his father, would prove to be crucial to his well-being. In no way would it be wasted time.

Similar thoughts to these had been present with him throughout his long journey through Gaul. Nevertheless, they were being brought into sharp focus as he approached the main gates to the family estate, riding ahead of a small cart and an escort of eight legionaries. Beyond the gates a short road led to the awe-inspiring estate villa. The dark red of the tiles on the roof contrasted vividly with the stark white of the painted walls of the three-winged, single-storeyed building. The two side wings reached out towards Decianus and his small group like two welcoming arms as they approached the main entrance in the centre of the building.

Decianus raised his arm, bringing his party to a halt. He dismounted from his horse, which looked as weary as he felt. Stepping back, he addressed his men.

"Rest here. I'll arrange with the estate manager for you all to be taken care of. We shall only be staying here for one night. I'll expect you all to be ready to leave early tomorrow morning. It will be our final day and when we enter the city I want you all to appear worthy of being my escort."

*

The welcome he received from Septimus was as he'd expected. Formal but with some warmth, it was just how a tutor might normally greet a cherished pupil rather than an only son. Like father like son, Decianus didn't give it too much thought. He was here for advice and not affection. An initial few words of welcome were quickly ended, Decianus speeding off to bathe, enjoy light refreshments and take a short rest.

*

"So! You've had chance to rest," Septimus commented later when the two men sat down to talk. "Perhaps you can tell me what has prompted this most unexpected visit."

Seated in the large garden immediately behind the central wing of the villa, they were enjoying the balmy evening air in the reducing light of a fast-approaching magnificent golden sunset. They were also being kept warm by the large pitcher of Septimus's favourite and most expensive wine.

"It's not good news, I'm afraid."

"Then let me top up my wine before you begin to burden me with it."

Decianus gave a little smile, not one of amusement, but one of resignation. He was expecting a cautious rather than facetious response. He proceeded to tell the full story of Boudica's rebellion as he'd experienced it, and as he wished it to be told. Full stress was given to the foreseeable problems which had been very likely to arise from Governor Paulinus's ambitious need to seek fame and military glory. His own role as Imperial Procurator, levying and collecting the Province's taxes for the Emperor, had been hampered and thwarted by Paulinus. The task had been difficult enough without his undue interference.

He decided to leave out his own unfortunate confrontation with Boudica. Her intransigence had ended in her outright refusal to obey the law. Refusing to hand over to him that which was rightly the Emperor's, had led to her flogging in front of her tribe. He felt his father wouldn't understand the necessity for his actions at that time. It would only confuse him. That would certainly be true of the punitive treatment of her two daughters which had also proved necessary at the same time. He wouldn't appreciate the finer point of ridding the two young princesses of their maidenhood in front of their people to warn them all of the terrible consequences of defying Rome.

He ended his tale by explaining how his brave attempts at preventing a rebellion, by taking the two princesses hostage, had come to naught. The rebellion had started because of the reckless absence of most of the army, away on one of Paulinus's adventures.

"In conclusion, therefore. I was left with no choice but to escape while I was still able, rescuing what I could of the Emperor's gold. When I first got to Gaul I discovered that I'd acted just in time. I learnt from legionaries based there that soon after my escape the one remaining Legion had already been ambushed, virtually wiped out, and Camulodunum was about to fall. I haven't received any other news on my way here. I now intend to give this account of events to Nero tomorrow."

"I see."

"I thought it would be useful if you could guide me on how best to do that. You must know him better than almost any other person still alive. There were rumours in Britannia of a growing change in his behaviour, if you get my meaning."

"What exactly have you heard? You can tell me, but I strongly advise you not to repeat any such rumours to anybody else, friend or foe."

"The rumours suggest that he's increasingly becoming more like those previous madmen, Emperors Tiberius and particularly Caligula, in his self-indulgent and cruel behaviour. He's said to be less and less like his uncle Claudius before him."

"Is there anything specifically mentioned in this gossip."

"Indeed. It's about the death of his mother, Agrippina, or should I say her murder last year."

"What's said about it?"

"That she didn't commit suicide as we are led to believe but that she was murdered by Nero himself in a mad fit of rage. What's your opinion?"

"It's not a matter of my opinion as to what might have happened. I know exactly what he did."

"Will you tell me? It could prove important in my dealings with him."

"Reluctantly, I feel I have to. You're in considerable danger for just being involved in what may turn out to be a catastrophe in Britannia. However, there is the added complication for you that Nero knows that I'm aware of what really happened to Agrippina and why. Because you are my son he may assume that I've told you. Therefore you may be in additional peril because of that."

"I agree. I really need to know what happened."

Septimus began by reminding Decianus of the common knowledge about mother and son.

"She was an evil, ambitious woman. She thought she could rule the Empire through her son when Claudius died suddenly and he became Emperor.

"It's an old rumour that she poisoned Claudius because he was having second thoughts about the fact that he'd nominated Nero to succeed him. Do you know that to be true?"

"I've resisted telling you about these things in the past. Perhaps the time has come to reveal all I know. Yes! It's true. She did just that. How do I know? Because Nero told me in confidence, during one of his many wild, drunken rages about his mother."

"Are there others that she's murdered?"

"Yes. Those that she perceived to be a serious threat to her son and herself."

"How did things get to such a point that he decided she had to die?"

"It's only six years since he became Emperor, but after just a few of those years he began to realise the power he had. He began to resent and then ignore her interference in his decision making. Increasingly he was relying on the advice of others he trusted. They included Seneca, who you know well, since he's another and perhaps the most influential of his former tutors. Then there was Burrus, who you haven't met. He's the commander of the Emperor's Praetorian Guard. And there was myself. She resented our influence over the young Emperor. They were dangerous times for the three of us."

"You mean you were careful what you ate."

They both laughed at this, relieving a little of the tension that had been building.

"However, even she wasn't prepared to take on the three of us."

"Safety in numbers, I suppose. But why did he decide to murder her?"

"The beginning of the end for her came when he fell in love with Poppaea. She's a woman of outstanding beauty. Unfortunately for him she was already married and very much in love with her husband, Marcus Otho. Nero was, and still is for that matter, married to Octavia, who was a great friend of Nero's mother Agrippina. She very quickly and publicly showed her disapproval of any steps her son was thinking of making to satisfy his desires. No doubt she could see that Poppaea was a strong, forceful woman who could eventually replace her at her son's side."

"Complicated!"

"Not for a young man who was coming to realise that there are no limits to his power, or that there wasn't anybody strong enough to resist him."

"So! What happened?"

"Nero stopped her from playing any role in government, making that clear to the Senate and others. Not only that, he took Poppaea as his mistress. She quite willingly accepted the role because of the power it gave her. But she did so only if her husband Otho was allowed to live. Nero solved that by packing him off as Governor of the Province of Lusitania."

"Neat! Why then did he still decide to kill his own mother if she no longer had a part to play? She was out of the way and he had the woman he wanted."

"This is where the madness really begins to appear. Until then he was becoming increasingly suspicious of everybody, imagining plots were being hatched to overthrow him. He convinced himself that she was behind them."

"Any truth in his fears?"

"Not that we were aware of."

"Then, presumably, he decided to act. How did he arrange it?"

"With the help of Seneca, and Burrus, since he was the commander of the Praetorian Guard, and very reluctantly, myself."

"YOU?"

"Yes! I was still one of his main advisers. He told us of his certainty of a plot to assassinate him, led by her. He commanded that we find a way to remove her before she got to him. It was as simple as that."

"What did you say? What did you do?"

"What could we say or do? When the three of us were alone I spoke against it but had no idea how we could refuse and live. The other two convinced me we had to act to save Nero's life. We decided to leave the arrangements to Burrus. He quite liked the idea."

"Did it take long?"

"Not really, although things went wrong at first."

"In what way?"

"We told Nero we knew of her intended visit to an offshore island to see an old friend. Burrus would have her shipwrecked and drowned. No blame could possibly be levelled against her son for such an act of the Gods. He was delighted, almost drooling at the thought that he would finally be rid of her."

"She didn't die that way, did she?"

"Unfortunately, no. We heard the witch was the only survivor, swimming quite a distance to the nearest shore to be rescued."

"Unbelievable!"

"Quite. And very inconvenient."

"What did you do then?"

"We acted quickly. Nero was in a state of extreme panic, a mixture of rage at our failure and terror that she would know he was involved and seek revenge."

"He's very weak and immature still, then."

"True. But very dangerous qualities for us all in an Emperor. He insisted we act quickly, regardless of how it looked. Burrus sent three men. They forced poison down her and made it look like suicide. Ironic, don't you think?"

"He owes you a great deal. Even he must have been grateful. Why did you retire so soon after those events?"

"It wasn't my choice. He learnt, probably from Burrus, that at the beginning I hadn't been fully in favour of her assassination. With Nero you are either 100% with him or you are against him. I thought I was going to die. He was probably considering it but chose to retire me instead."

"You were very close to him once. Wouldn't that have counted for something?"

"Perhaps. Nevertheless, he decided I needed to spend more time on my estate."

"Was there anything else that saved you?"

"I think Seneca will have played a part. In the absence of his mother, Nero still uses him as his main confidant. While he was hesitating about what to do with me, Seneca would have reminded him of my total loyalty to him over many years."

"You owe a debt to Seneca if that's the case."

"I do, and I've started to repay it by taking a risk in giving a warning to Seneca if he hasn't already thought of it. When Poppaea finally agrees to marry Nero he will have a new legitimate advisor. She's a formidable woman. His days then may well be numbered. I hope he leaves with his life."

"Do you really think he would be in such danger after all he's done for him?"

"I've reminded him that Nero's uncle through his mother's line was Caligula. I fear his madness is beginning to descend onto his nephew. If that is so, none of us are safe."

Septimus was the first to break the short silence which followed.

"So now you know it all. Let's hope that your understanding about the recent events involving myself and Nero will be beneficial when you meet him tomorrow. He may try to tease out whether you know about what really happened to his mother. It's your decision whether or not to admit what you know depending on whether you are forced to in order to save yourself."

"I agree."

"I'm pleased you came to see me first. It certainly wouldn't have aided the case for your lack of blame for Britannia if you'd mistakenly gone in there thinking you could draw on my 'wonderful' working relationship with him. Your situation is hazardous enough already."

"Thank you for your openness. It couldn't have been easy for you to confess to such a crime."

"Crime or service to the Empire? Only time will tell. That's enough for this evening. I think you should get some sleep, if you're to be at your best for tomorrow."

*

Decianus lay on his bed, his thoughts churning over the story he'd been told. He wasn't a stranger to, or averse to becoming involved in intrigue, as recent events in Britannia showed. In this instance, though, he must be careful. If necessary, he may need to distance himself from his father and the difficult situation he was in. He wouldn't admit to knowing anything of the events described that evening. He would make sure Nero was left with an understanding that he was a man to be relied upon to always provide unquestioning, utterly ruthless loyalty to his Emperor. That would be easy to demonstrate without a moment's hesitation when and if that situation arose.

His final thought before seeking sleep was that the information about Seneca and Burrus's part in the murder could prove very useful to him in the future.

Chapter 2

Since the defeat and rout of Boudica's forces there had been little opportunity for Julius Agricola to rest. Two days only for recovery from fatigue and the clearing of the battlefield had been followed by a three-day march back to Londinium. As soon as the fort had undergone initial repairs and the army re-established there, Governor Paulinus had ordered Tribunes Camillus Pecius and Julius Agricola, to take a small cavalry force to Camulodunum. They were to report back with what they found there.

The destruction suffered by Londinium had been expected by Paulinus. Most of it had been carried out by legionaries on his orders as a scorched-earth tactic to thwart Boudica, to deny her hungry followers the food and booty they expected. Camulodunum, however, had fallen victim to the full force of the hatred built up over years in the Iceni and Trinovante tribes. Reports filtering through at the time had spoken of the horrors committed in revenge against the defenders of the town.

Camillus, being a senior tribune, was to take command and decided on a cavalry troupe of 200 men. Although the enemy had been defeated and widely dispersed many miles to the south, groups of tribal warriors would be returning to their lands. Although likely to be much smaller than Camillus's troupe, they were still capable of causing trouble. It turned out to be an unnecessary precaution. The road linking the two towns had been virtually empty.

"I didn't expect to see so few Iceni making their way home," Julius observed.

"We must assume they're frightened to take to our roads," Camillus replied. "And it's not necessarily just us they fear. It's also the slavers using the roads to search for them, aiming to fill their carts with captives for the markets."

No sooner had he said this than a slaver's cart came into view on the road ahead as if to make the point for him. The cart was stationary and a great deal of activity was taking place at the rear. As the massed cavalry drew close it became clear that at the centre of the disturbance were the slave master and a young captive who was tied to the cart. The slaver was using a long heavy stick to beat the boy. He appeared to be not more than twelve or thirteen years old. Camillus manoeuvred his horse close up to the cart, which was filled with a dozen other captives. He shouted aggressively for the beating of the boy to stop. By then the youth had slumped onto the ground, broken and bleeding.

"What's going on here?" Camillus demanded.

"It's nothing to concern you, Tribune. I don't need you to help me to teach a lesson to one of these Iceni dogs."

"I'm making it my concern. Answer me!"

That had the desired effect. The flippant arrogance disappeared immediately.

"This treacherous Iceni savage tried to escape when we stopped here to attend to the horses. As I said, I'm teaching a lesson to this one and the rest of my cargo."

Julius had already dismounted and was examining the boy on the ground. He looked up at Camillus, still on his horse.

"This youngster won't learn anything. He just died."

Camillus lowered his head, pausing for a moment. Then he raised it and stared at the master slaver who, wilting slightly under his penetrating glare, threw his stick away before speaking nervously.

"Ah well. That's probably the best warning I could have given to these scum. It will have cost me money, but it might just save me a lot more. There will be plenty others where he came from."

Camillus jumped from his horse. The startled slaver stepped back a pace or two.

"I have a lesson of my own to teach before I move on," said Camillus, turning to face his men. "The life of a child has just been taken in front of our eyes by this Roman. We all know that a Roman citizen cannot be held to account for killing a slave who he owns. Therefore, as much as I'm tempted to, I can't punish the deed we've just witnessed. However, I think this man would benefit from a better understanding of the subtle art of chastising a wayward slave."

He moved to speak directly to the slaver.

"You need to experience what it feels like to receive a beating such as the one you've just given to that poor wretch. It will enlighten you. Hopefully, you will be able to carry out your role of slave master, with greater wisdom in the future."

Four cavalrymen were quickly delegated to the task, one which they appeared to relish. They used the same stick. It didn't take very long, enabling the tribunes and cavalrymen to continue their journey.

"You have the ability to surprise me, Camillus," Julius said. "I didn't expect such a strong reaction from you at what we witnessed. Don't get me wrong. I support what you did. I wish I'd thought of it. What made you do it?"

"Not many days ago that boy and those others in the cart were our enemy. Today, they're our responsibility. Besides, I have a son who is of a similar age. I haven't seen him in a long time."

Julius gave a thoughtful nod of his head. Few words were said after that until they neared the end of their journey.

*

They began to get warning of the horrors they were about to see before they reached the ruins of the town. All those in the troupe of horsemen were experienced in battle and would have smelt death before. Many days had passed since the slaughter of the Roman citizens who had tried in vain to resist the wave of terror. Afterwards, those responsible had marched on to their next objective, Verulamium. They'd done so in such eager anticipation of another victory and more spoils that the dead had been left to lie where they had fallen.

The riders halted just short of the devastation. In front of them, small groups of those who'd survived and returned had begun the process of disposing of bodies. The scale of the task they faced hadn't yet overwhelmed them but it would inevitably do so if they received no help.

"I think it's obvious what our first duty has to be, Camillus," Julius suggested.

"Yes it is. Deploy the men while I try to find someone who is prepared to assume some responsibility for the town until the army returns. It may have happened already but I doubt it."

Later that evening, sheltering as best they could from the cold and the occasional shower, the two tribunes were reflecting on the events of the day. It would help them to decide what still needed to be done before they could return with their report describing what they had found.

"I've experienced a few bad days in my short military career but I think this must be the worst," said Julius.

"It ranks up there with some of those I wish I could forget, but never will. Don't you ever forget this one either, my friend. I take it this is the first time you've seen such an overwhelming number of ordinary Romans, many of them women and children, slaughtered and mutilated by an enemy."

"That's what is so devastating. Men die in battle, sometimes not easily. But that is a glorious death. This was anything but that."

"This is the other side of war, Julius. Young men like you seek the glamour and glory of leading others into war. The deaths we witness on the battlefield don't necessarily lessen the feeling of rapture that men like you and I experience in victory."

"That slaver was not the only one to have been taught a lesson today, Camillus."

"How do you think Paulinus will react to what we describe? As one of his staff officers you have got to know him better than most of the rest of us."

"He'll want to come to see for himself. He's already bent on re-establishing his authority throughout the Province. This will only add to his need to set an example and take revenge. He's not a forgiving man, as some of the Brits are about to find out."

Chapter 3

"Gentlemen! The last few weeks have passed us by very quickly since we resolved our little problem with good Queen Boudica. By the way, has anybody seen her recently?"

Governor Suetonius Paulinus was greeting his senior military commanders, about twelve in all. He'd called them together to reflect on the situation he and his army were facing, the reconstruction and rebuilding of those towns which had been destroyed. His remarks were received with some amusement but no comments. The sudden calling of the meeting had placed everybody on their guard.

"Before I begin to explain the main reason why I've brought you together, I have another matter to bring to your attention. We lost a large number of our people because of that woman."

"Not nearly as many as she did."

The interruption, uttered by one of the more confident Legates, was met with loud laughter. An unsmiling Paulinus continued.

"I remind you that two of my staff officers died fighting while carrying out my orders during the height of the final battle."

Any remaining smiles, lingering from the previous joking comment, quickly disappeared.

"I've decided to act quickly by filling one of those vacancies with Tribune Titus Vespasianus, until yesterday a tribune with the 9th Legion. Although he was unable to take part in our final battle, he fought courageously when the 9th was ambushed by Boudica at the very beginning of her march of terror. It was because of Titus's efforts in that debacle that many brave men were able to survive the treachery by the Iceni."

Foot stamping and cheers of approval were aimed at the tall young man, who showed his gratitude by standing straight and puffing out his armour-clad, broad chest. Paulinus brought the applause to an end with a raise of his hand.

"Let us get back to the business in hand," he began, his expression a fierce grimace, his eyes staring coldly at his audience. "The devastation we see all around us here in Londinium is repeated in Camulodunum and Verulamium. I've seen some of it with my own eyes during my tour of some of the badly affected parts of the Province during the last few days. During that time our legionaries have had chance to recover. They've rested long enough. We need to get these men busy again or they will become bored and start to be mischievous.

"We shall begin by creating a new magnificent Governor's palace and other administration buildings here in Londinium to replace those destroyed in Camulodunum. They will be paid for with the money and treasure that we are currently gathering from our defeated enemy. It will demonstrate that Londinium is now to be the new capital of this Province."

"What will become of Camulodunum?" asked Julius Agricola. Having been based there since his arrival in the Province the previous year, he had a particular interest in its future.

"It will be restored but not to the size it once was. Only Romans will be allowed to own and farm land for miles around the town. The Trinovante and Iceni tribes will be kept to a mere shadow of what they once were. It will be a symbol and a reminder to the remainder of those followers of Boudica, and indeed other tribes throughout the Province, of the consequences of daring to defy Rome. Of course, that depends on whether I choose to allow any of that woman's tribe to return and live in those lands. They will make very good slaves, I am told."

Again, there was a display of partially controlled amusement among those present. But not in the case of Julius Agricola.

"With great respect, Sir, we need to give more thought to this problem. To deny them a return to their lands would be a mistake. Before the war they were a productive people making a valuable contribution to the Province's economy. They could be taught to do so again."

Paulinus glared at Julius, and a deathly quiet descended as everybody held their breath.

"Enough of that for now, Julius. You are distracting me. I will make a final decision on that matter at a later date."

It wasn't only Julius who released a quiet sigh of relief.

"I'm getting tired of living in make-do accommodation," Paulinus continued. "Start the rebuilding immediately. The rich merchants of this place will dig up their buried treasure and follow our example, competing with each other to be amongst the first to re-establish their businesses and make the most profit out of us. Any questions?"

There followed a brief discussion that established the division of responsibilities and tasks between the two Legions based outside the town. The discussion was brought to an end by an impatient Paulinus.

"I think we've all said enough. All is agreed then. However, before we break up there's one other matter."

Anxious faces amongst some of them suggested that they could be anticipating what was to follow.

"Immediately after our defeat of Boudica, I despatched an initial report to Emperor Nero describing our glorious victory. I pointed out that the triumph was his and it was on a par with that of his uncle Claudius when he first conquered these Brits sixteen years ago. A bit of flattery never goes amiss."

This caused more than a few smiles of satisfaction. They were to be short-lived.

"However, he will demand more than that initial glowing account later. I'm sure he will order me to give a fuller report on the circumstances that led to what we all know was a close-run thing. Therefore, I will be reviewing with each one of you, and others not present today, what part you played and where blame, if any, lies."

Paulinus paused, letting his words take effect. The exchange of worried expressions on the faces of his subordinates contrasted with the slight grin of satisfaction on his.

"That is all, gentlemen."

As they began to leave the room, Paulinus stared at Julius, catching his attention. He shook his head and Julius correctly took it to mean he wanted him to stay behind.

"I asked you to remain, Julius, because you disappointed, even angered me with your remarks about those unworthy Iceni rebels. They very nearly destroyed everything we've been working for with their hatred and barbarism. My previous regard for you saved you from humiliation in front of your fellow officers. Explain yourself."

"I apologise if I appeared in some way to be disrespectful to you, Sir, by appearing to be favouring the Iceni or to be beginning to excuse what they did."

"That's what it looked and sounded like. Regardless of your motive it was regrettable in front of all my staff."

"I lost many of my friends and fellow soldiers as a result of what they did," Julius countered. "I hated and despised what Boudica was trying to achieve, especially the barbarism which occurred in the Camulodunum massacre. I have no wish to defend them in any way."

"Then what was the purpose in your outburst?"

"I believe what I said. I think there needs to be more thought given to what good we want to come out of this disastrous experience. I regret my timing in making this point to you in that meeting was not the best."

"Indeed! And your choice of words, repeated now – 'more thought needs to be given to this problem' – was undoubtedly aimed at me. It wasn't one of your cleverest statements. Nevertheless, I take note of your comments. We shall discuss this subject again later, when I have less anger in me. You can go to join the others."

"Yes, Sir."

"One other thing before you leave, though, while I remember. I see you've taken one of Boudica's best warriors as a slave. I remember him as that arrogant, disrespectful young savage who escorted us on our earlier visit to meet her and her tribe. What was his name?"

"Olsar."

"Yes! I remember. I've been told that you rescued him from the battlefield having overcome and wounded him. Unusual in the circumstances. I also hear that you've been active in seeing he recovers from his wounds. All this, together with your actions today, is beginning to lead me to believe you are becoming too attached and respectful of these Iceni."

Julius was about to respond but was waved away by Paulinus, preventing any further words being spoken.

Outside, a small group had gathered to give a more personal welcome to Tribune Titus. Julius joined them just as the others finished. The group broke up, leaving the two young tribunes alone.

"My name is Julius Agricola. I'd like to join the rest in welcoming you, Titus. Like everybody else, I wish to hear first-hand about the action in your fight with Boudica."

"Likewise, Julius, although I already know of some of the significant part you played in trying to restrain her and prevent the rebellion. In fact, I was there when you came to warn my Legion of what was happening, and to ask our Legate to be ready to help defend Camulodunum. Obviously, we weren't introduced at that time."

"A lot of good that did, asking him to protect the town. He led the 9th into an ambush."

"Don't judge him too harshly until you hear his reasoning for what he did. I supported him."

"I admire your loyalty to your commander. I think we shall get along just fine serving Paulinus together."

"You stuck your neck out there with him in the meeting, didn't you? I admired your frankness, if not your wisdom, in giving your views about the future treatment of the Iceni. I thought he was going to eat you alive there and then."

"He very nearly did so after you all left."

"I detected you have a grudging respect for that tribe. I do also. They fought bravely against us. But it's not only that. I was protecting our chaotic retreat as our men tried to escape the ambush. I saw Boudica, with her daughter at her side, call off her warriors when they could have slain many more of us. I decided she was interested in defeating us, not massacring us."

"You say you saw Boudica and her daughter. Would you recognise them if you saw them again?"

"Not really, apart from the mother's red hair. They were too far off. Why do you want to know?"

"They weren't found after the battle. Paulinus would love to catch either or both of them."

"To pack them off to Nero, no doubt. May the Gods help them if that happens."

"As I've just said, I think you and I are going to get along very well together."

The two men grasped each other's arms, and exchanged nods, before going their separate ways.

On his way back to his quarters, Julius called into the medical area and entered the room where Olsar was still receiving treatment for his wounds.

"How are you today?" Julius asked.

"I shall soon have recovered enough to walk out of here unaided," Olsar replied. "I have you and your surgeons to thank for that."

"Don't be too grateful. Remember you are now my slave. To the victor come the spoils. I shall expect total obedience," Julius said, the smile on his face denying the harshness of his words.

"And you shall have it — for the time being."

Olar's show of defiance was to be expected by Julius. He would behave in just the same way if the roles were reversed.

"You will have to control your tongue and obvious defiance, especially in the difficult times ahead if you're to survive. There's a great deal of hatred for what Boudica and her supporters have done."

"The feeling is mutual."

"There you go again! I see we shall have to talk a lot more about your attitude."

"So be it."

*

Julius finally reached his quarters and the relative seclusion provided there. He began to go over in his mind the events leading to the war and his role in it. This last conversation with Paulinus had surprised him. He would need be more careful than he'd previously thought as the process of review and final judgement took place.

Chapter 4

Julius had suffered a twinge of conscience. It was approaching six weeks since the end of the war and so far he'd only sent a very quickly drafted message immediately afterwards to his parents. It told them what they needed to know at the time – he was alive and well. He'd decided he needed to write a further explanation of what had happened. His father would be particularly interested in some of the more dramatic military activities he'd been involved in. He hadn't progressed very far when a legionary entered his room.

"You wished to be told when Tribune Titus and his men returned from Isca, Sir. He's just been seen approaching the fort and will be here very shortly."

"Thank you. I shall come at once."

Julius grabbed his cloak, to try to keep out the chill wind, and headed for the central parade ground. His arrival was just in time to see a weary group of riders dismounting and handing over their horses to be taken away and cared for.

"It's good to see you back, Titus. You look as if you're in need of a hot bath and meal."

"More like a soft bed and a full day's sleep, but that's not going to happen. I must report to Paulinus straight away."

"Bad news? I can see you don't have Legate Postumus with you."

"It couldn't be any worse. I'll explain it to you later after I've been to see the Governor. I'm assuming I'll still be able to walk and talk after I've given my report."

"I hope the Gods are with you."

"So do I. Thanks anyway."

Julius was intrigued. Titus had been sent to Isca in the far southwest to bring back Legate Postumus with a military escort. Paulinus had ordered the two commanders of the 9th and 2nd Legions to report to him to explain their actions. Both of them had disobeyed his orders during the war against Boudica. Cerialis had confirmed he was due to arrive later that evening. Postumus, on the other hand, had appeared to disobey another order. Paulinus wouldn't be pleased that Titus and his men were unable to force him to attend. He hoped he wouldn't have to wait too long to discover what had happened.

*

Titus entered Julius's quarters, looked at him and blew his cheeks out, his body sagging.

"You look relieved and in need of a large drink of wine," Julius suggested. "Well! What have you told him and how's he reacted?"

"When I arrived at Isca, it was obvious Postumus had been expecting to be summoned to headquarters," Titus began. "The military escort to accompany him back was perhaps a surprise to him."

"I've met him in the past. He's a quiet, uninspiring man. My opinion was that his appointment to Legate had probably been a political one. He would make a better Senator than soldier."

"I agree. Or rather he might have done had he lived."

"I had his death as one of the possible reasons why he hadn't come back with you. What happened?"

"When we were alone, I immediately explained that, although I'd been sent with a military escort, his status meant he wouldn't be placed under arrest. However, he was to return with me without delay to give an explanation for his behaviour."

"How did he react and what was his excuse?"

"He began to rehearse his story with me. At the start of the rebellion, he said he'd received information about the size of Boudica's forces. The numbers had probably been inflated way beyond what they really were by the time they reached him. You know how rumours can exaggerate things like that. Anyway, he decided all was lost. To take his Legion to Londinium or wherever needed would only mean its destruction like the other three. He thought it was better if he stayed and kept control of the tribes in that part of the Province until the Emperor sent fresh Legions to defeat Boudica and regain control of the rest of Britannia."

"A politician's tactical decision," Julius added, "and not one of a loyal military commander. What did you say to that?"

"I told him he'd gambled and lost. He must make the best of the situation, and hope Paulinus would be sympathetic to the difficult situation he'd believed his Legion had been placed in. It might be accepted that in the end he was trying to act in the best interests of Rome."

"Not at all likely. However, more importantly, did he believe that just might be the case?"

"Not by the look of despair on his face. So he asked me what I realistically thought his fate would be."

"I can guess what you said."

"I decided to be more direct with my answers at that stage. I told him that in my view there were two possibilities. At best, Paulinus was likely to remove him from his command and return him to Rome. Nero would then decide his fate depending on whether he believed he was acting out of cowardice or loyalty to him."

"And at worst?"

"As you'd expect, he asked exactly the same question. I told him Paulinus would have him executed on the spot."

"Harsh, but most likely. Paulinus wants to show Nero he's very much in control and punishing those who made the task of putting down the rebellion harder than it needed to be."

"You know the man better than I."

"What happened then?"

"I left him alone to prepare for the ride back, perhaps a foolish choice, looking back on it. Anyway, that's what a furious Paulinus has just called it."

"Ouch!"

"Whatever! I did what I did. When I got tired of waiting I went to his private quarters. He'd made his own decision. He'd fallen on his sword."

"At least at the end he behaved with honour and like a soldier should."

"That leaves only my old commander, Cerialis, to face the inquisition tomorrow," Titus added.

"I think you should know I've been told by Paulinus that he wants me to join him in the merciless grilling he'll be giving him," Julius warned.

"That's unusual. I would have expected a Legate to be paid the courtesy of a face-to-face discussion between just the two of them. Cerialis will object to your presence."

"It will do him no good. Remember, I played a direct part in passing on Paulinus's orders for him to go to the aid of Camulodunum when the need arose."

"I can assure you Cerialis isn't the sort of man to fall on his sword, whatever the conclusion is," Titus added. "I've known him a long time. Did you know he's the brother-in-law of my father, Vespasian, who was also a Legate in Britannia at one time?"

Julius shook his head, raising his eyebrows in surprise.

"By the way, that's how my father prefers to be called, if you ever meet him."

"So! Tomorrow, we shall see if you now have two 'former' Legates in your family," Julius joked.

Titus gave a very tired laugh.

"Point taken. I'm off to rest. I've had enough for one day."

*

"I thought I would check if everything was to your liking, Sir." Titus was addressing his previous commander shortly after his arrival at the fort. "Old habits die hard."

"Yes. Everything is fine in the circumstances," replied Cerialis. "Of course I would have preferred to have had the luxury of a long spell in the baths, but I see the repair work on the partially destroyed bathhouse hasn't yet been completed. Our legionaries did too good a job at laying waste this town and everything around it before Boudica arrived. Nevertheless, with the help of the slaves allocated to me while I stay here I've improvised well enough. Have you settled into your new staff position? I suppose there's barely been enough time with all that's been going on."

"Yes, Sir. I've been made to feel very welcome."

Titus paused briefly. The pleasantries over, he decided to get on with dealing with the issue which had really prompted this visit.

"I think there are a couple of matters I needed to brief you on before your meeting with Paulinus. Old loyalties also die hard."

"Let's hope so. What is it you have to tell me?"

Titus realised his previous commander was still inclined to play the old, slightly stiff and pompous superior officer. He decided to ignore it and just say what he had to say for his own peace of mind.

"Firstly, you were not meant to be the only Legate about to be judged tomorrow on your conduct and decisions during the rebellion."

"I've been told that already."

"What you don't know is that Legate Postumus won't be attending. He's committed suicide rather than face the consequences for refusing to bring his Legion to the aid of Paulinus."

"Unfortunate but understandable. He could have had no acceptable explanation for his cowardly failure to obey such a direct order and carry out his duty. What's the other thing you wished to tell me?"

"Tribune Julius Agricola will be present during your meeting."

"Unfortunate again, and quite irregular. However, any objection on my part will be destined to fall on deaf ears. Given the circumstances I don't think any opposition from me would do me any good."

"I agree, Sir."

"Still, forewarned is forearmed, as they say. I appreciate your coming to see me. Nevertheless, I think the time has come for you to concentrate on your new loyalties. After tomorrow, depending on the outcome, it may not be to your benefit to have your name still associated with mine. Paulinus is a man who demands total personal loyalty from his staff officers."

"And he shall have it, Sir. That doesn't stop me wishing you good luck tomorrow."

"Thank you, Titus."

Chapter 5

The night had been much like the others recently. A thick mist filled the dense forest where the two sisters, Linona and Cailan, were trying to keep warm. Their position was becoming increasingly desperate. They had long since lost the horses which they'd stolen to flee after the final battle. Startled by predatory cries one dark night, the horses had broken from their tethers and fled into the surrounding forest. Since then, any progress in their hazardous long journey home was going to be on foot.

Without any means to speedily avoid capture they'd decided to travel at night from then on. The Roman legionaries had long ago given up the search for survivors from Boudica's defeated forces, leaving it to the freelance slave traders. There were many of them in small, heavily armed gangs. Unarmed as the sisters were, they would have great difficulty in avoiding capture. They had begun to discuss the frightening fact that their chances of ever making it back to their homeland, many miles northeast of Londinium, were rapidly diminishing without horses.

After the final battle, they'd been relieved to have escaped almost certain death or at best slavery. They'd been optimistic that by taking a long, indirect route home they could avoid their pursuers. However, that meant they were still miles to the west of Londinium, having only recently managed to ford the large river which flowed down through that town.

Bad weather had meant they were finding it increasingly difficult to find food and to keep warm. Added to their problem of growing weakness and weariness, Linona had become sick. It meant that the task of finding food, water and shelter had begun to fall on Cailan. Not particularly strong or self-sufficient at the best of times, she was finding it almost impossible to cope. The result was that they hadn't moved from their present shelter for two days.

"We need to find food soon, Cailan," Linona whispered.

"I know that. I've done what I can. I'm finding our traps empty. The forest is providing less and less. We need to find more meat somehow."

"There's only one answer. We are going to have to raid the nearest village."

"That's too dangerous! We'll be caught for sure," Cailan argued. "The villagers in these parts are allies of the Romans. There must be something else we can do."

"There isn't. We can go in the middle of the night. Nobody will see us. Even their dogs will be asleep."

"I'm frightened, Linona."

"I know, little sister, but we don't have a choice. We won't have the strength to go on unless we can eat fully for a day or two. Starvation will be the outcome in a very short time if we go on as we are."

"How can we be sure food will be there for us to steal easily?"

"We can't."

"The villagers will have weapons and we don't. How do we even know they will all be asleep?"

"We don't! But we have to gamble on both. We can reduce the risks by watching what happens tonight. From what we discover, we can settle on a plan for the following night."

Nothing more was said for a while as the perilous situation they were in, and how they'd got there, would have filled their thoughts. Linona was the first to speak.

"We were wrong in what we did."

"What are you saying?" Cailan asked. "I don't understand."

"Our father was correct in the warnings he gave us."

"You mean against going to war against the Romans?"

"Yes. Although we were always under Roman dominance, we prospered and we lived in peace. He tried to get us to realise that for the future of our tribe we had to ensure that arrangement continued. His wisdom was seen as weakness, born out of fear, by the rest of us. In the end, all the clan leaders were eager to respond to our mother's call to war."

"It was understandable, given what they did to us and our mother, our rapes and her whipping."

"Everybody was blinded by hate, Mother and I more so than anybody else," Linona admitted. "We couldn't see what an impossible dream of freedom we had. And now, our people are mostly dead or being sold into slavery, mainly because of us."

"You can't just blame yourself," Cailan pleaded. "Everybody joined in willingly. Nobody was forced to march to fight with us."

"Our mother was a clever leader. She could have chosen some sort of resistance other than total war if she'd wished to. Maybe I could have turned her away from war if I hadn't wanted to destroy everything Roman."

"Whatever! That's the past, to be put behind us," Cailan urged. "That is, if we still have a future."

"If we can survive, I'm certain of one thing. We must never reveal our true identities to anybody. The Romans will hate and curse the name of Boudica forever. That hatred will apply to her daughters if they were ever to discover us."

"We must get back to our own people, Linona. We'll be able to disappear amongst them."

"I wish it could be so. Can't you see we will come to be hated by our own people, by the ones who survived the horrors of what befell them? They too will blame our mother for everything. If we are identified I can't see us being allowed to live."

"I never thought… What can we do?" muttered Cailan desperately.

"I don't know other than to try to stay alive at all costs. We have to live through each moment and always choose to survive."

"Please let it be together."

"It will be so, little sister. I promise you."

*

Two nights later they were taken prisoner and after another two days a slave trader paid a visit to the village where they were being held. They were bought for next to nothing. The trader argued that they were hardly likely to last very long, given the state they were in. They were loaded onto his cart to be taken on a journey to the slave markets of Londinium, twenty miles downriver from the village.

Chapter 6

The area around the Governor's temporary headquarters had been cleared for the duration of the meeting on the orders of Julius. Even the usual sentries had been removed. He'd decided it was important for the Army's morale that the content of what was about to be discussed was kept secret and not overheard.

Julius had mentally prepared himself by recalling the discussion he'd had with Cerialis in those final days before the outbreak of hostilities began. He was as keen as Paulinus to hear why, instead of going to the defence of the citizens and legionaries of Camulodunum as ordered, he'd attempted to attack the Iceni forces which were gathering in their tribal lands. By doing so, and losing half of his Legion, he'd made the destruction of Camulodunum inevitable. He was quite clear in his own mind that Cerialis was told to help contain the rebellion until Paulinus and the full army could return from Mona to restore order.

Nevertheless, he reminded himself that he was going into a very difficult meeting with two very experienced and wily superior officers. Both of them would be determined not to be considered the main culprit by Nero for the breakdown of order and the great loss of people and resources in the Province. He needed to hold his emotions in check and to try to keep his mouth shut unless spoken to. The fight was between those two and he intended it should remain so. One or possibly both would be likely to be looking for a scapegoat for the more embarrassing aspects of the campaign.

"If you're out there, Julius, come in and sit down," Paulinus shouted. "I don't seem to have any staff around at the moment to show you in. Cerialis has been summoned. He will be here shortly."

"That is as intended, Sir," Julius replied as he entered. "I felt it to be advisable that nobody hears what we have to discuss."

"I see. It's inconvenient but probably wise in the circumstances. Take this seat beside me. When we get down to the serious business let me do most of the talking. You were there during the time he took his decisions and your presence will be important if there's a need to challenge the accuracy of anything he has to say."

"I understand, Sir."

Julius felt happy and relieved that Paulinus saw his role as he did. His instincts were right also. It sounded as if he was about to be used against Cerialis.

*

"Good morning, Paulinus. You wish to discuss important matters with me."

Cerialis had spoken as he made his entrance and before he'd reached where the other two were seated. When he did reach them he stood rigidly straight with his feet slightly apart and his chest puffed out arrogantly. He'd chosen to dress for the occasion in his full battle armour, emphasising his credentials as a military commander.

Julius, despite his efforts to the contrary, allowed a slight respectful grin to appear at the corners of his mouth. This man was not here to walk meekly into the lion's den. He'd made sure he had spoken first, seeking to take some control. He'd backed that up by referring to Paulinus by his name and not his title, as a subordinate would be expected to do. And he'd dressed and presented himself as the true warrior of Rome he undoubtedly considered himself to be. Julius decided this wasn't going to be quite the uneven contest Paulinus was anticipating.

"Take a seat, Legate Cerialis. This is not intended to be a casual conversation between fellow officers. Rather you should regard it as a formal enquiry of events and behaviour which will form part of a fuller report I have to send to the Emperor. Do I make myself clear?"

The challenge had been met by Paulinus and, as expected, dealt with adequately, Julius thought. He was aware also that Cerialis had deliberately failed to even glance sideways in his direction to acknowledge his presence.

"Indeed, Governor. I note what you are saying."

"Then let us get on. I take it you remember my staff officer, Julius Agricola."

Cerialis dipped his head towards the two men opposite in turn, without any change of his stern expression. Julius returned the gesture in a similar manner.

"I thought it might be helpful to us both if Julius was available. In my absence he took an unusually active part in some of the events which will form part of my report. Irregular as that is I think you can have no objection to it."

Cerialis delayed his acceptance, probably for effect, before waving his hand to indicate no objection would be made.

Julius couldn't but admire Cerialis's coolness in the face of an interrogation which may well be career threatening, possibly worse.

Paulinus, seeing the cool defiance also, got directly to the point.

"Why did you disobey my orders?" he barked, any pretence at a calm, gentlemanly approach to finding answers disappearing immediately.

"My understanding is that I didn't."

Julius noted he hadn't ended his denial with the respectful 'Sir'. It was more evidence that this man wasn't going to be anybody's scapegoat without a fight.

"We shall see," Paulinus snorted. "Let's start at the beginning. For the purposes of today that would have been when I informed you and the other three Legates here in Britannia that I intended marching to Mona in the north to solve this druid problem once and for all. Do you accept that as an appropriate starting point?"

Paulinus raised his eyebrows briefly, seeking agreement. Getting no reaction, he continued regardless.

"You all agreed then with my decision, and accepted the necessary division of our forces so the campaign could go ahead, whilst maintaining security here in the south."

The eyebrows were raised once more and were met with the same response.

"From this point on, since you aren't responding with your acceptance or otherwise, I shall not wait for your answer. If you object to anything I say you must make it clear, otherwise I shall take your silence as agreement.

"The 14th Legion and half of the 20th were considered sufficient for Mona. It meant one and a half Legions remained to keep an eye on things here in the south and east. That included yours which was the core of that force. It was the best trained and experienced."

A weak smile spread across Cerialis's face, the first change of expression since Paulinus had begun his recap of events.

"That placed a major responsibility on you."

"I agree entirely with that assessment of my Legion and my position," Cerialis emphasised.

Julius realised he was hearing the first part of the report to the Emperor which Paulinus had already drafted in his head.

"Did you raise with me any difficulties which my absence may have presented you with?"

"I understood the pressures placed on you as Governor to be continually aware of the need to expand the boundaries and peoples of your Province, and to deal with any tribe or group that are hindering that process."

"That's not the question I asked, but we'll carry on. Were you aware at that time of the extent of the limited unrest in the Iceni and the smaller tribe of Trinovantes?"

"The answer to that question is yes. However, my own main concerns, as you well know, were with the tribes further to the northeast where my Legion is necessarily based to maintain order. Nevertheless, my spies kept me well informed as to what was happening further south. It's my practice to deal severely with any spill-over of trouble into my area of control."

"Let's move on to that. During my necessary absence, the situation unexpectedly worsened considerably when Presutagus was taken seriously ill. You very quickly learnt of this, didn't you?"

"Yes."

"I had written to you emphasising the need for extreme caution and stressing the active role you may have to play in maintaining control."

"You wrote to me from Mona. I was also paid a visit at more or less the same time by Tribune Agricola. He was able to give me excellent first-hand and up-to-date knowledge together with his assessment of a very fluid situation. He confirmed my own belief that Boudica would provide a very different type of leadership to her tribe, should King Presutagus die or lose control to her. He also passed on your thinking in this matter."

"Then why, man, did you disobey my orders?"

"I repeat, I did not."

"We shall see. The tribune told you my thinking. What did you understand that to be?"

"He confirmed you were emphasising my role in the changed circumstances and in your continuing absence. I was to play an important part in defending the citizens of Camulodunum should the need arise. That would allow time for you to complete your task on Mona and return."

Julius had noted that the two men had mentioned Paulinus's absence several times, but their motives in doing so were very different. He was enjoying the verbal sparring they were engaging in.

"You were told that you were to take your Legion to the town to join up with those legionaries from the 20th who'd been left behind there in case some demonstrations of unrest were to occur. Together with the capable citizens of that town, you were to contain matters until my return. Admittedly this would have been very difficult but necessary."

"That was not my understanding."

Julius couldn't avoid sitting upright in his chair and staring at Cerialis. He wondered if he was about to become the scapegoat both men might be content with.

"What was it then?"

"I considered Tribune Agricola's opinion at that time to be that Boudica might be interested in causing trouble, but not engaging in an outright rebellion. He thought a limited siege of Camulodunum would be most likely to give her a stronger negotiating position when you eventually returned. We didn't discuss the precise deployment of my Legion in those circumstances. It was unnecessary since it was a matter for my judgement alone if and when she took action."

"Any comment on that, Agricola?"

"It may well have been the case at the time, Sir. However, Legate Cerialis recognised how unstable things were and that my view was they could change very quickly. Certainly, none of us could have foreseen the catastrophic action taken against Boudica and her daughters by Decianus, the whipping and the rapes."

Julius finished his reply by reminding them that the unpredictability of Decianus's actions meant they we are all in this together.

"Quite so," agreed Cerialis.

"Regardless of all that, it's not what you were in fact ordered to do subsequently, when the fighting began," continued Paulinus. "Is that not so? Agricola sent instructions for you to go to Camulodunum as quickly as you could. You chose to disobey the order sent on my behalf. You were meant to assist in the building of defences around the whole town, and then work with others to contain the situation."

An exaggeration, Julius thought. Even he didn't think total indefinite containment of the situation was likely to be a realistic option after what had happened.

"I will answer that point shortly. Before then I refer to that previous meeting with Tribune Agricola. I remember clearly both of us were assuming that a full-on rebellion was unlikely. I was being asked to come to the 'aid' of Camulodunum as required. I was not being ordered to go to the town then. I think we can all agree on that."

"Tribune, your comments on that please," Paulinus demanded.

"At that time, no. However, in the context of our discussion I was quite clear that coming to the aid whenever necessary, implied the physical presence of the Legion at Camulodunum, siege or otherwise."

"That may have been what was held in your head at that time, even your sincere belief now, Tribune. It was not what was said

41

then," argued Cerialis.

"Let us move on," Paulinus growled, appearing agitated by the way the interrogation was going. "What you cannot deny is that later you were told Camulodunum was going to be attacked by the combined forces of the two tribes led by Boudica, and your Legion was needed. Whatever the words used, man, you must have taken it to mean get the Legion there as quickly as possible."

"As far as I was concerned I was still being ordered to come to the aid of the town."

"Not again! Explain yourself!"

"My spies had earlier told me of the unfortunate and untimely actions of Decianus and his large force at Boudica's settlement. Once the inevitable reaction to that abuse had led to the outbreak of fighting I decided my Legion needed to act quickly. We were in the unique position to do so. You said earlier that my Legion was the core of our forces, being the best trained and most experienced, or words to that effect."

Julius wasn't surprised in the least that Cerialis had chosen to quote that sentiment back at the Governor. He would continue to use it outside this meeting whatever the outcome. He leaned slightly forward, eager to hear the crucial defence of his actions.

"I finally made a decision on an idea that had been building in my mind ever since the visit by the tribune. I knew it wasn't possible to defend Camulodunum against the size of force Boudica could gather together given time, and time was on her side. The town had no defensive walls, not even boundary ditches to hide behind. There were far too few men who could fight in support of my legionaries. In short, a decision to rush the Legion there, a ploy Boudica would be hoping for, would be doomed from the start. At best we would delay her march to find and join you in battle by a few days. I considered what my studies of Rome's past victories had taught me. I wondered how the great Julius Caesar would have reacted if he'd met a similar crisis when he first came to this land one hundred years ago and fought these Brits."

Julius felt like interrupting Cerialis's long speech by agreeing with him that it was never a bad idea to call on a great General from the past to support your case. That was particularly true if it was the most famous relative of the current Emperor, who was awaiting his explanation of his controversial action. Surely that hadn't occurred to Cerialis! He managed to supress a little chuckle.

Paulinus glared tight-lipped as Cerialis continued with his apparently well-rehearsed monologue.

"I decided the town and everybody and everything in it was going to be lost if we just waited, allowing Boudica to build an overwhelming horde before attacking. Attack is also sometimes considered the best form of defence, don't you agree?"

An answer or comment would not have been expected or desired and none came. He continued.

"I reflected on the fact you'd taken a gamble as well, in taking most of your forces away to Mona to deal with the problems there. I decided to take a gamble. It was my judgement call, being the senior military commander left here to deal with her. The gamble was to strike at her heart before she could gather her full force together. If I was able to capture or kill her or just set her plans back by a significant period it might just buy us enough time. My gallant gamble failed."

"You didn't just fail. You lost more than half your Legion in an ambush, with little effect on the Brits."

"I gambled to try to make the best of things, when I'd been faced with an impossible defensive position. At the same time you were involved in undertaking a gamble to extend this Province. We are both gamblers, brave and decisive. I didn't condemn your gamble. Taking calculated risks when the responsibility falls on us is part of the duty we have to accept. That's why we are given this Province to control."

He paused for breath. The other two remained silent, absorbing what had been said.

"I have one further thing to add. I'm sure the three of us have regrets about some of the actions and decisions we took or should have taken during these eventful times. I'm also sure each of us did what we did honourably at the time."

"Have you anything else to add?" Paulinus enquired, head bowed as if in defeat.

"I didn't disobey your orders. I made a legitimate judgement in a time of war."

Julius stared at him in grudging respect. He'd managed to explain away allowing his Legion to be ambushed. He had praised all three of them, instead of engaging in counter-accusations against the other two. A line had been drawn that suggested if one was to blame for the near disaster, they all were. Julius couldn't see him receiving more than a mild rebuke in any report compiled by Paulinus.

The meeting ended very quickly. The frustration Paulinus was feeling showed in his tightly clenched jaws and his brusque instruction to Cerialis to return to his legionary fort. He offered no summary or conclusion about the meeting.

Cerialis and Julius knew that meant no further action would be taken by the Governor. As Cerialis turned to leave the two of them exchanged no words, only blank stares. However, Julius couldn't help noticing the grin that began to appear on Cerialis's face, and how it broadened the closer he got to the exit. He decided this was a man to respect in the future, but also to be wary of.

When the other two were alone Paulinus's frustration and anger were released. Julius felt the full force of it.

"You let me down, Julius Agricola. I had thought better of you."

The use of his full name by Paulinus had never been applied in this way before whenever they were alone. Something had changed.

"In what way, Sir?"

"You failed to make it clear to that man what I required of him. He's escaped me as a result."

"I'm certain I did, Sir. I know when I left him he understood he was expected to take his Legion to Camulodunum when called upon to do so. This was clear even though times were uncertain and events difficult to predict. He's been clever enough to explain away his decision not to do that as being forced upon him by the unforeseen twists and turns of war. He sends a message to both of us. The Emperor Nero needs to be reminded of our glorious victory against almost impossibly large numbers. It was inspired by his very name. The villains in this story were Boudica and her followers."

Sounding like Cerialis in full flow seemed to be having a positive effect on Paulinus.

"You could be making a point I may wish to consider further," Paulinus acknowledged with much apparent reluctance. "However, I'm still disappointed. I've been prevented from punishing the two Legates who failed me so badly in my time of greatest need. I don't forget those who fail me. You may leave."

He waved him away.

*

Julius spent some time strolling around the camp thinking about the whole business of the meeting, what had been argued and why. He was particularly disturbed by those last few words with his commander, who until then had been worthy of his respect and admiration. He was beginning to realise he'd been blinded by this outstanding soldier, blinded to the flaws in the man. He knew for certain that the special relationship he'd enjoyed with the illustrious Governor of a Province, an arrangement he had seen as very beneficial for his military career, had begun to deteriorate.

Chapter 7

Following the advice of Septimus, Decianus had sought out Seneca, his father's old friend and fellow tutor, at the Royal Palace. With his help he'd been able to transfer to the Treasury the gold and coins which he'd tirelessly protected on his long and hazardous journey through Gaul. Seneca had been surprised at the amount Decianus had been able to rescue. He suggested that whatever story he had to tell Emperor Nero, of the part he'd been forced to play in the disaster that had befallen Britannia, he could expect some favourable response for the unexpected bounty the Emperor's Treasury would be receiving. Then again, he'd added it might not be as much as he would need in these increasingly unpredictable days.

Once the immediate task of arranging for the deposit in the Treasury vaults had been completed, the two men, prompted by Decianus, talked briefly about their shared experiences from the past, particularly involving his father. But not for very long. Decianus accepted the urgent advice from Seneca that nothing would be gained by delaying the moment when he faced Nero.

"Is that music and singing I can hear?" Decianus asked as they left Seneca's room and began their determined walk to Nero's suite of private rooms.

"It certainly is, and both are being provided by Nero himself. It's a new song written by him only a few days ago. He thinks it's his best work yet. We all agree with him, of course."

As he spoke these words, Seneca lightly touched Decianus's arm to make him look at him, causing them both to stop momentarily. The old man bowed his balding head towards him, his eyebrows raised as if in alarm. His mouth was slightly open and he took in a deep breath. He let out a big sigh but said nothing more. Decianus grinned his understanding.

"He likes to accompany himself on the lyre. He feels it brings out the true quality of his poetry. He'd decided none of the court musicians could match his own skill in that respect."

A further pause to add unspoken comment proved unnecessary for Decianus's benefit. He had known Nero quite a few years previously, before he became the boy Emperor at the age of sixteen. In his earlier discussion with his father he'd been reminded that in the years since, the once outgoing, always friendly youth had become a man of variable character. This could have been caused by the young man's growing eager zed that he had unlimited power over every single person in the Empire, and unrestrained use of resources to satisfy every need and whim.

Because of Septimus's role, Decianus had made many visits with his father to the Palace. He had become quite friendly with the boy Nero who at that time could have had no realistic expectations of succeeding Emperor Claudius, since he was only his adopted son. Certainly, Decianus hadn't anticipated it. Had he done so he would have paid him much more devoted attention. Even so, he'd begun to revive memories of the time when Nero had regarded him, an older and more experienced young man, as an apparently valuable friend, even a confidant. It occurred to him that those memories, if mentioned at an appropriate time, and shared by Nero, might yet stand him in good stead. As might be expected other long-forgotten memories were creeping back at this very moment.

"I can recall the boy was always interested in singing in front of Claudius and his family. Even then, I recognised the outstanding talent the boy displayed," Decianus lied.

He resisted an urge to show any lack of sincerity in his expression as Seneca had done. He still didn't know how much he could trust this man, currently one of the closest confidants of Nero.

"As we all did, and some of us said so at the time. Others amongst us were perhaps a little crueller in what we said to him," said Seneca.

That caused Decianus some alarm. Does this old man remember some remark, long forgotten by himself? Had he been less than cautious in what he'd said, either directly to Nero or to others? He was reinforced in his belief that he had to be wary of this apparent ally. At court you had no friends, only potential enemies. He changed tack slightly.

"Now we are closer and I can hear much clearer that wonderful voice. I can't hear the words of the song fully yet but I'm sure they will rival those works of our greatest Greek and Roman poets."

"You'll do well to continue along the lines of this reaction to Nero's performances, both in his presence and in conversation with any of his family and close confidants."

"I note what you're saying."

"We're almost there. There will be other opportunities to talk. One last thing before I take you into Nero's private reception room. I take it you haven't had time to be introduced to Burrus, commander of the Emperor's Praetorian Guard?"

"Not that I can recall, and certainly not since he took up his present position."

"Let me explain something very important to you," whispered Seneca, looking about him to check they weren't being overheard by anybody. "He and I have been Nero's closest advisers for most of his recent development years. He's trusted us more than anybody else. That was certainly true during those difficult years for him when he was dominated by his mother, particularly the period before her death. Fortunately, Burrus and I see eye to eye on most things. While we are not close friends, we do respect each other. We accept we each have our own particular area of expertise while agreeing on most shared matters."

"I realise that's the case considering you've lasted so long together."

"Having said that, things have been changing in recent times. He's acquired a special mistress. Her name is Poppaea. More of her later."

"My father explained a little of the relationship there."

"For now, it's important for you to realise he's becoming increasingly reliant on her. Her influence is growing in all areas. She will be the one listening to him in there. You can expect her to stay while you deliver your report. She'll be listening and taking note of what you say, even if at times she appears not to be doing so."

Decianus showed no sign of the turmoil increasing inside him.

"We've said enough. Follow me in and let me do the talking at first."

Walking slowly behind his newfound ally, Decianus slowed his pace even more, his jaw dropping in awe as they entered the room. Even by his own extravagant tastes he'd never seen the extraordinary luxury that met his eyes.

The room was large but not too overpowering. It managed to avoid the impersonal effect it would have produced had it been so. The furniture and fittings, however, were a different matter. They were there to overwhelm the senses. Sumptuous couches filled half the room. Each was draped with an ample supply of cushions made from brightly coloured silks. Between some of the couches provocative but still elegant sculptures of naked young men and women were arranged to stare down on those relaxing there. Elsewhere, miniature palms and other exotic plants from the warmer climes of the Empire brought the feeling of the Palace garden into the room.

Eventually, Decianus was able to raise his gaze to wonder at the spectacular tapestries hanging from all the walls. The scenes they depicted were a perfect backdrop for the sculptures and plants enriching the room.

Seneca had paused immediately on entering the room to ensure he didn't disturb Nero's flow. He'd succeeded. They stood just inside the room and waited patiently. Nero was in full voice again. Decianus realised it was fortunate Nero was seated with his back to them facing the only other person in the room, Poppaea. She'd briefly noted their interruption but continued giving her full attention to her lover.

Decianus could see why Nero had taken her as his mistress. Her beauty rivalled any he'd come across in Rome or his many travels. He considered himself a worthy judge of such female beauty, having made it part of his life's work to seek out feminine charms at every opportunity. In his case, though, they tended to be the most expensive slaves money could buy. Nevertheless, his gaze didn't linger on Poppaea for more than a few moments. Conscious that he couldn't be certain the three or four slaves he could see in the room weren't observing him, to report later on his behaviour, he quickly concentrated on Nero. He made sure his eyes were staring at Nero and that his face showed a look of pure delight.

Nero paused again as he had done so several times before. It couldn't have been the first time Poppaea had heard the new song because she immediately recognised the ending. She began her delighted applause. The two late additions to the audience joined in enthusiastically. Nero, slightly startled, turned to face them.

"Seneca!" he cried. "I didn't know you'd come into the room. I've made a few changes to my new song. They make it even better than before. What is your honest opinion from what you heard? Don't lie to me."

"Magnificent, Sir. I didn't think the previous version could be bettered but you were right. Only you could have spotted the need for those changes."

"How long were you there? Were you doing what you liked to do when you were my old tutor – quietly creeping up on me trying to find fault?"

Decianus recognised some remaining old insecurity of the young boy. Being Emperor hadn't removed it all.

"No, Sir, I only joined you towards the end of your performance. I had a rather urgent matter to bring to your notice. I'm only too happy I didn't wait too long to bring it to you, thereby missing what little I heard."

Decianus could see the look of self-satisfaction on Nero's face at the flattery he was receiving. It was something he would keep in mind for the future. For the moment, putting Nero in a good mood could only help him with his report.

"Who is this you've brought with you?" enquired Poppaea, only looking mildly interested.

"Yes, Seneca. I'd like to know as well," Nero added. "You gave me no notice. You know how I hate that. He looks familiar, though."

Decianus didn't like being talked of as if he were a slave. He further resented the restraining hand of Seneca placed on his arm preventing him from answering the questions directly.

"This is Catus Decianus, son of Septimus, who like myself, was one of your tutors."

"Septimus's son! Yes, I remember you even though you're a great deal fatter and older."

Poppaea's giggle at his remark produced a smile of pleasure of his own.

"You used to be around the Palace helping your father as I recall. Why are you here?"

"He has just returned…"

"Let him reply for himself for goodness' sake, Seneca. He has a tongue of his own. You do have one, don't you?"

"I do, Sir."

"Good! So, what is it you have to tell me? And please be quick about it. You can see I'm rehearsing. We great artists are always seeking perfection."

Poppaea let out a giggle showing her amusement at the way her lover was treating his old tutor and the stranger.

"I am the Imperial Procurator for the Province of Britannia, appointed by you to ensure the collection of taxes there."

"Then why aren't you there doing precisely that?"

"That's why I've brought him to see you," Seneca offered.

"Then you should keep quiet and let him get on with it!" Nero ordered, at the same time looking to Poppaea for further signs of her approval, giggles or otherwise.

A full account was given by Decianus on the situation in Britannia. He was aware that Nero would have received some much earlier reports from a variety of sources. He was careful to describe his first-hand experience of the faults of everybody else but himself in those circumstances leading up to the rebellion. He particularly spoke of Paulinus's unwise campaign in the north, leaving the south unprotected. The complacency and failure of previous Governors to build proper defences around the three main towns was noted.

"And what steps were you taking to continue collecting my taxes even if what you say is true?" asked Nero, glaring at Decianus.

"With the help of my brave soldiers I was able to continue my work despite the restrictions being placed on me by Paulinus and his officers in his absence. Through my firm dealings with the Iceni and other tribes I tried to curb any thoughts of rebellion they may have had. That even included Boudica herself."

"What do you mean regarding her?" asked Poppaea, who had begun to take more notice with the name of Boudica.

"I was carrying out my duty, having gone to her settlement. I went there to confiscate the wealth of the dead Iceni king. He died without leaving a male heir which meant the whole of his estate became the Emperor's. Boudica decided to argue that this was wrong and to resist me. I taught her a lesson in front of her tribe."

"How so?" asked Poppaea.

"I had her flogged in front of her people."

"What was that intended to achieve?"

"It showed her and all those thinking of supporting her what it meant to defy Rome and its Emperor. My men then went on to search her settlement and recover what was there for the taking.

"That's what I would have expected you to have done," Nero added while looking to Poppaea for approval.

"Continue," she ordered.

"Unfortunately, my small force and the meagre residue of legionaries left behind by Paulinus were insufficient to prevent the outbreak of hostilities. I took hostages but they were released by Paulinus's staff. Things became so bad I decided Britannia was going to be lost to us for a time. I did what I could to protect the Emperor's wealth. I gathered what I could and escaped."

"I can confirm he's brought a great deal of gold with him," Seneca added. "It's been safely stored in the Treasury."

"You can show me later," Nero cried gleefully. "Have you finished?"

"I only wish to assure you that I couldn't have done more to prevent the loss of Britannia."

Nero glanced at Poppaea, prompting them both to burst out laughing. Seneca looked amazed, Decianus confused, and Nero wriggled in delight.

"I don't understand," said Seneca, seeking an explanation for what was happening.

"Yes. Yes. You weren't here last night. You'd gone to bed early as usual. One of Burrus's men arrived with a message from Paulinus. I haven't seen you since to tell you about it. My Legions have given me a glorious victory. Boudica and her rebels have been destroyed. Soon all the people of Rome will know what a mighty Emperor they have."

"And a wonderfully talented one," insisted Poppaea.

Seneca gave a puzzled look at Decianus who could only stare at Nero with eyes and mouth wide open.

"So, Decianus. Taking so long on your journey back to Rome has meant you've been overtaken by events. You may or may not have behaved bravely, but you certainly acted a little too prematurely. However, you may still come out of this well. You probably saved some of my gold from being looted and taken by Boudica. Wait for me outside. I will join you shortly. We shall go to the Treasury. It will help me to decide what to do with you."

Poppaea waited until they were alone. "What do you think about this Paulinus then?"

"I don't have a great deal of experience of him. He was one of my mother's last appointments. There appear to be some decisions he made which need close examination. However, that can wait. There's no need to recall him for the time being. He and I are heroes. Let us bask in the glory."

*

Much later, outside the Treasury, Nero had taken Decianus to one side, still accompanied by Seneca.

"On balance I'm pleased with you. These gifts you brought me and the high regard I still have for your father just about outweigh your premature desertion of your post. Seneca's apparent support for you has helped. Obviously, I can't return you to your previous duties in Britannia."

The relief showed on Decianus's face. He gave a quick glance in the direction of Seneca, which Nero noticed.

"What does wise old Seneca suggest I do with you?"

"I think his wide experience in the Provinces would be very useful in my service, particularly in taxation matters."

"So be it then. Be about your business. I have to get back to my music."

Decianus expressed his gratitude to Seneca as they left the Palace. He realised how near he'd come to disaster. He knew he would have to be at his cunning and ruthless best to survive in the future. One interesting thought occurred to him as he went his separate way. Seneca's trusted and respected colleague, Burrus, had been given the opportunity the day before to let Seneca know the amazing and very welcome news from Paulinus. He'd chosen not to. What game might he be playing?

Chapter 8

Camillus Pecius had mixed feelings about the decision of the Governor to order the men of the 14th Legion to return to their base in the northwest at Viroconium. He understood the need for action. The longer the Legion was absent the more Paulinus would become concerned that the druid control and influence would return to that region.

He looked forward to the enjoyment he got from carrying out the responsibility of being second-in-command of a Legion in a restless area with troublesome tribes. On the other hand, he regretted leaving the new friends he'd made during the combined campaign on Mona and the suppression of Boudica. Chief among those was Julius Agricola. He'd decided to make sure there was sufficient time to see him in order to say a meaningful farewell. So, he was making his way through the fort to Julius's quarters early in the morning of departure. There was no need to wait to be told to enter.

"Good morning, Julius," he cried.

"And to you, Camillus. I see you've dressed in readiness for the long march back. Have you remembered to take your wet-weather cloak? From my limited time up there I seem to think you'll be needing it. Have we got one big enough to fit your bulk?"

"Very amusing," Camillus replied, his top lip curling in mock disgust. "I'm beginning to wonder why I bothered to come to say goodbye to my disrespectful friend."

"I'm glad you did. It's good to have the chance to wish you well. Although, thinking about it, I seem to remember we've done this a few times recently when we weren't sure if one or both of us would be alive the following day, considering the battles we were facing."

Camillus couldn't have helped but be aware of the presence of Olsar when he entered. He'd given him a mere momentary glance. Only now did he look closely at him to see if those remarks had had any effect on him. Olsar's expression, already sullen, hadn't changed. Julius noticed what was happening and couldn't resist an opportunity to comment.

"Olsar is still full of resentment over what happened, so one further unintentionally provocative remark from me isn't going to make him feel any worse."

Olsar showed his indifference at what was said by ignoring them. He continued to concentrate on the cleaning and polishing of Julius's armour.

"You know my opinion about Olsar becoming your slave," said Camillus, talking about him as if he weren't present. "I realise the respect you have for him as a warrior. I share it. Saving his life was understandable. Making him your slave and preventing his subsequent execution, when his identity as Boudica's cavalry leader became known, was brave and maybe even the correct thing to do. Unfortunately for you, Paulinus doesn't think so. I know for a fact that he's told our Legates he considers your actions to be provocative and potentially disloyal to him."

Olsar gave a little cynical laugh, showing he was taking note of what was being said.

"I can live with that," Julius replied.

He got to his feet, moved the few paces to Camillus and placed his hand on his broad shoulder.

"As before, when we've wished each other farewell, I have the feeling this isn't the last we shall see of each other, either here or elsewhere in the Empire."

"I agree," said Camillus, "and to increase the chances of that happening, remember the soldier's second duty is to fight for the Emperor."

"What's the first duty then?"

"Fight for yourself, to survive!"

Even Olsar gave a little smile and cough at this remark. Camillus, noting this, turned to speak to him.

"You owe this man your life. He saved it twice. If he can survive these turbulent times he will become a great leader. Protect him as he's protected you. Together you can make a powerful team."

Julius took a firm hold of his friend's arm in one last gesture.

"May the Gods look after you and keep you safe. That son of yours has been waiting a long time to see you again."

No further words were needed. They saluted each other and parted.

*

Later that day, as early evening was approaching, Julius strolled down to the river, swelling with the rising tide. He began to watch the feverish activity on the docks. Immediately, his attention was drawn to one particular ship which was being loaded by slavers. They were herding their latest shipment on board bound for Gaul. Even from his position some way away he could recognise by their dress that most of them were Iceni.

Moving much closer he became angry at the sight of one family of four – two parents, a boy and a girl – receiving the most violent encouragement to move closer to the ship. They were being whipped savagely by the slave master with a log length of knotted rope. Through terror or weakness, probably a combination of both, they had collapsed onto the floor into a little group. The parents were desperately trying to shield their children.

Reminded of the small boy on the road to Camulodunum, Julius rushed the few remaining steps to snatch the rope from the man's hand and throw him to the floor.

"How much for the four of them?" he demanded.

"They're not for sale," the startled slave master replied before he had time to fully consider his answer.

"What do you mean? They're slaves, aren't they?"

"There are too many for sale here. I'll get a much better price for them in the markets in Gaul."

"Name your price for them."

It didn't take long for a sale to be completed. The fury in Julius's eyes kept the slaver's demands reasonable.

"That's settled then," said Julius.

He turned to the family, still cowering on the floor, raising them to their feet.

"You are now my property. Listen carefully to what I have to say to this villain."

He turned to slave master.

"You will make a note of the names of my four new slaves. Give it to one of your men. He will come to the fort when you've finished your work here. By the time he arrives there I shall have had documents prepared to be given to my slaves."

He moved closer to the family again and with a much softer voice, gave them instructions.

"Those documents will be yours to keep. They will clearly state you are the property of Tribune Julius Agricola. They will tell all who read them that anyone ignoring that will have me to deal with and be liable to the severest punishment. You'll be able to return to your farm and work it for yourselves. Anything you grow or raise is yours to keep. I don't expect any rent or proportion of what you produce. From time to time I will call at the farm to check if you are prospering. Do you understand everything I've said?"

The parents nodded through tears caused by a mixture of relief and gratitude. Finally, he gave his last order to the slave master.

"You'll transport this family back to their land, making a careful note of the way to get to it and where I can locate them in the future. That note is to be addressed to me and given to one of the Governor's clerks, who will see that I receive it. Remember, if you fail in any of this, I have a very long reach through the Army. The punishment you've just given out will be nothing compared to that which you would receive from me."

The look of fear on the man's face told that failure to do as he was ordered wouldn't happen.

*

Returning from the docks, Julius began to think of Linona. Had she managed to evade slavers like these or had she gone to the slave markets in Gaul? Had she even been able to stay alive? In the last few weeks he'd fought back unwanted thoughts of what could have happened to her and Cailan. Even now he was trying to drive from his mind the idea which kept creeping in, that he would never see her again. He had to keep reminding himself that if anybody had the strength and determination to resist and survive against all the odds, it was Linona.

*

Two days after Camillus left with his Legion, Paulinus sent for Julius to join him in his office.

"You sent for me, Sir."

"I did indeed. Take a seat."

He pointed to the guard by the entrance.

"See that the tribune and I aren't disturbed."

Julius began to get a feeling this wasn't going to be a routine discussion about ordinary matters.

"Having sent the 14th Legion back to Viroconium, I've been giving thought to the other three Legions. I've asked the Emperor to appoint a new Legate to the 2nd Legion since a vacancy has arisen there. However, that's the only change I want to make in that case. The southwest is the quietist part of the Province."

No surprise there for Julius.

"In the east, Cerialis will continue as Legate for the time being. His Legion is to receive two thousand replacement legionaries in the coming months. It's no time to be changing the Legion's commander. Cerialis, for all his failings is a strict disciplinarian and will soon have the Legion back to functioning normally. Since I've mentioned the man, what do you think of him? Have you changed your opinion since that meeting we had with him?"

Julius decided it wasn't wise to either praise or condemn Cerialis in these times of reckoning and reconstruction. He chose his words carefully.

"Not to any great extent, Sir. My opinion before was that he was a shrewd and courageous commander. It hasn't changed. He certainly took a brave gamble, to quote his own words, in trying to stop Boudica in her tracks. Had it paid off he could well be sat in Rome expecting to be appointed by Nero to be a Governor of a Province somewhere in the Empire. The fact that it failed would make me more wary of him in the future. In answer to your question, I think I would add the slick skills of a politician to his others, after watching him perform at our meeting."

"I detest the man," growled Paulinus, probably reminded of his combative performance in their meeting.

That's not surprising, Julius thought. *He sees a rival and equal in him.* He decided to try moving off the subject of Cerialis.

"That leaves only the 20th, Sir."

"It does and that's why you're here. I want you to take a part of the Legion and go to the Iceni and Trinovante tribal lands for an extended period. I have a special task for you there."

"What's that, Sir?" Julius asked, half knowing and not welcoming the answer.

"I want you to complete what we've only just started. We need to clear and remove any major village or settlement, particularly those of Boudica, and the others associated with the clan leaders. I want it known that there's no such thing as an Iceni or Trinovante tribe any longer. There will only be individual families living there. Eventually it will be only new Romans who settle there. You are to be promoted to Senior Tribune. What do you say?"

"I have to turn down the assignment and promotion, Sir. I'm not the man to carry out that work for you in the way you wish."

Julius realised he'd just sealed his fate but it was the only answer he could give.

"Are you serious? Not only are you denying yourself a promotion, you are refusing to accept my decision. What's your reasoning?"

"I have indicated my feelings in this matter to you before, Sir. I think we should try to re-establish those two tribes. That would be the most effective way to bring these lands back into productive use. Their numbers are so reduced they could never be a threat again. In addition, we could ensure their leadership is entirely supportive of Rome."

"I think you appear to have grown a liking for these barbarians. You're taking of one of their highest warriors as a slave rather than kill him was not wise. Neither was your demonstration at the docks two days ago. Yes! It was reported to me."

Julius knew his actions wouldn't have gone down well in Londinium in these early days when emotions and hatreds were still raw. Paulinus continued.

"I think you are right. I now realise you're not the man to help me rid this Province of the curse of Boudica."

"I'm sorry to disappoint you, Sir."

"You do indeed disappoint me, Julius. So much so that I think your time in my service as my staff officer is at an end. Not only that. I think it best you seek to serve the Emperor in another Province, where your loyalties won't be so confused. I shall prepare documents for you to take back to Rome with you."

"I understand, Sir. May I say I've learnt a great deal from my time under your command and guidance."

"I shall not condemn you to Nero, Julius. On the contrary, I will tell him of the pivotal role you played in our victory and in my opinion you are a courageous and intelligent officer, destined for greater things. I shall explain we both feel you would now benefit from another posting to put your experience gained here to better use."

"I'm grateful, Sir."

"And so you should be. Begin to make arrangements for your departure in the next few days."

"Yes, Sir."

"One last thing. Take your new slave with you. I will be glad to see the end of him. Let me give you a word of advice regarding him. Don't be too quick to let people know the part he played in the rebellion, particularly Nero. They might not be as tolerant as you or I. While I'm giving you warnings, be most careful of Nero himself. You haven't met him yet. I have. People have found that the nearer they get to him the more difficult it becomes to survive."

"I understand what you say, Sir."

"Report to me when you're about to leave."

PART II

TIME OF SURVIVAL

61 AD

Chapter 9

The day's racing at the Circus Maximus had gone well for Nero. His favourite chariot team, the Whites, had won six of the twelve races. The Reds had managed three and the Greens two. Blue team had suffered throughout the day. Their best charioteer had been thrown violently from his chariot in the first race, barely escaping with his life. Badly injured, he'd been dragged to safety by the attendants.

When he and Poppaea returned to the Palace in the early evening, Nero's good mood didn't last long.

"One day I will take part in the races. I want to experience the power of controlling those white stallions. I want to hear thousands of Roman citizens cheering their victorious Emperor across the winning line."

"If you control them like the Blue charioteer did today they might just be cheering the idea of getting a new Emperor who could provide heirs for them," replied Poppaea.

"What do you mean by that?"

"The people want an Emperor who can produce a natural heir, not one who can ride a chariot. None of the previous ones have managed to produce their own child to succeed them so far, starting with Augustus. They want continuity and security for Rome."

"Not that again, Poppaea, please."

"Yes, that again."

"Why won't you divorce Octavia and marry me? I want to be the Empress of Rome, not just your latest mistress. I deserve it. You need me."

"You know you're everything to me."

"Everything but your wife."

"Seneca says it would go badly with both the Senate and the people if I divorced her. After all, she is the daughter of the God, Claudius. She's very popular, even loved, throughout the Empire."

"Seneca! Seneca! I'm tired of hearing his name. What does he know? He's still behaving as if he's your tutor and you his pupil. He can't accept or understand that you're the Emperor with absolute control over everybody and everything."

"I shall talk to him again to see what he can suggest."

"Don't ask him. Tell him there's a way to bring her down from her pedestal. Discover she has a lover, whether real or imaginary. Adultery will be seen as excuse enough for a divorce, even if she is Claudius's daughter. By the way, I'm pregnant. I'm going to bed."

*

Seneca didn't enjoy being summoned to see Nero before the midday meal. It usually meant something was troubling him or he hadn't slept very well. His mood would be suffering as a result. Whatever the cause, it was likely to be a difficult meeting.

"You called for me, Sir."

"Yes, Seneca. I have two matters needing urgent attention. I want you to make some arrangements for me."

"I'm at your service as ever, Sir."

"Firstly, I want you to arrange things so I can divorce Octavia immediately."

"You know I think that would be very unwise of you."

"That's only your view. It's also unwise not to have an heir for the people to identify with. That is soon to be resolved."

"What do you mean? Is Octavia pregnant?" said Seneca without thinking first.

"Don't be stupid. Poppaea is to have my child. Which means I will be marrying her once Octavia is finally out of the way. That's where you will do something for me."

"I… I don't know what to say."

"Don't say anything. Just listen. The answer to my problem is for me to announce that Octavia has committed treason by taking a lover."

"Who is it?" a shocked Seneca asked.

"There isn't an actual one as far as I know, you idiot. I will have to choose one. That's where you come in. Who can you suggest?"

"Such a person would be guilty of treason and would need to be executed."

"So! What's your point?"

"The person would be innocent."

"So?"

"I would find it very difficult to nominate a suitable candidate. It would need to be some someone who is a likely candidate and is expendable. I can't think of anybody."

"I can, if you're unable to give me an alternative."

"Who is it?"

"Marcus Galerius."

"He's been one of your tutors for some years. I recommended him to that post."

"That's unfortunate, but he's no longer necessary."

"But he has a wife and child."

"Compensate them when this is all over. There's plenty of funds in the Treasury. If you don't like my suggestion you have one last chance to come up with an alternative."

He looked at a distraught, tired old man who remained silent.

"That's decided then. Bring me a report detailing the crimes those two have committed against me."

"What will become of Octavia?

"Unfortunately I will have to be more magnanimous with her. Find me an island I can banish her to."

Seneca remained silent for a while, his body sagging in shocked resignation. Nero seemed to remember there was a second item for discussion.

"Oh, yes. The other matter is nowhere near as taxing for you. For your information it appears that Tribune Julius Agricola, the one who was very much involved in the defeat of Boudica, has turned up with a letter from Paulinus. He's waiting to be considered for reassignment."

"Do we know why, Sir?" Seneca whispered.

"Yes. The letter gives an explanation of sorts. I want to discuss it with him. I want you to find him to tell him to report to me immediately. Then you're released. Oh! You can have Decianus stand by outside my rooms as well. I have a feeling I might be calling on him."

Chapter 10

Julius wondered why he was feeling so nervous and apprehensive about what was soon to happen. It wasn't as if he was going into battle. Behind the door which he was approaching there weren't men waiting with swords drawn ready to attack him. The problem was that he faced an unknown situation with an adversary he'd never met before. The outcome was totally unpredictable. The power was all in his opponent's hands. Nevertheless, he'd to keep his wits about him to be able to give of his best in front of Nero.

"Welcome, Tribune. You fit the image that I've come to expect from the reports I've received about you. What do you think, Poppaea?"

"Every inch the powerful soldier," replied Poppaea, smiling broadly, her eyebrows raised in approval.

"Take a seat, Agricola. I prefer to talk to you informally about your recent experiences."

"Thank you, Sir."

Julius did as he was instructed. Informal or not, he wasn't going to lower his guard too quickly.

"You brought a letter with you from Governor Paulinus. I've had the opportunity to read it. He asks that you be assigned to a role elsewhere in the Empire. You have exceptional skills, he tells me. Not only in a military sense, of course but also as a diplomat."

Julius was grateful Paulinus appeared to be keeping the promises he made in their last meeting. Nero continued.

"However, he doesn't want you anymore. He suggests that your time as his staff officer is best brought to an end, and your development would benefit from a wider role. He also describes the vital part, to use his words, that you played in helping to defeat Boudica."

"A glowing report," observed Poppaea, "but like all reports we suspect maybe there's more to be said than is contained in it."

"I don't think so, Madam," Julius replied.

He now realised he had two adversaries rather than one.

"Then why your sudden return from Britannia?"

"I'd fought alongside the Governor in two campaigns, taking Mona and against Boudica. I'd learnt a great deal. In the necessary restructuring of the army following these campaigns, new staff officers were being appointed to give them experience. Men such as Titus Vespasianus deserved to be given promotion and to gain the experience I'd had."

"I know that young man's father. He was a Legate and later became a Consul of Rome. He was a distinguished soldier and politician. He's been retired for some time."

"That is as I understand it, Sir."

Poppaea yawned, then stared coldly at Julius as she continued her questioning.

"You obviously regard each other highly, but your sudden departure still hints at something being wrong. However, we'll leave that for the time being. We see that he's won a great war, but wasn't he at least partly to blame for causing it? Didn't his absence give that woman the opportunity she needed?"

"Not at all, Madam. The problem we were facing in the north with the Druids couldn't be left to get any worse. There was no immediate threat elsewhere to delay the campaign."

"I think it's time to introduce our other witness don't you, my dear?" Nero suggested.

Without waiting for a reply, he summoned a slave and had Decianus brought into the room. Instinctively, Julius's hand went to grasp his sword only for him to remember he hadn't been allowed to carry any weapon into Nero's presence.

"I know you're familiar with each other. Let's continue. Decianus has told me all about what he says happened in Britannia. There's quite a difference between what he says and what I think you are about to suggest. Decianus argues that we had a rebellion because the south of the Province was left unprotected. What do you say, Tribune?"

"It's not true," snarled Julius. "There was no sign of King Presutagus's illness when the Mona campaign began. When he became seriously ill, Paulinus sent me to represent him with Boudica. After he died, I got her agreement to wait to raise her grievances until the Governor's imminent return from his success in the north."

"She fooled you, didn't she?" scoffed Decianus.

"Speak when you're spoken to," demanded Poppaea.

The grin on Decianus's face quickly disappeared.

"So, you met her," continued Poppaea. "What did you think of her? She must have been something to raise an army numbering more than one hundred thousand in a very short time."

Julius didn't miss the significance of one powerful, dominant woman's admiration for another.

"At the time, I thought she was a dangerous but very shrewd and determined potential adversary. She was very much in control of her tribe. We needed to continue to handle her with great caution if we were to contain her approach, different as it was to that of her husband."

"Why then did she decide to go to war?"

"Because of what he, Decianus, did to her and her daughters."

Julius thought the truth was about to be revealed. He soon realised it wasn't that easy.

"Yes! Yes!" said Nero impatiently. "He told us all about that. He was lawfully, and quite correctly seizing what was rightfully mine."

"Paulinus would have done it anyway without a war if this fool hadn't destroyed any chance we had of avoiding it."

Both Decianus and Julius rose to their feet.

"Sit down both of you," Nero shouted as Poppaea giggled. He gave them a few moments for their anger to subside.

"I have two versions of what happened. Who do I believe? On the one hand I have the story told by my competent tax gatherer, who happens to be the son of my trustworthy and loyal former tutor, Septimus. On the other hand I have the report of Paulinus himself. He has given me and the people of Rome an outstanding victory against enormous odds. His story is confirmed by his staff officer who is also the son of a trusted friend."

Julius was surprised to hear his father being described as a friend by the Emperor. Since his father was a Senator in Rome he would expect him to know him, but hardly as a friend.

"I won't rush to judgement on this. Perhaps you're both correct in what you believe, while being mistaken in parts. So! What to do with you both? I've already decided on your new role, Decianus, working with Seneca. I won't change that."

"Thank you, Sir."

"As for you, Tribune Agricola, after the recent demands placed upon you I think you will benefit from a time away from the military environment. You need a time for reflection. Are you married? You appear to be of a similar age to me."

"No, Sir. The opportunity has never arisen." Julius couldn't help wondering what had prompted the question.

"You will come to realise it can be greatly to your advantage and peace of mind to find a woman with whom to share your life. I want you to retire temporarily to your father's estate. I will call upon you in the future when the right circumstances arise. In the meantime, get married. You'll find it a great help in whatever career I decide you should follow."

Julius nodded his understanding rather than risk a reply he might regret.

"You can both leave us."

*

Outside, neither man was eager to move away. After all that had happened before and because of what had just been said there was unfinished business. Julius was having great difficulty in controlling an urge to grab him by the throat, to end it there and then. He realised, though, that if he did he was sure to be accused of treason.

Decianus held a position on the staff of the Emperor and such an outrageous action in the Palace would be regarded as a direct action against his authority.

Decianus seemed to sense the threat of violence enough to step back. However, it didn't prevent him from behaving in character by provoking Julius further, perhaps relying on the safety the walls of the Palace provided him.

"Consider yourself lucky, Julius. You survived on this occasion. Your lame excuse, blaming me, won't protect you for long. Go to look after your father's cows."

He cackled with laughter designed to annoy.

"Consider yourself the desperately unlucky one because I have entered your miserable existence again," Julius countered. "There will be a time for my revenge. It can't be now, but it will happen. I will see you dead for what you did."

"Don't you realise I could go back in there to tell him you've just threatened to kill me? I could also tell him you told me you've heard and believe rumours that he has the musical skills of a goat. Of course I would be lying, but he wouldn't wait to discover that before he crucified you."

Again, he finished with a raucous laugh. Throwing his head back, exposing his throat, only made it more difficult for Julius to stop his hands reaching out.

"My day will come."

"Your days from now will be spent milking cows. If you go to the Palace stores I'm sure you will be able to requisition a pail and a stool to go with it."

Julius watched him scurry away. Hearing the laughter slowly fade away, his heart was full of hatred.

Chapter 11

During his life Seneca had been forced to face many difficult situations, both personal and in the service of three Emperors. Some he'd handled most reluctantly and it was those he lived to regret for long periods afterwards. Among those at the forefront of his mind at this moment included the time he'd fallen foul of Caligula. Expecting to be executed he managed to escape at the whim of that unpredictable lunatic. Much later, Claudius had banished him from Rome because he committed adultery with an important woman at his court. His involvement in the demise of Agrippina had been grossly repugnant, but it was also an act of self-preservation before she acted first by resorting to presenting him with one of her potions. This action he was about to take ranked amongst the worst for which he would subsequently despise himself.

He considered refusing to obey Nero but he knew he would be dead before the day had ended. He wasn't a brave man. The thought of the pain Nero would inflict on him, before death brought him relief, made him feel physically sick.

Therefore, it was with a heavy heart he walked from the Palace, the half mile through the centre of Rome, to the large villa the Empress merited. Knowing him as she did, Octavia would sense his dark mood as soon as he was shown into her reception room.

"It's a pleasure to see you again, Seneca," Octavia said, holding out her arms to embrace her friend. "But by the look on your face you aren't too happy."

"You know me too well, Octavia. Perhaps it's better if what I have to say isn't delayed by pleasantries."

"Then sit down and tell me what it is that is so obviously

troubling you."

Seneca embraced her first, enjoying the warmth of the gesture. He couldn't prevent the thought creeping into his head that this gentle woman had never done him any harm from the day he first met her.

"I fear you'll hate me for the rest of your life for bringing the message I have to give to you."

"You know that would never happen. Please give it to me. It's from Nero, isn't it?"

He looked at her, his face pale with the feeling of self-loathing that was beginning to overwhelm him.

"You guess correctly. I'm sorry there's no easy way to say this. He's divorcing you."

"So!" she whispered. "The coward has finally taken the decision that's been tormenting him for years. I can't say I'm surprised."

She began to speak louder, showing the anger building inside her.

"His latest mistress undoubtedly had a hand in the death of Agrippina. I suppose it was only a matter of time before she found a way to make this happen."

Seneca winced at the reference to Agrippina but quickly supressed his feeling of guilt.

"That, she certainly did. She's pregnant."

In blurting it out he was forgetting his intention to announce it sensitively to her. Octavia closed her eyes, sighing deeply.

"I suppose I shouldn't be shocked. It's the ultimate weapon she would be able to use against me. When is the divorce to be arranged?"

"Immediately, given the urgency the pregnancy brings to it. But that's not all I have to tell you."

"What else can there be?"

"They don't want you around. You're to be banished to an island of his choosing."

"For how long?"

"He didn't say. He will marry her within a short time of your departure. She will replace you as Empress and her baby, if it's a boy, will become his heir."

"I might as well be dead," moaned Octavia, using her hands to cover her face in despair.

Seneca gently lowered her hands, surprised there were no tears of sadness.

"I am desperately sorry for you. You don't deserve to be treated this way."

"Don't be sorry. He will be hated by the people for divorcing me. The daughter of their much-loved Claudius is to be replaced by that whore."

"He's thought of that."

"What do you mean?"

"He'll announce that the divorce has been forced upon him because of your adultery."

"My adultery," she gasped. "What's he saying?"

Seneca was a little surprised. He had expected her first reaction to be a vehement denial of the false accusation.

"He will say your lover is Marcus Galerius."

"He's mad. That man is an insignificant junior tutor. Nobody will believe it."

"And nobody will call Nero a liar. To do so would mean instant death."

"What false evidence does he claim to have?"

"He doesn't need it beyond Marcus's written confession which he will provide just before the torture he will undergo kills him. That way he won't be able to deny it later. You will be shipped out very quickly afterwards to avoid your voice being heard. In a sense that part is a blessing. Were you to fight and deny any wrongdoing your fate could be a lot worse. Nero has learnt a great deal from his mother including her skill at concocting certain potions, should we say."

"But that poor innocent Marcus. I take it he has a wife."

"And a child."

"What will become of those two?"

"I will see they're taken care of. I'm so sorry for the three of them. I've worked with Marcus for a number of years. He's been a good friend of mine," said Seneca, his voice beginning to break with emotion.

"I hear what you've advised me not to do, but I must fight this for everybody's sake."

"You will surely die if you do so and it will not save poor Marcus. You must survive so that you can fight another day. I will work tirelessly for your return. You have my word."

"How long will that take? Be realistic. You no longer have the influence you once had with him. She has virtually taken over that role. My return will never happen while he lives and he's still very young."

"You must not give up hope."

"Please leave me. Be assured I don't hate you for coming today to give me his message. I certainly don't blame you in any way, even for trying to get me to accept my fate. You did what you had to, and you have my survival at heart. I need what little time I appear to have to consider my options."

"Please don't do anything hasty."

"We shall see."

As soon as Seneca left, Octavia sat down at her desk and wrote a short note. Sealed and addressed, she gave it to her trusted slave with the instruction to deliver it urgently.

*

"Your note said to come quickly. Have you been injured?" Burrus asked.

"Close the door," Octavia ordered, wringing her hands nervously.

"What on earth is the matter, my love?"

"Hold me please."

She clung to him for a long while, the tears finally beginning to flow.

"Please take a seat. You must tell me what's happened to make you behave like this."

They sat down close together, hands gripped tightly. She gave Burrus the details of the conversation she'd had with Seneca, pausing occasionally to breathe heavily in alarm.

"What can we do?" she begged. "I can't bear the thought of being separated from you."

"Let me think for a moment."

"And there's that poor innocent man. He will die without knowing what it's all for. We must save him."

"How do you think we could do that?"

"We can expose Nero as a liar. We shall let the people know the real truth about us."

"And we shall be executed as well as Marcus, or at least I will be. Think about it. Since he's already been earmarked for death, he will still be forced to confess to add to your sins."

"We must do something. Please, Burrus."

"Unfortunately, there's nothing we can do which won't expose our love for each other. We have to accept for the time being that he has the power to do whatever he wants. But your banishment won't last for long."

"What do you mean?"

"I won't rest until I find a way to get you back. We'll defeat him in the end."

"But how?"

"I don't know yet. I need time to think. But it will happen. Don't forget I command the Praetorian Guard. That gives me great power also. The Guard has both made and removed different Emperors in the past. I promise you our love will not be denied."

Only whispered words of love followed from then on. For a long time they continued to cling to each other, kissing desperately as if to reassure each other all was not lost. Eventually they parted with great reluctance and sadness.

Chapter 12

Olsar had first heard tales of the size and magnificence of Rome from travellers he'd met in the markets of Camulodunum and Londinium. His occasional visits there had sparked an interest in how big the city could really be compared with those two towns. After all, they were the largest in Britannia. Some of the buildings were even made from stone, something his own tribe had never achieved or needed. Nothing in his imaginings came anywhere close to the reality of what he found.

Large parts of the city, particularly in the centre, contained enormous stone buildings which would dwarf those in Britannia. He had passed by the Circus Maximus, which Julius told him contained a seemingly endless horse and chariot racetrack. He thought it so large it might take half a day to stroll around its complete exterior walls. The buildings of the Forum, of which he'd only had the merest passing glimpse, seemed to reach forever into the sky with gigantic columns. They towered above the throngs of people crowding below them. Further out from the centre unimaginably beautiful villas had been built to house the richest citizens.

Although on a scale he could not have dreamt of, this is what he'd been led to believe was what the whole of Rome was like. However, there were just as many areas and buildings, if not more, which shocked him with their squalor. It seemed to him that throughout virtually the whole of the city, with the exception of the very centre, extensive areas of small, ugly buildings were intermingled with those richer dwellings. These, more often than not, appeared to be made of wood. They were crammed together, taking up every piece of land. The narrow passageways between the rows of houses were dark and oppressive. Quite often, gullies had been provided running down the centre of them. As might have been expected, in many cases these were being used as virtual sewers.

Overwhelmed by the sheer scale and misery, unlike anything he had witnessed in his own tribal lands, he'd asked Julius for an explanation. Julius could only suggest the need to accommodate the never-ending flow of Romans seeking the fortunes many others had achieved there. He was staggered when Julius added that his father believed the total number of citizens and slaves in the city now exceeded one million. It was a figure Olsar had difficulty visualising. He couldn't think of anything in his experience that consisted of a million. Even the stars in the sky, which he'd attempted to count on dark nights as a boy, couldn't number that many. It was with great relief that he and Julius had escaped this onslaught on his senses into the fresh air of the open country, initially heading south out of the city.

A short time later, the arrival at Julius's family home was a totally different experience. It was a large villa, set in rolling farmland about five miles southwest of the city. The fields, though a little less green and more parched, reminded Olsar of his father's own land. His yearning to be free and home hadn't diminished. Seeing the spectacle of the villa in the near distance, the look of delight on Julius's face had finally displaced the expression of gloom he'd displayed in Rome.

"What are you going to tell your mother and father about your new enthusiastic Iceni slave?" Olsar asked sarcastically.

"What should I tell them?"

"You could tell the truth and horrify them. Describe how I was one of Boudica's enthusiastic warrior leaders who tried to throw the Legions out of Britannia into the sea."

"I'm sure they would find that very interesting. They wouldn't be inclined to welcome you with open arms, though. No! I shall tell them a different truth. Yes! You were a warrior who fought bravely for his people. I can vouch for that, and your being wounded in battle will impress them. I shall say that I concluded that if you made such a dedicated and loyal warrior there was a good chance you would make an equally good slave. If I'm wrong I can always sell you to the navy as a galley slave for a decent price."

Olsar couldn't hide his amusement.

"You know I won't remain your slave forever. There will come a time when we have to settle this. Should it be in combat, I won't give you a second chance if I gain the advantage rather than you next time."

"Let's wait to see what the future holds for the both of us. Mine may be more precarious than yours at this time. I shall explain later when there's a better opportunity. As for my mother and father, they will treat you kindly and with dignity, as they do all our slaves. There are exceptions, of course. Those slaves who can't accept their important role in our family receive a different treatment."

"It will be interesting to both of us, which category I fit into."

Julius smiled, showing he was enjoying Olsar's defiant attitude.

"What did you think of our wonderful city?"

"It filled me with awe and disgust in equal measures."

"Then you share that opinion with a million others who live there. That first reaction is unlikely to change in the future except perhaps to feel more of the disgust. You'll understand after more visits why those who rule have built the Amphitheatre and the Circus Maximus. They lift the eyes of the citizens above the daily squalor and misery of their lives."

"Presumably the multitude of their slaves don't have that facility to cope with the agony of their lives."

The discussion ended there. Olsar had given vent to some of the feeling of anger the sights of the city had produced in him.

*

A young woman in a simple gown came rushing down the main steps in front of the villa and ran the short distance to greet the two riders. She took a loose hold of the saddle cloth on the back of Julius's horse, speaking with such speed and excitement that Olsar was unable to understand most of what she was saying.

"Slow down! Slow down please, Selima," Julius said with a chuckle. "Are you saying my mother and father aren't here?"

"Yes, Julius. They've gone to visit friends. They won't be returning until evening."

"Is Fausto here?"

"He's in the stables."

"Good. Please take these horses to him and ask him to come to see me in a short while, but not immediately. I shall be in my favourite room in the west wing."

Both men dismounted so she could take hold of the reins.

"This is Olsar, Selima. He'll be joining us."

Selima paused to take a good look at him. Her large, dark brown eyes looked him up and down before she gave him a broad smile of approval. He grinned in recognition of what had just taken place. She gave a little skip, leading the horses away.

"I now know Selima. But who is she?" Olsar asked.

"That's something we can talk about later."

Julius led the way up the broad steps.

"I will arrange for you to see the whole of the villa and its complex of buildings in due course. However, before then, my parents not being here has given me an opportunity to sit down and tell you what happened earlier today when I reported to the Emperor."

Julius took him into a small private room towards the rear of the building. They relaxed on two small couches facing each other.

"You won't like what I'm about to tell you. Today I met Decianus."

Olsar took a long breath in through his nostrils.

"You mean the beast who ordered the rape of Linona and her sister?"

"The same!"

"I have to kill him. My one hope in coming with you to Rome was that I could seek him out and slit his throat. He's caused so much misery."

"Wait! There's more to add. He's convinced the Emperor that he is somewhat of a hero. So much so, he's been appointed to his staff. If you tried to attempt to kill him now it's more than likely you would be prevented and slaughtered."

"I don't care for myself."

"Then care for my innocent family and everybody who lives here. Since you are my slave your action would be regarded by Nero as an attack and a conspiracy against him. That's the sort of man he is. None of us would be spared."

Olsar didn't respond. He was breathing rapidly, appearing to be trying to suppress his rage.

"I want him dead just as much as you for what he did to Linona and Cailan. Our time will come, but not yet. Do you hear what I'm saying?"

"I hear you."

"You must obey me."

"I have told you before I will do so, for now. I have no other choice."

Julius rose to his feet and began to pace the room. It allowed the tension between them to ease a little.

"The other thing you need to know is Nero has been told about you in a letter from Paulinus. However, you were only described as my Iceni warrior slave. He will want to take a look at you soon."

"Like some prized captured animal, fit only for entertainment in the Arena."

"Whatever his motive, it will happen. Whenever it does, you mustn't be provoked into giving away your true role alongside Boudica. If you do, he's likely to parade you before the people, and that might well be in the Arena. You aren't the prize she would have been, but you could take her place. It would be a popular gesture."

"You have no need to worry about that. I've just been given a strong reason to survive and remain here until I get my revenge and kill the rapist."

"That brings me to my last point. Will Decianus recognise you? Did he meet you on the day he took his large force to pillage Boudica's stronghold? If you took an active part in resisting him then he may well recognise you and your importance to her. It could well be fatal for both of us."

"That isn't a problem. I wasn't present on that day of shame. Had I been, I would have died trying to protect my Queen and her daughters."

"At least that's in our favour then."

A firm knock on the door caused Julius to move towards it, pausing briefly to end their conversation.

"We'll need to talk some more about these matters in the coming days."

A tall, slender, middle-aged man entered the room at Julius's bidding. He received a firm, friendly slap on his shoulder.

"Good to see you again, Fausto."

"And it's a pleasure to see you arrive safely from the war, Julius. Your mother and father will be delighted and very relieved. I take it Selima told you where they are."

"She did indeed. This is Olsar with me." He turned to address him. "Olsar, meet Fausto. He manages our estate for my father."

Both men gave a slight bow aimed at each other in recognition of their introduction.

"Olsar is my personal slave. As such he will answer only to me. He isn't to be given work or instructions by you or anybody else. I shall explain this to my father."

"I understand."

"I want you to spend the rest of the day giving him a full tour of the villa and surrounding buildings, particularly the bathhouse and especially his own quarters. Please choose the best available for him."

He turned to Olsar.

"I shall introduce you to my parents, probably not today. It's likely to be too late when they return. For myself I'm going to take a much-needed bath."

*

Julius's mother, Procilla, rushed into the main family room to embrace her son, followed by his father, Lucius.

"What a marvellous surprise, Julius. When did you arrive?"

"I got to Rome late last evening. I had to report to the Emperor, which I did this morning. He released me to come here."

"Welcome home, son," said Lucius.

"Thank you, Sir. It's good to see you both."

"We have so much to talk about. Your mother will have her own list. I want to hear all about the rebellion first hand. It's all people in Rome can talk about."

"I got that impression from talking to Nero."

Lucius was correct. Procilla did have a list and it lasted well into the evening. When it was exhausted so was she.

"I'm tired and your father has things he wants to talk about with you. We have still more to catch up with including what the future holds for you, but it can wait. I'm going to bed."

She embraced and kissed both of them warmly and left.

"I am indeed keen to hear about what went on over there, but it will take a long time and we can start tomorrow. No! I'm more intrigued as to why you had to report to the Emperor so directly and what was said."

Julius gave him a full explanation of the last meeting with Paulinus. He told him of the letter he was required to deliver to Nero and the subsequent meeting with him, including the part played by Poppaea and then Decianus.

"I think I understand what's happening but I'm beginning to feel my age like your mother. It's getting late and you've already given me lots to think about. Like I said, we have all tomorrow to continue."

"I agree."

"There is just one thing I want to emphasise tonight, though, something for you to think about. He's instructed you to get married. That man is being driven by whim increasingly these days. You may think it was a playful, casual comment, and he will forget what he's said. You mustn't ignore it. Whatever his motive you have to assume he is serious in what he's told you to do."

"I don't have the slightest interest in marriage at this time, Father."

"That may be so, but it is irrelevant. He's sent you here to give him time to assess you, to consider what to do with you and why. He's more than likely going to check on you to see if you've obeyed him. Personal loyalty is becoming an obsession with him as his paranoia deepens. Look what happened to his mother."

"I hear what you say. However, because of my personal experiences in Britannia, I have no intention of becoming committed to anybody in marriage."

"We shall see. Coincidently, your mother and I have been giving a lot of thought to this very thing in your absence. Your mother thinks she's found the ideal match for you, and I agree. It will feature very much in our discussions tomorrow."

Julius shook his head, showing his disapproval of what was being said. With the mood having turned slightly sour at these last remarks, they left it at that, wished each other a good night's sleep and parted.

Chapter 13

The walk along the corridor to the kitchen was just as Julius remembered, full of the sound of chatter and laughter. The sounds made by Selima were the loudest as usual.

"Do you think I will be able to eat my first meal of the day in something approaching calm and silence?" Julius asked with a smile.

"Good morning, Julius," Selima cried before anybody else had a chance to speak.

She ran across the room to fling her arms around him, clinging tightly. Standing on her toes she buried her face into his broad chest. He was knocked back slightly by the force of her embrace. Once he regained his balance he folded his arms around her, planting a gentle kiss on the top of her head, which almost reached up to his chin.

"Good morning, son," cried Procilla. "Come and sit by me. Have something to eat. But it won't be in silence. You know what it's like when Selima and the rest of the girls are preparing the meals for the day."

By girls she was referring to the four trusted house slaves who were her constant companions.

"Thank you, Mother," said Julius. "How are you this morning?"

"As well as I can be, having to listen to this one's incessant gossip."

"And how is Selima?" Julius asked.

"Much happier now you and your friend have arrived," she replied.

"Not again, Selima," Procilla demanded. "You haven't stopped talking about this tall, handsome stranger since the moment you walked in here."

"He is beautiful though," Selima added with a slight giggle.

"I take it I will be introduced to your friend later," said Procilla.

"And that applies to me also," added Lucius, entering the kitchen.

"I was intending to mention him to you both at an appropriate moment, explaining everything, but Selima has managed to change that plan for me."

He looked across at her just in time to see her make a disgusted face at him.

"He's not here as a friend. He's my personal slave. I acquired him in Britannia. He was an Iceni warrior."

"Oh, goodness. This gets better and better," Selima blurted out.

Lucius tutted, Procilla shook her head, the others in the kitchen laughed, and Julius smiled broadly at her.

"That's a little unusual," suggested Lucius. "Taking a warrior as a personal slave I mean, not Selima letting her tongue act quicker than her brain."

This time everybody laughed, including Selima. Then she stuck her guilty tongue out at Lucius, first having made sure he wasn't looking. The conversation then became a free for all as the food was prepared and eaten. Later, Fausto brought Olsar in to be introduced much to the delight of the women in the room. Olsar looked extremely uncomfortable with the attention he was receiving, only starting to relax when the discussion moved away from him. Eventually, Lucius brought the impromptu gathering to a close.

"Well! We all have things we should be getting on with. Procilla and I want to carry on with our conversation with you from last night, Julius. I suggest we find somewhere quiet."

He stood to leave the kitchen.

"And I shall take Olsar and show him the villa and gardens," said Selima.

"I've already done that," announced Fausto.

"And you'll have left most of the interesting things out, I don't doubt. Come with me, Olsar."

She grabbed his hand, dragging him away before he or anybody else could object. Tutting, head shaking, smiling and laughing followed once again from everyone else.

*

Julius's following discussion with his parents concentrated at first on the circumstances which led to Olsar becoming his slave. Their reactions were very much as Julius expected.

"You're taking a great risk by taking a sworn enemy of Rome as a personal slave," stated Lucius. "Revenge is a need some people can wait patiently for, even for a very long time, until the right opportunity arises for it to be satisfied."

"I hear what you say, Father, but there's something about this man that makes me think he won't seek revenge from me. What I am sure of is that he doesn't see himself as a slave forever. I'm inclined to agree with him. How he breaks free of me in the future will be an interesting challenge for both of us."

Procilla, with her next remarks, changed the emphasis.

"From what you've described these Iceni were a proud and sophisticated people, not the savage barbarians we're being led to believe they were. Nevertheless, I'm happy you're back home safe with us."

Julius thought his mother was still as shrewd and wise as she'd always been.

"What did you think of Olsar, Mother?"

"He looks to be the man you described. He has the bearing of a proud, dignified warrior, much like you. I can see why you like him. Hopefully, he will regard you in the same way eventually. I agree he doesn't appear likely to allow himself to remain a slave for too long, any more than you or I would. Let's move on."

Julius accepted they were in agreement on that matter. He could guess from her impatience what the next item was going to be. The outcome wouldn't be the same.

"Your father has told me what Nero said to you about marriage. You realise, don't you, that we would have been saying the same to you without his interference?"

"I do, Mother."

"And you could have expected Lucius and I to have been giving it a lot of attention in your long absence also."

"Yes, Mother."

"Lucius, tell him what has been achieved so far."

"You make it sound like it's been all my doing. Nevertheless, I'll begin and no doubt you'll keep interrupting."

Julius was happy to see some things about his parents hadn't changed while he was away.

"Your mother and I have been friends with Verus Decidianus and his wife for many years. He comes from a very old noble family. He's been a Consul of Rome, and a Senator like myself. Unfortunately his family have fallen on difficult financial times. They're looking for a marriage partner for their daughter, Domitia. They'd prefer someone from a wealthy background to help restore their family's longer term fortunes."

"That's where we come in," declared Procilla.

"I thought we might," said Julius, feeling his anguish beginning to grow. "So you think my marriage to her would be a mutually beneficial arrangement for both families."

"Precisely," declared Lucius.

"It seems to be a very good solution," added Procilla more cautiously, having seen the look on her son's face.

"I'm sorry to disappoint you both but I have no wish to get married, now or in the immediate future."

"We touched on this briefly last night. Because of Nero's intervention, you have no choice."

"I think I have. I don't know this woman and have no wish to become committed to a stranger."

"What has that got to do with it? Your mother and I hadn't met until we got married and we've had a happy life together."

"Did you meet somebody in Britannia?" asked Procilla, showing not a little female intuition.

"Not as such but it made me want to choose my own partner, one

I care deeply about before the question of marriage arises."

"I understand," offered Procilla, taking hold of her husband's arm to prevent him replying. "But I agree with Lucius. You no longer have that luxury."

Julius began to consider the truth in what they were saying without them realising it. He had to let the idea of Linona go.

"I've no wish to dishonour you both. You appear to have given some sort of understanding about this to Verus Decidianus. Therefore, I will agree to meet his daughter as soon as you wish. We shall see what happens after that. It may well be she's as opposed to the idea as I am."

*

Much later Julius found Olsar still in the garden with Selima. With some difficulty, he persuaded her to leave them alone so they could discuss private matters.

"What do you think of Selima?"

"She is the most astonishing woman I've ever met," replied Olsar.

"That's what most of us think."

"She's quite small but appears to have limitless energy."

"It's why she never stops talking."

"It must have been very interesting to have had a younger sister like her."

"She's not my sister. At least not my birth sister."

"But, the way she behaves, I thought…"

"Of course you did. Let me explain. Her parents came from the Province of Judaea. They became slaves of a family my mother knew and Selima was born later. Unfortunately, her parents died of the plague when she was only four years old. She became too wild to be controlled by her owners and my mother took her, thinking she was worth saving. She grew up here and I came to love her as my younger sister. Eventually, my parents acquired enough courage to adopt her. She's loved by every single person who lives and works on my father's estate. It looks like you will be no different."

"She looks so delicate."

"Don't you believe it. But enough of her. What about you? Have you seen everything?"

"Twice!"

Julius chuckled.

"I have something to tell you. It appears your master may well have to present you with a mistress soon. My parents, not to mention Nero, are determined to see me marry. Sit down on this garden bench and I shall explain it all to you."

Chapter 14

Linona had become accustomed to her new status as a slave owned by Quintus Tiberius Saturninus and his wife Julia. Her natural tendency to be fiercely protective of her independence, serving nobody, which normally would have led her to seek opportunities to escape, had been deliberately supressed. She had a different priority, the protection of her unborn child. She'd no love for the baby growing inside her because it was the creation of an obscene act, her rape by several Roman soldiers. Nevertheless, she felt the motherly need, the instinctive sense of responsibility, the natural protective urge to do whatever she could to give the baby life. The poor, innocent thing hadn't had a say on whether it was to be conceived or not. She hadn't wanted to give much thought to how she would feel, or what she would do with it when the child was born. She couldn't imagine ever loving it. Somehow she didn't think of it as hers. In any case, born to be a slave, others may well decide its fate for her. She'd shared these troubling thoughts with her ever patient and understanding sister, Cailan.

She was ready to give birth now. She and Cailan had determined the baby was well overdue. Repeated hot baths and long walks around the grounds of the villa, as suggested by Julia, hadn't persuaded the baby to leave the comfortable warmth of its present surroundings.

"I feel as if I'm going to burst if this child doesn't come soon," groaned Linona, "and don't you dare say it will be here soon, Cailan. I'll scream if you do. You'll be chased out of here if you repeat it one more time, except I can barely walk, never mind run."

They both laughed at her desperate attempt at humour.

"Even I'm tired of hearing myself say it," Cailan admitted. "I've been thinking, though. Why don't we try one last variation of what we've been doing?"

"Which is?"

"You take a really hot bath. Afterwards, I rub lots of olive oil on your great fat lump, massaging you till my fingers hurt. And this is the new bit. While I'm doing that, we sing some of the lullabies our mother and the other women of our tribe used to sing to relax us all when we were children."

"Now you're being silly."

"At least I'm trying to think of something. Never mind, it will be here soon."

Cailan just managed to avoid one of her sister's shoes aimed at her head. After a while they were able to stop their laughter, mainly because Linona said it hurt too much. The mention of their mother prompted a long period of talking about the shared happy times of their youth. It helped to lighten Linona's impatient, bored mood.

"I've decided to humour you. Let's give your idea a try. Get the olive oil ready for after I've taken a bath and we shall see what the songs can do."

Whether it was the effect of Iceni lullabies or just coincidence, the occupants of the villa were woken in the middle of the night by Linona's cries. At first they were mostly of relief as she went into labour. A large proportion of those living in the villa played a part in what followed, especially Julia. An exception was Quintus, unless nervously pacing the corridors of the villa and the paths in the garden could have been regarded as helpful. However, Julia told him he was being useless just as he'd been when she'd given birth to their own two daughters. Quintus had apologised and looked even more distraught.

*

Late into the morning a healthy boy with a fine pair of lungs became yet one more slave to be added to Quintus's list of assets. He proudly held the boy when finally he'd been allowed in by his wife to see Linona.

"He's a fine boy," said Quintus. "Have you decided on an Iceni or a Roman name for him?"

"I haven't given it a thought. Something will come to me." Her words matched the disinterested look Linona had shown from the moment of birth. "I'm exhausted, too tired even to think."

"Of course you are," Julia added. "Let's all leave the room and let her get some much-needed sleep."

The following morning a much-rested Linona had asked for Cailan to come to her room.

"How are you feeling?" Cailan asked.

"A mixture of relief and something I hadn't expected at all. I think I'm going to love this beautiful little thing next to me."

Cailan, as was her tendency, couldn't control her emotional response. She pressed her tearful face against her sister's, clinging to her. Linona, not one to readily show her emotions, echoed her sister's sobs of joy. With some difficulty, they gained control. Linona began to look her serious self again.

"In the middle of the night, after the second or third feed, I was shocked to realise how precious my little boy was."

"Your little boy?"

"Yes! Despite how he came to me, he's still MY wonderful boy."

"I'm so happy for you. I always hoped that would happen for the sake of the baby, but just as much for you."

"After that first realisation, there was plenty of time in the quiet of the night for me to do some serious thinking."

"What about?"

"The future for the three of us. Doesn't that sound strange? The three of us. That's what I thought. We've concentrated our minds, both before and after our capture, on our survival. We've talked of a possible future escape if the opportunity arose."

"But you thought we wouldn't be welcome in our own homeland."

"I still think that. Added to that, this little boy would make an escape and survival practically impossible in the foreseeable future."

"What are you saying then?"

"Survival for the three of us for some years to come is best achieved here. We can hide our true identities with these good people. We can live here, maybe even prosper, in relative security."

"But we will still be slaves, Linona."

"I know that. And you know I won't accept that forever for either of us, I mean the three of us. I give you my word we shall be free again one day. In the meantime, there will be some joy in our lives again. Today has proven that to me. I have found hope again for us after all you and I have gone through."

"I really need you to be right. I agree with everything you've said."

"Our future is in our hands again."

Cailan hugged her sister before turning her attention to the baby.

"You still have to name him."

"I know. I'm at a complete loss."

"Bearing in mind what we've just been discussing, I have a suggestion."

"Please tell me."

"Early this morning, Julia and I were talking about your beautiful new baby. We both became quite emotional. She confessed to me one of the regrets in life she and Quintus both shared was that they had never had a boy. Had they done so, they would have called him Marcus after her father who she loved dearly. If you were to call this little one Marcus it would go some way to thank them for saving our lives, even as slaves."

"In a way, it will also set the seal on what we've just decided about our immediate future," Linona added. "I agree. Please find them and ask them to join us. We can tell them together."

Chapter 15

Septimus felt more than a little uncomfortable entering Nero's palace after such a long time. It was the first time he'd been there since his retirement. He was there to meet his son. They'd been invited to join Nero's group for a day at the chariot races held in the Circus Maximus. He hadn't needed much persuading. Like most of the citizens of Rome he marvelled at the spectacle they provided, especially on a day such as this, the religious festival of Claudius the God. It would also give him the opportunity to see whether Decianus's sometimes unhealthy love of gambling from his youth had diminished any during his time in Britannia. If it hadn't, he could try once again to teach him the error of his ways, something he'd failed miserably to achieve in the past.

Calling here first, presented him with the additional opportunity to see his old friend Seneca. It was why he was pleased to find them both in Seneca's workroom.

"I think it's time you two put away your documents and scrolls for the day, don't you?" he said.

"We do indeed, Father. Seneca just needs a little nudge from the right person. Someone like you for instance."

"Welcome, old friend," said a smiling Seneca. "It's good to see you. I hope life is being good to you."

"Well, it has so far. From memory, I recall these days at the Circus as having a tendency to be a bit fraught with danger. An excess of wine, gambling and partisan support for the four racing teams always carried the potential for trouble."

"Sounds like an excellent reason for us to join the activities," Decianus quipped.

Before anyone could comment further they were interrupted by the entrance of Burrus. He looked surprised at first to see Seneca wasn't alone. He murmured a quiet greeting to Septimus, completely ignoring Decianus.

The dark, menacing expression on Burrus's face suggested to Septimus something very serious was causing him great concern. His next words confirmed it.

"I need to talk to Seneca urgently about our arrangements for the races today. Alone!"

"Would you please excuse us, gentlemen?" Seneca added. "We'll see you later in the Emperor's royal pavilion."

Outside in the corridor Decianus looked annoyed.

"What could have caused that ill-mannered display?"

Septimus sniggered a little. "Could have been anything. However, he's probably concerned about something involving Nero which might not go to plan today. Still, his intervention allows us to get to the stadium in good time."

"I hadn't been expecting this invitation to the royal pavilion," said Decianus.

"No. But since we've been provided with one, we mustn't be late."

He didn't reveal that he felt uncomfortable at the thought of getting close to Nero again.

*

The royal pavilion in the Circus Maximus had been virtually filled to capacity with Senators, nobles and their wives, anxious to show their loyalty to their God. The ample supply of free wine had ensured a light, friendly atmosphere full of humour and some careful sarcasm.

The impressive structure was positioned towards the end of one of the extremely long straights, adjacent to the winning post. As well as the best view of the finish of races it also gave a clear sight of the spectacular struggles and crashes as charioteers fought and manoeuvred for position, urging their horses around one of the two 180-degree turns. Nero had extended it considerably, adding a long balcony to provide unrestricted views of the racing.

Septimus had received many a genuine warm welcome from friends, some of which he hadn't seen for a few years. He was feeling the loss of these good people.

It reminded him that that was one of the curses of retirement from court.

The atmosphere suddenly froze as the word was passed around that the Emperor was approaching the pavilion. Accompanied by Poppaea, he made his entrance to loud applause and cheering from those gathered there. Closely in attendance, almost breathing down their necks, came Seneca and Burrus. Their faces bore the forced expressions of delight at the rapturous reception the royal couple received. So genuinely delighted was Nero that he turned to Seneca and asked for him to pass his lyre.

"Friends. I'm so pleased so many of you have come today to honour my predecessor. Your happy, joyful reception makes me want to add to it by sharing with you my latest poetry. I have written it especially for this occasion. Would you all like to hear it?"

The cries of support were deafening.

"You won't be disappointed," he boasted.

The rendition took a considerably long time with Nero repeating some of his better passages to ensure everybody had understood them. The faces of those present showed varying degrees of disbelief and amazement.

Septimus was reminded there were benefits that flowed from retirement from court.

The end of the performance was met with rapturous cries of wonder, with some appearing to try to outdo one another. The result was a burst of ecstatic giggling from Nero. When order was restored, Poppaea seized the initiative.

"I think the only thing that could follow that is the commencement of the day's celebrations."

"I agree," said Nero, moving into the full glare of the burning sun shining down on the balcony and terraces of the gigantic, elongated oval arena.

He was met by a wall of sound from the voices of the many tens of thousands who had filled it. Septimus knew Nero would be thinking the cheering was for him. He also knew most of it came from those who'd almost given up hope in the heat that the racing would ever start. Their shouts were really cries of relief. Nero gave the signal and the opening parade began.

First to enter the racing track from the entrance, just to the right of the royal pavilion, were the musicians. They immediately strolled past Nero and his guests, bowing to him as they did so. The noise from the terraces meant few were able to hear and enjoy the music being played.

A short distance behind these, came row upon row of dancers, doing their best to hear and follow what was being played for them. They were eventually followed by a group of less organised children carrying large baskets filled with flower petals. From time to time, they rushed to the spectators nearest the edge of the track, throwing handfuls over them.

The last group to join the parade were the charioteers who would be risking injury and death in the races to be held for the crowd's enjoyment. They were all on foot and led by the four main charioteers of the competing teams. Pompously ambling past each section of the terraces, they received praise approaching worship.

At the rear of the whole parade came a chariot pulled by eight amazing horses. The chariot, much larger than those used for the racing, contained three track attendants. One held the reins, struggling to contain the spirited animals. The other two carried a huge bust of Claudius, garlanded with flowers. The applause wasn't nearly as enthusiastic as that given to the charioteers.

As if planned, the inevitable happened. One of the eight horses happened to empty its full bladder, followed soon afterward by another emptying its bowels. It caused much amusement amongst those who could see this undignified display. It included those on the royal balcony.

"I see the offerings to our God have begun," suggested Nero, causing even more laughter.

He paused for it to die down a little before making a further comment.

"I do believe it's a message from dear Claudius. I note the insignia decorating the heads of both the guilty horses were those of the Red team. I must change my practice of betting on White. By the look of it, those Red horses should be considerably lighter and faster as a result of their generous offerings."

The parade completed, the constant loud noise was replaced by a much quieter excited murmuring, anticipating what was about to follow. Nero and the others had withdrawn from the balcony temporarily to seek the welcome shade, and perhaps to refill empty wine goblets.

What began as a low continuous background sound, gradually built up into a full-bodied chanting of the name of Claudius. It spread throughout the arena. Nero, Poppaea and the others returned to the balcony to marvel at what was happening. Septimus wondered why Seneca and Burrus had moved to stand much closer to the royal couple than they'd done until then.

Nero was pleased. He would see it as a confirmation of the love for him being expressed by this show of admiration for his predecessor. His expression began to change as the name the crowd were chanting gradually started to alter.

"What's happening?" enquired a puzzled Poppaea. "What are they saying?"

"They are calling out the name of Octavia," shouted Burrus urgently.

His loud reply could be heard by all those on the balcony.

"Why would they shout that witch's name?"

"She's the daughter of Claudius, and has always been a great favourite of the citizens of our city," replied Burrus.

"Perhaps they're making a point about her absence today," added Seneca, speaking just as loudly as Burrus had.

Just at that moment, large white flowers began to be thrown onto the racing surface immediately below the balcony. The gesture was being repeated at intervals all along the edge of the track.

"And what is that all about?" she demanded. "I thought the parading and flower throwing had all ended."

"White lilies, which they appear to be, were Octavia's favourites,"

Seneca explained. "She was known throughout Rome for that."

"We're leaving!" Poppaea ordered, looking directly at Nero.

"Why, my dear?" Nero protested. "We've not long since arrived and the racing hasn't even begun."

"I've begun to feel unwell. This child of yours has decided it wants me to spend the rest of the day vomiting. Please clear the way," she ordered, turning to face the exit.

Seneca and Burrus stood to one side as she and Nero stormed past. Septimus saw a brief smile of satisfaction pass between them before they followed on behind. Knowing them as he did, he began to realise what might be occurring. He felt he might be understanding the significance of the earlier anxious interruption by Burrus into Seneca's room, and the close attention and ready explanations they'd given to Nero and Poppaea at a dramatic point in the proceedings.

It reminded him of the enjoyment of intrigue that retirement had taken away from him.

When Nero's little group had gone, everyone else who'd remained gradually recovered from their shock at how events had taken an unexpected turn. They began to gossip excitedly. A voice, protected by the anonymity of the back of the pavilion probably summed up what most of them were thinking.

"It could be baby sickness. Then again, it could be bad poetry, or even an allergic reaction to flowers, especially lilies. We shall never know for sure."

Much appreciated, the comments restored the humour and excitement of earlier.

*

"What's going on?" Poppaea demanded.

She and Nero had finally arrived in the Palace, after a difficult short journey through crowds, who like those in the arena were carrying white lilies.

"It's further evidence of the affection our citizens have for Octavia," Seneca replied.

"Some of them were shouting personal abuse at Poppaea," Nero added angrily. "Why didn't you arrest them on the spot, Burrus?"

"There were too many. I only had a small escort. I was intent on getting you here to safety."

"Then, why don't you put together a much larger force to go and find them and have them executed?"

"It would be impossible to find the culprits now to arrest them. In any case their numbers would appear to be too great."

"Go to arrest any street vermin then and say they did it, Burrus," snarled Poppaea. "Executing a significant number would set a good example for the future."

"It would also be extremely provocative in the current situation."

Nero began to walk to and fro across the floor, wringing his hands. "What can we do, Seneca?"

"Stop pacing. Calm down!" shouted Poppaea, attempting to gain control.

"I have something to suggest," Seneca offered.

"Anything," pleaded Nero.

"You've sent Octavia into exile to an offshore island. Perhaps the people think it was too severe a punishment for the daughter of their new God. You could still maintain her in a form of exile, but let that take place in Rome."

"That doesn't make sense."

"It does if she's exiled to her own villa. She could be banned from having any normal contact with the outside world."

"She would be living here in Rome, when I want her out of my life!" screamed Poppaea.

"She would be a prisoner in Rome playing no part in the city's life, whether it be social, political or anything else."

"Would that make the people love me again?" Nero asked.

"I'm certain it would," Seneca replied, smiling at him supportively.

"Then I accept. Arrange it immediately. I want things back to normal. How can I perform my poetry and music with the depth of feeling it demands when I'm troubled in this way?"

Poppaea stormed out, quickly followed by Nero. Another silent smile of satisfaction, broader this time, passed between Seneca and Burrus.

*

"You're too weak and foolish for words at times!" Poppaea yelled in rage. "Those two still dominate you. I will have to get rid of them once and for all."

"You misunderstand me, my love. What is worse, you underestimate me. I'm manipulating those two, not the other way round."

"What are you talking about?"

"I shall get you what you want."

"How? I want her dead, out of our lives."

"She will return to Rome. After a short time I shall invent another grievous act against me by her. After this wonderful public show of mercy to her, I shall have no difficulty ending her miserable life. Being the daughter of a God won't save her a second time."

"You promise?" she whispered, snuggling up to him.

"I give you my word. Soon we shall find a way to be free of her."

*

Much later, Septimus had gone to look at the small house Decianus had recently purchased close to the centre of the city.

"What do you think of it?" asked Decianus, not really interested in a reply.

"It appears comfortable and ideal for your new position with Seneca."

"Exactly! Now, would you like a drink of wine to celebrate?"

"No, thank you. I've drunk too much already today for a man of my age. Did you enjoy the races?"

"They were spectacular. I'd forgotten how much pleasure they gave me."

Decianus hadn't had much time to think about the day they'd shared, but he began to realise how good his new life was going to be.

"Even after losing all the money you did? You really must learn

101

how to control yourself on these occasions."

"Please not again, Father. Can we talk about something else?"

"In that case, what did you think about the Octavia incident?"

"I thought that was extraordinary. I would never have expected such a spontaneous outburst from that crowd."

"Perhaps it wasn't so spontaneous."

"What do you mean?"

"I got the clear impression Seneca and Burrus weren't surprised at all. Perhaps they were half expecting it."

"You mean they could have organised something along those lines between them?"

"Maybe. I wouldn't put it past them."

"But why would they want to cause such a fuss about her? She's been found to be an adulteress. She deserved to get what she got."

"I think they would both like to see her pardoned and returned to Rome, but perhaps for different reasons."

"Such as?"

"Maybe I will tell you more later. It wouldn't help you to know at this time what I think might be the case. These are becoming increasingly dangerous times, being made worse by our Emperor's new wife. Remaining ignorant about some matters, while concentrating on your new limited role at the Palace, will be in your best interests for now."

*

Decianus was intrigued by his father's teasing comments. Behaviour that was quite like him. After Septimus had left him to return home, he contented himself with another drink of wine. Far from accepting that he should remain ignorant about whatever was being hinted at, he'd been frustrated. He had to find out what was behind his father's veiled comments. A far as his new post was concerned, he viewed it as only a temporary holding position.

Chapter 16

"Isn't this the most beautiful morning? Julius, I swear there isn't a cloud to be seen."

Procilla had entered the kitchen from the garden at the rear of the villa, her arms full of freshly picked flowers. Without breaking her stride she passed them to one of the household slaves and went to sit next to her son at the small dining table. He'd just finished a light snack before he was heading off to speak with Fausto and Olsar.

"Good morning, Mother. I'm running a little late today – too much wine and catching up with Lucius."

"Talking about the war I suppose."

"That and other things. He told me to expect Domitia and her parents this evening."

"That's good! I thought he might leave it to me to break the news to you."

"Don't worry, Mother. I won't embarrass you both. I'll give you my answer soon. Let's see what this evening brings."

"Changing the subject, Lucius held his wine better than you last night, or had less of it. He left early this morning to go to the Senate. He wants you to meet him there."

"That's strange. He didn't mention it last night."

"Huh! Too much wine!"

"Did he say why and when?"

"Only to meet him at the Senate House soon after midday. He'll explain why when you get together."

The conversation ended there, interrupted as conversations

tended to be by Selima rushing into the room, eager to gain everyone's attention.

"Julius! I'm glad to see you. I was going to leave you a message with Mother."

"I'm here and I'm listening."

"Good. I just wanted to let you know Olsar won't be available today."

"I told you he only receives instructions from me, Selima."

"It's not an instruction I've given him. It's a request. He's taking me riding to show me how to ride my horse bareback, Iceni style. We'll see you all later. Bye!"

"But…" Julius didn't have time to complete his objection before she dashed out, waving her arms vigorously.

"None of us could ever control her. Perhaps her new love can."

"What new love?"

"Have a word with your sister."

"I most certainly will."

*

After his absence in the less than sophisticated frontier territory in the far north, the architectural wonders of the Forum filled Julius with pride and awe. He wandered around for a while, soaking in the splendour. Eventually he made his way into the Senate House. He was directed into a minor meeting room by one of the guards at the entrance.

"Your timing couldn't have been better, Julius," said Lucius. "Please take a seat."

"This is all a little unexpected, Father."

"Yes. Sorry I forgot to mention it last night. I suspect it was a combination of age and being totally absorbed in your exploits with the Brits. Still, let me tell you why you're here. You remember Senator Piso don't you?"

"I've met him when he's visited the villa. I remember him being a charismatic, distinguished-looking man from an old noble family."

"That's him. He's one of the most influential and respected members of the Senate. He's asked me to join him and several other Senators at his villa here in the city."

"What's the reason?"

"He didn't say other than it was important. He also said it was part social, which is why you have been asked to attend."

"Why me?"

"He's asked the former much admired Consul of Rome, Vespasian, to be there. Piso said your invitation was prompted by him. It's a bit of a mystery to me."

"Not to me, perhaps. I served briefly with his son in Britannia."

"That could explain it. So! It's time we went to meet them."

*

"I want to thank you all for coming," said Senator Piso. "You all know each other, so introductions aren't necessary, except perhaps for Julius, Lucius's son. He's just returned from playing a key part in defeating Boudica."

Vespasian, Seneca and all three Senators present introduced themselves briefly.

"Julius has been asked to attend so that you can learn directly from him all about the rebellion and how it was ended. Vespasian is particularly interested since his son Titus also played a part, and in fact is presently serving as staff officer to Paulinus."

"I am indeed interested," Vespasian added. "Titus has suggested I get to know you, Julius. He sends his regards."

"Thank you, Sir."

"You can call me Vespasian. I stopped being a soldier many years ago."

Julius smiled his appreciation of the old General's move to help him to relax.

"Having introduced you, Julius, I have to beg your forgiveness for what I'm going to ask of you," said Piso. "I need to talk to everyone else here about a confidential matter concerning the work of the Senate. My wife, who you met a few moments ago, is standing by to look after you for a while. She will show you around our little home."

"I fully understand," said Julius, leaving as requested.

"What I'm about to say would lead to my death, probably by torture, if Nero was to hear of it," Piso began. "When I say I would trust each one of you with my life, that's precisely what I'm about to do."

"I have a suspicion of what you're about to tell us," interrupted Vespasian, "and it makes me feel uncomfortable. However, I will hear you out."

"Thank you, old friend. Let me begin. Like most of you I managed to survive the reign of that lunatic, Caligula. I did so because I was only a junior official in his administration. I'm no longer able to hide from the glare of this latest increasingly unstable ruler. The same applies to all of you as it did to those Senators and others who've already met their death in recent times, either executed or forced to commit suicide to protect their families."

"What are you suggesting?" asked Seneca.

"I'm asking you all to consider whether we just carry on with things only getting worse as that man's madness develops, or is it time for us to do something to bring about change?"

"You are talking about assassinating Nero," suggested Lucius, looking concerned.

"That's one option. The Praetorian Guard got rid of Caligula."

"I don't see the current commander of our Guard here," Vespasian noted.

"I don't know him nearly well enough to include him at this stage of my thinking. That's why I asked Seneca to join us. He knows him better than anyone. What does Burrus think of Nero, Seneca?"

"He has the same opinion as virtually anyone who has to deal with him. He's rapidly losing faith in him, and like the rest of us becoming increasingly uncertain about his own future. However, I don't think he would be in favour of anything drastic at this time and I would agree with him. He would realise the need to be sure he could carry his men with him, particularly his second-in-command, Faenius. That takes time and would be very dangerous."

A general discussion began, mainly about the defects in the personality of Nero. Seneca was asked to pass on the experience he'd gained of the new Empress and the effect she was having on Nero. Seneca was honest in his description of the reducing influence and restraint he and Burrus were able to apply. Vespasian, having made virtually no contribution until then, raised his hand signalling his intention to speak. He waited until he had everyone's attention.

"I share the concerns the rest of you have. Like you, I would wish we had an Emperor worthy of the people who make this Empire great. We haven't, and an alternative to Nero at this time doesn't exist. There is no legitimate heir. Nero and his predecessors between them have managed to wipe out every single member of the family of Augustus. Not only is there no legitimate heir, there's no obvious successor anywhere else strong enough to establish order. If we assassinate him there would be chaos. There would be civil war again. Having an Emperor, even with the faults of Nero, prevents such horror. With a lunatic in charge, at least the few of us that die at his whim are nothing compared to the tens of thousands that are wiped out when we fight one another. I will play no part in a plot to remove Nero, now or in the future. However, you have my word I will keep today's discussion a secret."

Nobody argued against the logic of what they'd just heard. Instead a silence fell on the group, contemplating the immediate future ahead of them. Piso broke the silence.

"We hear what you say, friend. Your courage and wisdom is what we need. I only ask all of you to take away the thought that sooner or later action may be forced upon us. I will be ready. I would ask you, Seneca, to keep me informed of the attitude of Burrus. He would need to be a part of a plot, mine or any other."

"I share Vespasian's views," Seneca replied. "I'm not interested in any plot, but I will do as you ask regarding Burrus."

Lucius said nothing. The other Senators' comments were more supportive of Piso's intention to play a waiting and watching game, perhaps seeing themselves as likely to be the ones who could fall victim to one of Nero's whims.

"That's perhaps sufficient for today. Let's all relax," Piso added finally. "I would just add that some of what Vespasian just said has reminded us that it is the Senate, the people of Rome and our Legions that make our Empire great. Let's bring back one of our gallant young tribunes to share his recent experiences with us."

*

Julius spent a long time answering questions. By the end he began to hope this was going to be the last time he would have to describe what happened in Britannia. Somehow he doubted it. Eventually Vespasian and Julius chose to walk around the garden to talk privately.

"My son, Titus, says you became good friends in the short time you were in Britannia, Julius."

"Indeed we did. One of my regrets in leaving was we didn't have more time to work together."

"And the other regrets?"

"Mainly a feeling that I would have liked to have played a part in rebuilding what the war had destroyed, and I don't just mean the buildings. Paulinus saw things a bit differently."

"In his correspondence, Titus hinted at a difference of approach you had with the Governor. Not very wise for a junior officer. Is that why you returned to Rome?"

"It would have been difficult for me to remain on Paulinus's staff. I think he genuinely thought I had more to offer the Empire than reverting back to being a legionary tribune in an outlying fort in that Province. I agreed with him."

"I'm sure you're both right. Certainly, Titus has suggested I try to use any influence I may still have on your behalf. My retirement looks like continuing, so I'm limited in what I can do. However, if I can help, I will."

"The only person likely to decide on my immediate future is Nero, but thank you all the same."

"You met my brother-in-law, Cerialis, no doubt."

"I did indeed."

"What did you think of him?"

"I thought he was a shrewd, courageous military commander."

"A little flattering, but mostly true. What about the loss of half his Legion?"

"He gave a good account of himself, which is why, despite his own preference, Paulinus has kept him as Legate of the 9th."

"He lacks wider tactical awareness, and could improve his diplomatic skills, but I would have him as one of my loyal commanders anytime."

"I fully understand. Whether I would enjoy being his subordinate is another matter."

Vespasian gave a little chuckle.

"I can see your bravery extends beyond the battlefield. Your honesty even when it might be detrimental to you is appealing. I would welcome you as my subordinate if the situation ever arises again, and who knows, in these precarious times stranger things could happen."

"Thank you Si… Vespasian!"

"It's time we went back to the others."

*

Back at their villa Julius and his father were taking the opportunity to enjoy a relaxing period in the bathhouse. Julius had been given a full account of the discussion which took place in his absence, including the views of all those present.

"That was a potentially very dangerous move by Piso," Julius asserted.

"Don't be too alarmed. Piso is a very astute man. He knows each of those present wouldn't betray him or each other."

"I share Vespasian's view about the consequences of anything as foolhardy as was being suggested by Piso."

"So do I," Lucius agreed, "but it wasn't the view of everyone. We must remain separate from any action doomed to failure, however attractive it may appear. Enough of this, though. Your future bride will be here shortly."

Julius's solemn expression went unnoticed by his father.

*

Julius's day until the early evening arrived had been reasonably satisfying, if a little disconcerting. There was the hint of troubling things about Selima and Olsar, and his learning of Piso's intentions. Then things got a lot worse.

"My father won't appreciate you taking me into this room alone for us to discuss our marriage," argued Domitia.

"He has no choice. This is between the two of us. You have to realise I haven't the slightest wish to marry you or anyone else for that matter at this time."

"What has that got to do with it? It's what our parents want and need. That's all that's necessary."

"From what I've experienced of you this evening, I have an instinctive dislike of you. True, you're an attractive young woman. But it isn't sufficient reason for me to agree to marriage. To add to that you're five years younger than I am."

"That is all irrelevant. By the way, the dislike is mutual. In addition, I can't say I'm filled with delight at marrying into a socially inferior family, but I recognise my family's economic necessity."

"What are you expecting from me, then, from a marriage which appears to be doomed from the start?"

"Children! And you are helping me to do my duty, to honour my parents' wishes. It's the Roman way."

"Doesn't nature's way, attraction and affection, come into your thinking?"

"Only as a supplementary ideal. I've said all I wish to on this matter. Earlier, I could see my father giving yours some very angry looks in his direction. Tonight was supposed to be a formality. Commitments have been given previously and the financial arrangements agreed between them. We've delayed things long enough. We must re-join them."

"What If I tell them I won't agree to their bargain?"

"Don't be silly."

"If we do marry we shall both regret it."

"Don't most married couples, whether there's love or not to start with? That's why there are lovers, mistresses and divorces. We shall be going into this marriage with our eyes wide open. I shall have children and a husband who my father thinks is destined for greater things. You will benefit from the undoubted influence my father's name carries. We shall make the most of it and become successful. I'm going back in there."

*

The following evening Olsar was walking slowly to join Julius in his rooms. That morning he had been told by Julius he wanted to discuss something important with him. Work pressures around the villa had prevented them getting together earlier. In the less busy parts of the day he'd given some thought to what it might be. His final conclusion, as he knocked on his door, was that it must be connected with the visit Julius and his father made to the city.

"Come in, Olsar."

"You wanted to discuss something important with me."

"Two things, actually. Take a seat. First things first. Get yourself some wine. I'm going to get drunk."

"You look and sound as if you're halfway there already. Are you ordering me, your slave, to get drunk with you?"

"Suit yourself. I'm full of self-pity and self-loathing. You're going to sit here and listen to me tell you why, whether you get drunk with me or remain sober."

"In that case, I choose the wine."

"Do you know who visited last evening?"

"Selima has spoken to me about it."

"She has, has she? That's the other thing for us to talk about later. So, you will know that the very attractive young lady who came is intending to be my wife."

"Congratulations."

"Drink your wine quicker. You have some catching up to do. Your good wishes aren't appreciated. I'm feeling almost suicidal."

"Be my guest. At the rate you're going you'll achieve that with wine."

"Your humour is in poor taste and is also not appreciated. Well, perhaps not."

"It might be worth you starting to tell me what it is you want to say, while you still can."

"Last night I agreed to go along with my parents' wishes to get married to that young woman."

"What's the problem? It's a normal practice in your society for parents to do that, as it was in mine."

"It's not *my* normal! Have another drink. Every inch of me was saying no, but I said yes. Why did I do that?"

"You tell me. This wine is very good. I don't get much opportunity to drink it these days. We should do something about that."

"Very funny! The reason is I gave my love to somebody else who I can never have. I've taken a coward's way out and surrendered. You wouldn't understand. Have another drink."

"It must be the first time in your life you've ever considered yourself to be a coward. You have no idea of what I understand about the matters of the heart. Finally, I don't need any encouragement to drink anymore. I'm almost up to full speed."

"You sound annoyed. Does wine do that to you?"

"No. In your case it appears to make you depressed, and repeat yourself."

"I am very depressed. Do you want to know who the woman was who came to mean everything to me? It may shock you."

"You're going to tell me anyway."

"It was Linona."

Olsar stopped his drink of wine halfway to his mouth. He couldn't stop staring at Julius.

"Well! Say something."

"I am shocked, disbelieving. And yet it shouldn't surprise me if any man fell in love with her. I did."

It was Julius's turn to be shocked. Then they spent some time telling each other how, when and why they'd become smitten.

"She hated me, you know," moaned Julius.

"I know. I did at the time. I only loathe you now."

"Very funny again." Julius laughed. Olsar joined him.

"In my case she told me she only loved me as a friend. I don't know which is worse."

"Do we think she's still alive?" Julius speculated, as much thinking aloud as asking a question.

"Until I hear differently, I will always think so."

"I'm getting married because, whether she's alive or dead, I will never see her again. Would you ever marry?"

"Until recently, I would have thought not."

"That brings me to the other thing I wanted to say. Have another drink. My mother said yesterday that Selima has another love. Do you have any idea what she means?"

Olsar's face went a deeper red than that already caused by the wine.

"It's you, isn't it? You're in a worse situation than me."

"I have never met anyone as fascinating as Selima in my life, not even Linona. I'm sure she feels the same about me."

"You realise it can't go anywhere. She will be my father's responsibility for a few years yet. Given that he knows you fought alongside Boudica, he would never approve of her marrying you, even if I gave you your freedom to make it possible."

"Sometimes love finds a way."

"Have another drink."

Chapter 17

Decianus had a problem. How was he going to expose Octavia and Burrus without it becoming known generally that he was the source of the information which led to the final downfall, even the death, of Octavia? Burrus certainly wouldn't escape execution. Events several months ago had demonstrated her popularity throughout Rome leading to her return. While he could ensure he received some initial recognition from Nero and Poppaea he had to be careful. There would be many others who held her in such great affection they would be sure to try to discover who betrayed her and seek revenge.

His father's veiled comments had prompted him to look deeper into the motives behind Seneca and Burrus's efforts to secure her release from exile. Seneca had proved to be above suspicion. That was only what could be expected, given his well-known long friendship with her. Burrus's intentions were much less innocent. His frequent visits to her villa since her return had been noticed by Decianus and appeared to him to be way beyond what was necessary to ensure she was complying with the strict terms of her confinement. Decianus had used money from the Treasury to offer bribes to slaves from her household to keep him secretly informed of happenings at the villa when Burrus was with Octavia. The information he'd received showed clearly they were lovers.

He found the solution to his problem when Seneca had gossiped with him about the tensions existing between Burrus and his openly ambitious second-in-command, Faenius. He gave the information he'd gained to Faenius on the understanding that if he used it he would not disclose his source other than to Nero and Poppaea.

Decianus was about to improve his future prospects considerably.

Not only would his standing rise with Nero, but he would have gained a very valuable future ally in the undoubted replacement Commander of the Praetorian Guard.

*

Burrus was being forced onto his knees by two powerful men from his command. They stood either side of him, each with a firm grip of an arm. Behind him, a third had a tight grip of his hair forcing his head back. To one side stood a grinning Faenius.

"You disappoint me greatly, Burrus," snarled Nero. "All these years I've honoured and trusted you. This is how you betray me."

"What is going on?" cried Poppaea as she came running into the room. "Why is Burrus on his knees?"

"This dog has betrayed me."

"How?"

"Faenius has discovered he and Octavia are lovers."

Poppaea's hand clutched her throat in shock.

"Admit your treason. Tell me how long it's been going on," Nero demanded, leaning close to his face, his lip curling in hatred.

He didn't get an answer to his question, at least not one he was expecting. Burrus, with great difficulty, forced his own face slightly forward to fully empty the bloody spittle from his mouth, full into the face of Nero, who staggered back, screaming.

"Poppaea! Poppaea!"

"Faenius," she barked. "Take this animal away and torture an answer to your Emperor's last question out of him. Don't return until you have it."

When they were alone, Poppaea was able to calm her distraught husband.

"How could he do such a vile thing to me, and in front of my Guards?" he bawled.

"It will be amongst the last things he ever does," she replied. "He doesn't have to confess. His vile act said it all."

"What are we going to do with the two of them?"

"The Gods have answered my prayers. Don't you see? We can dispose of the two of them without any fear of similar unrest like last time. She has shamed herself before everybody. No one will expect her to be pardoned this time. However, we will act with swift justice, just in case."

A long time later a crestfallen Faenius returned.

"Well!" demanded Nero. "Where is he? How long has it been going on?"

"No matter what we did, he wouldn't confess. His only words were to say she wouldn't be condemned by words from his mouth. Eventually his body gave out. He died a few moments ago."

"That's unfortunate, Faenius," said Poppaea. "But, it's no serious matter. We still have her. We won't allow her to die before she confesses. Go to arrest her and bring her here without any delay. On your way out, arrange for Seneca to come to see us immediately."

"Why have you sent for him?" Nero asked when they were alone.

"He worked closely with Burrus as your adviser for years. He may well have known of her adultery. If he did and didn't tell you he's just as guilty as they are."

*

"You wish to see me," said Seneca.

"We do," replied Poppaea. "We've sent for Octavia. There's a matter we want to discuss with her. It may involve you."

"Can I ask what it's about?"

"It's a delicate matter. We prefer to wait."

What could have been a very awkward period was partly rescued by a general discussion about the level of reserves in the Treasury. They also discussed the favourable progress of Decianus.

Octavia's expression showed her concern and uncertainty when she was led into the room by Faenius.

"Why have you brought me here, Nero?" she demanded indignantly. Her stern gaze passed from him across the face of Poppaea to settle in a smile on Seneca.

"How long has your affair with Burrus been going on?" Nero

demanded.

"Don't be ridiculous."

Seneca looked startled and puzzled. "What is this all about?"

"Be quiet," Poppaea ordered.

"I know you've been having an affair. What I want to know is how long this treachery has been taking place."

"Who has been spreading these lies?"

"It's you who's lying," Poppaea said. "Burrus has confessed."

"That can't be. You're trying to trick me."

"I think it might be a good time to bring the two lovers together, don't you, husband?"

Nero showed his agreement by ordering Faenius to have Burrus brought in. The three guards from earlier strode in, carrying between them the broken and bloodied body into the room. They flung it onto the floor at Octavia's feet. She gave a long agonised scream. Seneca let out a deep gasp of anguish.

"You monster," was all Octavia could say.

"Tell me how long and I will let you live."

Octavia didn't reply immediately. She stared blankly at Nero, appearing to gain control and collect her thoughts. Then she spoke.

"I have no wish to live now you have slaughtered the love of my life."

Poppaea smiled broadly.

"You ask me how long. The answer is for several years. It was the only way I could stop myself from following you into insanity. His love gave me something to live for. You've destroyed it. Do your worst. You are a madman and I've no wish to live in a world that allows you to be Emperor."

"Take her away," Nero ordered. "She's very stressed. My wife and I will come to tend to her later. I will give her a little potion which will help her to sleep."

Poppaea giggled. Nero laughed. Seneca moaned.

When the three of them were alone Seneca was interrogated extensively about what he knew about the affair. Poppaea noticed he appeared to have aged considerably from when he'd entered the room. He looked a weary and broken man. He would no longer be her rival for Nero's ear. She had listened to him and decided he had nothing to answer for.

"I am convinced. You were innocent. Don't you agree, my love?"

"I do," replied Nero. "You are free to go."

"I have a request to make. I've served you for most of your life as tutor and advisor. I'm getting old and feel very tired. I feel I'm no longer able to give you the guidance you need. I ask you to reward my years of faithful service to you by allowing me to retire."

Nero seemed surprised and looked unsure of what to do. He turned to his wife. Poppaea knew exactly what to say.

"You've served your Emperor well. You are released."

Seneca stumbled out of the room and Poppaea gave a big sigh before continuing.

"Well, my love. This has been a rewarding day. Many problems have been solved and obstacles removed. We are now free to rule unhindered."

Chapter 18

"You do realise I've met Poppaea before, don't you?" Domitia boasted.

"Lucky you," mocked Selima.

Making sure Domitia wasn't looking at her, she screwed her face up and stuck her tongue out at her. Looking pleased with herself she looked at Procilla for approval, only to receive an angry, cold stare from her.

"Yes!" Domitia continued. "When she was married to her first husband, Otho, they were good friends of my parents. They would make frequent visits to our villa. She's very, very beautiful."

"That must be why Nero stole her," said Selima.

"That's quite enough, young lady," Procilla warned. "Have you met Nero before, Domitia?"

"Not that I can recall. However, my father was a good friend of Emperor Claudius. So it's quite possible I may well have done so when I was a child."

"Well! You'll meet both of them later when they come to spend part of the day with us."

"Has all the food and wine been arranged?" Lucius asked nervously for the third time that morning.

"Yes! Yes!" Procilla shouted. "If you ask me one more time I won't answer you."

"Have I told you I've invited Vespasian and his wife to join us to give us moral support?"

"Yes! Three times. Now will you please relax? Go for a walk

around the garden. I'm sure Vespasian will be here soon to calm you down. He wouldn't want to arrive after the Royal guests. You can go with your father, Selima. Talk the nerves out of him. By the way, there's no need for you to join us all later. Since neither you nor I can control what you say, it wouldn't be in the interests of your father's good health if you were to engage in a conversation with either Nero or his wife."

"Thank you so much, Mother. Come on, Father. Let's escape."

*

To Lucius's great relief the meal was going well. Nero appeared to be enjoying the casual conversation which was taking place.

"Are you enjoying your retirement?" he asked Vespasian.

"It's a good life, if somewhat quiet."

"You had a long and successful career I believe, both as a soldier and a politician."

"By some people's standard, I suppose."

"You could still be of use to me. I shall keep you in mind."

Vespasian gave a little shrug of his shoulders as if to indicate what will happen, will happen.

"And you, Julius. Are you enjoying your temporary role helping your father to run this wonderful estate of his?"

"It's certainly different from my life in the recent past."

"Speaking of which, I have yet to meet your pet Iceni. Have him brought here. He could prove entertaining."

Lucius, no doubt noticing the look of agitation appear on Julius's face, intervened before any damage could be done. He gave an instruction to one of the slaves present to fetch Olsar without delay. Nero continued to show interest in Agricola.

"I was pleased to hear from your father that you'd taken my advice and got married to this charming woman."

He pointed to Domitia who looked suitably coy.

"I wasn't aware, however, until I arrived today that you'd gone one step further and made this beauty pregnant."

Julius was saved the difficulty of trying to sound enthusiastic in his reply by Poppaea's intervention to question Domitia.

"How much longer have you to go before your baby is to be born?"

"I'm told by Procilla that she thinks there are still three months before it is due."

"I suppose you will want to provide Julius with a son and heir as I'd hoped for," added Nero. "Let's all hope you won't be disappointed as we were."

The room went deathly quiet.

"I told you, my love. Our daughter is perfect for us," Poppaea insisted. "We shall have a son next time."

Awkward silence returned until it was broken by Domitia, who must have assumed her comment would be useful.

"The Empress and I have met before when you used to visit my parents with your first husband."

"I can't say I recognise you," Poppaea replied, her voice full of menace.

Domitia was saved by the timely return of the slave closely followed by Olsar. Julius signalled Olsar to stand close to him. The last thing Julius would want, following Domitia's insensitive comment, was for Olsar to take a seat before being given permission.

While Nero was having a brief, quiet conversation with Poppaea, Julius took the opportunity to whisper into Olsar's ear.

"Call him, 'Sir' or 'my Emperor'."

"I know. Trust me!"

"So, you are Julius's Iceni slave, one of those ferocious Brits," Nero observed. "Do you have a name I can pronounce?"

"Olsar, Sir."

"And how have you found our glorious Rome, Olsar, compared with your barbarian land?"

"There's much to be admired, Sir."

"Indeed there is. Take the Amphitheatre for instance. That's where the gladiators, mostly ex-warriors, as you were, I believe, fight to the death for the glory of Rome. Most of them are slaves just like you."

"I understand that to be the case, Sir."

"I think you would make a valuable addition to their ranks by the look of you."

Julius couldn't hide his discomfort, shuffling in his stance. Olsar stood rock-still, his blank expression unchanging. Poppaea gave a little snigger.

"Don't be alarmed, Julius. I just felt in need of a bit of fun. I'm not about to rob you of your well-earned trophy slave. Nevertheless, the Empress and I really do want to talk to someone who fought as one of Queen Boudica's savage horde, someone who knew her. That's you, isn't it, Olsar?"

"I was one of the commanders of what you would call her cavalry, and yes I did meet her."

"Did she really lead men into battle?" Poppaea asked, looking disdainfully at him. "I still find it hard to believe."

"She led women also. We fight as a tribe."

"You used to," Poppaea pointed out with contempt in her voice.

This prompted Nero to burst out laughing, followed quickly and obediently by others of his support staff in the room. Olsar didn't laugh. Neither did Julius, and neither did Vespasian. Instead he took up the conversation.

"I fear Olsar's tribe is typical of those in Britannia. There are many more, and they can be fiercely independent, capable of resisting to the death, as we've discovered. We underestimate them at our peril."

"Ah, yes, General! I remember you were in Britannia, commanding a Legion which was part of Claudius's conquering army there," said Nero. "Are you saying we should be frightened of them?"

"No. However, I think we have to be very careful to choose our Governors and Legion commanders very carefully to go there in the future."

"I agree. Incidentally, you will be interested to know, Julius, and maybe you too, Olsar, that I found it necessary to replace Paulinus as Governor. He's returned to Rome and tells me he wishes to be appointed to the Senate. I've agreed for now."

"Is it true she drove a chariot into battle?" Poppaea asked, still eager to discuss Boudica.

"She did."

"I find it hard to believe. She must have really been an unusual woman."

"She was, but not because of that. Driving a chariot into battle was a skill many of us learnt, men and women. She wasn't our leader in war because of that."

"Why was she then?"

"Because she was our best leader," Olsar stated, looking surprised by the nature of the question.

"You say you drove a chariot also?" Nero asked.

"At times, as others did."

"How many horses did your chariots have?"

"Two."

"At our races they are pulled by at least four. Which reminds me, in two days I'm going to the Circus Maximus to drive a chariot around the track for the first time. It's because I intend to take part later in the next full day of races. You're all invited to my pavilion to watch me. That includes you, Olsar. You will learn something more about why we are superior in all things."

It was Poppaea who changed the topic of discussion.

"You haven't forgotten what you wanted to do for Lucius and his family, have you?"

"Indeed not," Nero replied. "I think it's time for me to reward you for your hospitality today, Lucius. I've brought my lyre and will treat you all to a selection of my songs and poetry."

*

The Gods had heralded Nero's first appearance as a charioteer in an unfortunate manner. Thunder and lightning and rain had been a feature throughout the night. It hadn't helped the condition of the track. However, the warm sun since dawn had dried out most of it. The exceptions were parts of the two 180-degree turns at either end.

The thirty or so guests, included Nero's current favourite Senators and nobles with their wives, and of course Lucius's family. Vespasian was the only one not able to attend, having developed a convenient chill. There was a tension in the air because of the unique nature of the occasion, and the unpredictability of the outcome.

That tension only got a litter stronger when Poppaea entered the rear of the pavilion accompanied by the new Commander of the Praetorian Guard. Faenius had dressed in his full ceremonial uniform to make sure everyone there recognised his new status. Most of those present were amongst those who'd treated him with less respect than he might have merited in his climb through the ranks. His pompous stance, close beside his Empress, indicated those days were no more. Any show of disrespect now would be unwise.

"The Emperor will be appearing down below on the track very soon," Poppaea announced. "I will expect all of you to show the same delighted enthusiasm as I do throughout the whole sequence of events."

She wasn't wrong about the timing. Barely had she and the others taken their seats when a test chariot appeared from the entrance. It was being driven by a powerfully built young man, one who, as lead charioteer of the White team, was recognised by most of those present. Julius and Olsar had taken seats well to the rear of the pavilion. Julius was anxious that Olsar played as little a part in events as possible. He didn't want him to become involved in giving a commentary about what Nero was doing well or otherwise which Poppaea might hear. Events proved it to have been a wise move.

The charioteer started off slowly at first, doing two full circuits of the track.

"He's getting the feel of the track conditions," Olsar whispered into Julius's ear. "Not only that, he's letting his horses do the same. He's also giving them time to remember that he's controlling them and what his commands through the reins mean."

"Be careful what you say when the Emperor takes over. Make sure only I can hear you."

"I shall. This man is in full control of those magnificent beasts. He has my full respect and admiration. To watch four chariots such as this competing at speed on this track must be spectacular."

The charioteer slowly built up speed until he achieved normal race speed.

"This is a magnificent display of power and beauty," cried Poppaea to nobody in particular, although everyone either nodded or shouted their agreement.

"He's having difficulty with the bends," Olsar murmured. "The surface appears to be treacherous."

"I agree," said Julius. "He only just made the last turn."

Perhaps because of that the chariot began to slow down to a trotting pace which the charioteer maintained until he left the track. A short delay occurred until a trumpet blast, echoing those of race day, announced the arrival of the same chariot drawn by the same equally spirited horses. This time the charioteer was Nero, his face displaying a mixture of puzzlement and fear. The horses were behaving erratically as the chariot passed the royal pavilion.

"He's holding the four reins as one in both hands. Instead, he should be holding them separately between his fingers." Olsar explained quietly to Julius. "The horses don't understand what he wants. On some occasions, each rein has to give a separate command, but at virtually the same time. If he continues like this for very long they will understand only one thing, to run as fast as they can."

Manipulating the first bend at a trot proved to be chaotic. It was accompanied by frequent gasps of alarm in the pavilion, not least from Poppaea.

"Did you see that the horses were badly confused all the way round the bend?" Olsar whispered. "The inner, most experienced horse would be expecting a command to take it slower than the others to help pull the rest round. If he goes any faster it will be a disaster."

"Perhaps he's learnt from that turn to take things gradually."

They didn't get a chance to find out. As predicted the horses took control, letting their instincts to run take over. By the time they reached the next bend opposite the pavilion they had reached almost top race speed. Nero was pulling back hard on the reins as the chariot went into the turn. Any slight chance he might have had at a more controlled turn was made impossible at that speed by the poor condition of the track. The result was the chariot at first went into a brief slide until it turned completely over, flinging Nero high and wide across the track. His body lay motionless in the damp earth.

There were those in the pavilion who began to scream uncontrollably. Not so Poppaea. She leapt to her feet and ran towards the exit, closely followed by Faenius.

"Nobody must dare to leave until I return. Place guards on the door, Faenius."

Guards weren't needed. The force and hidden threat in her cold command was sufficient.

*

"All of you will be very relieved to know your Emperor's life is not threatened by his unfortunate accident. I've given instructions for those treacherous horses to be destroyed and their remains to be fed to the animals destined for the Arena." She paused. "You're all silent. Aren't you overjoyed by my news?"

She got the cries of relief and gratitude she was demanding.

"However, he's broken a few small bones and as a result will be bedridden for a while. I, with the help of Faenius and a few others, will rule in his temporary absence. Is that clear?"

It was.

"There's something more for you to understand. What really happened here today is to remain a secret. In the hands of some this could be put to evil use, particularly while my husband is indisposed. The Senate and people will be told the Emperor suffered a few minor injuries today here at the track. He did so in a selfless and courageous attempt to rescue me and some of you from a breakaway, driverless horse-drawn chariot. We were down on the track congratulating him on a breath-taking display as a charioteer. That is what you will all say if asked."

"It certainly took his breath away," whispered Olsar so quietly even Julius could barely hear him. The fact he did resulted in a sharp elbow jab into Olsar's ribs.

"I shall point out which of you were those with me on the track."

Fortunately, none of Lucius's group were chosen. She went on to describe in more detail her fictitious account of how Nero had become injured.

"If anything of what really happened comes to be known beyond us here today, it will have come from one of you. Nobody from the Circus Maximus was allowed to watch what was happening earlier. Therefore, if word gets out, Faenius and his men will root out the traitor from amongst you. You can imagine the fate awaiting that person. Have I made myself clear?"

Everybody nodded or said they understood.

"Good! I suggest you forget completely what has happened here today. Your lives may depend on it. You can all leave."

*

Lucius had spoken to those who'd been with him earlier as soon as they had reached the privacy of their villa. Domitia and Julius weren't a problem. They indicated they didn't feel overly threatened by what Poppaea had said. Olsar, being a slave, wasn't a problem either. Any indiscretion by him could easily be dealt with. Procilla had been different from the others. It had taken him some time to reassure her Nero would soon recover despite his injuries. What happened today would very quickly be forgotten. Having convinced her and calmed her down, he sought out Julius.

"She demonstrated today what a powerful, determined individual she is, Julius."

"Ruthless is a word I'm inclined to use."

"I know what you mean and it concerns me. There would be nothing to stop her ordering Faenius to arrest and dispose of everyone who was there."

"True, but I don't think she will. There were some influential people there and members of some old noble families. To execute so many of us would create a major outcry and people would try to find out why. She and Nero wouldn't want that. She was quick to assess the situation today. Then she chose her strategy to play the incident down."

"It's a good thing Piso wasn't there to see Nero become incapacitated," said Lucius. "He might have chosen to take the opportunity to progress his wishes."

"Not with Faenius eager to show his loyalty to Nero and Poppaea. Certainly, he would have been impressed as we were if he'd seen her perform as if she were Emperor uninhibited by Nero's absence. No! Things are pretty much as they were. Our situation hasn't changed. Except we now have Poppaea as well as Nero to try to outlive."

Chapter 19

The distance between Selima's room in the main villa and that of Olsar in the adjoining building occupied by the estate slaves was no more than a hundred paces. In terms of their social standing their separation may as well have been a thousand miles. That at least is what Selima was thinking as she made her way through the dark to meet her lover. She had to talk to Olsar about their future, to get him to agree with what she'd decided was necessary.

Her urgent but quiet knocking was answered by Olsar, pulling the door open and dragging her into his eager arms. They clung together with a yearning desperation.

"I thought you weren't going to come to me tonight, after all," he whispered into her moist lips between breathless kisses.

"You know I can't bear to be separated from you, not for a moment. But, we can't go on like this. Something has to change."

"Later! Later!"

He walked towards the bed breathing heavily. By the time he reached it, the few clothes he'd been wearing were lying on the floor. Selima paused only for a moment before she told herself discussing the future could wait until she'd experienced once again the exquisite pleasures of the present. Her clothes quickly joined his on the floor.

With a giggle she placed her hands forcefully against his heaving chest, causing him to fall backwards onto the bed. She dropped to lie on top of him, pinning his arms down. For a moment or two he allowed her to kiss him as she wished.

"I think I'll get Julius to relinquish you to become my personal slave," she murmured, "my sex slave to be available to satisfy my every need."

"Even I could learn to accept that sort of slavery, but not tonight."

Completely overpowering her, he flipped her over onto her back, this time pinning her down.

"Tonight you're my slave and you'll do everything I say."

"Yes, Master."

*

"It's late and there's something we have to discuss before I go back. We have to tell my mother and father about our feelings for each other. I include my mother in that, but I'm sure she guessed long ago. She knows me too well. I need to tell them I want to be your wife."

"Your father would never accept it."

"He has to!"

"We've had this conversation before. I'm a slave. I would only be allowed to marry another slave. Besides, what Julius says is correct. If somehow I was free, your father still couldn't bring himself to consent to you marrying a barbarian."

"He'll just have to get used to the idea. I know we've talked about this before but things are different this time."

"Why? I'm still a slave. I've told you we have to wait until I'm given my freedom. Or what is more likely, since that will take too long, when I decide to break free. When that happens you must be prepared to go with me."

"I'm pregnant!"

"What! You can't be. You mustn't be!"

"How can you talk like that? I've just told you we're going to have our very own child and you react in that way."

"Don't you realise my life could be at stake! Your father, when he finds out, could do whatever he wishes with me. A common slave has taken advantage of his daughter."

Alarmed at the look of deep concern on Olsar's face, she clung to him, fighting back her tears.

"What can we do?"

"I need to speak with Julius. He saved my life once before. It could be he may have to do so again."

"I want to be with you when you talk to him. You know how much my brother loves me."

"We must do it without any delay."

"I thought you would be happy with my news, not angry like this."

"And I'm more than happy, my sweet Selima. I'm sorry I said what I did. I was shocked and confused. I spoke out of panic for a few moments. I will find a way through this, I promise you."

*

"You both know why I've brought you here. You need to talk sensibly to each other and with me," said Procilla. "This is the worst crisis this family has had to face for a long time. At the moment you're not helping to solve it by not talking to each other. We aren't leaving this room until we've decided what is to happen."

The room in which Procilla was speaking was the largest in the villa. Normally it was used particularly for entertaining visitors but on this occasion it provided the ideal neutral and impersonal territory for her to get what she wanted from her husband and son. She knew it wouldn't be easy. Both had reacted badly to the news about Selima's pregnancy, but for very different reasons. She had thought carefully about her opening remarks and was pleased to see by their sulking silence they were at least considering what she had said so far. She decided to trust her instincts to continue to aggressively direct the discussion.

"I'm disappointed in both of you."

Lucius shuffled as if he was about to take over.

"Let me finish what I have to say before you interrupt. Then you can reply. In fact, I will insist on both of you explaining yourselves."

Lucius huffed a little and Julius couldn't prevent a little smirk.

"You've both spoken to me separately about your concerns, but not enough to each other. You seem to be forgetting this isn't about how either of you are affected. It isn't just about Olsar, and what should happen to him. It's really about Selima and her unborn baby.

What can we do that's best for them?"

Julius's nod and Lucius's blank stare confirmed to her where the main difficulty lay.

"Bearing that in mind, I want you to tell me what it is you're having difficulty with. You go first, Julius."

"My problem is simple to explain. They both came to see me to explain the deep love they have for each other. They didn't really need me to explain to them the difficult situation they were in. Olsar particularly knew marriage to Selima was impossible because he's a slave. He said he'd explained that to her. Her simple solution was for me to make him a freedman."

"And you refused."

"Not so directly. I told them that in my judgement he doesn't deserve it yet. He didn't completely deny it when I pointed out he continues to mistrust everything Roman. Understandably, he hates what we did to his tribe. I felt if he was freed now he would flee to Britannia, taking Selima with him."

"And you, husband, what have you to say?"

"Slave or freedman, he's not worthy of our Selima. He's betrayed us. He's a Brit, still a barely controlled savage. I don't want to lay eyes on him again in this villa. As Julius says, he hates us. I haven't yet decided what I'm going to do with him."

"I remind you he's *my* slave. Only I will take any decision about him," Julius insisted.

Procilla was not surprised at what they'd said. She'd anticipated what they were likely to say. As a result, she was ready to challenge them.

"Julius. You think he should remain a slave, and your father appears unable to contemplate him staying here. It seems to me you are both pointing in one direction. The solution for both of you is for him to be sold. To get the best price we should sell him to the slave-master at the Amphitheatre to become a gladiator in the Arena. Don't you agree, Julius?"

"The Arena is for criminals and thugs," Julius replied. "He's neither. He's a brave warrior and leader. If he'd been born a Roman we would all be proud of him."

"And you, Lucius. What do you think will happen when we finally tell them they can never marry? Even worse than that, how do you think they will react when they're told they are to be separated? I'll tell you what they will do, the same as I would. They will be gone the day after. You will never see your dear Selima again. Neither would I and that isn't acceptable to me. We both adore that young woman. Take a few moments, both of you, to think about what I've just said."

Procilla sat back and waited. She knew them both and was reasonably confident her words would have had some effect. Whether or not it would be enough, she was about to find out. When she thought they'd had sufficient time she continued.

"There is only one solution. This is what's going to happen.

"Julius! You will give Olsar his freedom with immediate effect. However, it can only be if there is a commitment from him that he will swear his allegiance to this family and Rome. If he's the man you appear to think he is, and he truly loves our Selima, he will do so and keep his word.

"You, my husband, will have to take note of that. Olsar will be a freedman and eligible to marry Selima. In the same way that you can't seem to forgive his people, he may continue for some time yet to be unforgiving of us for the horrors of that war. But, he will have to put that behind him, as will you. You must think of Selima's happiness and give them your consent. If either of you can't accept what I've decided, then say so. We can carry on our discussion until you do."

The deathly silence didn't last too long before Julius burst out laughing and went to Procilla to clasp his arms warmly around her. Lucius looked startled for a moment before laughing even louder and joining in their embrace.

"I take it we're all agreed then," concluded Procilla.

A knock on the door was followed by the urgent intrusion of one of the older female slaves.

"My apologies, Mistress, for entering without your permission, but Mistress Domitia has begun to give birth and needs you urgently."

*

133

The baby's cry had been so distinctive and loud coming from the next room Julius knew he'd become a father for the first time. The crying had lasted only briefly. Still, he had to wait.

"Even now, when I hear the child uttering its first sound, I still don't feel any differently from before. No excitement, no reaction whatever."

His confession was to Olsar who'd waited patiently with him for many hours. They'd had ample opportunity to discuss many things including Julius's complete lack of any emotion, good or bad, regarding his unborn child.

"If Domitia and I shared a love like you and Selima do, then maybe I would be excited. But I feel nothing, except perhaps a sort of sadness for this child."

These few hesitant, troubled sentences were ended by the sound of the baby crying again as before. Olsar said he thought that appeared unusual, but neither man was sure or could suggest why. Julius continued to wait patiently, if a little gloomily, until Procilla appeared.

"You may come in, Julius," she advised. "However, I think you should prepare yourself for a shock."

"What do you mean?" said Julius, jumping to his feet.

"You'll have to see for yourself."

Julius didn't get beyond the doorway of the room being used for the birth before he let out a disbelieving gasp. Domitia lay propped up on the bed, exhausted but awake and alert. Cradled in each arm was a tiny baby, content and fast asleep for the moment.

"Twins!" he cried. "Boys or girls?"

"Neither, or should I say both," answered Procilla, struggling to get her words out before the emotion of the previous few hours finally overwhelmed her.

She fought through her tears to add a few more words.

"We have a boy and a girl. Both babies are perfect. They are well, as is Domitia. It's time you four were left alone. I will tell Lucius our good news."

Julius took hold of each baby in turn. He was amazed to discover how small they were, how incredibly vulnerable they seemed to him to be. He had a sensation at the back of his throat like nothing he'd experienced before. It was as if he'd swallowed something large which had stayed there. Eventually, he felt able to speak.

"Did you suffer a great deal, considering there were two to deliver? It seemed to last forever."

"It's something I will never wish to experience again. I now have all the children I wanted, a boy and a girl."

"We have to discuss what names to give them."

"No discussion is necessary. I've already decided. He's to be called Alexus and her name is Livia. Please don't object. I haven't the energy left to get into yet another argument with you. Can you please leave? I need to sleep."

Julius took one last smell of each child, placing a light kiss on their foreheads before he left.

*

"What is it, a boy or a girl?" asked Olsar.

"Both! I have a boy and a girl, twins."

"That's amazing! It's a pity you feel the way you do about them."

"That's all changed."

"What has?"

"The moment I held them, smelt them, looked closely at their frail little bodies, something happened. They are mine. I have an overwhelming urge to take care of them. Circumstances are not ideal as I've explained to you, but I'll overcome that."

"Can I see them?"

"Take a look in through the doorway. Domitia will be going to sleep."

Olsar came back after a short visit, smiling broadly.

"I see what you mean. You're very fortunate. I hope it will be me very soon. Will you be there for me, Julius?"

"Nothing will stop me."

Chapter 20

At the time, Decianus could hardly believe his good fortune. Both Seneca and Burrus had gone. The responsibility for the Treasury that Seneca had carried for a long time had been passed on to him by Nero. Even so he had the growing suspicion it had been at the suggestion of Poppaea. At first he'd thought it was possibly a reward for bringing back the gold and jewels from Britannia. However, he'd since come to the conclusion she'd seen something in him from the start that had suggested to her he could become an ally in the Treasury. He realised she had a desire to have unrestricted access to all the wealth and wonders contained in there.

While Burrus had been around, things had been different. Both he and Seneca had many important friends in the Senate. Amongst them were the Senators who'd been delegated the task of monitoring and reporting back to the full Senate on the holdings and transactions of the Treasury. Decianus had been told by a proud Seneca that as a result there had been no known corruption during their time as Nero's advisers. Burrus particularly had ensured that access and support had always been given to those carrying out this role on behalf of the Senate.

With Faenius things were different. Decianus had soon realised the new Commander of the Guard was besotted with Poppaea. She had noticed also, and she took great advantage of his weakness. Very quickly she'd got him into the state where he wasn't able to deny her anything. The result was that he escorted her on her frequent trips to the Treasury.

At first she paid her visits on the pretext that she was then able to reassure Nero the contents, including the continual additions, were being securely received and protected. Before long she began to acquire for her personal use some of the objects held there. They'd been sent as part of the taxes sent from the Provinces. There were jewels and gold and silver ornaments that caught her eye. She took whatever she wanted, insisting no record was kept of them ever arriving or where they had gone. Decianus assumed that if Nero noticed any of them, wondering where they came from, she could always claim they were only for temporary use to be returned later to the Treasury. Of course, there would be those she couldn't bear to give back. In those cases, Decianus supposed, she could describe them as coming to her originally as gifts from her first husband and his very wealthy family.

She also took large amounts of coins, presumably to reward those particular allies she had undoubtedly acquired in the ranks of the Senators. They would be paid handsomely to keep her informed of the views of their colleagues about Nero, and more importantly about herself. Faenius's role was to help her to transport her newly acquired wealth back to the privacy of the Palace. The result of all this was the records kept for the Senators to monitor became practically meaningless. Their previous control had gone without them realising it.

Decianus enjoyed the enormous opportunity she was presenting to him without her realising it. Even in the relatively short time he'd been in direct contact with Nero, he'd come to realise he didn't need a soothsayer to forecast for him this Emperor, sooner or later, would most likely meet the same violent end as Caligula. That wouldn't happen while Poppaea was by his side. However, if for some reason she ceased to be there his time as Emperor would be limited. He would then have lost the last of the three shrewd and strong advisers who could save him from himself.

To ensure his own survival when that happened, he decided he would need to avoid being accused of corruption on a massive scale, until after he was able to disappear for good. He'd done it before in Britannia. To be able to escape successfully this time, he would need considerable wealth of his own to build a new life anonymously, somewhere in a Province in the far reaches of the Empire. Poppaea had provided him with the means to accumulate that wealth.

Each time she had taken objects, gold and silver or coins, he'd made a secret record of the items and amounts of money. However, to each of those lists he'd added his own considerable number of items, indicating they had been taken by her. In this way he met both his objectives. In the event that Nero and Poppaea were removed from power by one means or another, it was very possible that he would be immediately held to account for the relatively poor state of the Treasury finances. He could produce his own lists showing she was the guilty one. Not only that, in making his lists, he could be seen to have been trying in his limited way to protect the Treasury's assets, by making them recoverable from the tyrants. If that failed to save him he would still have his hidden wealth to use in his escape.

His only problem had been where to store his growing hoard. He couldn't use his own small property. It was too close and easily searched. He came to the conclusion that it had to be hidden somewhere on his father's estate. At first, Septimus had denied him that solution. Not only did he consider it corruption at the heart of the Empire, it was extremely dangerous for them both.

Decianus didn't accept his resistance for long. He merely pointed out that being a party to the murder of the Emperor's mother might be regarded as a much more serious crime. He explained that, while he would try to keep Septimus's involvement secret, who knew what future pressures might be placed upon him? This could be particularly likely if he were he to be prevented from using his newly found wealth to avoid possible arrest. His father had quickly taken the implied threat seriously and agreed to take care of the horde.

On a bright sunny morning his mind was full of happy thoughts about his future as he looked forward to the next likely visit of Poppaea that day. He'd sent a message to her that the latest shipment of taxes from the Province of Thracia had arrived and were ready for her inspection. However, a particularly beautiful golden brooch inlaid with rubies and sapphires was something she wouldn't get chance to see. He'd hidden it in readiness for it to be added to his own collection.

He was disappointed to see only Faenius enter his room.

"Where is the Empress? Is she following on behind you?"

"She's not coming. I've been sent by the Emperor. He wishes to see us both, together."

"Do you know what it's about?"

"I've no idea. I can only think it's important. He looked tense."

"Will Poppaea be present?"

"No. She's not in the Palace today."

"Do I need to bring anything with me?"

"He didn't say so."

*

"If there's one thing I will not tolerate it is corruption," Nero shouted, "especially by people whose appointments were made with my direct approval."

Decianus turned pale. Standing rigidly upright, he risked a quick glance to see if Faenius was looking as concerned as he himself felt.

"Poppaea agrees that the culprits, once identified, should be punished most severely. The two of you will agree also, won't you?"

They were both speechless, but managed to nod their agreement.

"There's a problem in the Province of Asia with the Governor there."

Two very relieved men started to breathe again.

"I've received a confidential report claiming he's involved in a scheme to defraud me of large amounts of taxes. Gold that should be reaching the Treasury is probably being syphoned off before it ever leaves there. Or it's being diverted soon after it is on its way here."

"If the gold never reaches us in the Treasury it will be impossible for me to help in identifying the culprit or culprits," Decianus pointed out.

He was anxious to avoid too much close attention being concentrated on himself and his work.

"Poppaea was quick to identify that difficulty also. That's why she's suggested instead we send somebody directly to the source of the problem. That person will be nominally appointed to act as an aide to the Governor in carrying out all administration of the Province. He will also have the more important task of reporting back to me secretly on any corruption he finds."

Decianus immediately understood the reason for their summons by Nero. He began to suspect he'd been earmarked to be the one to go. It wasn't going to be Faenius. He began to think quickly about how he might avoid it.

"Poppaea has suggested you as an obvious choice, Decianus, because of your previous experience of tax matters in the Provinces. She was reluctant to do so because of the help you give her and the Senators to monitor the Treasury assets. Therefore, she thought you might be able to recommend an alternative to you who could more easily be spared."

"I agree my absence from the Treasury so soon after the loss of Seneca would not be advisable, Sir. However, there is somebody who I think would suit the situation admirably."

"That was what she was hoping for. Who do you suggest?"

"I think Tribune Julius Agricola would be very suitable. Like myself, he's gained experience in provincial administration including taxation matters."

"Yes, but as you point out he's a tribune, a soldier. He's more accustomed to fighting barbarians than collecting taxes."

"As you know, he was also Paulinus's Staff Officer. As such, he gained experience in the administrative and other responsibilities of a Governor. He should know what to look for, to identify where and how corruption is taking place."

"I hear what you say."

"Not only is he the right choice for the reasons I've given, but his appointment solves another problem."

"Go on."

"On his return from Britannia, you will recall you had mixed feelings about him. So you decided to take some time determining what was to be his next appointment. This could be the ideal solution."

"That's enough for now. You've given me something to think about. I will discuss it with Poppaea and let you know in due course what I've decided."

*

Decianus thought, even by his own standards that had been a masterstroke. He was confident he'd avoided being sent to carry out a very difficult task in a far-off Province. He would have lost his very lucrative present post, increasing the chance of his own misdeeds being discovered. His sworn enemy would be sent there instead of him.

He'd heard Julius had recently added twins to his family. It appealed to him, knowing Julius would be reluctant and inconvenienced to leave Rome at this time. He also liked the idea of him having to get involved in the daily boredom of setting and monitoring the collection of taxes. It was something that would drive him to despair if it continued for any length of time.

There was another added advantage. It removed one of his worst enemies from Rome. He would feel a little safer as a result. His final thought on it was to contemplate the fun he would have at a later date informing him it was his idea to send him there rather than himself.

Chapter 21

The short ride back from the city seemed to Julius to last forever. Earlier that morning he'd received a message from Nero summoning him to the Palace. As he was leaving the villa, Procilla told him she was hopeful Selima's baby might arrive that day or very soon afterwards. The baby was long overdue. She was very concerned, stressing it was important for mother and child that the birth happened without any more delay. Riding as fast as safety allowed, Julius was hoping he could honour his promise to Olsar to be there for him when his child was born. It all depended on the Gods.

"I was right, Julius," cried Procilla, running to him as he climbed the steps into the villa. Selima has begun to bring her baby into this world. I'm going back to be with her. Olsar is waiting for you."

Julius found what he'd expected, having gone through the same thing recently. The normally courageous, self-confident, capable young man was anxiously pacing around the same room they'd been in the last time.

"Thank you for returning. How did it go with Nero?"

"I'll explain in a moment. How are you feeling?"

"Not the same as you did at this stage. In your case, you felt indifferent towards your unborn child. I know that very quickly changed afterwards. I want to see and hold my child. It's everything Selima and I have dreamed of and talked about these last few months. I desperately want to see her safe. She looked so exhausted by the time she got the first signs the baby was finally coming.

"I'm pleased for you. It will soon be over."

"Can you tell me what happened with Nero? It might take my

mind off what's happening."

"It's not particularly good news. Nero has finally decided what to do with me. I'm to be sent to Asia."

"How soon?"

"Almost immediately. However, I managed to convince our impatient Emperor I needed as many as five days to finish my work here to be able to hand things over satisfactorily to my father. I think the fact that he's a well-respected and influential Senator helped me to get this concession."

"Will you want me to go with you?" Olsar asked hesitantly.

"No. You're still thinking like a slave. You're free to make your own choices. I don't think you would want to in any case. My role is not primarily a military one. Your task for the immediate future will be to take care of your wife and child. You can help to keep an eye on my two for me."

"Thank you, my friend."

Julius realised it was the first time either of them had used that word. He felt a warm satisfaction that after all they'd been through together they could come out of it friends.

*

Not long after the first baby cry was heard from the next room, Procilla appeared in the doorway. However, the broad smile of last time was replaced by a look of deep concern. She leant against the frame of the door to steady herself.

"You both need to come quickly."

She didn't wait to answer Olsar's urgent question as to whether he had a girl or boy.

The baby girl lay cradled in Selima's arm. Around the bed, stood three of Procilla's most trusted slaves. They were quietly sobbing. Procilla's self-control finally crumbled.

"I've sent for Lucius," she murmured tearfully. "He'll be here at any moment."

"What's happening?" Olsar gasped. "Selima! Is our baby alright? Is there a problem? Please answer me!"

Lucius came rushing into the room looking anxious. Procilla raised her hand sharply enough to stop him in his tracks and prevent him saying anything.

"We are all here now," she whispered. "The baby is fine, Olsar. Selima fought bravely to give her baby life, to save her life. But she couldn't save her own. She lost so much blood and struggled so hard her heart eventually gave way. I'm desperate. I've lost my precious girl. I couldn't save her."

Procilla collapsed with a sob onto the floor as her strength finally gave way.

Lucius knelt down to comfort his wife, crying also. Julius bowed his head, fighting back his tears. Olsar stood stiffly, staring at Selima. Slowly he walked over to the side of her bed. Taking hold of her hand, he gently brought it to his lips. Placing her arm back across her body, he lowered his head to kiss her several times on her peaceful face. Between each kiss he whispered to her, so quietly the others in the room couldn't hear.

Eventually he stood up straight to stare at the others. From all the competing mixture of emotions he must have been experiencing only one showed on his face. With his eyes half-closed, jaw and lips set tight, his anger was there for all to see. Without saying a word he strode out of the room. He'd made no move to hold or even look at his daughter.

*

"It's three days since we all lost our beautiful little Selima," said Procilla. "I understand Olsar hasn't left his room in all that time, not even to see his baby. We don't know what we are to call her yet."

Lucius, still deeply overcome with grief, didn't comment. Julius shook his head in dismay.

"I have to leave for Asia in a day or so. I'm going to have to speak to him before then. I owe it to him. I have to help him. He has to see his child."

"You're right," agreed Procilla. "He will see she looks just like her mother. He needs to know he's not alone, without Selima. I already have so much love for that child. I want to convince him they are both part of this family now. They're welcome to stay here forever.

He can make this his home. I've realised in these last few months why you and Selima came to think so much of him. Your father will need more time, but he will get there."

Lucius looked at Procilla, as if to show he was listening, but he made no comment.

"I think he needs to be told all this, preferably by you, Mother. I'm not going to delay any longer. I have to make him face his future."

*

Fausto was where Julius expected him to be, in the stables ensuring the horses were being fed and groomed.

"Have you seen him at all in the last few days?"

Fausto didn't need to ask who was being referred to.

"He's emerged several times, after sunset. I think he went for long walks in the dark."

"Do you know if he's eaten?"

"I don't think so but there's no real way of knowing. Are you going to try to see him? Do you want me with you?"

"I think it's time, don't you? It's best I see him on my own though."

"I thought of doing it myself. I've come to regard him as a friend. He's a good man."

"That's why I have to force him out of his room, out of his desperate grieving."

Julius then went to stand outside Olsar's door. Having knocked several times without receiving any response, he was considering forcing his way in when the door opened slightly. Olsar didn't say anything, neither did he close the door again, having seen who was there.

"We need to talk. I only have a day or two before I have to leave. There are assurances we need to give each other, and my mother wishes to speak to you."

The door opened slowly, allowing Julius to enter. He was expecting Olsar to be in a poor physical and mental state. He was surprised to find nothing of the kind.

"I'm glad you came to speak to me, Julius. There are things I need to say also. First of all, I apologise to you and the others, who I know care, for retreating for so long. I just had to have time to think."

"I understand. I also want you to realise that in making your way through this tragedy Procilla wants to take care of you and your little girl. You can be a tremendous help to Lucius in my absence."

"I was going to ask your mother to look after Selima's baby. I know she will try give her the love and care she'll need without a mother of her own."

"That child is yours to care for also."

"I know that. But at the moment I'm not going to stay here."

"What do you mean?"

"I need to escape for a time. There will be too many raw memories of Selima here at present. At the moment I feel only resentment towards the child for taking Selima away from me. I expect you to think that's unreasonable and unjustified, but it is there. I also hope I will change given enough healing time. That's why I have to ask something of you."

"What is it?"

"I need you to rescue me once again. I want to go with you to Asia."

"You're no longer my slave. This isn't a military appointment. I may fail in what's being asked of me. Nero won't forgive me if I do. You would suffer if you're associated with me."

"I understand all that. I've thought about nothing but this in the last few days. Despite everything you say, and some of my own doubts, it will give me a challenge to concentrate on again. I want to do something that will help me to get rid of all this anger, take it away from my child."

Julius turned away from him to show he was weighing in the balance what had just been said. Moments later he turned back.

"I will agree, but there are conditions."

"Tell me what I must do."

"Firstly you have to come with me to see your daughter, to hold her and give her a promise you'll return to her."

"Agreed."

"Secondly, you have to come to tell my mother and father what you've just told to me and explain what you're asking them to do."

"That will be more difficult but I agree."

"Thirdly, you have to tell me what you're going to call her."

They smiled at each other as the tension melted away.

"Selima told me her birth mother came from Judaea. She said that if we had a baby girl, she wanted her to have her mother's name. She is Sarah."

Chapter 22

The short debate in the Senate that morning had been attended by Nero himself. That in itself was not unusual. However, what was different about this one was the particularly active part Nero took in the discussion on the question of the growing influence of those calling themselves Christians. Lucius had been startled at first at how agitated Nero had become when even the name of this relatively new religious cult was mentioned. He shouldn't have been surprised since it was Nero himself who had insisted the issue be raised.

Lucius was taking time later to explain to Julius what had been the outcome.

"We believe they call themselves Christians after their dead leader," said Lucius, as they strolled through their vineyard.

The high humidity of the morning had been reduced by a short heavy shower just before midday, making it much more comfortable than expected for Julius to be shown the progress of the season's grapes.

"I used to talk to Selima about them," Julius replied. "She was interested because this man they follow, they refer to him as their Messiah, came from Judaea as did her parents."

"She never mentioned them to me. Come to think of it, you didn't tell me of her unwise interest either."

"That was because we both knew you wouldn't approve. As far as I know, she hadn't any intention of becoming one of them. She just found some of their ideas intriguing. That alone would have been enough to give you nightmares if you'd found out."

"It certainly would. It's an idea that is doomed, as are all those who choose to believe in what their leaders preach."

"In any case, when Olsar came along she could only think of him. So it ceased to be relevant."

"Has he been to see his child since you both returned from Asia?"

"Only once. I'm afraid he still blames her for Selima's death."

The next few strides were made without further comment, both of them staring thoughtfully at the ground rather than the vines.

"Why was the subject of the Christians raised by Nero?" Julius eventually asked.

"He's been told by those close to him that their numbers are increasing rapidly, particularly involving the poor, and especially among slaves. Does the cult have a following in Asia? After all, that Province is much nearer to where I understand it began in Judaea."

"It was known of but I can't say it caused a great deal of concern amongst the authorities and normal religious leaders there. It was just regarded as one cult amongst many. Why is he so upset by this group, these Christians?"

"He's come to realise they believe there is only one God. Therefore, they are scornful of all our other Gods, refusing to sacrifice to them. He sees this as liable to bring the anger of the Gods down upon us, endangering the Empire. We all agreed on that. He says it can't be allowed to continue. He was particularly furious they'd refused to sacrifice to Claudius. Some are said to even practice cannibalism."

"Surely that was ridiculed as pure fantasy by you all when it was suggested."

"Not since it was being suggested by Nero."

"What then was the outcome of the debate?"

"Senators have been told to regard a refusal to make sacrifice as an act of treason. A Christian who will not pay homage to our Gods in this manner is guilty of a crime. The punishment for them is death. We're required to reinforce this to all our citizens. They're to be made aware of the Emperor's views, his intolerance of Christians and their beliefs."

"What do you all think about that?"

"We're genuinely supportive of him. If the number of citizens, or more especially our slaves, becoming Christians gets out of control, then we're all threatened. If they consider this Messiah to be more important than our Emperor, the Empire won't last."

"He runs the risk of creating martyrs amongst them, but I can understand the concern a man like Nero would have. I think he must see himself becoming a God one day like his uncle."

"There was something else I discovered this morning which you'll be interested in. You've only just arrived home so you won't know that Titus Vespasianus is in Rome."

"That's a surprise! Why has he returned from Britannia?"

"He's here only temporarily to deal with matters on his father's estate before he goes on to join him shortly."

"Join him! What do you mean? His father is retired, living on his estate."

"Not any longer. You obviously haven't heard. It only happened a short while ago. The Senate appointed Vespasian to be the Governor of the Province of Africa. It's one of those few where the Senate still has that responsibility delegated to it."

"Yes, but why Vespasian? He isn't even a serving Senator."

"It was Piso who nominated him. His military record together with his previous service as a Senator and Consul made the decision easy for us."

"But why would Piso recommend him after all this time?"

"Think about it. Some time ago he got a group of us together to consider working to replace Nero. Seneca and I showed our reluctance to become involved, but Vespasian was clear in his total opposition to the suggestion. It wasn't just Nero he was protecting. It was his firm belief that the removal of the Emperor would almost certainly lead to chaos and civil war."

"I remember you telling me that."

"I can only assume Piso still has his desire for change. Not only that. I suspect he's begun to firm up on a plan. He will have seen Vespasian's blind loyalty to the status quo as a possible dangerous obstacle, given his standing and influence with both Senators and citizens alike. So he's got him out of the way. The next year will be very interesting. I shall keep well clear of Piso, as must you."

"I agree. Is Poppaea still exercising a powerful grip on things?"

"More so than ever. She has both Nero and Faenius under her spell. Even Piso must know he could never succeed if he has to overcome all three. We shall see."

"I would like to see Titus before he leaves for Africa. Hopefully he'll still be there when I ride to his estate in the morning."

"Be careful not to mention anything of what we've just discussed, particularly any mention of Piso."

No reply was needed from Julius.

*

"I understood you to be in Asia, Julius," said Titus. "It's good to see you again."

"Likewise. I only returned two days ago. I found out late yesterday you were here."

"You're fortunate to catch me. I'm leaving to join my father first thing in the morning."

"What will you be doing?"

"Anything he wants me to do. It will be similar to our roles as staff officer in Britannia but with much more authority to act."

"Speaking of Britannia. How are things there?"

"Recovery is well advanced everywhere with the exception of Iceni territory. I know you were concerned about what was happening there. You were right. The area is still sparsely populated, and looks likely to remain so for some time."

"I take it Boudica or her body was never found. We would have heard."

"Correct!"

"What about her two daughters, Linona and Cailan?"

"You still remember their names after all this time! Astonishing! It's the same with those two. There hasn't been a sign of them, not even a rumour. Mind you, there aren't many around to start rumours.

Paulinus was replaced eventually, as you must know."

Julius ignored the comment about Linona and Cailan.

"He became a Senator again, but little is heard of him. A flawed genius, I fear."

"I came to the same conclusion. Talking of which, Cerialis has also left Britannia. He's now the commander of a Legion in Germania."

"So I hear. That should keep him fully occupied."

"What's going to happen to you here?"

"I'm waiting to hear what Nero has planned for me. We only touched on it briefly when I reported back to him on what I found to be taking place in Asia."

"Which was?"

"Corruption on a massive scale. He was pleased with my findings and report. So, I'm well and truly in his line of sight. I will have to wait for him to decide what my next duty for Rome will be. He hinted he was considering appointing me to some sort of role within the city. I envy your move to Africa, the relative obscurity and simplicity of your appointment to your father's staff."

"If ever the opportunity arises would you welcome the chance to join my father?"

"From what I've heard of him it would be an honour."

"Then let's both hope it will happen. Come and have meal with me. We can reminisce about our time with Boudica."

Chapter 23

The death of her daughter when she was only a few months old had sent Poppaea into a deep depression which had lasted for many months. Nero had described the child's death as an act of the Gods. To any other observer this would explain the absence of any display of grief by him at the time she died or since. It could be seen as the reason why he hadn't mentioned her name since then. Poppaea knew the real reason. She'd decided he was only interested in having a male heir to succeed him. The result was his failure to fully understand the depths of her despair.

However, he did finally come up with a suggestion to help her, which Poppaea at first didn't like and rejected. He proposed she withdraw from the noise and other distractions of Rome and seek a period of rest and recuperation somewhere in the country. She considered the real motive behind the suggestion was to give him a rest from her dark moods. Nevertheless, the more she thought about it the more it began to appeal to her. In the end, she'd chosen to spend several weeks back at her family's villa near the town of Pompeii.

It had been a success. She had gradually felt her health returning to normal. Visits to friends and places from her childhood had begun to remind her she'd already achieved success beyond even her own wildest dreams. She was the Empress of Rome. On many occasions she could well have been the Emperor, taking decisions for Nero when he'd dithered over some very important matter of state. She began to get her confidence back. Nero needed her strength. More than that, the future of the Empire required her presence back in Rome. The certainty of a male heir was needed to end the negative speculation she was certain had begun again when her poor daughter had been born. Her future role was no different from what it had been before. The Gods required her to produce a male child and it wouldn't happen while she remained in the comfort and seclusion of her past.

*

"I'm told my husband isn't here, Faenius. Where is he?"

"The Emperor has gone to your villa at Antium, Your Majesty," replied Faenius nervously.

"Didn't he receive my message that I was intending to return today? I sent it three days ago."

"He did, Madam."

"And?"

"He left two days ago."

"For what purpose?"

"He didn't say, Madam. He only ordered me to remain here to be at your command until he returns."

"And when will that be?"

"Again, he didn't say."

"Didn't he just? Get out," she cried. "Leave me alone."

Crestfallen, Faenius hastened to the door. Taking hold of the handle he turned as if to make a comment.

"OUT!" she screamed.

An hour later, Faenius was tensely fidgeting with documents in his office. A gentle, hesitant knock on his door only just got his attention.

"Come in," he shouted unnecessarily harshly, his own anxiety apparently affecting his mood.

"I've been sent by the Empress, Sir," whispered one of the Palace female slaves. "She's ordered you to attend her without any delay."

"What's her mood like? Don't be alarmed. You may answer in confidence. It will go no further than this room. You'll be doing me a favour if you speak the truth."

"Thank you, Sir. She's been acting as if she was very angry for a while. However, she appears to have calmed down. She even gave me a little half-smile when she told me to bring you."

"Return to your mistress. I will follow you very shortly."

"Faenius! Come to sit here by me."

Poppaea, relaxing and smiling broadly as she sprawled on one of her large couches, tapped the vacant space next to her.

"Leave us!" she barked at the three slaves still in the room.

"Why are you hesitating, Faenius? Please come here."

He ambled across the room before lowering himself into a stiffly upright sitting position, as far from her as the frame of the couch allowed. He might have been expecting some mention of the unusually harsh way in which she had treated him an hour earlier. At best he might have wished for an apology. He got nothing.

"I'd forgotten how magnificent you look in your Commander's uniform. Have you missed me?"

"I have, Your Majesty. Did you enjoy your time away?"

"I did indeed. The period of rest has certainly given me lots to think about. I've lots to say to you, lots of ways in which you can be of service to me. But that's for later, not today."

She took hold of his hand, squeezing it suggestively. Faenius sat up even straighter, if that were possible. He coughed slightly, looking around the room as if to check no one had been told to remain hidden behind a tapestry or an item of furniture. Poppaea laughed out loud, withdrawing her hand.

"There's no need to be alarmed. I can see you think I'm trying to trap you. I'm only engaged in a little playful teasing. I'll stop as it obviously disturbs you. Your reaction is quite charming, though."

Faenius gave a weak smile and yet another embarrassed cough.

"I asked you to come so I can tell you I shall be going to Antium tomorrow. Obviously, I will need you to accompany me."

"I shall arrange for your carriage and escort to be ready for you from dawn onwards."

"There's something else I want you to do. Don't send any message ahead to my husband. I want it to be a surprise for him."

"I understand, Madam."

"Good. You know, I feel really excited to be back at the centre of things again. I think we shall finish this day with a short inspection of the Treasury. There might be something I can borrow to wear tomorrow."

Faenius at last began to relax.

"One last question. What do you think of our Palace and the small villa Nero owns behind it?" she asked thoughtfully.

"I think they are both something the people are very proud of. They're known throughout the Empire."

"Hmm!" was all she chose to add in response to his comment. "Come! Let's go to see Decianus."

*

The guard from the front of the villa lost the race to get to warn Nero of the Empress's arrival. He'd been told by him not to allow any intrusion into his private rooms until the entertaining had come to an end. He hesitated after knocking on the door, not daring to enter unless ordered to. He tried again, delivering a second, louder series of blows to the door but it was too late. Poppaea pushed him aside so that the urgently following Faenius could restrain him while she flung open the neglectfully unlocked door.

"Good morning, my dear husband. I thought I would surprise you! I can see I've succeeded."

It wasn't only Nero who'd been surprised. Two of his closest Senator friends were desperately attempting to find their clothes from the pile strewn around the room.

"You two get your pathetic bodies covered and leave immediately. If you're in here by the time I count to ten, Faenius's sword will see to it that the Senate will have some vacancies to fill. Those whores with you can get on their knees and remain where they are."

Stumbling and still half naked, the two panicking Senators just made it in time. Nero had managed to dress. He had correctly taken Poppaea's outstretched arm and pointing finger as a sign to remain seated on his couch. He was trembling in terror, unable to take his eyes off Faenius's drawn sword. Poppaea walked slowly amongst the six females, lifting their terrified bowed heads, looking to see if she recognised any of them.

"Well, husband. What are they?"

"What do you mean, my darling?"

"Don't play the cringing fool with me. Are they slaves, whores or high-born ladies, perhaps even a combination of those? If some are in fact noble ladies, I need to be introduced to them."

"They are neither slaves nor from the nobility."

"Then they're all whores merely plying their trade."

She told them to dress and wait while she decided their fate.

"I've decided on your punishment. You're fortunate my anger is aimed at someone else in this room. Today, I'm inclined not to take it out on you. However, you won't be paid your fees. Get out before I change my mind."

Faenius was unable to hide his amusement at the Empress ridiculing the Emperor of Rome. She was facing him with the humiliation of being seen to be paying for sex as if he were a miserable low-born common citizen.

"Faenius! Will you escort those whores from the premises and leave my husband and me to share a happy reunion?

"So! This is how you've amused yourself while I've been away."

"I swear it was the first time. Those two Senators, who I thought were my friends, have misled me."

"Don't be pathetic. I know you too well."

"How can I show you how much I truly love and need you?"

"We shall come to that shortly. You may have noticed I'm no longer depressed. Your suggested remedy, or your scheme to get me out of the way of your orgies, has worked. I've made a few decisions on how you can make my life complete."

"Anything. Anything you desire is yours, my darling."

"I shall explain more to you later. It's sufficient for the moment to mention only one thing. You need an heir and I need a child to replace the one I lost. You seem to be in need of sex this afternoon. So, get your clothes off again. We're going to commence our task right away."

Nestled contentedly in Nero's arms much later, Poppaea woke him up from his deep, snoring sleep.

"Did your day finally go as well as you thought it might, my love? It certainly wasn't as crowded as it had been earlier."

Her remark, and the slight giggle from her afterwards showed she appeared to have forgiven him. He certainly took it to mean as much.

"We must never be parted again," he cooed. "You are the most amazing woman I've ever met, in or out of bed."

She gave him a playful dig in the ribs, followed by another short giggle.

"If we are to get the child we both want, you will need me to be amazing again in a few moments."

"As usual, I'm always willing to take your guidance."

"However, there's something I want to ask of you first. It's very important for my future happiness."

"What can I give you? Just ask."

"I want you to build a new home worthy of us here in the centre of Rome."

Nero sat up straight, greatly surprised for the second time that day.

"Are you serious? We already have a magnificent Palace. In addition, we have our villa close by where we can retreat to for our privacy."

"Please lie down again. Hear me out."

He did as he was told and she snuggled back in his arms once more.

"Where has this idea come from?"

"My time in Pompeii, or more correctly the small retreat nearby called Herculaneum."

"I know of both of them. Quite a few Senators own properties in that area."

"As you know, my parents live there. I was able to visit many old friends, spending time in their villas. The citizens of Rome think our villa is luxurious, but it can't compare to those I saw. Things are different there."

"In what way?"

"To start with, there's a lot more space. So the villas are much bigger. As a result there are many different rooms. More importantly, they are new! There are wonderful modern mosaics in every room. Our villa is small, old and the mosaics are drab."

"You can't say the Palace is small. That is enormous."

"But it's also very old, and draughty, and it's used by many others."

"I don't know what to say. Our villa is surrounded on all sides by areas containing many important buildings. They include some sacred temples, government buildings, at least one forum, and many villas and commercial properties. Most, owned by very important and old noble families, have been theirs for centuries."

"You don't have to say anything today. I just want you to begin to think about it. Now, what were we talking about before I changed the subject? Oh yes! Come here, my Emperor."

Chapter 24

More than a year had passed since Seneca had been remotely interested in revisiting the city of Rome and he hadn't regretted a moment of it. From what he'd heard from his frequent visitors, things, if anything, had become much worse than before. It sounded as if Poppaea was the Emperor in all but name. Many, including Seneca's friends among the Senatorial class, had been executed, forced to commit suicide or exiled for the most trivial of matters if Nero had taken offence. He saw conspiracies everywhere, particularly among Senators. Poppaea, aided by her tame Faenius, was only too ready to relieve her husband's stress by removing those who he imagined to be a threat. Others were liable to be severely punished for any perceived slights to their authority.

It wasn't surprising, therefore, that Seneca's heartbeat began to increase when he realised the rider approaching the front of his villa was none other than Senator Piso. It was the first time he'd ever been to his home. He could only assume something serious must be about to be disclosed to him.

"Welcome, Senator. It's a long time since our last meeting. Please come into the shade. Your horse will be looked after."

"Thank you, my friend."

Piso dismounted, handing his reins to the nearest slave. He paused to stretch his spine before striding up to Seneca, taking hold of the arm held out in greeting to him.

"I'm getting too old for such a long ride these days. Perhaps I need to get myself a carriage, although they can be worse on your spine than riding horseback."

"Come inside. I can provide soft cushions and a hot meal. Both can only help you to recover."

Sometime later, when Piso had eaten and was surrounded by those soft cushions, Seneca asked the question both knew was long overdue.

"Why the visit, then, Senator? Is it in some way official?"

"Not in any sense of the word. It's quite the opposite. I came unescorted to keep my journey here totally secret, for the sake of both of us."

"I fear I can guess something of what you're going to say. If I'm correct, my answer is still no. I'm not interested."

"Please hear me out."

"Go ahead."

"I spoke to you and a few others some time ago of our need to replace Nero. Although it was the right thing to do, I accepted it wasn't the right time for a number of reasons. Vespasian's total opposition to it, and the influence his presence in Rome still had, ended any wish I had to proceed with my plans. Things have changed since then."

"So I understand. I heard you nominated him to be Governor of Africa. That should help you."

"I see you haven't lost your liking for sarcasm."

"Nor for my liking to stay alive."

"Other things are different."

"I'm not really interested but I know you'll carry on. I'm listening."

"Nero was bad then. He's now a monster, unrestrained by the likes of you and Burrus. The Senate has ceased to function, other than to do his bidding, however horrific it may be."

"That was the case with Caligula and he was eventually removed. It will happen to him. However, it will not be as you wish, by a conspiracy of a large number of noblemen and Senators. Like Caligula, it will happen when the Praetorian Guard decide it is time."

"There are many Senators and noblemen who think as I do. With your support, even if it's only passive, we could persuade many others."

"You aren't listening to me. Do you yet have the support of the current Commander of the Guard?"

"Not at the moment but…"

"Is it true the beautiful Poppaea has him love-struck and totally under her control?"

"Yes, for the time being, but…"

"Then forget it! You will fail. Vespasian was correct then and still is. You will create a civil war if you were by chance successful. There's no obvious successor to Nero. Although, perhaps you see yourself in that role?"

"You do me a great disservice, my friend. My only objective is to rid Rome of the last Caesar. I and those who will join me have the same dream, to restore the Republic, the one Julius Caesar and his descendants stole from us all."

"I had the same dream as you. But I came to realise something a long time ago. That's all it can be, a dream. The Republic has gone forever. Our only hope is that the future Emperors learn the necessity of becoming worthy of the Senate and people of Rome."

Neither spoke for a long time. Seneca expected Piso to get up and ask for his horse at any moment. His guest spoke instead.

"It's no wonder you lasted as long as you did as adviser to that madman, maintaining his confidence. You're always honest in your advice, even when you know it isn't welcome. I would welcome an invitation to stay the night if you can tolerate me. There are many other topics we could enjoy discussing together. I know we both share a love of the Greek philosophers for instance."

"Of course you're welcome to stay. The evening is going to be warm. Since my retirement I've grown even fonder of sitting outside at night and contemplating the world around me and the stars above. A few drinks of wine will help to loosen our thoughts and our tongues."

*

"I can remember when I would have been insulted if somebody had offered me a stool to help me to mount my horse," said Piso. "Now, I'm only grateful for it, old friend."

"The value of the onset of old age is that you don't have to bow to your own unhelpful pride. Life becomes so much more acceptable."

They both laughed and clasped arms in a farewell gesture.

"I didn't get what I came for. But I've listened to you and thought about your words of warning through the night. Once again I note what is said about the Commander of the Praetorian Guard. I won't move as quickly as I might have done. I will wait for the right time, but Rome cannot suffer forever. May the Gods go with you."

"And with you, my friend, especially those Gods of Caution and Wisdom. I've forgotten who they are but I'm sure they'll forgive me."

Piso, smiling and nodding his approval, pressed his heels into his horse and moved off down the track.

Chapter 25

64 AD

Centuries of unplanned, uncoordinated building projects had resulted in every spare piece of land in the city being put to use. This was particularly true of the central area. The result was a jumbled mass of properties of every kind crammed together, allowing the bare minimum of space to provide access. Narrow, dark streets meandered chaotically, making the movement of people and goods dangerous and frustrating.

It was this noisy, smelly almost unfathomable panorama that was exciting Poppaea as she gazed down on it from the roof of the Palace. Built as it was, high on the central Palatine hill, it gave views in almost all directions for considerable distances.

"Do you see what I'm saying, Faenius? You can make out my small, totally inadequate villa over there. The buildings surrounding it are many and varied, almost completely overwhelming it. Rome needs a villa to be proud of to reward its Emperor. We need to build a new one which would become the eighth wonder of the world. To do that we need to create space, the space down there which has been totally occupied by buildings. They would have to be removed. Some of them would be easy to acquire, either by purchasing them or by commandeering those whose owners objected and were reluctant to sell."

"I can't see there being too many of those who own them becoming brave or foolhardy enough to deny the wishes of the Emperor."

"That would certainly be true of the simple commercial and trade owners. However, they are not the problem. It's the other owners who are likely to be difficult. Many are from rich and influential families. Or they are the many religious leaders and magistrates all extremely protective of their temples or public buildings. They are monstrous piles of stone which have been there for more years than anybody can remember."

"Couldn't they be persuaded to come to some agreement to make their land available to you? The Emperor mustn't be denied anything he thinks is necessary for him to rule the Empire."

"Well said! The difficulty I have is, I can't persuade my husband to agree with me that having a much bigger, and certainly newer, private villa is absolutely necessary. Not if it means taking on the Senate, the old noble families and some powerful religious leaders all at the same time. He prefers to keep what we have."

"Is there nothing that can be done?"

"That's where you come in. I want you to identify for me which owners might be those most likely to be a problem. Then I want suggestions on how we might apply pressure to change their minds. Physical intimidation and threats of the ultimate kind can be considered if absolutely necessary."

"May I involve anybody else at this stage?"

"Such as?"

"Decianus is one, for instance. He could provide a great deal of information about who owns which buildings and what taxes they pay. He's also cunning enough to come up with ideas on what might be effective with some of those involved."

"I agree. But involve only him at this stage. Only the three of us must know about this. My husband mustn't hear of it."

*

"I've given this a great deal of thought," declared Decianus. "The conclusion I've come to may not please you, and especially not Her Majesty."

"I don't like the sound of that, but continue," Faenius growled.

"Intimidation is not the answer. There would be too many

important people involved who will be fiercely reluctant to grant Poppaea what she wants. It certainly couldn't be done without Nero finding out about it. When he did, and if as she suggests he's against disturbing them, then we could say goodbye to our careers, even our lives, were he to consider we'd been scheming against him."

"I'm disappointed in what you've said. I'm not looking forward to telling her what she's wanting isn't possible."

"However, I have an idea of my own."

"Go on."

"I need your word you won't involve me in any way if you decide to carry out what I'm going to suggest might be an alternative solution. More than that, I don't ever want to receive any credit for coming up with the idea."

"I give you my word. If your suggestion is acceptable to Poppaea your involvement will have ended when I leave this room of yours."

"Poppaea needs the land to expand her villa. That land has buildings on it. It's the existing buildings that are the problem. Do you agree?"

"Of course."

"So! If the buildings aren't there, if they are destroyed, Nero and Poppaea would find it much easier to acquire the land for their new villa. There wouldn't be the same determination to retain just a plot of land."

"But that's ridiculous. If Nero, most likely using my men in the Guard, carried out the task of destruction, it would be worse than trying to intimidate all the owners."

"It wouldn't be worse if he, or anyone acting on his behalf, wasn't suspected of having been the cause of the destruction."

"How could that possibly be achieved on the scale we're talking about? There are tens of buildings involved, over a large area."

"Accidental fire!"

"How could that happen in such a way that it destroyed the buildings involved without it being obvious to everybody that they've been burnt to the ground to make way for the subsequent new villa for Poppaea?"

"That's your problem to solve. The Commander of the Night Watch reports to you in times of need, as I understand it. His men are there to fight and control fires in the city, aren't they? With his help, I'm sure you could come up with a plan using his most trusted men."

"I think you just might have the answer. I shall put it to Poppaea."

"Remember I'm not involved, or ever was."

*

"I like the general idea of using fire to destroy the buildings standing in my way," said Poppaea. "However, it will be seen as too much of a coincidence by Nero, and probably by many others. He knows I want that space. It's too dangerous, even for me, to defy him so openly."

"What I have in mind will overcome that."

"Then please explain!"

"The fire will be started in a place some distance away, and made to appear to spread by chance to the buildings which interest us."

"Where do you propose to start the fire?"

"It would depend on the direction of the wind at the time."

"I can see how that might work. Tell me more. Who would be involved?"

"The large number of men under the city's Commander of the Night Watch are responsible for policing the streets, particularly at night. They are also responsible for combatting fire. Their skills and experience are such they could create the fire and then channel it to run through the area we require. The right men could easily ensure that they would appear to any witnesses to be trying to put out the fire. They would eventually do that once our goal was achieved."

"I understand. However, it's vital the finger of guilt cannot be pointed at us. Who can be trusted enough to ensure it never becomes known how the fire really began?"

"The Commander of the Watch is totally loyal to me. In any case, he will understand his life depended on complete secrecy."

"What about his men who'll carry out this task?"

"The same applies to them. Their number only needs to be small.

They will be handpicked by the Commander. They will be his most trusted men, and like him they will understand the consequences for them if it ever became known how the fire began."

"What about the rest of the many men of the Watch?"

"They will be unaware of how the fire began. When released at the appropriate time they will fight bravely to protect property and citizens."

Poppaea took a few moments to reflect on what had been said. She paced around her room, watched anxiously every step of the way by Faenius.

"I agree! Begin to get your team together and prepare them for when I give the command to go ahead. My husband and I must not be in the city when this takes place. I will arrange for us to go to our villa in Antium for a few days. You will be well rewarded for this when it's all over."

Chapter 26

Julius paused only momentarily in his room to find his sword and dagger.

"Ask Olsar to join me immediately, Fausto," he ordered. "And tell him to bring his weapons with him."

Fausto left immediately leaving Julius alone with his mother.

"Did the two soldiers from the Praetorian Guard say why they wanted to speak to my father?"

"I didn't get an opportunity to ask. When I told them in which room he was working they brushed straight past me without another word."

"How did they appear?"

"They had obviously ridden hard from Rome. It's quite a cool morning but they were sweating profusely. Their faces, despite obvious attempts to disguise the fact, were showing plenty of alarm. I'm very concerned for Lucius."

"Were they carrying weapons?"

"Yes. They appeared to be fully armed. In fact the junior of the two kept fiddling with the hilt of his sword. That may of course just have been caused by his state of nervousness rather than meant as a physical threat."

"You sent for me," cried Olsar, as he ran into the room. Sword in hand, he quickly looked around.

"There's no need for your sword just yet, Olsar. I want you to come with me. We're going to Lucius's room. He has two members of the Guard with him."

"Has the Emperor sent them?" Olsar asked, striding down the corridor alongside Julius.

"We don't know but I can't help thinking about Senator Piso. I pray he hasn't started some mischief."

They entered Lucius's room without knocking and came to a confused halt. All three were having a quiet conversation.

"I'm glad the two of you have come to join us. Please take a seat. I've just been asked to attend an extraordinary meeting of the Senate later on today. I'm afraid these two Guards have brought terrible news."

"Has the Emperor come to some harm?" Julius asked, his thoughts about Piso no doubt still uppermost in his mind.

"No! It's still dreadful, though. The city is on fire. It's spreading rapidly and is already out of control."

"When and how did it start?"

"It began long after the city had settled down for the night," explained the senior of the two Guards. "As to how it began, it appears to have started in the shops outside the Circus Maximus. It quickly spread despite the brave efforts of the men of the Watch dealing with it."

"I've just been told the Forum, and all its buildings, aren't thought to be under threat, given the direction of the wind," added Lucius. "Hence we're able to hold a meeting of the Senate there."

"Where is the Emperor?"

"He was in his villa in Antium last night when the fire started," replied the Guard. "A message was sent to him at dawn. He's expected to return with the Empress later this evening."

"I'll leave immediately, with these two as my escort," Lucius concluded, rising to his feet.

"Olsar and I will come with you. We'll give whatever help we can. Mother needs to be told what's happening before we leave."

"Because you are my son and have carried out work for the Senate, you should be allowed to accompany me into the Senate meeting. You'll get first-hand knowledge of the tragedy as it's unfolding. However, you won't be permitted to take any part in the debate."

"I understand."

"You, Olsar, won't be able to attend the meeting, but I fear your courage will be in great demand before this horror is over."

*

"What has gone wrong?" Poppaea screamed at Faenius. "You assured me that the Commander of the Watch and those carefully chosen men would control the fire."

"The problems began with the wind last night. It had been increasing throughout the day. By nightfall it had become strong enough for us to consider abandoning our plan."

"Then why didn't you?"

"It was too far advanced. Too many people were involved. The wind could carry on at that strength for days, perhaps beyond your expected return from Antium. With a long delay, there would be a strong possibility our intentions would become known. I decided to go ahead."

"Maybe you acted correctly, maybe not. Nevertheless, there's no going back. We have to deal with what we face. The Emperor has gone to meet the Senate. What's the position with the fire at this time? The smoke is everywhere."

"A price has already been paid. When the strong wind began to have its effect the Commander of the Watch and his chosen group fought to keep control. The rapid expansion of the area being affected and the relatively few men involved produced panic in the citizens. That brought out the looters. So, between the raging fire and those murderous bands, the Commander and his trusted few were amongst the first to perish."

"Are you saying that, apart from you and me, all those who knew how the fire started are dead?"

"Yes!"

"That's better. The first bit of good news today. What about the fire still being able to give me what I want?"

"You will get that and much more. I'm afraid a great part of the city will be destroyed before this fire dies away."

"All of it can be replaced."

"There will be countless deaths amongst both citizens and slaves."

"They can be replaced also. The city, even the Empire as a whole, has become too overcrowded. This is beginning to turn out better than I could have hoped for. I must take steps to ensure Nero is seen to be doing everything he can to help the citizens of Rome in their time of greatest need. It will make him more popular than ever with the people. You must do the same with the Praetorian Guard. Involve them in everything. Be the heroes of the day. It would help if you lost some more men dying bravely. We shall find somebody to blame for causing the fire when it's all over, looters and the like."

*

"This unfolding tragedy has had no equal since the fall of Troy. You are my Senators. Tell me what has to be done," shouted Nero as soon as he entered the debating chamber. "I'm in despair. All my children are dying, suffering horrific injuries and becoming homeless."

"Everything that can be done is taking place," replied the Leader of the Senate. "The men of the Watch are using every one of their skills and vast experience. Every piece of equipment is being put to use."

"What about calling on others?"

"We've sent messengers to the nearest towns to send help."

"Where's the Commander of the Watch? Have him brought here."

"Sadly, he was the first to forfeit his life for the rest of us. He died bravely."

"Then we must appoint another one, just as brave if not braver. However, let's hope he's cleverer than the last one. He must be able to do what's needed yet stay alive, at least until the fire has ended."

One or two bursts of laughter from the tiers of seats were met with a ferocious stare from the Leader of the Senate, who was the next to speak.

"When you joined us, we were already in the process of debating who we should appoint to the post on a temporary basis to deal with this crisis."

"Well then. How far have you got?"

"There were several good candidates, but we'd narrowed it down to just two. One was Julius Agricola and the other w…"

"Say no more. I have first-hand knowledge of this man Agricola. Send for him so I can set him about his task."

"He's already here."

"Then step forward, Agricola."

Julius came out of the shadows at the back of the debating chamber to stand in front of Nero.

"I take it you have no objection."

"None, Sir."

"Good! This is a challenge as great as the one you faced against Boudica. Again, you are asked to fight for Rome. You are to save as much of the city as it is humanly possible. Money is not a problem. The assets in the Treasury are there to provide what's needed. You will report to the Prefect of the City in all matters. Have you any questions?"

"No, Sir."

"Then, you may leave us to begin your battle."

*

"We are going to find the Prefect," Julius told Olsar. He'd explained to him what had happened in the Senate debate.

"I shall tell him I want you as my second-in-command over all the men. If he objects I shall have a quiet word with the Emperor. He seems to favour me at the present."

"Are you pleased with your promotion, albeit only temporary?"

"It will be good to command a large body of men again in dangerous times. I only wish the circumstances were different."

Chapter 27

The third day of the fire had come and gone and there was no sign of the fire burning out. Julius estimated at least a fifth of the city had already been affected, mostly burnt to the ground. Those of his men who weren't dead, were either injured or at best exhausted. He'd resorted to using money from the Treasury to bribe citizens to allow their slaves to help in the dangerous work of fighting the fires.

At least the number of people dying daily had reduced to almost none. The initial panic in the areas first hit by the fire had caused many deaths. Slaves particularly had suffered. Many had been ordered by their owners to remain in buildings to protect against looters. They died in large numbers as a result. Either it was because they left it too late to escape for fear of their masters, or they died at the hands of the looters while trying to protect their masters' abandoned property.

Julius had managed to end both unnecessary reasons to die. Firstly, he'd sent some of his men to patrol the territory in front of the advancing fire. They were instructed to search all properties and order any citizen or slave who they found to leave and seek refuge away from the path of the fire, preferably outside the city boundaries. The Prefect had supported him by issuing a decree banning the punishment of a slave just for escaping from the fire, when ordered to stay by a fleeing master.

Secondly, he'd withdrawn a number of his men from the main task of fire-fighting and formed a force commanded by Olsar. They had the task of protecting the others from the looting. In the early stages of the fire the looters had resented the men of the Watch trying to prevent their thieving. The result was they had ruthlessly murdered anybody who got in their way. Olsar's men met and fought these thieves, nearly eliminating them all. Virtually all of the looting had ended.

Julius was increasingly concentrating on trying to make the fire go in a direction he wanted rather than be at the mercy of the wind direction. Destroying wooden buildings to create fire breaks was having a limited effect.

It was while heading towards his next possible target area that he came across Olsar, who was in command of a group of men concentrating on a group of buildings where the fire was beginning to take hold. The fire fighters were using several of their large pumps to douse flames which were beginning to appear. In addition, they were attempting get ahead of the fire by also spraying water on other smouldering wooden structures. The pumps were mounted on the back of carts, and were being operated by two men per pump. Despite their obvious exhausted state, they were still managing to raise and lower their levers at a constant rate.

"I see there aren't any looters preventing our men from doing their work."

Olsar gave Julius a weary smile. Before he could reply they were startled by the house just a few paces away, which had become almost filled with smoke. It suddenly burst into flames. Almost instantly, a young slave woman who had until then avoided detection came screaming from the house.

"My husband and my child have been overcome by the smoke. They're in the back room. Please help them."

Olsar was the first to react. He took a cloak from the back of a cart, pausing only to douse it in the water coming from the pump. Before Julius or anyone else could stop him he entered the building, hiding as best he could under his woollen shield.

"Why are you still here?" Julius asked the woman. "You should have left long ago."

"Our master ordered us not to leave under any circumstances."

"The Prefect has issued an order preventing him from doing that."

"He said it didn't apply to him. If looters stole anything he would sell us to the Amphitheatre to be used in the Arena."

A steaming hulk appeared in the doorway, paused, and then staggered forward a few paces before halting. Three of Olsar's men dashed forward to drag him to safety. Julius pulled the cloak away to reveal Olsar staring at a small, charred bundle in his arms. The slave woman let out a shrill scream and collapsed.

"May your Gods forgive me, Julius. I couldn't save them. I thought this little girl was still alive when I found her in there. But I knew I was too late when I held her in my arms."

Julius was lost for words. At first the water on Olsar's face may have appeared to those surrounding him as having dripped from his cloak. Then a loud, long, desperate sob that escaped from him left nobody in doubt they were tears of despair and sorrow. He continued to stare at the little dead child in his arms.

After a while Olsar placed her in her mother's open arms and turned to address everyone there.

"Let this be a lesson to us all. We must be vigilant in clearing houses before the fire arrives."

"I stress what Olsar says," Julius added. "Some slaves are still more frightened of their masters than they are of an approaching inferno. All our men will be told of what happened here today. The battle goes on."

*

On the fifth day of the fire Nero was on the roof of the Palace as dusk was approaching. The irony of the flame-coloured sunset filling the sky wouldn't be lost on those present. They were gazing at the still-raging fires in the distance. With him were Poppaea, Faenius, the leader of the Senate, the Prefect of the City, and Julius.

"I'm told that the fire is likely to continue for another day, maybe two," said Nero. "More than half of the city will have been affected by the time it's over. Hundreds, perhaps thousands, will have perished. I've called all of you up here because it provides the most fitting backdrop to my performance. I'm going to sing you the song I've written to commemorate our great loss. It will go down in history and be remembered alongside our other treasured Greek and Roman poems and songs."

Julius, wishing he was anywhere else but there, risked a glance across at the Prefect to see him returning his brief stare. The others appeared transfixed, eyes firmly watching Nero pick up his lyre. A long time later, verse after verse had made Julius realise what Nero had been doing in the last five days to help Rome in its great time of need.

When the performance ended, Poppaea was in tears. Faenius and the Senator were applauding and speaking their enthusiastic praises. Julius, with only the slightest moment of delay, mirrored by the Prefect, gave his similarly enthusiastic applause.

"Thank you all for showing your appreciation. As soon as Julius tells us the fire is at an end I shall be calling a meeting of the Senate to discuss the future. I want you all to be there. You will have the pleasure of hearing my new song again. In the meantime we must continue with our titanic struggle."

Outwardly, like the others, Julius showed his enthusiastic approval for a repeat performance. Inwardly, he screamed loud enough, if it hadn't been a silent one, for the whole of the citizens of the sorely injured city of Rome to hear as their agony went on.

*

"Seven days ago, this great city of Rome was faced with a challenge sent by the Gods," Nero began. "I, assisted by you Senators, have met that challenge. I have proved worthy to the Gods and saved this great city. More than that, I've saved the Empire. For without Rome there is no Empire. My name shall go down in history as a result."

Not a sound was to be heard. Recent experience of Nero meant the Senators would be anxiously wondering if someone was to be blamed for what had happened. And the enormous cost of recovery would have to be borne by everyone, but some much more than others.

"To commemorate this great victory over adversity, I have written a new song. I shall shortly give the first public performance of it to you here today."

There followed a lengthy period of polite cheering and applause.

"Before then we have to discuss what has happened and what must be done. To do that we need the attendance of the Prefect of the City and the acting Commander of the Watch. Have them join us."

The two men marched in and approached Nero. At first a slight hesitant applause greeted them. It was as if those doing it weren't quite sure if it was appropriate. Then, the whole gathering of Senators rose to their feet, cheering in grateful relief. Nero only allowed the applause to continue for a short while, perhaps not wanting the day to be remembered for the reception they received rather than his song.

"You can see and hear the gratitude Rome has for the brave and indescribable results you two have achieved during the last seven days. You will be rewarded appropriately. As for today, you've been invited to attend to hear what is to happen in the immediate future. Take a seat while I speak to the Senators."

Julius was able to seek out the proud smiling face of his father in the time it took him to find a vacant seat.

"We shall build a new city," Nero began. "This one will be made of stone. Wooden buildings won't be allowed. It must be planned properly with wide streets and open public spaces. All the public and religious buildings and monuments destroyed in the fire will be replaced with grander and better ones. The Prefect will be given greater powers to regulate the city and the numbers of his men and those of the Watch will be increased significantly."

Applause broke out again, everybody straining to look at the reaction of Julius and the Prefect.

"While I'm referring to those two again, I have decided they will work closely with a body appointed by the Senate, tasked with bringing about the changes I've just described. To facilitate that, Julius Agricola will be appointed deputy to the Prefect. He will be active in all the areas of responsibility of that Administration as delegated by the Prefect, and he will carry the same authority as he does."

Julius was showered with supportive slaps on his back and shoulders from those immediately around him.

"Finally, I raise the matter of the cost of bringing about the changes I've described. Not only the surviving citizens of Rome but the whole of the Empire will be honoured when asked to raise the money that will be necessary. An initial assessment will be undertaken by the Senate and the Treasury to determine what's needed. The task beginning today is for you gentlemen to decide what taxes, new and old will be identified and levied throughout the Empire specifically for this purpose. I shall eagerly await your proposals. I declare the meeting over. Bring me my lyre."

Chapter 28

Military campaigns can prove to be very demanding of a soldier if they extend over a long period of time. Julius had experienced that when the Army undertook the task of searching for and destroying the druids on the Island of Mona in Britannia. Individual battles lasting from dawn to dusk can test the physical endurance of a legionary or warrior to the limit, as was the case in the Boudican rebellion. But Julius had never felt the like of the total exhaustion his mind and body were suffering when he was finally able to return home after the fire ended. He sought his bed the moment he entered the villa and sank into a deep, dark sleep. When he finally woke it was mid-afternoon; the first thing he noticed was a terrible hunger and thirst. He dressed and urgently made his way to the kitchen.

"At last!" Procilla cried. "We had to keep checking if you were still alive."

"How long have I slept?"

"Nearly a day and a half."

He gave a brief whistle of surprise.

"That's never happened before."

"You never had to fight a fire for days and days before, with very little rest and sleep. Here, you'll need this."

She placed a pitcher of fresh milk and fresh bread and cheese in front of him.

"I suppose the same thing has happened to Olsar as myself?"

"Not exactly. What happened to him during those seven days?"

"Why do you ask?"

"When he got back to the villa, he didn't go immediately to his bed like you. He went straight to see his child. Sarah was fast asleep. He sat by her side for a long time, holding her hand until he finally collapsed. Fausto had to carry him to bed. He's still there. So! What happened?"

"He needs to tell us himself," Julius replied thoughtfully, "but I'm sure it has something to do with a tragic little girl we came across in the fire."

*

At the same time as Julius was eating his simple, life-restoring meal, a meeting of a small group of Senators was taking place in a small side room of the Senate House.

"As we know, massive tax demands have been approved," said Piso, "and the Senate has been ordered to apply and enforce them. We've all greeted the decision with dismay and anger. Many of us will have to contribute very large amounts to the Treasury in addition to meeting our own rebuilding costs. All of this is good news for our cause."

"There's more to give us optimism," suggested one of the other Senators. "A rumour is spreading that Nero started the fire so he could build a new city to be named after himself."

"There will be many rumours," Piso replied. "Some, like this one, will have been started by me."

Nervous laughter and a general discussion broke out with this comment. Piso raised his hand to bring it to an end.

"Our time for action to remove this tyrant is fast approaching. We need to identify and talk to others who will come to accept that the overwhelming need to move against Nero is worth the risk of failure. However, be careful in doing this. The Praetorian Guard aren't with us yet. At the moment, Faenius still only has eyes for Poppaea. To approach him now would be suicide. Nevertheless, the time is coming soon when his ambition will get the better of him. He will be persuaded to join us. Then we shall be ready to strike."

*

"My men tell me the people are already looking for someone to blame for the fire," Faenius reported.

181

"That's only to be expected," replied Nero. "A Senator who has his ear to the ground has told me there's even a rumour spreading that I am the guilty one."

"Why! What's being said?" asked Poppaea.

"They are saying I started it for my own reasons, to allow me to build a new city in my name. Everybody knows, or will do soon, that I was in Antium at the time of the outbreak."

"Nevertheless, it would be dangerous for us to ignore this threat," Poppaea added nervously. "Faenius and I have been discussing this need to identify who is to be held responsible. We think we have an ideal candidate, or more accurately candidates, to take the blame and solve another of our problems at the same time."

"Go on! Who do you suggest?"

"The Christians!"

Nero's eyes lit up.

"They're already universally disliked for their sacrilegious beliefs," Faenius added. "Arrests and punishments occur many times every day."

"I'm very interested. Anything else to add?"

"Perhaps the most important point. They're well known for insisting the world, and by that they must mean our Roman world, is about to end. They claim their God will appear at that time. It can be argued that by starting the fire they were trying to hasten that day."

Nero looked even more excited with the idea.

"It would also be a gesture to our Gods that these sacrilegious barbarians will not be tolerated by us," he added. "Their deaths will bring us good fortune as will the rebuilding of our sacred temples."

"Exactly!" Poppaea said, glancing slyly at Faenius.

"Then let it be known, Faenius, that I've concluded that the Christians are the culprits. Liaise with the city's Prefect to have likely suspects arrested and get them to confess their evil. This will give us the opportunity to be rid of them forever."

"It will begin immediately, Sir."

Chapter 29

Quintus Tiberius Saturninus was like most men of his advancing old age. He spent a good deal of his time churning over in his mind the various phases of his life. At times he could become quite depressed, dwelling on the mistakes and poor decisions he'd made. And there were the bad times also which fate had confronted him with, ones which had been totally out of his control.

On the other hand there were times when he'd counted his blessings. Times when he knew what he'd achieved was the result of his own efforts and choices. And yes, he'd been presented with his fair share of good fortune by the Gods.

Naturally, more recent times were at the forefront of his mind when he pondered on the good and the bad. The rebellion and its aftermath had been the worst part of his life. In the fairly recent past, he'd received yet another blow. His wife, Julia, had finally succumbed to the physical and emotional fatigue caused by that war.

Her devastating death had been followed soon afterwards by the loss of his two wonderful daughters when they married and left the family home. The total emptiness in his life caused by the loss of these three almost destroyed his will to carry on. The best decision he ever made helped him to survive. The two Iceni slaves had increasingly filled the void left in his life. He chose to free and then adopt them.

This had presented him with one additional blessing. One major regret he and Julia had shared had been that they'd never had the little boy they both yearned for. Because of the adoption he'd acquired a remarkable grandson, Marcus. They'd become inseparable. It brought Quintus immeasurably joy he couldn't have dreamt of only a short time before.

This particular evening his reflections were about his latest dreadful mistake. Without giving it enough careful thought, he'd taken Lucia and Flavia to the Games. As could have been expected, Flavia had been appalled at the violence on display. However, Lucia had been fascinated by the gladiatorial contests taking place, particularly the exhibition bouts between female gladiators. She was especially interested to learn they were volunteers fighting for prizes.

As a result, he and Lucia had paid a visit to the gladiator training school earlier that afternoon. She'd persuaded him to use his influence to take her to watch the gladiators in training. Not content with just being an observer, Lucia had somehow persuaded those in charge to allow her to take part. Her obvious fighting skills had so impressed them she'd been asked to return later to make arrangements for her to join the school.

Quintus and Lucia had argued continuously about it on the journey home.

*

"Why are you doing this, sister?" Flavia demanded.

"For two reasons. Firstly, only our immediate future is secure here with Quintus. What happens to us when he dies? His two daughters have made it clear to me that they only gave Quintus their blessing to our adoption if he made it clear in his will they will inherit all his estate. So when he dies we shall be free but with nothing of our own. I've found a possible way we can solve that problem, securing our longer-term future."

Lucia could see her sister wasn't convinced.

"Secondly, I'm now known to the world as Lucia. However, deep down inside me I am still Linona, as you are Cailan. I still need the thrill and excitement I got from facing a physical challenge, of meeting danger full on, overcoming it. Helping to run this farming estate hardly provides that. Inside me is still the warrior princess."

"But you will risk serious injury, even death in the Arena. We saw it happen. What would become of Marcus and me if you died?"

"I accept that death occurs sometimes with the male gladiators. However, in the case of the women, they only perform in demonstration bouts. Fighting to the death in our case is not allowed. Yes, there is the possibility of injuries, particularly in contests including various wild beasts. We can deal with that if and when it happens."

"It is still too big a risk."

"You worry too much, sister."

"When do you begin your training?"

"Tomorrow."

Chapter 30

The first anniversary of the great fire was fast approaching. Throughout the winter and spring the reconstruction work had gone ahead at a pace surprising everybody. The massive inflow of taxes from all parts of the Empire had made this possible. At first, Nero and Poppaea were indifferent to the unrest this was causing in every Province of the Empire. However, rather belatedly, they'd become concerned at the increasing displays of unrest. The main focus for this had been the construction of their enormous new villa estate.

Poppaea's initial desire for a relatively modestly grand villa had changed into something outrageously extravagant. Money and particularly space were no longer an obstacle. Initial objections by the owners of the scorched land being used were quickly brushed aside by Nero once the buildings were no longer there. His seizure of the area he needed had been supported by the Senate. The latest disturbance resulting in several deaths had prompted Nero to hold a special debate there. The outcome was to try to placate the citizens in the time-honoured fashion. The first anniversary of the fire would be marked with a festival of gladiator contests and chariot racing at the refurbished Circus Maximus. It would be financed by Nero himself.

"I have acted on your advice, and given instructions to the Senate," said Nero.

"Which particular piece of advice is that?" asked Poppaea.

"We shall involve Christians as part of the entertainments at the Games. It's a reminder to everybody that they were to blame. It will refocus the current unrest and anger onto those who rightfully deserve it."

"Talking of the Games, you know I'm not in favour of you taking part as a charioteer, particularly since you're to become a father again. I realise you're determined to do so, but you were badly injured before."

"This time, I've spent some time with the White team for a few weeks. As with everything I do, I shall win. I've become an expert in handling a chariot and team of horses."

"It will have one big advantage. For those who gamble on you, as almost everybody will, they get to win their bets. Their affection for you will increase."

The day turned out to be a fateful one, but not for the reasons either could ever have imagined.

*

The parade at the start of the day's festivities started as usual with musicians and dancers. However, on this day there were double the normal number of both. The message being sent by the organisers was to mark this as a very special occasion.

Immediately behind them marched a group of approximately eighty men, led by a centurion. They were representatives of the Night Watch. In the front rank were four of their horse-drawn pumps. Each man following the pumps carried and waved his preferred piece of fire-fighting equipment. These included buckets, axes, mattocks, picks and long-handled hooks. They received a rapturous welcome from the grateful citizens on the terraces, showing they hadn't forgotten their heroism of a year ago.

Those cheers quickly changed to howls of derision and anger as the next group entered the stadium. A small group of twenty men and women were being herded slowly down the track by nearly as many gladiators with their swords drawn. Dressed in the dirty rags of slaves, half of them were being forced to carry large wooden crosses on their backs. Nero had insisted the crowds should be reminded later of his message about these Christians.

The ecstatic applause returned as a collection of chariots was the next to roll onto the track. In the first of them, the charioteer was wearing a large royal purple cloak. A fanfare of many trumpets greeted his raised arm. The Emperor was making a performer's entrance onto the stage. His only regret at that moment would be that very few amongst his audience were close enough to see the tears of ecstasy streaming down his face.

As Nero passed the royal pavilion, Poppaea gave a well-rehearsed greeting. She stood on an improvised raised platform so that the thousands on the terraces could see how near she was to giving them a new heir. She blew her beloved husband several exaggerated kisses. Her final gesture was to throw a bouquet of flowers in his direction. On cue, the rest of the special guests in the Pavilion roared their support. As if anxious for the entertainment to start, Nero stirred his horses into action and the chariots quickly left the track. The parade was over.

*

The initial gladiator contests had taken place as planned. They were intended to excite the spectators just enough to leave them wanting more. Therefore, none of the contests had been to the death. Nevertheless, there had been sufficient spilt blood to whet the appetite of the more bloodthirsty members of the crowd. Nero had joined his guests in the pavilion soon after the end of the parade. He would re-join his fellow charioteers later.

"I hope he's learnt the art of being a charioteer since we were last here," whispered Olsar.

Julius glared disapprovingly at him, but didn't risk a reply in the crowded pavilion.

"I'm sure you all enjoyed our gladiators," said Nero. "We're about to involve them again. This will please every man and woman here today."

To astonished applause, two centuries of legionaries ran onto the track. They formed a shield wall at each end, sealing it off. A spear protruded between each shield facing inwards. When they were set, other legionary archers appeared at intervals all around the stadium. The lowest terrace where they had positioned themselves had been built high above the track to protect the spectators from wayward chariots and horses.

Olsar took hold of Julius's arm, concern written all over his face.

"It won't be what you're thinking," said Julius. "Those archers aren't a threat to the crowd. In fact, it's the opposite. Along with the two shield walls, they're providing a protective ring. If I'm right in what I'm thinking this won't be to your liking."

Doors were opened in the side walls beneath the terraces. The twenty Christians from the parade were being prodded and pushed onto the track. When they were far enough away from the crowd the gladiators withdrew and the doors closed behind them. Everything went quiet. Then, gasps and screams from the terraces greeted the entry of the first enormous lion. It was quickly followed by five others. Terror-stricken, the Christians ran in all directions to try to escape, prompting the starving lions to attack. The first to be brought down was an old woman who could barely run. The force of the male lion's initial blow dropped her onto the ground, face down. It sank its huge fangs into her neck, breaking it.

"This is barbaric. What sort of people can enjoy this as entertainment?" Olsar asked in not much of a whisper.

"Quiet!" Julius ordered.

"My people would never have tolerated this level of depravity as entertainment."

"Quiet! If Nero hears you defending his hated Christians you'll be joining them on the track."

Before too long, all of them had been killed. Those who escaped the first attack had made it to the two lines of legionaries only to be driven back by spears towards the lions. Some were already satisfying the hunger of the lions. The shield walls began to approach each other. When the area between them had been reduced to half the previous size, they halted. Doors opened immediately, spilling twenty gladiators onto the track. Running at speed, they attacked the lions. Their war cries drew the attention of the feasting lions and the battle began. All the lions died. Only one gladiator was badly mauled.

*

A variety of chariot races formed the second and most important part of the festivities. Eventually, the climax to the day's festivities arrived. There was just one race to come.

"We are about to witness a great athlete," Poppaea boasted. "I hope you've all bet on him to win."

The fanfare announced the arrival of the four final chariots. The charioteers' cloaks, including the purple one were discarded and the four contestants drew up in a straight line across the track. By some lucky chance Nero had drawn the most advantageous lane on the inside. His luck didn't end there. It appeared the other three charioteers weren't concentrating when the starting flag was lowered. As a result, Nero was at least a length ahead when he carefully manoeuvred around the first bend.

"Don't say anything!" Julius insisted, fighting back a smile.

"I could have won this race driving my first ever chariot pulled by one mule, judged by the pace at which they're competing," Olsar muttered.

By the end of the last circuit Nero had won by two lengths. The spectators greeted the victory with a thunderous roar.

"It's been a wonderful day. I'm sure you all agree," said Poppaea to her guests. "Go to your homes to celebrate."

The pavilion began to empty.

"Julius Agricola! Wait a moment," she commanded.

She waited until the room was almost clear.

"I'm not pleased with what I've observed today. On occasions I noticed expressions on your face, and particularly that of your Brit, suggesting you weren't in full support of the proceedings, especially your Emperor's efforts in the last race. Both of you will come to see me in the morning to explain yourselves. Leave me."

*

Late that night a very drunken Nero was helped back into his private rooms by Faenius. He was placed on a couch facing a fuming Poppaea. He sat up straight and looked sheepish. She looked very unhappy with him.

"I am sorry I'm a little late. I've been celebrating my victory with my fellow charioteers."

"Leave us, Faenius, but stay close by," Poppaea ordered. "I might need you again."

Nero, having a little trouble focusing, stood up.

"Where are you going?" she demanded.

"To bed. Where do you think at this hour?"

"Sit down. Do as you're told."

Nero was reminded of how much she reminded him of his mother at her worst.

"Not only am I going to bed now, but tomorrow I'm taking my charioteer friends with me to Antium for a few days of fun."

"You're not going there whoring with anybody! We've a lot of business to get through."

Nero nodded. He wasn't accepting what she said. He was agreeing with himself that his mother would have said exactly the same thing.

"You need to behave properly, like a responsible father for the sake of this child inside me if for no other reason. Don't be so selfish."

That's it, he told himself. His worst fears could have been realised. Had she come back from Hades to have her revenge? Is the unborn child in her a girl? Is it Agrippina?

"It had better be a boy this time," he said. "If it's a girl, I shall have the pair of you strangled when it's born. Then I can marry again and have a son."

Poppaea jumped to her feet, closing the distance between them in three strides.

"How dare you say such a thing? You drunken swine."

Her hand struck him a fierce blow across his face, forcing him backwards.

"Now I know you're in there, Mother," he shouted.

A puzzled look on Poppaea's face was wiped away by Nero's return vicious blow. She screamed as she fell onto her side on the floor. Without hesitation he stepped forward to land several savage kicks into her heavily swollen body.

"Take that, Mother. When you come out, there'll be a lot worse to follow."

Nero stormed out of the room, passing a patrolling Faenius in the corridor.

Faenius, having responded to Poppaea's cries for help, was

standing by the couch holding her hand.

"I've sent for a surgeon. He'll be here shortly. Please stay calm."

"He's become insane. We must stop him."

"Please don't upset yourself. Have you had a fall?"

"No! No! Don't you understand? He deliberately tried to kill my baby. He thinks I've been possessed by his mother, Agrippina."

"What has he done?"

"He knocked me to the ground and kicked the child in my womb to try to kill it."

*

By dawn the following morning Poppaea and her child were dead. Nero had had a good night's sleep.

Chapter 31

"Gentlemen. We've obtained the final missing link to complete the chain. Faenius is with us."

Excited cries from the men in the room greeted Piso's triumphant words. One Senator was so overcome with emotion he began to shed floods of tears.

"We've waited so long for this," he explained, wiping his face with his toga. "I thought the time would never come."

"Well it has, my friend. All we need to do now is to agree with Faenius when, where and how we end the life of this tyrant and bring back the Republic."

"Let it be soon," demanded another of those present. "Every day we wait carries a risk for us all."

"It's just a matter of days, I can assure you. Faenius wants him dead as soon as possible after what he did to Poppaea."

"What about the rest of the Guard? Can Faenius bring them with him?"

"Sabinus, his second-in-command, is still very loyal to Nero and must be eliminated at the same time. The rest of the men are content with Nero for now. However, Faenius assures me they will follow his lead when there's no longer an Emperor to protect and the bribe is large enough."

"What about Seneca?" asked the Leader of the Senate.

"I've just come from visiting him again to persuade him to join us finally. I've explained everything to him. He still refuses to be one of us. His excuse now is he's too old to become involved in the chaos he insists will result. He's not the man he once was. We no longer need his name to help justify our cause. Are you all with me?"

To a man, they gave their enthusiastic support.

"Then go to brief the rest of our group. We shall meet here in the Senate house in two days, unless you hear differently from me before then. Bring your weapons with you! It won't be the Ides of March on this occasion but it will still be an historic day."

*

Decianus had been depressed since the death of Poppaea. It wasn't because of any affection or respect he may have had for her. No! It was because a very important ally in building his wealth had been lost. Not only that, his access through her and Faenius to the Emperor had diminished. Nevertheless, he needn't have been concerned on that score. His luck was about to change once more.

"Can I come in, Sir?" Milichus asked.

"I'm very busy. What is it?" Decianus growled. He wondered why people thought they could constantly bother him.

"We haven't met before, but a mutual friend told me you may be prepared to help me with a very important matter that's troubling me."

"If it's money you're after, you can get out. I'm not a rich man. The money you see here isn't mine." *Not yet anyway,* he thought.

"It isn't about money. It's a great deal more important than that."

"What's more important than money to you, me or even the Emperor?"

"There's a conspiracy to kill Nero."

"There are always rumours of that sort. It is about money, isn't it? Get out."

Another scoundrel, was his conclusion.

"It isn't a rumour. I'm part of the conspiracy! I should know."

"Are you mad? Who are you anyway?"

"My name is Milichus. I'm a freedman. Once I was the slave of the Leader of the Senate, but I bought my freedom a long time ago."

"If what you say is true, why are you stupid enough to tell me? I must report you to Faenius immediately. You're a dead man."

"Faenius has joined the conspiracy. That's why I'm here. I can't go to him or trust any of his men. I know you aren't involved and could go directly to the Emperor."

"What of Sabinus?"

"The second-in-command isn't involved yet. I understand he's still loyal to the Emperor. But I don't know for sure."

Decianus's thoughts were in turmoil. He told himself he couldn't ignore what he'd heard. Whatever he did could be dangerous for him if he made the wrong move. He made his decision.

"Wait here! You mustn't leave while I'm out. If you do, you'll be found and be dead by nightfall."

*

"There's a conspiracy to kill Nero," declared Decianus. He was speaking to Sabinus in his office. "Do you wish to join it?"

Sabinus stood up from his desk, drawing his sword.

"You traitor. You're under arrest. I want the name of everybody who's involved."

Wait!" shouted Decianus, thinking with relief he'd made the right decision. "I had to be sure you weren't one of them since your commander is."

"What lies are you telling? Speak quickly. You have an appointment with the torturer shortly."

Decianus speaking rapidly but carefully told him what had just happened. Milichus was brought in and repeated his story.

"We shall go to see the Emperor. If this turns out to be false you are both meat for the Emperor's lions."

"There's only one question I want to ask you, Milichus," said Nero. "Before I decide whether to have the truth cut out of you, why are you here if you're one of them?"

We asked that, thought Decianus. Would Nero believe it as they'd done? He felt nervous.

"I'm only an ex-slave. My former master still tries to dominate me. He thought I'd be loyal to him because he granted me my freedom. He considered I would be useful to his group. I decided to break free from him once and for all. My Emperor is everything to me."

I like the last bit, Decianus thought. *He's not as simple as he looks.*

"I've been convinced."

He turned to Sabinus.

"As from this moment you are the new Commander of my Guard. Arrest all of those traitors who he's named. Start with Faenius and Piso. Torture them to find out who else is involved as well as those identified by Milichus. Then torture them all before you execute them. You, Milichus, will hide with Decianus night and day until this is over."

I knew there would be a downside to this somehow, Decianus thought.

*

Two days had passed. The same four men were in Nero's office.

"You are free to go, Milichus. You've proven to have done me a great service. As a reward you are granted full citizenship. In addition, you will receive riches you could only have dreamt of a few days ago. Go and use them wisely."

Milichus bowed then exited proudly to start his new life.

"You have had your reward, Sabinus. Which leaves only you, Decianus."

A large estate in a prosperous part of the Empire would be appropriate, Decianus imagined. *As long as it's not in Britannia.*

"You are to be appointed the personal assistant to Sabinus. You'll have special responsibility for my future security. You can build a network to look out for traitors. I will never trust a single Senator again. So you have my permission to keep a special eye on all of them and their supporters."

Decianus expressed his overwhelming gratitude. However, his first thought had been that Julius Agricola had better be very careful in the future. Any more threats from him, against Nero's special security adviser, could be regarded as treason against Nero. He felt good.

"And now I want you both to stay and witness my final performance in this treacherous tragedy. Bring in Seneca," he shouted at the guard by the door.

"Why have I been arrested?" Seneca demanded before anything else could be said to him.

"All your friends are dead. Piso and Faenius were made to commit suicide in my presence for their treachery. The twenty or more co-conspirators were tortured before being executed."

"Then you will know I wasn't one of them. I accept some had been my friends but I can't be judged a traitor because of that."

"You are a traitor because you knew of their plot to remove me and said nothing."

"Piso approached me as he must have done with many others who didn't join him. I told him he was wrong to plan to remove you. So, I didn't just turn him down, I opposed him."

"But you didn't warn me."

"Because I thought he would never get to put a plan together and carry it out. I thought he would never get the support of the Praetorian Guard. I was right."

"You were very nearly wrong. He almost succeeded."

"But he didn't, and I repeat that I took no part in it."

"Enough of your banter. I pronounce you as guilty as those who took a more active part. You will be allowed to commit suicide like the other two. However, you can do it at home in front of your family. I have no desire to witness it. Guards! Take him away."

Seneca didn't look surprised or alarmed. He may well have been expecting his life to end in this way one day. He did have the last word, though.

"You've killed many Senators and nobles alike in the last few years. No doubt you will carry on and kill many more before you've finished. Nevertheless, the one person you won't be able to destroy with your paranoia is the one who will soon succeed you through whatever means. Whoever he is, he will be somewhere this very moment, the next Emperor of Rome."

Chapter 32

Vespasian had been summoned from his country estate to meet Nero in the city. Six months had passed since the Piso conspiracy. During that time, he often wondered if the earlier meeting Piso had involved him in would somehow become known. If so, he could have expected to be dealt the same fate as his good friend Seneca. However, nothing had happened up to the present.

One period of real anxiety had occurred three months previously when he'd been brought back from Africa. He knew his period as Governor was coming to an end, but the failed conspiracy could still have been the reason. With this man you never knew for sure. His fears were groundless. He'd gone into semi-retirement again, waiting for any further call to service. An unexpected call had come late the previous day. The sense of urgency in the message raised a nagging doubt once again. He wondered if he would ever be free of it.

Walking through the Forum, Vespasian couldn't help wondering why the meeting had been arranged for late morning in a back room of the Senate building. He very quickly found out.

"Good morning, Vespasian," Nero said. "The weather is wonderful. It's the sort of day for making very important decisions. In this case it involves you."

Vespasian wondered if this was finally it. Would his explanation be better received than Seneca's after all this time?

"I expect you're wondering why we're meeting here. The answer is simple. I've received some very important information needing immediate action. Those continually troublesome Judaeans have started a full revolt. The Governor has been assassinated and our Legions badly mauled."

Vespasian sighed quietly with relief.

"I've debated the situation with the Senators this morning. The main decision which we've all agreed upon is that you are to be sent there to put down the revolt. Do you accept the role of General? I ask because someone in the debate had an initial slight reservation since you haven't been in charge of a full army for many years. That didn't receive any support at all. I take it you don't share a similar concern."

"Not in the least. I'm more than delighted with the honour I'm being given."

"We need to talk about the resources you'll need."

"You say our forces have suffered losses?"

"Yes. So, you will have to make an urgent assessment of the size of the army needed. I want this problem solved once and for all."

"I shall look into it immediately. What about my Legates and support staff?"

"Choose who you want."

"I shall take my son Titus as one of my Legates. Also, there's someone I would welcome on my personal staff. He's had past experience in putting down a revolt."

"Name him."

"Julius Agricola. My son served with him in Britannia and he speaks very highly of him. However, I understand he's doing a vital job in rebuilding Rome."

"You're correct. I will be reluctant to release him. Do you insist his support is vital to you?"

"I do. I wouldn't be so crass as to ask for him unless it was so."

"Then I agree. But if things are sorted out there very quickly, I will demand his return."

"I understand."

"There's one other thing. You mentioned your son Titus going with you. You have a second, younger son, Domitian. I think it would be a good idea if he came to stay here at court with me. It will be a gesture to show the need for trust between us while you're away."

Vespasian's expression showed no change as he stared coldly at Nero, choosing not to comment.

"Good! Everything is settled then. You'd better have your sword sharpened and your old armour polished."

PART III

TIME OF WAR

66 AD

Chapter 33

Joseph had only ridden into the town of Tiberias in northern Judaea that morning. The main part of the Roman army was several days' march away. There was still sufficient time for him to carry out his task. His visit had been expected. So, it had been relatively easy for him to gather together a large number of citizens in the main town square. His armed escort of twelve men, standing around him, raised their swords. The noisy, alarmed discussions taking place throughout the square came to a gradual halt.

"You will have received a message several days ago from Jerusalem notifying you all of my visit. The leaders of our revolution there have appointed me to the position of Commander of this whole region of Galilee. My name is Joseph, son of Mathew. I bring a message to you from them."

"Why should we take any notice of you?" came a cry from the crowd. "We don't come under the control of those southerners in Jerusalem."

"We are all Judaeans," Joseph countered. "Hear me out. You don't know what I have to say."

This brief exchange of unfriendly words provoked a multitude of discussions and arguments in the square once more. Joseph let it go on unchallenged. It was similar to the reception he'd received in nearly all the towns he'd visited during the last few days in his new area of command. Gradually the discussions died down and expectant faces turned towards him again.

"Some months ago these Romans were guilty of yet more outrages in the Temple and elsewhere in our beloved Jerusalem. We southerners, as you call us, courageously drove out the Legion from there, virtually destroying it. That showed our leaders we can fight for and win our freedom, particularly if we all band together. I'm here to help you to organise to resist our enemy."

"We knew why you were coming today," replied a self-appointed spokesman. "We've been told of your message by our friends in the towns you've already visited. We've had time to consider what you're asking for."

"Then you're ready to join us."

"Half of us are. The others won't take on the might of Rome. We know their new General has arrived at the port of Ptolemais with three Legions and thousands of auxiliaries to replace the defeated one. Our town's defences, as good as they are, couldn't withstand a force of that size."

"What are you saying then?"

"Those who wish to join you to fight them will go with you. The rest will stay here to seek terms when the Roman General arrives."

"Is he speaking for you all?" Joseph shouted.

He was left in no doubt he was by those massed in the square.

"Then those of you who wish to fight can leave with us at dawn. We are gathering all our forces at the fortress town of Jotapata. I pray the Romans don't take their revenge for their disgraced Legion on those of you who are remaining."

Joseph gathered his escort together as the square emptied.

"I want half of you to take control of the men from here in the morning. Make sure they get to our fortress. I will ride on ahead. There's much work to be done there."

*

"This Judaean rebellion won't be an easy one to put down," said Vespasian.

He was reviewing the current military situation with his son Titus and Julius Agricola. In front of them, in his tented headquarters at the centre of his temporary campaign fort, were various maps of the huge area of Judaea. Months had passed since their arrival in the port of Ptolemais to assemble an army of three Legions. That number of fifteen thousand men had more or less doubled when the auxiliary forces were added.

"Nero will be getting impatient," Titus added. "He will have assumed it would be like the uprising by Boudica. In that case, it was all over in a matter of months. That's about the same time we've been here already. I take it there hasn't been any enquiry from him as to why you haven't crushed the enemy yet."

"Correct," Vespasian replied. "Let's hope he has other things to occupy him to keep us out of his thoughts."

"Whatever he would like to happen, he isn't going to get what he wants," Julius offered. "In Britannia the situation was entirely different. There, Governor Paulinus faced an enemy marshalled into one single force, desperate to meet him on the battlefield. Boudica realised she couldn't hold her army together much beyond the end of summer. It was too large and ill-disciplined. She played into our hands."

"I agree," said Titus. "The enemy here is completely the opposite. When we approach their forces, large or small, they withdraw. The whole area we've covered so far has many fortified towns to sustain them. When we eventually break a siege or enter unopposed we find the same thing. Most of their fighting men have escaped."

"I need a sizeable victory to boast of to Nero. That would pacify him, buying us the time we need for a total victory. That means only one thing. We have to defeat the major part of their forces, and destroy Jerusalem, the focus for their cause. So long as that city stands with its sacrilegious temple to their one and only God, we shall never have lasting peace in this troubled land.

"Part of the reason I asked you to join me this afternoon is to consider the latest success we've had," he continued, moving the discussion on.

He turned to face the guard at the entrance. "Bring in the tribune!"

The tall young tribune from the 10th Legion entered, then stood stiffly to attention.

"Relax, Tribune. I want you to repeat what you told me this morning."

"Yes, General," he replied nervously. "As you all know, my Legion is active in the northeast of Judaea. My Legate sent me to report we've just taken the fortified town of Tiberias. We'd expected to undergo many days of siege there. The area is part of this land of Galilee and the town is built by the side of a large inland lake. It has a strong defensive wall."

"So! What happened?" Titus asked impatiently.

"They surrendered without a fight."

"Did they ask for terms?" Julius asked.

"No. They said they were loyal to Rome."

"And you believed them," Titus commented cynically.

"Not at first. However, we did after a long discussion with the town leader."

"What did he say to convince you?"

"He told us that a few days ago they'd been visited by the commander appointed by the rebels to be responsible for the whole of this northern part of Judaea. He announced that his name was Joseph, son of Mathew. Unlike those in the town, he was a southerner born in Jerusalem. He asked them to join in his cause."

"They obviously didn't," Titus remarked.

"Half of them didn't. There was a split amongst them. The ones remaining do appear to be loyal to us. The others wishing to fight us left the next day with the commander's men."

"Did the town leader tell you where they were going?"

"To a town called Jotapata, somewhere to the south."

"Repeat what you told me earlier about what you'd learnt about this commander," Vespasian ordered.

"This commander stayed the night in the town. The leader said the message he brought hadn't been well received by these northerners. They resented him trying to tell them what they should believe in. It so happens he let it be known he'd recently returned from Rome to join the revolt. He'd been there for two years."

"What was he doing there?" Julius asked.

"He claimed he'd been a diplomat, sent by those in Jerusalem who are now leading the revolt."

"Interesting," Julius commented. "Why would he mention that to the town leader?"

"We asked the same question. The town leader said the commander had told him in confidence about what he'd seen and learnt first-hand about us in Rome. The commander appeared to be having strong doubts that the revolt could succeed in the long run. However, he would continue his recruitment of supporters to their cause out of loyalty to the idea of independence."

"We must seek out and kill this man. He's dangerous," Vespasian observed.

"I think I may have met him when he was in Rome," said Julius. "I was introduced to a diplomat called Josephus by my father in the Senate building one time. If I recall correctly, he was from Judaea."

"That may prove useful," Vespasian noted. "So! Let's see where this Jotapata is located and how long it will take a Legion to get there. It sounds as if we might just be able to get a significant victory there at last."

Chapter 34

The town of Jotapata had been located in the ideal place to be turned into a fortress. It was built on the top of a large hill in mountainous country. It was surrounded on three sides by steep ravines which made an approach only possible from one other side, from the north. Even this way into the town was difficult. It was relatively narrow with slopes on either side, the ground rising steeply in the approach to the only entrance. To add to the natural defences a high wall had been built all around it. It was particularly high right across the northern approach side. The only weakness it had was the lack of any significant water source. It was a weakness Joseph had quickly identified.

On this bright sunny morning he stood on the wall above the town gates. He was able to gaze down on the results of several weeks of attempts by the Romans to build a flat platform in front of the wall. From such an area of flattened surface they would be able to position their siege machines to break through the walls. He came to the conclusion that it was likely they were capable of an initial breach in a matter of days if nothing was done. Something was done.

Those building the ramp had protection from as many legionaries as the narrow area of the approach to the town allowed. A sizeable force, it was still too small to resist the attack of several thousands of Joseph's warriors as they poured through the hastily opened gates in the north wall. Virtually all those working on building the platform were put to the sword, as were many supporting legionaries before the rest retreated back to Vespasian's camp in the rear. They were sent on their way by a huge cry of victory from the town's defenders.

When the gates had been secured and the celebrations were over, Joseph called a meeting of the town leaders and his twelve most trusted men.

"Today, we've shown the Romans how strong we are."

His remarks were met with cheers all around.

"But we've only bought some extra time. The end will still be the same, defeat."

This time he was faced with astonished, angry silence and stares.

"I know of this Vespasian. He's an experienced General. He's fought in many lands, against all types of enemy. He will continue to hammer on our walls until they fall."

"Then we will die taking as many of these murderers with us as we can, Joseph!"

This comment came, not as Joseph might have expected from one of the more militant warriors, but from the town's most senior leader. Joseph ignored the comment.

"I've sent a message to our leaders in Jerusalem telling them we can't hold out much longer. Our water supplies have lasted many weeks but eventually they will be gone. I have asked them if we are to fight to the death here. I suggested an alternative to them."

"Which was what?"

"As many of us who are able should escape to continue our struggle elsewhere. Those wishing to stay could do so, to seek terms of surrender. The decision is with those in Jerusalem. Their reply is expected any day."

"The choice is ours. It isn't to be taken by some group of men we've never met," shouted a different leader this time. "We stay to fight."

"Is that the view of you all?" Joseph demanded.

There were no dissenters.

"Then we fight. Many thousands of us will die or be taken prisoner in the next few days. I hope our deaths will be an inspiration to others and don't prove to be wasted. To your posts."

*

The platform had finally been laid and siege machines used for several days. Those manning the assault towers and battering rams had been attacked with every kind of weapon from the hundreds of defenders on the walls. The result was a stalemate.

"This has gone on long enough," Vespasian shouted angrily at Titus and Julius. "I was told days ago a captured rebel had confessed that the town had no water. Yet they are still there. It was a lie to confuse us. They are still there, mocking us. Then I was told by my engineers that the platform and siege machines, that we spent many days building, would get me inside that miserable place. I'm still waiting. I'm about to send every man I have against the place now unless you have any other ideas."

"We would lose too many good men if we tried that," objected Titus.

"Then what do you propose if not that?"

Titus paused, apparently at a loss.

"I have a suggestion," Julius offered. "An idea came to me when I interrogated the captive who told us about the water. He'd been tortured to loosen his tongue. In return for his life he told us of a way we might take the town."

"I'm listening," said Vespasian, as was Titus.

"The whole of the defenders are exhausted, perhaps thirsty as well. The men guarding the walls are at their weakest and most vulnerable just before dawn."

"We could hardly send in Legions to attack in the dark," scoffed Vespasian.

"No, but you could send me with a good-sized group of our best men to secretly scale the walls at that time. Once inside we could dispose of the sleeping guards. They wouldn't be expecting such an attack. Then we could open the gates for our legionaries. They would create panic and chaos amongst the defenders. The town would be ours with minimal losses."

"What do you think, Titus?"

"I like it. It needs some refining, but I think it has a good chance. There's one thing though. To increase the chances of success we need to scale the walls from both ends. If Julius leads one assault I insist on taking the other. He's not having all the glory."

The two friends exchanged broad smiles. Vespasian was silent for a while, giving the proposal some consideration.

"You are both vital to the success of this whole campaign. What guarantee do I have the both of you will return?"

"None!" answered Titus quickly. "We are at war. All of us are at risk. Didn't you get an enemy arrow in your foot yesterday? I understand your inspection of the platform, and the limited damage done to the walls, took you dangerously close to one of their bowmen? Perhaps that's why you're in such a bad mood."

Vespasian laughed before replying.

"Let's do it!"

Chapter 35

Occasionally, the half-moon broke through the patchy clouds racing across the sky. When it occurred the fifty or so men in Julius's command stopped in their careful approach, dropping silently to the ground so as not to be spotted. Julius knew the same would be happening at the other end of the front wall. He hoped the two groups would still arrive at their destinations at the same time. When they did arrive, the plan was to show a small flame, hidden from the view of any guard above on the wall, to the other group. It would indicate their readiness to begin. The signal would be given periodically until a reply was received and acknowledged. Then the action could begin.

Julius couldn't help but remember the last time he'd led a group of men in a pre-dawn secret attack on an enemy. He'd been on Mona. That had been a success. He realised he was experiencing the same feeling now as he did then. He couldn't imagine failure. His men were the best. Any one of them would make a champion gladiator in the arena. The fighting which was about to start demanded close man-to-man merciless combat. Speed was everything if all the guards were to be silenced and the gates opened. His men arrived and settled close against the wall, staring upwards for any sign they'd been seen.

"I think I saw the signal as we came to the wall, Julius," whispered Olsar. "They're ready for us."

"We weren't ready though. We are now. We need to wait a few moments for their next try. There it is!" Julius murmured. "Light our flame."

Having done so, another return signal was received instantly. Julius gave the command to prepare the five ladders they'd brought with them. When they'd been placed carefully against the wall, Julius placed his foot on the bottom rung of one of them. He paused only for a moment to glance sideways and nod at Olsar, who was waiting at the foot of the next ladder.

"Go!" he ordered.

Each man had been given a number to climb their particular ladder to avoid any confusion. The result was all fifty men were quickly on top of the wall and heading along it towards the gates. As expected, virtually every guard they came across on the top of the wall and in the buildings below was deep in the sleep of the malnourished and exhausted. It was a sleep from which none of them would awaken.

"So far so good," Titus whispered to Julius when they met behind the gates.

"This is where things could start to go wrong," Julius replied. "Those hinges on the gates are going to make a lot of noise when opened. It's a sound that will be familiar to everyone in this town."

"You take six men to open the gates and give the signal to tell the legionaries to come running. I will take the rest to deal with the first of the enemy who come to see what's happening."

"Let's hope we have very fast runners in the front ranks of our legionaries," Julius added.

When the gates were fully open, Julius heard the familiar sound of a large number of men beginning to fight at close quarters behind him. He felt that old tingling excitement every true warrior feels as he goes into battle. He looked to see where the thickest of the action was taking place and went to join it.

"We need those legionaries soon while we still have the advantage," shouted Titus. "The word is getting out in the town that we've broken in."

"Our men are coming," Julius replied, just avoiding a blow aimed at his head. "They should be here by now."

No sooner had he said it than a huge terrifying roar came from the torrent of legionaries surging into the town. The inevitable panic and terrified confusion throughout the town meant the main fighting was over by mid-morning. The mopping up of those hidden and still resisting had begun.

In one of the large hiding places in the town, especially dug into the hillside for such a feared occasion as this, Joseph was with thirty of his men.

"The town is lost, but there's still time for us to escape," Joseph urged.

"We wouldn't get more than a few paces," replied one of the older men. "Legionaries are everywhere."

"Then we should surrender. If we stay alive there's always hope."

"What hope is that? God has abandoned us. If we're going to die today, we don't want it to be at the hands of those filthy Romans. I think that's why we've all come here, to end it ourselves. When they find our bodies it will show them that we true Judaeans prefer to kill ourselves rather than surrender to become their slaves. This final act of defiance will send a message to encourage our brothers in Jerusalem."

"Who is prepared to join me to try to escape?" Joseph pleaded.

Only one other man supported him. Joseph hung his head.

"Joseph can no longer lead us," the older man stated. "The decision has been taken. We are to die here. However, we shall not take our own lives. We shall have the honour of carrying out the task for each other. To determine the order, we shall draw numbers. Only the last man must take his own life."

Joseph decided not to stay until the end. Somehow he would survive and tell his people of the heroism and defiance he'd witnessed at Jotapata. He left the hiding place to surrender. He asked to be taken to Vespasian.

*

"So you are Joseph, or should I call you Josephus?" Vespasian asked.

"I see you know I've spent time in Rome."

"You asked to speak to me. Why should I waste any more time? You're a rebel commander and I'm eager to have you executed for what you've done."

"I'm more use to you alive than dead."

Vespasian laughed, as did Titus and Julius. Those two had been delighted at the news that Joseph had been captured. They'd made sure they were present to enjoy his being held to account for his treachery.

"Explain what you mean. Your rebellion is ultimately doomed. You and your fellow rebels will soon be forgotten."

"Defeated perhaps, but not forgotten."

"You've seen at first-hand what we have in store for the rest of Judaea."

"I've known since my time in Rome that we couldn't win. I've said this many times to my people, but I couldn't persuade them. I fought you because I'm a patriot, just like you."

"I don't believe you."

"Too many of us are dying. I could work with you to try to persuade my people to surrender as you move on through the rest of Judaea."

"I think not. So! Is there anything else before I help you to meet your one and only God?"

"It is written in our sacred scriptures that a new ruler of the world, a Messiah, is coming and he will be from Judaea. I believe in this prediction and it is about to happen. I repeat that he is said to come from this land. But I see now he won't be a Judaean. He will be a Roman. I have experienced the power of your Empire in Rome and here. The entire world in the future will be Roman, ruled over by one man as predicted. While that may be true, the question is which one. I learnt in the great city of yours of the high esteem that you're held in by the people. I predict when Nero is dead you will come from Judaea to become the ruler of the world. Our scriptures are foretelling it."

At first silenced by what he'd heard, Vespasian began to laugh loudly, joined by all the others present in his tent.

"You are either a fool or very clever. Nero is a very young man with lots of years ahead of him. I, on the other hand, am just an old soldier. If Nero doesn't leave an heir, the next Emperor will be chosen by the Senate, from one of our very old and distinguished noble families. My family is quite a relatively modest and insignificant one. I think perhaps you are cleverly trying to gain my favour by the use of flattery."

He thought for a while then smiled mischievously.

"I've decided to delay your execution until I return to Rome. I want you to tell your story to my Emperor to see how he reacts to your prediction. I think he will be greatly amused before he sends you to the Arena. In the meantime you will be my slave, on display for all Judaeans to see."

Chapter 36

"Let me have your report, Julius," Vespasian ordered. "How did the skirmishing go today? You look frustrated again."

"It went as every other day since Jotapata fell a month ago. The Judaeans come out of nowhere to attack us, only to flee when they've done their damage. The Legion lost another twenty men today. We killed at least that many of them and took some prisoners for interrogation. We could have done more but we dare not chase them too far in case they're setting an ambush. They've caught us out before with such tactics. This war is going to last a considerable time if they won't meet us on the battlefield."

"Not for you, Julius. I'm afraid your part in this war is over."

"Why, Sir!" protested Julius. "Have I failed you in some way? Tell me how so I can defend myself."

"Calm yourself and sit down so I can explain."

Julius did as ordered, taking a chair to sit facing Vespasian across his desk.

"I don't want to lose you. My son is particularly dismayed that you have to leave. We don't have a say in the matter. Nero has ordered your return."

"But my role in your campaign is nowhere near finished. He must know that from the reports he's had about how the enemy is choosing to fight."

"It appears he has other important work waiting for you in Rome."

"What did his message say?"

"No more than what I've told you. It said only that you are to return at once on the ship which brought his message. It's waiting in the port of Ptolemais. The messenger said he'd been sent on the fastest ship available."

"I shall collect my things immediately. Can I ask one thing of you?"

"Ask it."

"I may be walking into great personal danger. I will need every friend I can get to rely on. Will you release Olsar from his command within the auxiliaries? I have no more loyal friend than Olsar."

"I agree. But Titus won't be pleased. He's come to rely heavily on your friend."

Vespasian stood and walked round his desk to stand close to Julius, who'd risen from his chair.

"There's one thing you can do for me when you get back. You know my younger son Domitian is being kept there by Nero as some sort of hostage to ensure I don't fail in the task he's set me."

"Yes. You told me that in confidence right at the start, Sir."

"That was a measure of the trust I have in you. I want you to tell Domitian everything that's happening here. Reassure him I will return triumphant from putting down this rebellion to secure his release. Not only that. While you're there, I want you to do what you can to look after his interests, as your Olsar does for you."

"You have my word of honour, Sir."

"That's enough for me. Now go to say your farewells, particularly to Titus."

Chapter 37

Very few Romans had reason to visit the Province of Lusitania. It had no strategic value being situated at the far western edge of the Empire. Beyond it lay the unknown waters of the mighty ocean. Throughout history it had been suggested that the legendary land of Atlantis lay somewhere beyond the setting sun. Nobody who'd sailed westward in search of it had ever returned with proof they'd found it.

The contribution of Lusitanians to Rome lay in their provision of two main products, olive oil and a deep red wine. There was a never-ending demand for both throughout the Empire. Decianus had taken a keen interest in this possible refuge ever since his father had originally suggested it to him. The time for decisions to be made had arrived.

"It's as far away to the west from the city of Rome as Britannia is to the north," said Septimus. "However, unlike the northern equivalents, the peaceful native tribes have come to accept they are part of our Empire."

"An important point in its favour. Little attention will be paid to it," Decianus replied.

He was lounging on a very comfortable seat in his father's villa.

"You are still intending to go ahead with this plan then?"

"Indeed. Every day that goes by makes me more certain Nero's days are numbered. When he goes I shall disappear. I've made too many enemies in the Senate. Men regaining lost power will be interested in seeking revenge for the deeds of our Emperor and some of those who served him. I need a new identity and place to live where I can enjoy the benefits of my hard-earned wealth."

"Which brings me then to why I sent for you," said Septimus.

"I've found the perfect country estate in the south of Lusitania. It has recently been confiscated by the Province's tax authorities when the present owner died leaving considerable unpaid debts."

"How did you hear about it?"

"One of my fellow Senators with connections there learnt of it. Very few people, if anyone, will be interested in buying it. Everybody is reluctant to speculate in these uncertain times."

"How do I acquire it without it becoming common knowledge? I'm as closely watched by my enemies as I keep my eyes on their antics."

"You can leave that to me. There are ways of purchasing the estate so it can never be traced back to you. All I need is the money and your new name."

"Go ahead. I shall give you the money. Get the best price you can. As far as the name to use goes, very soon I think I shall become Alcimus Leonius. I will be a just a purchaser from another Province. That way, my origins will soon be forgotten in my new home. I think the growth of a full beard will help my disappearing act."

*

The day after his return from visiting his father, Decianus was summoned to see Nero. His look of surprise aimed at Julius already waiting outside Nero's room was met with a snarl of pure menace from him in return. Julius's mind began to race, wondering what possible reason there could be for this villain to be present while he reported his return to the Emperor. The presence of Sabinus was fortunate in that it prevented anything more than a mere exchange of looks of hatred.

"It's about time," Sabinus growled. "He's not a patient man. If he asks me for an explanation for the delay you'd better have your excuses ready."

They were led into Nero's private room to be greeted by him pacing to and fro.

"Sit down, all of you, and be quiet. I'm thinking."

He continued his relentless strolling for some time before he came to a sudden smiling halt.

"That's it! You'll be pleased to know I've just completed the last four lines of my latest poem. Well, Sabinus. Why have you three asked to see me?"

"You summoned us, Sir."

"Ah, yes. So I did."

He sat down opposite them.

"It was your return from Judaea late last night that prompted it, Julius. I'll listen to your report later when there's more time. Explain what's happening in Gaul, Sabinus."

"Governor Vindex of Central Gaul has started a revolt there, advocating the removal of our Emperor."

Julius realised that this must be the reason for his order to return.

"But how can he?" Julius asked. "How could he hope to win? There are no Legions based there to support such a move."

"Exactly," cried Nero. "Tell him what this mongrel did, Decianus."

"This traitor wrote to nearly all his fellow governors telling them of his plan, asking them to declare their support for his proposal."

"What! To support him as Emperor?"

"He doesn't actually suggest that. He only advocates a new Emperor being appointed."

"What has been their reaction?" asked a troubled Julius. He wondered if Vespasian had received such a letter after he left Judaea.

"Aware of my special task to identify any plots against the Emperor, almost all were wise enough to tell me what they'd received. They were anxious to point out they were ignoring it."

"You say almost all."

"There was one who didn't."

Julius had a moment of panic. Surely it wasn't Vespasian. If it was, in the next few moments he had better brace himself for what Nero was about to accuse him of.

"You look alarmed, Julius," Nero noted. "As was I. It was Galba, Governor of most of Hispania."

Julius's thoughts were racing as he tried to grasp the importance of what was being described.

"What can Vindex hope to achieve by contacting people in this way?" Julius asked.

"Although a Roman citizen, he's a Gaul by birth," Sabinus added. "He's reported to be gathering an army of warriors, fellow Gauls. It's said there could be many thousands of them. He must be hoping his action will be repeated in other Provinces."

"That's why I've called you back from Judaea, Julius," said Nero. "I'm sending you to meet him."

Julius wondered what he was expected to achieve alone.

"You're experienced as a go-between with native tribesmen in times of revolt. This isn't Britannia, but these northern barbarians are all the same."

"What do you want me to achieve, Sir?"

"Get him to understand the hopelessness of his actions. Get him to surrender. Bring him back with you. I want you to end this so-called rebellion without the use of Legions. I don't want it to appear bigger than it is. I need it to be recognised as just one man's fantasy."

"What do I have to offer him?"

"A quick and relatively painless death as opposed to being crucified in the Forum if he has to be defeated in battle and taken prisoner. You can offer him the lives of his family if you wish. That's all I have to say. Speak with Sabinus to determine what documents you need from me to take with you. He will also arrange whatever military escort you think is appropriate. That will be all, gentlemen. You have your instructions."

Julius had many questions about the near-impossible task he'd been set, but he realised he would never get the chance to ask them.

Outside, he was stopped in his tracks by Decianus grabbing hold of his arm. He had the broadest grin, stretching from ear to ear.

"I couldn't have planned it better," he teased. "There isn't anyone else I would rather see carry out this simple task for the Emperor. You have my best wishes."

He marched away, laughing almost uncontrollably. Julius made a move to follow him. His arm was grabbed again, this time by Sabinus.

"Come with me! We have work to do."

All Julius could think of was that one day he would put an end to that foul life.

Chapter 38

"You've arrived two days too late, Agricola. The rebels have been defeated. Governor Vindex, or to be more precise, the ex-Governor, is dead. He committed suicide yesterday."

Julius had just sat down opposite Verginius Rufus, Governor of Germania. They were in his campaign command tent in the centre of a temporary legionary fort outside the town of Vesontio in central Gaul.

"I suspected something had happened when I witnessed the buoyant mood of the legionaries on my arrival in the camp. At least I won't have the task of persuading him to obey Nero's command to return with me."

"You wouldn't have stood a chance of doing that, young man. I brought three Legions with me. I met with him as soon as I arrived intending to do more or less the same as you. I tried to point out that his makeshift army of Gallic tribesmen was no match for twenty thousand seasoned legionaries and auxiliaries. He appeared to have accepted his cause was hopeless. We agreed a truce while we sorted out the terms of his surrender."

"Then what happened? Why did he choose to fight you?"

"He must have heard that Galba in Hispania was supporting his revolt and had gone further by declaring himself Emperor."

"If Galba has named himself Emperor," stated a disbelieving Julius, "then he's as mad as Vindex. This must have happened as I've journeyed from Rome."

"It would appear so. As far as I know, no other Governors with Legions to command have moved to join him yet. That means he only has one Legion in his Province to support his claim."

"I must return to Rome as soon as I've rested. What shall I tell the Emperor you intend doing next?"

"You must report what you see. I shall stay here with my Legions until the situation returns to something like normal before I return to Germania. Now you must excuse me. I have meetings planned with this town's senior Magistrates. However, one of my Legates has asked to see you before you leave us. I believe you fought together in Britannia. His name is Camillus Pecius. I suspect he'll be outside my tent waiting to talk to you."

*

"It's so good to see you again, old friend," said Julius.

The two men grasped each other's arms warmly before starting a leisurely stroll around the fort.

"I heard you'd been given your own Legion in the north. I never dreamt you would be here."

"It's good to see you also, Julius. My Legion is normally based in Lower Germania although we keep an eye on a much larger territory, including northern Gaul. You seem to have reached a position of some power yourself. Am I right in thinking you're here as a special envoy of Nero, sent to quell a rebellion singlehandedly?" Camillus teased.

"Hardly! And if I was, I've just been told I'm too late. What happened?"

"I'll try to summarise as briefly as possible. When Rufus heard of the revolt he didn't wait for orders from Nero. He brought half the Legions based in the whole of Germania to frighten Vindex into an immediate surrender. You know by now that didn't happen. Having appeared to agree to talk peace he changed his mind."

"What did he do?"

"We were arranged in the fields outside town preparing to accept his surrender. Instead his army launched a full-scale attack without warning."

"What was the fighting like?"

"It was a complete mismatch. They were a badly organised and poorly trained mass of warriors. They were motivated by long-held grievances together with deep resentment of the huge extra taxes Nero has levied to build his new city. They didn't have a hope. It was a massacre. We lost relatively few of our men."

"What are your feelings about Galba's bid for power?"

"It doesn't come as a complete surprise. I mentioned the resentment here to the extra tax demands. The same is felt throughout Gaul, Germania and Hispania that I know for certain. I'm led to believe it's mirrored throughout the whole Empire. Nero's days must be numbered."

"Why do you say that?"

"When the men of these three Legions heard of Galba's declaration they almost rioted. They hate him. He was Rufus's predecessor as Governor in Germania. He treated his legionaries as if they were slaves, beneath his contempt. He was also a merciless disciplinarian."

"What stopped them from rioting? Was it loyalty to Nero in the end?"

"Loyalty to Rufus. They demanded he declare himself Emperor. They have no wish to see Nero continue or Galba replace him. It would appear to be the same view held by the men in the other Legions Rufus left behind."

"That is amazing. Rufus could be very powerful with that sort of support. He made no mention of it to me."

"That's because he refused them. He says he has no ambition ever to be Emperor. He told them it's for the Senate to decide who will succeed Nero when the time comes."

"How did they react?"

"They are displeased to a man. They will fight Galba if asked to, but it won't be out of love for Nero."

"What then do I tell Nero of Rufus's true intentions?"

"That will be difficult for you. He will be like most other Governors and Senators. They recognise the loathing for Nero throughout the Empire. However, they're all waiting to see how events unfold. No one other than Galba and possibly one or two others will be willing to rush into opposing Nero. Since Piso's plot, too many innocent men have been executed on the slightest display of disloyalty."

"It would seem we are about to witness events that will go to the heart of the Empire as it has existed for a hundred years."

"Let's put that aside for a moment or two. We've time later to discuss it more if you need to before you leave. I have a more immediate problem you may be able to help me to solve."

"How can I help?"

"I saw you arrive with your armed escort. I noticed your Iceni commanded them. If I remember correctly, his name is Olsar, I assume he's no longer a slave. If so, my request involves him."

"You're correct. He's a freedman. One day he'll be granted citizenship of Rome when he's earned it, and is ready for it. If what you have to say involves him, then we should go to speak to him."

"You know Camillus," said Julius to Olsar. "He has something to say to you which is of interest to both of us. We are all ears, Camillus."

"I shall be brief. In the unfortunate battle that took place a few days ago I lost some good friends. Some of them were commanders of my auxiliary soldiers. They were men who I've trusted with my life. They were special men, leaders who will be very difficult to replace. I know Julius must regard you in the same way, Olsar. But, I would like you to come to join me, to command my Legion's auxiliaries. You will gain invaluable experience."

The shocked silence that followed was to be expected. Olsar eventually spoke first.

"What do you say, Julius?"

"It's not my decision, Olsar. You're free to make it alone. You aren't tied to me."

"I know that. I have my own immediate reaction to what I've heard. I would just like to hear yours."

"You two are the most important friends I have," Julius answered. "I know you would serve Camillus loyally. For his part, he's the best commander I've ever served under. It's an honour for anybody to be part of his Legion. His gain would be my loss. Nevertheless, I think it would be a great opportunity for you to move towards citizenship for you and your little girl."

"When do we begin our journey home?"

"Things are changing at a pace. However, I think we need a day of rest before we leave."

"I will give you my answer then, Camillus."

*

"Farewell, Julius. I'm sure our paths will keep crossing," said Camillus. "The Gods seem determined to make it so."

"I agree. We do seem to live charmed lives."

"Tell my little Sarah her father will send for her when the time is right," Olsar said to Julius. "She's probably much too young to understand, but I need you to say it for me."

"You have my word on it. You can be sure also that my mother will continue to care for her. She loves her as if she's her own grandchild."

Julius exchanged one final smile with each of them, saluted, then he dug his heels sharply into his horse. He gradually disappeared into a cloud of dust raised by the horses of his accompanying escort.

Chapter 39

To his great relief, Julius discovered Nero wasn't in Rome when he got there. He had gone to his villa at Antium and wasn't expected back for some days. It allowed him to continue his journey and head straight to his family's estate. It would give him the opportunity to find out from his father what was happening. The closer he'd got to Rome on his journey back, the wilder were the rumours he'd been hearing. If only some of them were true, the next few weeks were going to be very dangerous. Those concerns were temporarily forgotten when he was met by his mother's beaming face.

"Welcome home, son. You look hot and weary. You need to come to relax in the cool, comforting shade of our reception room."

Julius, giving her a weak, tired smile readily took up her suggestion.

"I'm so relieved you're back here safe and sound. According to your father, things are in a state of turmoil. I know he could hardly wait for your return to bring you up-to-date. In return, both of us want to hear all about your latest experiences in Gaul, but it can wait until he's here."

"Where is he? I looked for him briefly in the Senate House, but was told he hadn't attended for several days."

"He's gone to visit a fellow Senator. He'll be back by evening. By the way, where is Olsar?"

"He didn't return with me."

"Oh no! He hasn't been killed, has he?"

"No. No! I'm sorry. I've alarmed you unnecessarily. It's good news as far as he's concerned. He's been given a new and important command of auxiliaries in a Legion in northern Gaul."

"Will it take him away from us for a long period?"

"Who can tell in these uncertain times?"

"That's a great pity. I had a special surprise for the both of you."

"I'm here, at least. What is it?"

"Wait! I'll be right back."

She hurried out of the room only to return a few moments later with a slightly built young woman with short-cut, dark brown hair. She was dressed simply, but not as a slave. Julius face displayed a puzzled expression, as if he was trying to recognise her.

"This is Miriam," Procilla announced excitedly. "She's Selima's older sister."

Julius's jaw dropped. Miriam chuckled.

"But you can't be. She didn't have one."

"I am so, and she certainly did," Miriam declared.

"I think I should start, Miriam. Then you can tell Julius what you told me."

Miriam gave a slight nod to show her agreement.

"Miriam was ten years older than Selima. They were slaves when their parents died. Selima came to us and Miriam was sold to another family. Your father and I wanted to buy both daughters but were too late. Miriam had already been sold.

"I shall continue," said Miriam. "I was fortunate. My mistress was like your mother. She very soon began to treat me as one of her own rather than her slave. Sadly, she died less than a year ago. Shortly before that, she gave me my freedom. Her love for me didn't end there. In her will she left me some money to help me find a new life."

Miriam paused slightly, her voice faltering with emotion. With a smile, Procilla clasped her hand encouragingly. Miriam continued.

"I had only one thought after the realisation of what freedom meant to me. I had to find out what had happened to my little sister. I had to work for her freedom also. With the help of my mistress's family my search ended here. Sadly, I arrived too late to see her. At least I have the comfort of knowing she died a free woman."

"And we have little Sarah to remind us of her," Procilla added.

"I'm only sorry Olsar isn't here to share this," Julius noted. "I shall write to him about you. I thought I recognised you when you entered. Now I can see why."

"When you do write, you can tell him Miriam is now part of this family. She wants to help me take care of Sarah until Olsar returns for her."

Julius, sighing deeply, stepped forward to give Miriam a warm, welcoming embrace.

*

The whole of that evening was spent by Lucius and Julius bringing each other up-to-date on what had happened since they last met. Julius was amazed at how rapidly things had changed while he'd been away, how Nero was losing touch with reality. More importantly his long-held tight grip on power appeared to be fading away. The Senators had more or less dispersed. They did so half in fear of what Decianus and his spies might accuse them of at this late stage, and half in an effort to hasten the isolation of Nero.

Julius had a restless night despite his travel weariness. Towards dawn he decided he had to go to the Palace to speak to the one man who would know better than anyone else what was happening. Amongst other decisions and actions he needed to take, he needed to honour his promise to Vespasian to look after the welfare of his son, Domitian. Early in the following morning he made straight for Sabinus's office.

"Good morning, Julius. I was told you arrived back yesterday."

"Good morning. I did, and now I want to report to Nero. When is he due back from Antium?"

Julius considered the usually supremely confident Guard Commander was looking nervous and agitated.

"Who knows? Rome is descending into chaos with evermore disturbing rumours. I can hardly find a Senator to speak to. Add to that Decianus has disappeared."

"I know about the Senators. What is this about Decianus?"

"He's nowhere to be found. His house here in Rome is empty. I sent men to his father's estate but he wasn't there. His father hasn't seen him for a while and has no idea where he might be. I think the cunning rat has decided to escape the sinking ship."

Julius supressed an urge to cry out in frustrated anger. History was repeating itself as far as that slippery villain was concerned.

"He has many reasons to flee," Sabinus continued, "not least his fear his role in the great fire may become known."

"What do you mean?"

"Faenius confessed to me before he died that the fire had been started by a trusted few of his men following the instructions of Poppaea. However, the original idea came from Decianus."

Julius wondered why he was suddenly being given such dangerous confidential information. What else might he learn?

"Nothing I hear about that man's evil surprises me. Was Nero involved?"

"No. He only learnt of the truth when I told him after Poppaea died."

"What was his reaction?"

"Total indifference."

"That's not a surprise either. But what can you tell me of all these rumours?" Julius asked.

"Galba, supported by two Legions, has begun his march to Rome. You'll know from your mission what happened in Gaul. The latest I've heard from there is that Rufus and his Legions are neither supporting Galba nor declaring loyalty to Nero. Elsewhere, more and more Provincial Governors are rumoured to be openly stating their dissatisfaction with Nero. Some are even said to have become brave enough to declare for Galba. I have no way of knowing what the truth is."

"What of your men in the Praetorian Guard?"

"They are still for Nero at the moment. He's always paid them well."

Julius couldn't help but notice he'd referred to their loyalty as possibly being only for the present. His feeling that he had to act decisively was becoming overwhelming.

"Where is Domitian? I have news to give him from his father."

"He's still here in the Palace. He's become a great friend of the Emperor. I was surprised he wasn't asked to join him in this latest debauchery at Antium."

It wasn't exactly what Julius was wanting to hear.

"Where is he now?"

"I'll have you taken to his rooms."

*

"I want you to leave with me. I'm taking you to stay with me for a while," Julius instructed Domitian.

"And I choose to remain here, thank you," the young man replied. "I'm being exceedingly well looked after by Emperor Nero."

"After just talking with Commander Sabinus, I fear he may not be in a position to do that for much longer."

"That sounds like treason to me. I shall have to speak to my very good friend Decianus about you."

Julius had anticipated something like this from what Lucius had described to him the night before. He'd told of the unsavoury experiences Domitian was known to have shared with Nero. However, the mention of Decianus's name was enough to make him angry. He decided he couldn't waste time arguing with this young fool.

"I have here a document bearing your father's seal. Read it!"

He threw it into Domitian's lap.

"You will see he wishes you to do as I ask, should I decide you're in any danger. That's the situation I believe you to be in. Get your things."

"What's the danger you imagine me to be in?"

"There's a very real possibility Nero may be overthrown. Anyone associated with him is likely to be disposed of with him. I can't take that chance with you. I repeat. Get your things before I have to drag you out of here! We're leaving."

"I won't forget this insolent arrogance, Julius. You've made an enemy today."

"Be that as it may. Honouring your father's wishes is all I care about."

"I want to see my uncle before we leave. I will take his advice."

"What do you mean?"

"My uncle, Senator Petillius Cerialis will be in the Senate building. Surely you know of him."

"I do indeed. We're wasting time. He'll agree with me."

"Let me hear him say so. Then I will go with you."

"Greetings, Julius. It's a long time since we both fought Boudica in Britannia," said Cerialis.

He smiled and nodded a welcome in the direction of his nephew.

"Indeed it is," replied Julius, his jaw set firm with tension.

"What can I do for you both?"

Julius took some time to explain his assessment of the situation they all faced. He finished by telling Cerialis what action he'd decided to take. Domitian merely stated he wished to stay.

"I understand your reasoning, Julius, but Domitian will be safe with me. I shall take care of him."

"You've seen what Vespasian has instructed me to do, Senator," Julius countered, trying to control his temper.

"I have. However, there are things happening you aren't aware of."

"Such as?"

"Should Nero be deposed, the Senate will appoint Galba in his place. I will be party to that decision, and would have nothing to fear from Galba. So, with either Emperor there won't be a problem for Domitian."

"You're taking a risk, remaining in Rome. You gambled in Britannia and you lost then. I repeat that I need to take Domitian to his father."

"And you are assuming authority you don't possess, as you did in

Britannia. I am instructing you to leave the responsibility for my nephew in my hands. I shall write to Vespasian telling him of my decision."

"As will I," Julius stressed.

"Good day!" Cerialis growled.

Julius stared at Domitian, receiving a smug smile in reply. He took one last glance at Cerialis before storming out of the room.

*

The news reached Sabinus that Agricola had been to the Palace and ordered a reluctant Domitian to leave with him without coming to see him first for permission. Under normal circumstances he would have sent a force to have him returned immediately before Nero heard of it. He'd considered doing just that for a while. However, the fact that someone as shrewd as Julius Agricola was prepared to act in such a treasonable way was yet one more confirmation that people were assuming Nero's reign was coming to an end. His thoughts for the rest of the morning were concentrated on his own personal survival. The Gods came to his aid that afternoon. At least that was his conclusion much later when he looked back on events.

Just after a light midday meal he was disturbed by one of his men.

"We've arrested a man who was trying to gain unauthorised entry into the Palace, Sir."

"Why are you bothering me? Interrogate him."

"He's produced a sealed document which he says is for your eyes only. He amused us by saying it would mean certain death to any one of us who broke the seal to read it."

Sabinus chuckled.

"Did he identify who it was from?"

"He wouldn't say."

"Have you searched him for hidden weapons?"

"There are none, Sir."

"Then show him in!"

"Who are you, and what have you to say?" demanded Sabinus.

His first impression of the man was that he was no ordinary villain. He was dressed in expensive clothes, with the bearing and manner of a man of some substance, used to being taken notice of.

"My name is irrelevant for my purpose. It's also not what I have to say that is important. My purpose is to pass on what Emperor Galba has to say."

Sabinus thought it very strange to hear anyone described as the Emperor other than Nero after all these years. Could this be a trick by Nero to catch him out?

"What makes you think I will fall for this trickery?"

"Galba anticipated your reaction, which is why he gave me this document bearing his seal. He assured me that, because of your position, you're aware of every Governor's personal seal."

"That's true. Hand it to me!"

Sabinus was expecting a demand for the surrender of himself and the Guard, and to rely on his mercy. Maybe there would be an instruction to assassinate Nero as a way of avoiding his own execution. He was pleased to read something which gave him a way forward.

"It states that Governor Galba is offering to retain me as Commander if I can persuade the Guard to declare their support for him as the new Emperor."

"That's correct."

"But he has only two Legions and they are at the edge of the Empire. How can he hope to replace Nero?"

Sabinus was trying to flush out confirmation of any of the current rumours.

"He has the written support of many more Governors and Legions. However, I'm not at liberty to name them. It's not in the document, but I have been authorised to tell you he's secured the support of the majority of Senators. You will have noticed there are very few of them in Rome at the present time.

"Regardless of whether that's true or not, he would argue he has their support, wouldn't he?"

"He thought you would say that. You can contact the leader of the Senate for confirmation once you have given me your written declaration of support. I would then show it to the Leader to give him the confidence to confide in you."

"You appear to have thought of everything. I will give you my answer this time tomorrow. You may leave."

Sabinus decided he didn't need confirmation from the Senate Leader. Senators would support whoever he and his men supported. At the moment it would still be Nero. If he decided on Galba he needed to change the current loyalty of his men.

*

At a hastily called meeting of his officers and centurions they had confirmed what Sabinus had known. The men of the Guard were still loyal to Nero. It wouldn't be sufficient for their leaders to order them to suddenly support Galba. They would demand a substantial bribe. In the end it was agreed Sabinus would confirm he had an assurance from Galba that each man would receive a grant of a year's pay when he became Emperor with their support.

It proved to be sufficient incentive for them to be prepared to pledge their loyalty to Galba when called upon. However, he was told they wouldn't be party to the assassination of Nero, someone who had always treated them well. Sabinus would take note of that when the time to remove Nero eventually came.

He didn't overly concern himself that Galba was unaware of the promised bribe. It would be his problem if and when he became Emperor. If he wished to remain as such he needed to pay the bribe as one of his first acts. Therefore, he gave his reply to Galba's messenger, confirming he'd won the future support of the Guard for him. No mention was made of the bribe it took to get it. A refusal by Galba to agree to it at this late stage would create too great a confusion.

Chapter 40

68 AD

"What is going on, Sabinus?" Nero demanded.

He was sweating heavily and his clothes were full of dust from his journey back from yet another stay at Antium. Recently he'd been spending as little time as possible in the city.

"This morning, I found my Guards had disappeared from my entire villa. I returned immediately with only my friends for protection on the journey here. You can see the exhausted and dreadfully distressed state I'm in as a result. It's completely intolerable. You must have those who deserted me executed by others in the Guard. Let it be a lesson to all of them. They need to be taught the necessity of obedience and loyalty to their Emperor."

"They are well aware of that," Sabinus replied. "That's why they acted as they did."

"What! Explain yourself."

"Yesterday, the Senate voted more or less unanimously to declare you an enemy of the Empire and to appoint Servius Galba Emperor in your place. The Praetorian Guards are therefore being loyal to their new Emperor."

"Have you gone mad? I'm loved by my Guard, and all the citizens of Rome. It's another plot by those treacherous Senators. Send for Decianus. I want them all arrested and executed. They shall be poisoned. I will arrange for the most painful potion to be made and applied."

Nero's words and actions were becoming increasingly frantic as he paced the marbled floor of the Palace.

"Don't you remember? Decianus has already disappeared. It's your arrest and execution that's being demanded by the Senate."

Nero stopped his pacing, his face showing his shocked disbelief at what he was hearing.

"I must get away until things settle down. I know what to do. I shall go to Macedonia. They appreciate my poetry and performing artistic skills there. They will protect me. No! I shall go to Alexandria. I have sent most of my personal wealth there for safe keeping. I shall use it to build a mighty army to return and kill everyone in this city who has betrayed me. Don't they realise I am destined to become a God like my uncle Claudius?"

Emotionally and physically out of control because of his total surrender to panic, he slumped onto his knees in tears.

"I'm required to arrest you immediately and to hand you over to the Senators. They have plans for your immediate trial and humiliation, no doubt to be followed by your torture and final public execution. However, I owe you something for what you've done for me in the past. I shall delay your arrest until later today. It will give you time to recover and come to terms with your reign being over. You have the chance to end your life in a dignified manner as befits a former Emperor, rather than what the Senators have in mind for you."

*

Sabinus's last words hadn't had the desired effect. Nero exited the Palace unobserved. He was accompanied by his most trusted personal slave, Andreas. Together they made their way to the villa of a long-time trusted friend of his mother. He knew she would help him to escape the city.

Nero explained the treachery of the Praetorian Guard to her when he was given reluctant admission to the villa. Andreas stayed with him while the rest of the villa's occupants made themselves scarce. After a short while Andreas was asked to join the owner of the villa in an adjoining room to the one where Nero was trying to rest after his desperate flight through the city.

"I've just been given grave news, Master," he stated on his return.

"What could possibly be happening now?" he murmured.

"Guards have been sent for. No one here wants to be accused of hiding you from them."

"Then we must leave at once!"

"There's nowhere left to run to. Sabinus will know by now that you've fled the Palace. He will feel betrayed and men of the Guard are searching everywhere for you. Who knows what will happen when they find you?"

"What are you saying? Clearly, I can't stay here."

"The time has come for you to meet the Gods."

"Noooo! I can't."

"I will help you."

"How?"

"I've just been given this knife by your friends. The Guards will be here very soon. You mustn't let them capture you. If they do, you'll be guaranteed a slow and painful death."

"Please help me then. I can't do it alone."

"Hold this knife against your throat and I shall guide your hand."

Trembling and sobbing, he slowly did as he was asked.

"Have you any last message you want me to pass on?"

He thought for a moment before pointing his tear-covered face upwards, looking to his Gods and addressing them.

"What an artist the world is losing!"

Andreas's hand moved swiftly and a cruel, wasted life came to an end. For him, it was indeed a quick, painless death, something he'd denied the countless victims whose lives he'd destroyed over many years.

Chapter 41

The disastrous civil war that Seneca and Vespasian had predicted and wanted to avoid had followed immediately after the death of the tyrant. Galba brought a sort of hope and peace for a matter of months before being assassinated by the followers of the first Provincial Governor to support him, Otho. He'd succeeded him, only to last a similar period of time before being defeated in battle by another clamant to be Emperor, Aulus Vitellius. Ominously, he had only been appointed Governor of Germania two months earlier by Galba. He was a man hardly qualified to rule the world. He'd nevertheless obtained the precarious loyalty of most but not all of the Legions from the north and west of the Empire.

Those of the east and south, had made their own choice of Emperor, dividing the Empire into two camps. They'd chosen an experienced General who had held virtually every administrative position the Empire demanded of any citizen. He had earned the respect of all those who served with and for him.

His name was Flavius Vespasianus, known to his family and friends as Vespasian.

*

Julius first heard that the Legions in Judaea, Syria and Asia had declared for Vespasian while staying at his father's villa. It had proved to be a safe retreat for him during all the turmoil. Lucius, although a Senator, wasn't considered a threat to any of the various factions struggling for power in the city. Julius, similarly generally well regarded, had been able to take his time to decide where his future loyalty lay. The indecision ended with a letter from Vespasian.

"I have to leave immediately," Julius informed Lucius, showing him the message he'd received.

"Vespasian is ordering me to go to Dalmatia to represent him. The Legions in the east have declared their support for him against Vitellius. The commanders of those legionaries will have received his plans for fighting the war by the time I get there. They will also have been told of my role in representing him. I have to get there by the swiftest means."

"Then you have to go east across Italia to the coast," Lucius added. "There, you can take a ship to make the relatively short crossing of the Sea of Adria to Dalmatia. The alternative of going entirely by land would take you north and then east through Italia into lands likely to contain your enemies."

"I agree. But what about you? What do you think your position will be, once it becomes known I've gone to join Vespasian?"

"Don't concern yourself with that. I know which Senators and nobles will be the main allies of Vitellius. They all respect me. They know I remain aloof to the political manoeuvrings in Rome and elsewhere. They also know I'm not interested in scheming for any particular candidate. We shall all be safe. You must do as Vespasian asks, free of concern for us."

Julius gave a grateful nod to his father.

"There's still the problem of Domitian."

"That's no longer yours to solve. Cerialis has taken over the role of his protector. He has to leave immediately with him to be safe. If he doesn't, the best he can hope for is that Vitellius considers them to be useful hostages, not traitors to be executed."

"With Cerialis you can never be sure he'll take the obvious course."

"One thing is certain, Vespasian is no longer expecting you to rescue his son. Otherwise he would have said so in his message to you."

"I see what you are saying."

"I think it's time for you to prepare for your journey. Go to say your farewells to your mother and children."

*

Apart from suffering from acute sea-sickness, the journey had been uneventful for Julius. His arrival in Dalmatia had been expected. Sitting in the bathhouse, recovering from the travels, he was concentring on the council of war which had been called for first thing the following morning. To bring him up-to-date, he'd been given an initial brief explanation of Vespasian's plan. The fact that summer was at an end had meant the normal campaigning season would soon be over until the following year. The coming months would be a time of preparation for what could be a long war.

This first assessment had begun to trouble Julius. The last year had shown how fluid the political scene had become throughout the Empire. The past one hundred years had benefited from the rule of one dynasty. That had ended with Nero's death, together with the certainty it had brought. Recently, Julius had seen allegiances could change rapidly and frequently. Vespasian's strategy was to proceed with a slow, careful campaign. He might not be aware of the potential need in this situation for a measured urgency to capture and secure the throne.

Julius hoped he could accurately represent and explain what would be behind his leader's thinking without the benefit of having seen the full plan yet or discussed it with him.

*

Julius was surprised at the number and seniority of the men who'd met to discuss Vespasian's plans. When the introductions were completed he'd counted three Provincial Governors and seven Legates, each with an accompanying senior tribune. He'd begun to realise this was not going to be an easy meeting given that some of those present would be anxious to meet the enemy without delay. He'd now read Vespasian's cautious plan fully. It wouldn't provide that opportunity to those so inclined. To his surprise the discussions were started, not by the Senior Governor there, but by Antonius Primus, one of the Legates.

"Gentlemen! I propose we begin our deliberations by taking a short while to remind ourselves of the details of our General's plans to take us to Rome. Any objections?"

There weren't.

"Excellent. To get us started, I shall summarise the main features.

The first point is to identify the territory we currently hold. The General has gone to secure his neighbouring Provinces of Aegyptus and Africa. In that way he will secure Rome's vital grain supplies for us and deny them to our enemies. Titus is remaining behind in Judaea. The action against the revolt there will fully occupy him. Then there's the Governor of Syria, Licinius Mucianus. As you all know he's an experienced General and Statesman. He will play the most significant part in our plan."

Julius wondered if the switch to 'our' plan was a deliberate tactic.

"We control the two Provinces of Asia and Thracia with the straits that divide them at Byzantium. And finally there are the Provinces of Dalmatia, Moesia, and Pannonia. The whole of the eastern end of the ocean is therefore bordered by our territory, and we have the ships and marines to control it. We have at least as many Legions as our enemy. More importantly, ours are fully committed to our cause. I don't think Vitellius could say the same."

That brought out a few chuckles.

"Don't forget something important, Antonius," Marcus Aponius, the Governor of Moesia, pointed out. "Some of our Legions, maybe as many as half, are still needed here to secure our borders against barbarian incursions from the east."

"Vitellius has the same problems, particularly in Germania," Antonius argued.

He paused, allowing an exchange of comments to take place. His natural control and authority was beginning to impress Julius who considered whatever was decided at this meeting would most likely be what this charismatic, natural leader was wanting.

"Let me continue with what our General has outlined as the main stages and timing of our military strategy. We can then discuss our role in it. The timescale stretches over one year. The autumn and winter will be used to build and prepare our forces. The following spring and perhaps summer will see our total victory."

"But that will allow Vitellus the same time to build and prepare as us," cried one of the Legates. "He won't sit idly by. From what we hear about the lack of enthusiasm in his Legions, he will welcome all the delay he's offered."

"I note your concern and we shall discuss it, but let me finish. Mucianus will march from Syria, through Asia and Thrace. From there he will bring his Legions up the eastern coast of the Sea of Adria. All the time he will be building our forces. Eventually he will decide how he will use his army. He could choose to cross the Sea of Adria to land on the coast of eastern Italia. That would be the quickest way to Rome, but has risks. Vespasian prefers the alternative, Mucianus would continue his march north to join us here before moving into the north of Italia. We shall then march south to Rome with superior numbers to remove this pretender. That concludes my summary of the plan. Now we can discuss it in full."

The following discussion was at times heated, although Antonius easily kept control. Julius was most impressed at how he was able to do so with the three nominally superior officials in the room.

"It seems we're splitting into two main groups," Antonius eventually noted. "On the one hand we have those who seem to think the General's plan is a good one and should be fully supported. On the other hand at least as many of you appear to be disappointed with certain aspects of it. I think those concerns can be summarised as being that the plan is too cautious, to the point of being potentially fatal to our cause. I have a suggestion. Julius Agricola has been sent by the General to represent him. Let's hear what he has to say."

Julius had known he would be asked to comment sooner or later. The two opposing arguments mirrored the confusion he felt within himself.

"Like the rest of you, I don't have the benefit of having spoken directly with the General about his plan. In fact I only saw it in full for the first time today. But I do have the benefit of having fought alongside him recently. I also have his trust not to mislead you.

"The first thing I would say is that he's a leader who tries to balance caution with the need not to suffer any unnecessary delay. I understand this plan has the appearance to many of you of being too cautious, to the point of being difficult for you to fully support it. The other thing to note about the General is his deep respect for his legionaries. He will try to balance the need for quick victories with his duty not to needlessly waste the lives of his men. I see his use of a blockade of food supplies to Vitellius's forces during the winter as his attempt to achieve those balances."

The looks of concentration on the faces in front of him gave Julius the encouragement to go a little further in his assessment of Vespasian the soldier/politician.

"He's likely to be thinking that a combination of partial starvation and our advancing, disciplined and committed army could produce a realisation by Vitellius that he is woefully unqualified to be Emperor. It could be followed by his abdication. That way many citizens who unavoidably become involved in civil wars may be spared this one. Those are my thoughts. If the view of you all is that the delay is too long, perhaps we can find a way forward which implements the plan in a way that brings more urgency without rejecting the General's overall wishes."

Antonius seized his chance.

"Then, I have a proposal. The blockade of grain will continue. The march of Mucianus must begin, and given more urgency. The majority of you will wait and prepare your Legions to join him when he arrives. In the meantime I shall move on with a small force, maybe one other Legion in addition to mine. We shall advance along the Via Postumia, the road that stretches westward from the city of Aquileia, just to our north, to Cremona in the north of Italia."

He was temporarily interrupted by offers to be the one to join him from three other Legates. He raised his arm to show his appreciation for support, but also so he could carry on.

"I feel I can clear the territory most of the way there at good speed if, as I suspect, there aren't too many significant enemy forces to slow me down. Some of you may ask – what if I'm halted in my advance? Then we can decide whether I hold our position and await the arrival of Mucianus, or we could decide to commit more of our Legions for me to go on to try to capture Cremona, before winter sets in. That way we would control the whole of that major region. We would be in a much stronger position to march down the road from there to Rome when Mucanius is ready in spring."

The three Governors still had their reservations but eventually gave way to the pressure from all the Legates and Senior Tribunes supporting Antonius. They said they couldn't give their full approval, but wouldn't prevent him putting his exploratory plan into action.

"What do you think Vespasian will make of our decision?" Antonius asked Julius when they were alone later.

"If I'm honest, I think he would have supported you if he'd been here," Julius replied. "Your proposal had a lot going for it. However, he wasn't here, was he? You'd better succeed. Victory will get his and everybody else's full support, including those three Governors."

Antonius laughed and nodded his agreement.

"What will you do now, Julius? I would welcome you joining my small army."

"I will on one condition."

"Name it."

"I'm still more of a soldier than a diplomat. Vespasian wasn't clear what he wanted me to do after our council of war. I think he would expect me to join in a fight if I got the opportunity. I will join you if you can give me a command."

"I agree. We can sort it out later."

Chapter 42

Things had gone better than even Antonius had imagined. His rapid advance had persuaded those attending the original council of war to agree to increase his force to five Legions. Mucianus had accepted the need for urgency in his long march north, but was still at least at a month away from Antonius's current position. This was the town of Bedriacum, just twenty-two miles from Cremona along the Via Postumia. The legionaries had built temporary camps there to allow a plan of assault to be prepared by Antonius. His deliberations were interrupted by the arrival of two very important pieces of information.

"Send for Julius Agricola," Antonius ordered.

Within a very short time Julius entered the large campaign tent Antonius had insisted upon.

"You want to see me?"

"I do indeed. We've just been joined by a Senator from Rome."

Julius was intrigued by the use of the word – joined.

"Is he an emissary from Vitellius suing for peace, or a refugee escaping execution?"

"More the latter, I suppose. He claims to be Senator Petillius Cerialis, the brother-in-law of our General."

Julius gasped with astonishment, his mind racing.

"I see from your reaction you know of him. I thought you might be able to confirm his identity for me. You can nip any trickery in the bud if necessary."

"Oh! I'll be able to recognise him for sure. And I will have a few questions to ask him myself."

The uncontrolled hostile glare from Julius when Cerialis entered and the grin from the Senator confirmed to Antonius they were known to each other. He was who he professed to be.

"Where is Domitian?" Julius demanded, fearing the worst.

"Back in Rome, the last time I saw him. He was under guard as I'd been. We were both being held hostage by Vitellius."

"I told you to leave Rome in order to protect him when you had the chance."

"And that is what we were in the act of doing when we were arrested by some Praetorian Guardsmen who then separated us. They were eagerly awaiting the arrival of Vitellius and saw the opportunity to earn some praise and money."

"Can you two pause there," Antonius insisted. "Tell me what has happened, particularly as I heard the name of Domitian."

It took a while for their history together to be explained. Julius eventually felt his anger subside.

"So! I know how you escaped and made your way here, Cerialis," said Antonius, "but I don't know why."

"I thought it would be obvious. I want to secure my brother-in-law's bid for power."

Just as arrogant as ever, Julius thought.

"To do that I want a command befitting my status and experience."

Julius sighed deeply.

"We can discuss that later," Antonius replied. "Can you tell me anything about Vitellius which will be useful to me?"

"Indeed. I was helped in my escape by fellow Senators. They confirmed there's very little enthusiasm for him in Rome apart from the Guard. His Legions are ill-prepared. The men are growing fat and lazy assuming there will be no serious battles until next year. There are two main Generals supporting him. The best is Valens, waiting in Rome. However, he's old and his poor health has virtually immobilised him. The other, Caecina, is commanding the Legions here in the north. He's less able and his loyalty to Vitellius is much in doubt."

"That's good to hear. This morning I received a request to meet him to discuss switching his allegiance to us, bringing at least one Legion with him. I thought it a trick. From what you say, it might be genuine."

"We need a meeting of all Legates to discuss this urgently," Julius proposed, excited at the thought of a major bloodless victory.

"Arrange it immediately," replied Antonius.

*

"We're all agreed that I talk to him, then," said Antonius to his officers. "So, this is what I shall do. He proposes I meet him on the Via Postumia at the marching post which indicates four miles to Cremona. He says he will have a Legion with him for safety purposes. He expects the same from me. The meeting will take place at noon tomorrow."

"Which Legion will you take?" joked one of the Legates.

"Not mine. It won't be a specific one. I want to rely on speed. Therefore I shall take four thousand of our cavalry and only two cohorts of legionaries, one thousand men. The rest of you remaining here will need to keep on the alert. It may yet be a trick."

*

Antonius had arranged his force on flat terrain, either side of the road. He commanded from the centre. Julius led half the cavalry on the right, assisted by a tribune. Cerialis had insisted his status and experience entitled him to lead the left. Antonius had reluctantly agreed, putting his best tribune in support. They didn't have to wait long for something to happen. From the direction of Cremona, three of his scouts approached at a full gallop.

"There are two Legions, with a small number of cavalry approaching, Sir," one of them gasped, dismounting in front of Antonius.

"What trickery is this?" Antonius shouted.

"They're coming to fight, not talk, Sir."

"Get your breath and speak slowly and clearly. Tell me how you know."

"We approached four of their scouts to tell them where you were waiting. They attacked us without warning, killing one of us. We fought them off, capturing one. We got him to tell us why they'd attacked us. He said the legionaries had refused to agree to switch sides as their General had said he wanted them to. They've imprisoned him in the town."

"Who's in command?"

"The two Legates, since they don't have a General anymore. There are just those two Legions defending the town. However, he told us they've sent for more to arrive this evening."

"I shall worry about those later. How far away are they?"

"They will be here at any moment."

"You say two Legions. Any support?"

"They didn't have a great deal of time to prepare many auxiliaries. They don't have a large cavalry support either."

"At least we won't suffer a surprise attack. Well done."

Antonius summoned Julius and Cerialis to join him.

"We aren't going to retreat. We haven't much time to plan our defence. I shall send for our Legions. With our cavalry advantage we shall hold the enemy until they get here. At least we brought our two best cohorts with us. It looks as if the battle for Cremona has begun. Good luck, gentlemen."

*

By late afternoon the first cohorts of the two relieving Legions began to arrive. Julius was exhausted. He'd lost many of his men by continually charging and frustrating any advance from the enemy's superior numbers of legionaries. On the other flank, Cerialis had suffered a similar fate. From time to time, Julius had been able to observe the battle he was having on the opposite flank. He grudgingly admired the way Cerialis had joined this army only the day before and yet he was fighting alongside and directing his men as if they had been with him for years. For all his insufferable arrogance, he was truly a worthy leader.

*

By early evening Antonius's legionaries had started to push the enemy lines back towards the town. Since the two opposing armies were both made up of experienced legionaries, trained and organised in the same way, there wouldn't be an easy victory for either side. Even so, Antonius had taken the opportunity to discuss with Julius and Cerialis the possibility of seeking the town's surrender before nightfall. The Gods have a way of interfering at times like that. It certainly happened on this occasion. A mighty roar came from Vitellius's legionaries, their slow retreat coming to a halt.

"I think our discussion has to be a quick one, gentlemen," said Antonius. "Their relieving Legions appear to have arrived. Dusk and darkness will soon be here. Therefore, they will expect not to have to fight tonight. They will be assuming most of them will withdraw to their camp to rest after their long forced march here. We must make the fighting carry on all through the night."

"What are you thinking?" demanded Cerialis. "We are all exhausted also."

"The fighting will be very limited by the darkness and spasmodic, but they will have to defend themselves, be on their guard everywhere. They won't be allowed to leave the battlefield. I can't think of a better way to show them our total determination to defeat them. By morning their desire to fight on will have withered away. We shall greet the dawn with a mighty roar. They will realise it is more relieving Legions coming to our aid as theirs did. They will crumble and Cremona will soon be ours.

*

The enemy's mass panic did occur soon after dawn as Antonius had predicted. Some fled into the town before the gates were closed. The less fortunate retreated to their camp only to be slaughtered or captured there. Which left the still-defiant town to be taken.

Antonius, perhaps because it was the usual thing to do, decided to offer surrender terms to the besieged citizens and refugee legionaries. He sent Julius to apply his diplomatic skills. No one was more surprised than Julius when he succeeded. The gates were opened and Antonius triumphantly accepted the formal surrender from the town dignitaries.

"Is there anything you need, Sir?" the leading town official enquired.

"Yes indeed!" Antonius replied. "An immediate long, hot bath!"

Julius and Cerialis joined him. It was a decision all three would spend the rest of their lives regretting.

One of the Legates eventually found the three of them relaxing in the frigidarium, but he was too late to prevent the slaughter. The Legate could only partially explain what had started it. He suggested the fatigue of fighting for a day and a night was certainly a factor in the mass loss of self-control. Many men had lost long-time friends in the fighting and wanted revenge. Some of the worst troublemakers had begun to complain that they had lost the opportunity to sack and loot the town, denied by the terms of the surrender. Whatever the cause the whole of the army became involved in the outrage of murder, rape and theft.

Antonius appeared as outraged as the others. Nevertheless, he decided after the short spontaneous mutiny had come to an end that if he punished any one man he would have to punish the whole army. It wasn't possible. He argued that this was an army he needed to take to fight again in Rome. He needed their full support. Julius eventually persuaded him at least to issue a statement utterly condemning what had occurred. It was subsequently read out to all legionaries on parade by their Legates.

In the following days, the burgeoning friendship between Julius and Antonius came to a temporary end. Julius told him they would all live to regret his failure to set an example by harshly punishing the worst offenders, those leaders in the orgy of violence against citizens who had formally surrendered. Julius said he still had a duty to accompany Antonius to Rome, but he would find it difficult to take command of the men from his Legions, those soldiers who had carried out this rape of Cremona.

Chapter 43

The defeat at Cremona began the collapse of the resistance of the forces of Vitellius. The still-ailing General Valens had gone to southern Gaul to try to bolster faltering support there only to be captured by supporters of Vespasian. This meant that what forces Vitellius had left were concentrated in the southern half of Italia. Antonius's army marched relentlessly down the road to Rome either capturing or accepting the surrender of towns still loyal to Vitellius. Any enemy forces were being defeated in skirmishes, sometimes surrendering or switching their allegiance without a fight.

Antonius's ultimate gamble, to try to be in Rome before the onset of the winter, had paid off. Or more accurately, it was about to. All his Legions were camped within very few miles of the city. General Mucianus had reached Cremona and so was less than two weeks' march away. This had set Antonius a problem. Was he content just to besiege the city, letting Mucianus arrive to accept the surrender of Vitellius? He would then get the fame and glory of the final victory. This way was likely to spill the least blood. However, why waste the next two weeks? There could be little hope and fight left in the soldiers and citizens occupying the city.

It was a choice he'd begun to discuss with Julius and Cerialis. The deteriorating relationship between the three very forceful leaders, each motivated by differing desires, didn't help.

"We should wait for Mucianus?" Julius argued. "Such a show of force would result in their unconditional surrender."

"I disagree," said Cerialis. "We must strike without any further delay. They are defeated already. An all-out assault around the city will see an end to it in days."

"With the unnecessary loss of many lives," Julius reasoned. "If we must do something now, we should send emissaries to offer terms of surrender."

"Gentlemen! I have a suggestion. Let's try both. We shall invite the Senate to send us envoys so we can offer them a relatively painless way out. At the same time we shall probe their defences in a limited fashion."

"I agree," said Cerialis. "I insist on leading the first test of their defences."

"And you, Julius. What's your response?"

"Send your message to the Senators first to gauge their resolve. Cerialis can carry out his little adventure later if they need encouraging."

*

The closeness of Antonius to Rome meant he had the advantage of receiving a constant supply of information on what was happening inside the city from those Senators, citizens and even soldiers, loyal to Vespasian. He learnt several things which sealed the fate of the hapless defenders.

The receipt of the message to the Senators suggesting a negotiated settlement to end the war had prompted a debate in the Senate, which included Vitellius himself. He announced at the end of it his intention to abdicate on the understanding that the Senators would insist on his survival and subsequent comfortable exile as part of a negotiated surrender.

Then he'd surprised everybody by going without further delay to the Forum to make his abdication speech. The citizens loyal to him had gathered there, together with many from the Praetorian Guard, to hear what he had to say. They refused to accept his abdication. Vitellius was escorted back to the Palace by the crowd, still the Emperor. There would be no negotiations. The attempted abdication was seen as a weakness and seized upon by Vespasian's supporters in the city. A minor revolt broke out. It lasted a day before it was mercilessly put down.

Cerialis's attack on one of the gates followed and was met with much fiercer resistance than he had expected. As a result he'd suffered many casualties. Antonius called another meeting with Julius and Cerialis.

"I think the decision has been made for us," Antonius declared. "Our supporters trapped within those walls fear there will be a massacre if we don't act quickly. It appears the Guard and the Night Watch are fiercely loyal to Vetillius to the point that they refused to let him abdicate or negotiate."

"They obviously feel they are dead men whatever happens," Julius added.

Cerialis was strangely quiet.

"We are all agreed then."

It was a statement of the obvious not a question. Both men nodded.

"We shall attack at every gate at dawn. With every available man. I want you both to stay out of the fighting on this occasion. After the victory, our task will be to create order and govern Rome until Mucianus arrives to prepare the way for Vespasian."

The other two prepared to leave.

"Before you go I have some extra news of interest to you both. We know where Domitian is."

"Do the Guards have him?" Julius asked anxiously.

"No! In the chaos of the failed revolt in there, he was rescued and is being hidden by our friends."

"He's still in great danger," said Julius.

"That's why I've assigned my best cohort to go straight to his rescue when we breach the walls. We must not lose him."

*

Rome fell very quickly despite a suicidal defence by the Praetorian Guard. Some parts suffered the same fate as Cremona with great loss of life. Other districts were hardly touched. This time there wasn't a formal surrender to deny the legionaries their thirst for bloody revenge and almost limitless bounty.

Vitellius was not as careful in the choice of hiding place as Domitian. The legionaries found him cowering in the Palace. His short reign came to an end in the streets of his capital. With his hands tied behind his back, he was paraded through the streets to be physically abused and spat upon. His misery was eventually brought to an end by a legionary's sword.

Domitian, the son of the new Emperor, had somehow survived captivity for months. Sheltered by his new guardians, his rescuers had little problem reaching him. Raising him high on their shoulders, they called him Caesar. That night Domitian celebrated his father's succession with a wild drunken orgy.

Julius sought out many friends, Senators and citizens alike. He was relieved to hear from them his father hadn't been in the city.

Cerialis sought out Domitian to explain why he'd been unable to include him in his earlier escape, and to try to convince him he'd been fighting ever since to come to his rescue. He wasn't invited to the all-night celebrations by Domitian.

Antonius was lauded by his fellow officers before joining Domitian's party.

Mucianus and his Legions eventually finished their march of several thousand miles just before winter set in. He took over the Government of the city from Antonius, and then the rest of the Empire on behalf of Vespasian. At times he struggled to remind Domitian that the father was the new Emperor and not the son.

Vespasian eventually arrived in Rome months later in accordance with his original plan.

Chapter 44

70 AD

"Who would have thought it, Julius? Who would have predicted only a year ago that a rough-arsed old soldier like me would be standing here in this luxurious Royal Palace, the new Emperor of Rome? Not only that. In another year it's likely I'll be called a God, just like dear old Emperor Claudius. Do you suppose he's looking down at me at this very moment?"

"I confess I've called you a few things in addition to General in the past. I'm only relieved you never heard them at the time, especially now you've become the absolute ruler of Rome, with the power of life or death over us all."

Vespasian grinned at the less than respectful remarks. For a while he let the discussion continue in a similar light fashion before he became a lot more serious.

"You'll have realised already that I've asked you to come here for a reason other than to wonder at this room and take part in a little light banter."

Julius nodded.

"Now the war is over, have you thought about what I might ask you to do for Rome?"

"These have been hectic times, Sir. I've not had much time to give it any real thought."

"I doubt that. I know you well and you're not a man to miss an opportunity when it arises, or to be reluctant to push for what you want."

"To be honest, I know one thing. I wouldn't make a very wise and servile counsellor in your court. I'm a soldier and warrior at heart. If I'm to be allowed a choice I would prefer to continue to serve you in that role somewhere in the Empire."

"You can relax. I agree with you. What did you think of the Province of Britannia and those little Brits when you were a young tribune there ten years ago?"

"You want me to go back there, don't you?"

"Yes. Britannia concerns me greatly. It's vital for the wealth it can bring. And yet, I'm being told that there's considerable unrest and indiscipline in the Legions based there. At the same time those unruly tribes, particularly in the north and west, continue to resist us and cause disruption."

"What's Governor Bolanus doing about it?"

"He hasn't been in the post for much more than a year. He's a career politician, not a soldier."

"Why don't you replace him?"

"At the moment he's doing just about enough to survive. So, let me tell you what I want from you. You're being sent to assist Bolanus with the two main tasks I'm setting him. Firstly, as you would expect, he'll be very firmly reminded by me that he has to meet the levels of tax that the Province has been set."

"And his other main task?"

"Military progress. As with any Provincial Governor, it's his duty to protect lands and people we've already conquered, by maintaining our borders. He must then go on and capture more lands and peoples to expand the Empire. So, he needs an efficient, disciplined army. This is where you come in. You are to do whatever is necessary to end any unrest and indiscipline in the Legions. Bring them up to the standard you and I have always demanded."

"Won't the Governor object, probably even obstruct, a mere tribune attempting to play such a broad role in the army? And what about the Legates commanding the Legions? I know I wouldn't stand for it in their shoes."

"That's why I'm promoting you to General."

"Bolanus could easily overrule me if he disagreed with any action I wanted to take."

"It's true you'll be subordinate to him in administrative and political matters, but not in military matters. In those you'll have the freedom of reporting directly to me. I shall put this division of responsibility in writing so that there won't be any confusion. Now have you any further questions?"

"Only one. When am I expected to take up my new duties?"

"When you leave this room."

Julius stood up and saluted.

"Thank you for my promotion and the trust you continue to place in me, Sir."

"And I thank you for your loyal service, past and future."

They shook hands. It was both a farewell gesture and a display of their respect for each other. For Julius, it was a decision that would change his life in a way he could never have imagined.

PART IV

TIME OF REVENGE

71 AD

Chapter 45

The ship's captain had made Lucia pay a high price for her intended journey to northern Gaul. Her Iceni accent hadn't helped and she'd noticed the look of surprise on his face when she said she could pay for herself and three others in gold coin.

"Four of you? Now that changes things!" he exclaimed. "I'm not sure I have the space to take four of you. I shall have to reconsider the price I just quoted. To make room and be sure I can fit all of you in the one crossing, I shall have to disappoint others or take less cargo from some of my regular customers."

Until then Lucia had been happy to play the role of Roman gentlewoman of considerable standing. However, when provoked her natural instincts of a former warrior took hold. Overcoming a natural reluctance to get too close to a foul-smelling oaf, she stepped up to him to take a firm grasp of the front of his greasy tunic.

"We agreed a price," she growled, "and an already exorbitant one at that. I strongly recommend you don't make yourself an enemy of me by trying to squeeze out even more money. Don't be fooled by my appearance as others have done and regretted it later."

The captain looked startled but not overly afraid. A smile began to break out on his heavily bearded face.

"And I suggest you withdraw any threats, my dear lady. Perhaps you hadn't noticed the effect your words have had on my crew. Their financial welfare is very much bound up with my wellbeing. I think they are about to join our conversation."

His men had broken off from their task of loading cargo from the dockside and had started to move towards Lucia.

"And you have no need of a quarrel with a member of General Julius Agricola's personal staff."

Olsar, who'd been delayed while taking care of his and Lucia's horses, was speaking loudly so everybody, whether on board or ashore, would hear him. He walked up the gangway and stood with his hand clearly on the hilt of his sword. His fierce grimace left nobody in any doubt about his intention.

His comment about being on the General's staff was not strictly the truth. A few days earlier General Agricola had released him from his role on his staff and given him his permanent discharge from the army. It was done so he could escort and protect Lucia as she began her journey to Rome in search of a new life. However, Olsar had decided he wouldn't rush to discard his staff officer uniform since it might prove an advantage in the long and dangerous journey ahead. That was already proving to be the case as the captain's men had a sudden change of heart and returned to their previous duties.

"I happen to be one of the four passengers in the lady's party," Olsar continued. "I think you'll agree I shouldn't be charged for the voyage."

"The reason being?" the captain asked rather timidly.

"It's obvious I can offer extra protection to you, your crew and your very valuable cargo, if we are unfortunate enough to meet bandits or pirates on our travels. I'm sure there are people with prying eyes on the dock watching us this very moment. In addition to passing on information about your cargo and destination to others with evil intent they will also warn of my presence."

"I take your point," the captain replied grudgingly.

That had quickly resolved matters and a departure was set for early the following day.

*

That evening when all the preparations for the following day's journey had been completed, Lucia and Olsar were relaxing in Quintus's town house in Londinium for the last time.

"So much has happened since Julius returned to Britannia," said Lucia. "It's hard to believe that it's only a year ago."

"All our lives have changed beyond recognition and here we are leaving our homeland perhaps forever," Olsar added. "A year ago I was commanding auxiliaries in northern Gaul and you were a Roman lady, albeit a gladiator fighting in the Arena as well. I doubted you'd survived the war although I'd hoped you were still alive, even if you'd been taken as a slave."

"I was so sure you were dead. I thought I saw you die in that final battle. If Julius hadn't come back we probably would never have known what happened to each other."

"Do you regret his return? The subsequent events it provoked led to your sister's death and also Quintus's."

"I regret their deaths, of course I do. But I don't blame Julius for any of that. They died because of the evil of Gaius Marellus. That could have happened if Julius had never arrived."

"What did you think of Julius then and how has it changed?"

"A year ago I thought he was out of my life forever. I hated his memory. When he appeared I would have willingly killed him given the chance. Then over those following months I learned the truth, what he'd done to save both our lives and the work he did to give us the freedom and opportunity we have today. Now? I think if we stayed together he would become the love of my life."

"Then why not?"

"It can't be. He has a wife. He's a Roman General. His work is here. Whereas I can't stay. I must leave or I will be discovered sooner or later and I would die."

"Maybe one day we can all be together again."

"Who knows? For now, let's see what tomorrow brings."

*

The high tide was expected to occur mid-morning. A light breeze that had greeted the dawn had increased slightly. The ship, although secured to the dock, was still able to move against its moorings as if it was agitated and eager to break loose, allowing it to move into the free-flowing waters of the wide river.

The captain looked relieved as Lucia arrived with her small group of four. In addition to Olsar she'd brought her ten-year-old son, Marcus, and Caris, her companion. Marcus could hardly contain his excitement as he gazed up in awe at the sheer size of the ship.

"I can't wait to see the ocean, Mama," he cried. "Olsar tells me it's much bigger than this enormous river."

"You'll just have to wait and see, won't you? Please walk up the gangway and climb on board. Don't rush and be careful!"

Caris was showing her anxiety by hanging well back from the others. For all her long life, or what she could remember of it, she'd been a slave. For many years that had been on the estate of Quintus Saturninus, the wealthy Roman landowner who had adopted Lucia some eight years previously. His recent death had given Lucia the opportunity to grant Caris her freedom. Despite that, she'd freely chosen to continue to be there for Lucia and particularly for young Marcus, who she'd grown to love as her own child.

"Come along, old girl," the captain shouted. "This tide won't wait for anybody, not even you."

Calling her 'old girl' was bad enough but when he followed it with a loud belly laugh she'd had enough. She rushed forward to the gangway, replying in kind to a rapidly retreating captain.

Whether it had been his deliberate intention or not, Caris's speedy arrival on board removed the last obstacle to the ship's departure. Mooring ropes were released and the ship slowly moved away from the dock and into the full flow of the greyish-brown water.

*

A short time later, content that everything was progressing satisfactorily and under control, the captain turned his attention to Lucia.

"I thought I recognised you yesterday and now I'm certain. It was your accent, a mixture of Roman and Iceni that confused me."

Lucia's heart almost stopped. She didn't reply immediately, her mind in turmoil. Fortunately, an urgent summons from a crew member in the bow of the ship drew the captain away. Lucia gripped Olsar's arm and whispered her dread.

"Do you think he's recognised me from my past? Does he somehow remember me from ten years ago? My heart skipped a beat. I was expecting him to say he knows I'm really Linona, daughter of Boudica. He might still return from the bow and say just that. Surely I'm not going to be recognised now after all we've been through. I'm leaving these shores for good, to avoid this very thing happening."

"Stay calm," Olsar urged.

"How could he know?" she continued, as if she hadn't heard his advice. "Only you and Julius know the truth. "I haven't even dared to tell Caris and Marcus. How could he have recognised me? He isn't Iceni or even from these lands. He sounds as if he comes from Gaul."

Her quick-fire comments betrayed her panic. Still, it wouldn't prevent her from taking decisions. With Olsar helping her, she could quickly take command of the ship if her worst fears were realised. She would have no other choice.

"Hold fast," Olsar pleaded. "Wait until he speaks again. Let's see what he knows and wants."

As usual, she thought, *he remains coldly calm when danger threatens.* She tried to do as he asked, controlling her breathing, steadying her racing mind, concentrating her thoughts as she'd once done in battle or the arena.

The captain, looking quite relaxed once his problem up front was resolved, came back to join them. His head nodding vigorously, he continued where he'd left off.

"As I was saying – I recognise you, even though you look very different from when I last saw you. Your clothes are obviously very different, and you were quite a way away but I got a clear view of you. I know who you are."

"Really," Lucia offered, trying to keep calm and look disinterested.

"Yes. I saw you fighting in both the recent games in the Arena."

"Ah!" sighed Lucia.

"You're the gladiator who fought in the unique, never to be forgotten fight to the death with the opponent from Gaul. You can't deny it."

"I'm not going to."

"You cost me a lot of money that day. I bet on the woman from Gaul."

"I'm sorry, but I did have a bit more at stake than you."

"Accepted," he replied, laughing loudly, "but then I went and bet on YOU in the next games you fought in. Bad decision! I lost my money again because you went and got wounded and were defeated."

"I'm sorry for you again. Thankfully that contest was merely for display, even if it proved a little painful for us both."

All three now laughed in what had developed into a relaxed and friendly atmosphere. Lucia squeezed Olsar's hand.

"At least I know I have two great warriors to protect me and my ship. With this strong favourable wind, if it holds, we will make a good start to our long sea journey."

A loud groan came from a short distance away, causing the three of them to turn and look in the direction of Caris. Whether she was expressing her dislike at the thought of having to stay on board this hateful ship, or she was showing the first signs of sea-sickness, wasn't clear.

*

"Thank you for coming to see me," said Governor Bolanus. "Let me explain why I've brought you all together."

He was talking to three members of one of Londinium's wealthier and therefore more respected families.

"We were happy to comply with your request," said Tullius Marellus, "and hopefully will be even happier when we find out the reason for it."

This was a man who didn't tolerate fools too easily, and readily showed his impatience and anger when it suited his purpose. He continued with his reply.

"Why, for instance, have you asked the three of us to come here to your headquarters at very different times and to enter the building using a variety of entrances?"

"I did so because I don't want General Agricola to be aware I'm having a meeting with the three of you together, the brother and two sons of Tarquinius. His recent death has been a blow to us all."

"His death? His murder, you mean. He was assassinated, not directly by him, but by the Iceni savage who was with him at the time. I believe he's called Olsar. You know all this because it happened before your very eyes, here in this building, and you've done nothing about it."

"And we still haven't had a satisfactory explanation as to what happened," added Cassius, the elder son. "We all know it was that Iceni vermin who delivered the fatal blow. Why hasn't he been arrested and executed for his crime? Why is he still free? We demand..."

"I shall explain," interrupted Bolanus, more than a little angrily, showing his eagerness to regain control. "I'm sure you're all aware of what I shall call the business arrangement that existed between Tarquinius and myself. You have all benefited significantly from it in the past."

"Please continue, Governor," said Tullius.

"Agricola had discovered what was happening with the army and navy supplies. He produced evidence to show the very lucrative if somewhat irregular dealings Tarquinius and I had in the provision of those supplies. He threatened to disclose what he'd found to his friend, Emperor Vespasian."

"How had he found out?"

"That no longer matters. He made his future silence about my part in what had been taking place conditional upon me taking no further action against the Iceni murderer. He also demanded I abandon any ideas I might still have of bringing that gladiator, Lucia, to trial for the earlier murder of Gaius, your other nephew."

"Both of them must die for what they've done to my father and brother," cried Paulus, the younger brother.

He was unable to contain his anger any longer.

"If you can't or won't arrange it then we shall see to it. Don't try to prevent us."

"That's enough, Paulus," Tullius ordered, eager to speak before a furious Bolanus made the young man regret his words. "Please excuse him, Governor. He still feels the loss of a father and close brother very deeply as you can see."

For a while nobody spoke. They could use the opportunity to think about the crossroads each of them had reached in their own way. Bolanus was the first to speak again.

"I think my time here as Governor is now very limited. Agricola has control of the dice. He will use his influence to ensure Vespasian recalls me to Rome, replacing me with his own man."

There was no reaction from the others. They had probably come to a similar conclusion.

"Before then, I wish to maximise my rewards for governing this miserable, damp island on the edge of the world. Are you willing to cooperate?"

"We'd already discussed this," Tullius replied, "and would have approached you soon with our own proposal, had you not beaten us to it. We've agreed I will continue to concentrate on running my own estate, while Cassius will take over the responsibility for his father's estate."

"And I shall assist my brother," said Paulus, "but only after I've taken time to do what circumstances prevented you from doing. I will seek out those two Iceni scum and get our revenge for the deaths of our father and brother."

"Then you must be prepared to travel very far and be patient," replied Bolanus. "One of your dead brother's spies has reported they sailed together for Gaul only two days ago. I can't see them returning soon, if ever."

"That changes things," Tullius decided. "You must leave as soon as possible, Paulus, while their trail is still warm. Take two of our best men with you. We have many trade contacts, both throughout Gaul and in Rome. I will provide you with letters of introduction."

Paulus nodded his acceptance of the change of plans.

"All is agreed then," Bolanus concluded. "Leave the way you came in."

*

The advice to Julius from his surgeons, to rest his shoulder for a few more days, had fallen on deaf ears. He'd had enough of idleness and decided his legionaries needed to see their General out and about. If nothing else it would put an end to any rumours being spread by troublemakers that the knife wound, which he'd received from the treacherous Tarquinius Marellus, had become infected, endangering his life.

Despite the pain and the risk of opening up the wound, he was determinedly struggling to fit into the final pieces of his full military uniform. The difficulty he was having didn't help his temper any, as his verbal abuse of his personal slave, Sirca, demonstrated.

"Are you sure it's wise in your condition for you to carry out a full inspection of the fort and the guards on all official buildings in the town, General?" asked Livius. He was one of the staff officers who shared the support duties provided to Julius.

"Not you as well, blast it. I've told those surgeons, with their endless potions and ointments, I've had injuries nearly as bad as this while shaving. Ahhh! Be careful. Damn you, Sirca. That part is still a little sensitive."

Rather than cower in fear, Sirca was doing his best to hide a broad grin. He'd explained to others, more fearful of the General, that in his experience some apparently fierce dogs, with a tendency to bark a lot, seldom resort to biting. It wasn't a pearl of wisdom he dared to share with Julius. Livius didn't try to hide his amusement, but he did decide to change the subject.

"I've just received some interesting news concerning Governor Bolanus, Sir."

"Leave us, Sirca. I can finish without your assistance."

When they were alone Livius didn't need to be told to carry on with his report.

"It appears that Bolanus has had a 'secret' meeting with the brother and two sons of Tarquinius Marellus."

"It doesn't surprise me, either the meeting or the fact that the fool tried to keep it a secret. And what in your opinion was the reason for their little get-together?"

"It must be to re-establish, with the brother at least, the corrupt arrangements Bolanus had with Marellus. I'm not sure why the two sons would need to be there at this time."

"It's very likely to mean one of the things Lucia was afraid of, and which was part of her decision to leave Britannia for good. The family Marellus will try to avenge the deaths of father and son, Tarquinius and Gaius."

"Do you want them arrested before they can do any harm?"

"No! Not on the strength of one family get-together. We shall wait until we have more credible evidence of their evil intent."

"Then you'll require us to give them even closer attention than we already do."

"Exactly. But it might be more easily said than done. By now they must already know Lucia and Olsar have gone. However, it won't end their desire for revenge. They're likely to send someone to try to find them."

"What do you want me to do?"

"Nothing for the time being. I've already sent a request to my good friend Legate Camillus Pecius to use his legionaries and auxiliaries to protect Lucia and Olsar on their journey, should they pass through those lands he controls."

"I know you've been a close friend of Olsar for many years. I've also seen you become very close to Lucia since you returned from Rome. Her loss must be affecting you."

It was an unusual, potentially foolhardy personal statement from a junior Staff Officer to his General. However, it was evidence of the respect between the two men that the comments were added to by Julius.

"Indeed. Circumstances have separated us for the present, but that part of my life hasn't ended. When Vespasian considers my work here is done and he calls me back to Rome, who knows what will happen?"

There was a brief, slightly awkward pause.

"So! This fully recovered General is about to stride out, vigorously and pompously, for all to see, soldiers and citizens alike. Join me, Livius, and keep whispering in my ear, reminding me that I am a mere mortal."

Both men laughed heartily as they left the room.

Chapter 46

The sea voyage had been trouble free. The moderate north-westerly winds prevailing for most of the time meant the journey had been completed in very good time. Whilst the wind had caused the waves to become troublesome at times, the captain was able to cope easily and was grateful for the swift crossing to the northern coast of Gaul. However, his obvious pleasure wasn't shared by his passengers, particularly Caris. Her first action, when the ship had finally been secured to the jetty in the harbour of Bononia, was to drop onto her knees to humbly thank her Gods for bringing her safely to dry land.

"That has been the worst period of my life," Caris moaned. "I thought I was going to vomit myself to death many times."

The captain and crew roared with laughter. Even Lucia was capable of displaying a slight smile on her still ghostly pale face.

"How can you bear to do that repeatedly?" asked Caris. "You can't possibly have stomachs like normal people."

"Can you please leave the ship immediately," the captain replied mischievously. "We're very hungry and need to have a full meal before we begin to unload our cargo. We have to begin our return voyage to Britannia tomorrow."

Caris groaned as she rose uncertainly to her feet with the assistance of the outstretched hand of the captain. He turned to speak to Lucia.

"You'll need to have a place to recover from the voyage for at least one night before you begin your journey south. I understand you've been to Gaul before, Olsar. Have you a place in mind?"

"We have plans," he replied, "but I agree with you. It will soon be evening and we need somewhere to stay just for tonight. What can you suggest?"

"I have a friend who owns the best inn here in Bononia. When you're ready I'll take you there."

*

The inn had proved satisfactory and once Caris and Marcus had been settled for the night, Lucia and Olsar went to speak with the innkeeper.

"As we said earlier we intend to be on our way tomorrow," Lucia began. "We need to buy four suitable sturdy horses and two mules. Do you know where we can get them?"

"I can supply them, and at a reasonable price," he replied. "You say you're going to Rome. That's a long, expensive and dangerous journey, particularly for two women and a child. If you're interested, I can arrange for you to hire four good fighting men, retired legionaries, to escort you."

Although Lucia had asked the question his reply had been made to Olsar.

"Have the horses and mules ready for me to inspect first thing in the morning," Lucia replied pointedly. "If they are suitable I shall talk about the price and maybe other provisions. If I decide to take an escort we shall find our own."

She took hold of Olsar's arm and marched off.

*

"These are four old nags," Olsar said angrily the following morning. "They wouldn't last ten days. They're fit only for dog food."

"They're the best you can buy from the few traders we have in this town. You won't get a better deal elsewhere."

"We shall see," Lucia added.

She walked a few paces to where Caris and Marcus were waiting.

"We aren't buying those old horses are we, Mama?" Marcus pleaded.

"Don't be alarmed, son. We're going to look elsewhere."

"Have you any ideas, Olsar?" Caris asked.

"I know the tribune who commands the small garrison guarding this port. He may be able to help. Let's go to meet him and see what he can suggest."

*

"Our Legate, Camillus Pecius, sent a message that we might come across you, Olsar," said the young tribune. "We were told to pass on his warm regards if we did. I understand you commanded auxiliaries in our Legion."

"That's true."

"Julius must have told Camillus to expect us," Lucia noted with a broad smile.

"The Legate has also instructed me to give you whatever assistance I can."

"That's very good to hear," Olsar replied. "We need three things we've already had some difficulty with."

"What are they?"

"Firstly, we need four healthy horses and two mules to carry ourselves and all our provisions. It appears we'll have some difficulty in buying those here."

"I know what you mean. I don't have any spare horses here in the garrison. However, you can take the best we have. I can send for replacements."

"Then there's our need for provisions."

"That's no problem. Just tell me what you need."

"Finally, I think we'll need an escort, at least until Lugundum in central Gaul. We can reassess the position there."

"How many men would you need?"

"Four would be sufficient to add to myself and Lucia. The six of us would be able to handle any group of bandits."

The tribune took a momentary glance at Lucia. Her firm stare made him quickly turn his attention back to Olsar.

"That's a real problem. As it is, we barely have sufficient men to guard this frontier port."

"I seem to remember there was a small fort in this region manned by a cohort of five hundred auxiliaries, mostly from Germania. Are they still there? If so, they could easily spare the men."

"Yes they are, but they're more than a day's hard ride from here. It could be three days before they get here."

"I don't want to stay another night here," Lucia said sharply.

"I have a possible answer which could satisfy you if you have to leave today."

"What is it?"

"There's a large village to the south of us which you could reach in three days at the rate at which you're likely to travel. I could arrange for the auxiliaries to meet you there in three to four days."

"Excellent!" said Olsar. "Let's get things started."

*

The innkeeper had called together four of his friends to share a drink of wine.

"I tell you it's an opportunity we can't afford to miss. They left soon after noon without any escort. They'd managed to get four excellent horses and two mules from the garrison."

"Won't they be branded?" asked one of the four.

"Leave that problem to me," replied the innkeeper. "I've solved that before. Then there are all their provisions. They could bring a fair return."

"That's still not enough to tempt me."

"Then there's the money they'll be carrying."

"What's that? How much? Have you seen it? Who's carrying it?"

The questions came at the innkeeper from all of them, now he'd gained their full attention.

"I haven't seen it. But think about it. They are travelling all the way to Rome. They wear the clothes of the rich, and were eager to pay to buy the best. The money is there, I tell you. We may even be able to sell the four of them to others who could hold them for ransom. Are you with me?"

He got their enthusiastic support.

"They only have a one-night start. You could easily catch them up by tomorrow night. You only have one thing to concern you. That man looked as if he was used to combat. But, remember you only have him to deal with. The others are two women and one child. Good hunting!"

Chapter 47

The walk to the Governor's palace in Londinium was not one Julius enjoyed, particularly when he'd been summoned by Governor Bolanus. It didn't help his mood when black threatening clouds started to empty their contents just before he began his short journey through the streets. He'd considered ignoring Bolanus's summons. However, in the end he decided relations were bad enough between them without making things worse. He would spare him a few moments of his time.

"You asked to see me, Bolanus," said Julius, throwing his wet cloak angrily to one side. "Make it brief."

He couldn't help but notice Bolanus looked downcast, deflated. He hadn't made any attempt to greet him in his usual manner, with a pretence of friendliness.

"I hope this drenching you've forced upon me is worth it."

"I'm sure you'll think it worthwhile when you hear what I have to say. But first of all, what are your current proposals regarding the continuing unrest in the north with the Brigantes and their leader Venutius?"

"I'm drawing up provisional plans for a campaign to put down the rebellion. We will need to recruit many more auxiliaries and get the support of some friendly tribes. We need to treat this problem with some urgency."

"Well, it seems the continuing problem with the Brigantes has had an effect on our Emperor."

"What are you saying?"

"I've just received a written instruction from him informing me

I'm to be replaced as Governor of Britannia."

Julius was momentarily shocked. However, he wasn't really surprised except for the timing of it. It had come a lot sooner than he'd expected.

"Why have you specifically mentioned the Brigantes? What has he said?"

Julius was anxious to hear if there had been any specific complaint against him since he'd been given responsibility for military matters.

"That's the main reason for my dismissal. I've lost the confidence of Vespasian. He thinks I'm not capable of working with you to end the revolt. He believes Britannia needs a stronger Governor, one who is a more experienced commander, able to provide the leadership in all matters including the military."

Julius had mixed feelings about what he was hearing. A new ally with better understanding and enthusiasm for a military campaign against rebels would be welcomed. However, he could very quickly turn into a rival if it meant his own responsibility and authority was reduced. It all depended on the replacement.

"Has he told you who will replace you?"

"He has indeed. It's someone who I think will be known to you," Bolanus replied with a smirk on his face. "He was involved with you in putting down Boudica's rebellion in this Province. It's the Emperor's brother-in-law, Petillius Cerialis."

Julius's jaw dropped. His history with Cerialis ten years earlier and recently during the civil war, didn't bode well for a successful future partnership controlling the Province. He would need to think long and hard about what it meant for him. For now, he needed to part company on the best of terms possible with this man.

"What is to happen to you?"

"Fortunately, our new Emperor still remembers I didn't respond to Vitellius's request to send him some of Britannia's Legions to join him to fight against Vespasian's forces during the civil war. If I'd done so, he accepts the military balance in Gaul and then northern Italia could have been a different one, causing him many more casualties, if not perhaps ultimately the throne. Because of that I shall not be returning in total disgrace. However, he pointed out I was originally appointed Governor by Vitellius. He says he wants to see me as soon as I get back to discuss my future and to be sure my loyalty is to him and not to the surviving supporters of Vitellius. He has reason to believe they're still around and plotting against him. So, I'm still under threat, suffering a great blow to my status and prestige. Nevertheless, I'm certain I can reassure him and will be allowed to return to the Senate to rebuild my career without too much delay."

Julius was tempted to make a sarcastic comment about his proven corrupt dealings but decided to let sleeping dogs lie.

"That means your immediate future is still partly in your own hands."

"We shall see. For the moment I have things to say to you, Julius, on a personal level. I see your hand behind this temporary humiliation. You've used your influence with Vespasian to bring about my removal. Don't try to deny it."

"I do deny it, but that will never be believed by you."

"Correct! Our paths will cross again in the future in Rome or elsewhere. You can be sure I will be looking to repay you for what you've done to me here in Britannia."

"If that is your intention, so be it. Just beware of what you could bring down upon yourself. Farewell!"

The walk back to his headquarters was slow despite the downpour having worsened. His own future had become more precarious. However, he couldn't stop thinking about the dangers facing Lucia. She had escaped her enemies in Britannia by seeking a future in Rome. She would be unaware that one of them, Bolanus, was also on his way back there. If he came across her he would undoubtedly use his influence against her. Julius began to realise that unlike in the past, he might be unable to be there to protect her. The rebellion in the north could occupy him for some time. In the meantime, he had no way of knowing where to find her to be able to contact and warn her. He had to work to get his recall to Rome as soon as possible.

Chapter 48

"How long does it take to get used to sleeping in these military tents?" Caris whined. "I'm not young like the rest of you."

"Normally, it takes a Legionary only his first night," Olsar replied. "To start with he will have marched for twenty or more miles with his full kit on his back. Then at the end of the march the first thing he has to do is to help to set up an overnight defensive marching fort before he can think of sleep."

"A fort like General Agricola's outside Londinium?" interrupted an excited Marcus.

"Not nearly as big and grand as that, Marcus. Nevertheless, it has to be a strong one. A trench has to be built with a rampart behind and a palisade made of wooden stakes on top. It has to completely enclose the area where the tents and carts are placed. Only then can they rest and eat their evening meal. After that they are so tired they could sleep anywhere, even standing up."

"I think I'll try that tonight," Marcus suggested.

The other three laughed which brought out a puzzled look on the young boy's face.

"We only have to camp in the tent tonight, Caris," Lucia commented reassuringly. "Tomorrow we'll reach the village where we can stay a few nights."

"Thank goodness. Please ignore my complaints. I'm sure it won't take me too long to get used to it."

"Talking of sleep, it's time we all did exactly that," said Lucia.

"I shall build up the fire to last the night," Olsar added.

Hidden in the trees approximately one hundred paces away, the four men from the inn were taking note of the sleeping arrangements as their prey retired for the night.

"The two women and the boy have gone into the nearest tent," observed their leader. "The man went into the other one with all their equipment. It makes it easy. Two of us will deal with the women and child. The other two will wait outside the other tent. The women's screams will bring him out. Disarm him and hold him fast."

"What if he puts up a fight?"

"Only kill him if you have to. We need to find out from them where they've hidden their money first. For the time being, we sit and wait until we think they're all asleep."

*

Caris had only been half asleep, but it still took her a short while to realise the man who'd entered the tent and taken Marcus out, with his hand covering his mouth, wasn't Olsar. Her scream immediately wakened a startled Lucia who staggered out of the tent to be knocked to the ground with a blow to her head. Hearing the same scream, Olsar had dashed out to receive a similar blow before he was held captive by one man either side of him.

"Don't resist us or we will kill you all, starting with the boy," the leader yelled.

He had a firm hold of Marcus with a knife at his throat.

"Please don't hurt him," Lucia begged.

"What is it you want?" Olsar growled.

"To start with, your money. Where is it?"

"We're only a poor defenceless family. Please don't harm any of us," Lucia pleaded.

"We won't if you tell us where you've hidden it."

"I buried it in the trees behind us. I'll have to show you. Please, please don't hurt us."

Handing Marcus to the remaining man, he walked over to Lucia. He grabbed her arm, twisting it up her back, placing his knife across her throat. Olsar's struggling caught his attention.

"If there's any more trouble from him kill the boy. By the way, what's your name?"

"Olsar."

"You've heard what I said, Olsar. The boy's life is in your hands."

He turned, dragging Lucia in the direction of the trees.

*

"He's been gone too long," murmured the one holding Marcus.

He shouted out the leader's name but got no reply.

"Something isn't right. I wouldn't be surprised if he's killed her and taken the money for himself, especially if there's a lot."

"You'll have to go and see what's happened. We both need to hold on to this one."

"What about the boy?"

"Leave him. He can't do anything."

Marcus ran to Caris as soon as he was released and his captor headed for the trees.

"One wrong movement from you, Olsar, and my knife slits your throat and my friend's opens up your belly."

Olsar continued to stare coldly ahead of him, appearing to be concentrating very hard.

*

"I don't like this. We've called out to both of them and neither has replied. They've been gone too long."

"You two can still get out of this alive if you release me immediately and leave," Olsar warned.

The two of them laughed loudly and for too long. It meant they didn't hear the last few steps Lucia took to come right up behind the one with the knife at Olsar's throat. In one movement she took a firm hold of the hand with the knife in it and turned it into his own throat.

Before the other man realised fully what had happened Olsar's forehead smashed into his face, crushing his nose. It sent him crashing semi-conscious to the floor. Olsar grabbed his knife and bent down over him.

"No more killing!" Caris demanded.

*

"What took you so long, and what happened to the other two?" Olsar asked later. "Since our money was under my headrest in my tent, not in the trees, I guessed what you were going to do. I also realised you would attack from behind."

"The leader was very suspicious so I had to choose my moment very carefully. He shouldn't have threatened to kill Marcus. He was a dead man from that moment on. The other one is unconscious with a broken arm in those trees. How did you react so quickly when I struck?"

"I heard you when you were four or five paces away. I tried to give them a chance."

"What shall we do with these two live ones? They deserve to die."

"We release them!" Caris insisted. "Put them on their horses and send them on their way."

"I agree," said Olsar. "That would still leave two of their horses. They will be useful to us."

"I think we have another problem," Caris noted.

"What's that?" Lucia asked.

"We need to talk to Marcus about what happened tonight. For someone his age he seemed to enjoy the danger too much, especially the killing of the man in front of him."

"We three shall talk about what's to be said to him first, Caris. But not tonight. Thankfully, from tomorrow we should have an escort to prevent a further attack happening."

Chapter 49

Paulus Marellus had learnt that Olsar and Lucia, his hated enemies, had gone to Gaul in a ship making frequent voyages between there and Londinium. Finding the captain of that ship had become a priority if he was going to get off to a good start in his search for those Iceni traitors. His latest information had led him one gloomy evening to an inn close to the riverside wharfs in Londinium. Deep in conversation with his two companions, he didn't notice a large, swarthy man with a full beard approach him from the shadows at the back of the room. Close behind him was a group of men who were dressed in rough, dirty clothes.

"I hear you're looking for me," he said.

"That depends on who you are," Paulus replied.

The inns in this town were well known for the violence and crime that occurred frequently. Earlier Paulus had placed his knife on the table in front of him as a precaution. His hand moved to cover the handle.

"I'm a ship's captain and these are my crew. I would suggest you take your hand off that knife if you want to live. If you look behind me you'll see you are greatly outnumbered. So, stop wasting my time. If you have anything to say, get on with it."

"I'm looking for the captain of the ship which recently took a family of four to Gaul. Two of them were Iceni scum. Was that you?"

"Might have been. Why are you wanting to know?"

"I'm wanting to find them. I need to know where to start looking in Gaul."

"Why are you searching for them?"

"You don't need to know that. Are you the captain I'm looking for or not?"

The captain smiled at this aggressive response and sat down next to Paulus.

"I am. I can take you there but it will cost you."

"Then let's begin to bargain."

*

"We shall be docking in the port of Bononia very soon," said the captain. "The inn where they stayed is only a short walk from where we tie up. I'll take you there. That was what you paid for. After that you're on your own."

"That's what we agreed."

"I suspect the reason for your mission to find them is not a friendly one. Am I correct?"

Paulus just stared at the captain without replying.

"Suit yourself. I don't need your answer for me to give you some advice. You look to be a young man who could handle himself in a fight, as do your two companions. However, the two Iceni you're obviously hunting won't be easy prey. In case you don't know she was a fearsome gladiator in Londinium."

"I know that."

"What you don't know is she has already made her mark in Gaul."

"What are you saying?"

"It's not for me tell you. Ask the innkeeper."

*

"I wonder what the captain meant when he said she'd made her mark."

The question came from one of Paulus's two companions as they waited for the innkeeper to finish talking to a group of legionaries seated at the opposite end of the large communal room in the inn.

"We shall soon find out," Paulus noted. "He's coming over to see us as he said he would. Let me do all the talking."

"Well, gentlemen! My friend the captain from Britannia told me you're wanting some information."

He pulled up a stool to sit down with them.

"That's correct. He said you'd be able to help us find some people we're searching for."

"Maybe I can help. Maybe I can't. Information doesn't come cheap in this town."

"We can pay well if we hear anything useful to us."

"We appear to have got off to a good start. So what is it you want to know?"

"Our understanding is that the group we're looking for stayed here recently. There was one man, two women, one much younger than the other, and one young boy. The captain introduced them to you in the same way he brought us here today. Do you remember them?"

"Possibly. I get a lot of travellers staying in my inn. What's your interest in them?"

"That's our business. You don't need to know that."

"Oh! Don't I? Then I shall wish you a safe journey, wherever you're going."

Pushing the stool backwards, he stood and turned to leave them.

"Wait!" cried Paulus. "Sit down! What do you want to know?"

"I told you. Why are you interested in them?"

Paulus gave a quick, nervous glance at his two friends before replying.

"You must treat what I tell you in confidence. If you don't, we have some powerful friends."

"Now you're frightening me," he replied mockingly. "Get on with it."

"The man and the younger woman have done great harm to my family."

"What exactly?"

"He killed my father and she slaughtered my brother. They have to pay for that with their lives."

"I have some sympathy, but it will take more than the three of you. Many more!"

"What do you mean?"

The innkeeper then took a while to give Paulus the details of what had happened to his four men.

"Look at the two men in the corner over there, looking sorry for themselves. They are the two who lived. If you look closely you will see the broken nose and arm."

"They couldn't have been particularly good at what you sent them to do," Paulus scoffed.

"They were the best. I've used them before. They were all former, battle-hardened legionaries. And it gets worse for you."

"How?"

"You saw me talking to those legionaries earlier. I'm on good terms with the men at the garrison. I've since learnt that by now they'll have an escort of auxiliaries to journey through Gaul. That means there could be six or more of them able to fight you. You will need at least double that number of men."

Paulus had gone pale. The other two looked down at the table top.

"As much as I would like you to avenge the deaths of my two men, I would advise you to completely rethink your plans. They appear to have some very good friends and influence in the Army."

*

"Don't be too downhearted, Paulus," said his uncle Tullius. "After what you've told me, I'm pleased you decided to return for us to decide what to do next. It's as well you didn't catch up to them and try to do the same as the innkeeper's men. You could well have suffered the same fate."

"Even so, I can't just accept we can never do anything to them."

"Me neither. And we don't have to. Something happened to help us in the short time you were away. We just have to be patient."

"What happened?"

"Bolanus is no longer Governor."

"How can that possibly help us?"

"He's being sent back to Rome shortly. He hopes he won't be totally disgraced and will be allowed to re-join the Senate. After this he will be just as determined as we are to destroy Agricola and those two friends of his. As soon we hear he's there and ready to help, you can go to Rome. With his assistance you will find them and we shall have our revenge. Waiting a while is nothing so long as we eventually succeed."

"I can wait, but not indefinitely. I shall go to see Bolanus before he leaves."

Chapter 50

The last time these two men met in Londinium the town was a burnt-out ruin. Legate Petillius Cerialis was being threateningly interrogated by the Governor, Suetonius Paulinus, assisted by a young Tribune, Julius Agricola. In the ten years since, they'd met on occasions, even been allies in the civil war. Allies they might have been, but neither would call the other one a friend. For some reason the Goddess of fate had determined that Cerialis had been given authority over Julius in Britannia.

Julius had entered the Governor's Palace to welcome his new commanding officer and to receive any fresh orders from the Emperor. More significantly, he wanted to get a first impression of how Cerialis saw their future working relationship. Even though Julius knew him to be pompous and head-strong, nevertheless, he could be a brave and competent military commander. He felt it was important they got off to a good start if they were to bring about a swift end to the northern rebellion. It was essential if he was to get an early recall to Rome to be able to find Lucia.

After a polite formal exchange of greetings, the two men retired into the Governor's private office to begin the report from Julius about his military activities in the Province. It was Cerialis who sat down first in the large sumptuous chair behind his desk. He then asked Julius to sit down in the plain workmanlike chair opposite him. The clear message presented by these tokens of status, whether deliberate or not, was not lost on Julius.

"It's nearly ten years since we did something similar to this, Julius," Cerialis began, "although our roles are somewhat reversed."

Julius noted the warmth in Cerialis's smile and decided he was trying to be friendly by his remark rather than provocative.

"I seem to remember you weren't particularly disadvantaged by being this side of the desk on that occasion," Julius countered, returning the warm smile.

"I think we might just get on quite well together in our new positions, Julius, bearing in mind we've shared a keen loyalty to our new Emperor over the years."

"Not to mention both having survived the keen attention of a previous one named Nero."

They both laughed freely and Julius began to relax a little more.

"We've lots to discuss, but before we begin I have something of a personal matter to bring to your attention."

Julius's expression changed to one of confusion at this sudden change of direction.

"When I was about to leave Rome, your mother came to see me. She gave me a sealed message to deliver to you. Here it is."

He passed the document over.

"Obviously, I haven't read it. However, I am a friend of your father and mother and I know the purpose of it, if not the detail. I suggest it might be appropriate if we took a short break for you to withdraw into a side room to read it."

Julius, intrigued and eager to find out what his mother had to say, did as was suggested.

In the quiet of the small room, Julius took a few moments before he broke the seal he recognised so well. His imagination was working at great speed wondering what the message might contain. Finally he opened the document and began to read.

My dear Julius,

There's no easy way to tell you this.

Your wife Domitia is dead.

I would have preferred to tell you face to face. You deserved that. I intended to do so when you returned from Britannia. I know you and she weren't very close. In fact I was always surprised you didn't get divorced some time ago. Nevertheless, she was your wife, and knowing you, this news will be met with some sorrow.

When I heard from your father that Petillius Cerialis was going to Britannia. I realised he would know of Domitia's death from your father or others. Her family are very prestigious and it was well known in Rome. He would assume you knew when he first arrived and met you. Therefore, I asked him not to say anything before you'd had time to read this and learnt about it from me.

The circumstances of her death were a shock and unusual. Her father, a long-standing friend of Vespasian as you know, had been appointed by him to the position of Governor of Aegyptus. However, he was not a young man. Since her mother was dead, Domitia decided to accompany him to assist him in establishing himself there. She also confessed to me her wish to see those temples and monuments of that ancient kingdom, particularly those pyramids we've all heard about.

I hope she got her wish because soon after her arrival she was struck down by a fever and never recovered. It was a double tragedy for her family since her father was also taken in the same way.

I'm sure your first thought will be of the twins. I can assure you they are fine. With Miriam to help I am taking care of them.

We all anxiously await your return.

Your loving mother,

Procilla

Julius stared at the document in his hand. His immediate reaction was indeed sorrow, but it was mainly for his children who had lost the love of their mother. Domitia and he had led more or less separate lives over a long time. He was consoled by the knowledge that Procilla would care for them. His longing to complete his task here as quickly as possible had grown even stronger.

"I know it must be very unwelcome news for you, Julius," said Cerialis when Julius returned.

"Thank you for bringing me my mother's message. It was a shock, as you can imagine. However, in case you're wondering, I'm ready to begin our discussion."

"Excellent! Let me begin by telling you what Vespasian has

ordered. As you can expect he wants the rebellion to be put down quickly. He wants to link it with the final defeat of the Judaeans. The Emperor will be able to boast of two great victories at opposite ends of the Empire, the perfect start to his reign."

"I have already been making plans to launch a campaign from the west using the fort at Viroconium as my main base."

"So I understand from Vespasian. That's excellent. I've been giving some initial thought to an overall strategy using the particular knowledge we each have. Before and during the Boudican revolt your experiences were up the western side of the Province. Mine were up the eastern side. I see us launching a twofold campaign, you attacking with two Legions from the west while I take the other two and attack at the same time from the east."

"It would work," Julius added enthusiastically.

"I'm pleased you agree. As soon as I've got control of my new administration we shall get our campaign underway."

*

Later, Julius left the building in a much lighter mood than he'd entered it. He now had a Governor he could deal with. They appeared to see the solution to the Province's main problem in the same way. Any difficulty that could have been there from their previous dealings with each other seemed to have disappeared. He felt good about the immediate future.

Chapter 51

The ride south to Lugundum for Lucia and her companions proved to be largely uneventful. There'd been no sign of any threat similar to the one they'd experienced soon after leaving the coastal town of Bononia. However, that didn't mean the trek had been boring and tedious as far as Lucia, Caris and Marcus were concerned. The scenery they were riding through, particularly in the later stages of the journey, had been a constant source of amazement to all three of them.

During his short life, Marcus had lived on his grandfather's farming estate a few miles west of Londinium. The countryside around the villa, with the river gently flowing down to the town, consisted of flat or gently rolling fields and woodland. He'd barely witnessed a hill of any size compared to the snow-capped mountains he'd marvelled at in the far distance.

Caris, although much older than Marcus, had shared a similar experience to him throughout her life. She'd asked the others in her travelling group how those distant mountains could have snow on the top of them when they were enjoying the gentle warmth of early summer. No one could give her an answer.

For Lucia it was a vindication of her decision to seek a new life and experiences for herself and Marcus. At a similar age to her son, she'd had no reason to believe the rest of the world was any different to the more or less flat lands of her tribal territory. Until she left the shores of Britannia she hadn't seen a great deal of evidence to make her think much differently. She could never have imagined there could be such awesome beauty as that which the Gods were constantly displaying to them.

Olsar and the four auxiliary soldiers in their escort had seen it all before and had been able to concentrate of the road ahead. Their particular delight was in seeing the large town of Lugundum finally and safely come into sight. Olsar had visited the town in the past if only briefly. So he knew where to go to find a place to stay.

*

The first open revolt against Nero, as his control over the Empire began to evaporate, had occurred in this region, led by Vindex. Because of that, a full Legion was now based in a fort immediately outside the town to ensure future loyalty to the new Emperor. Having settled Lucia and the others temporarily at an inn to rest and enjoy a welcome meal, Olsar had gone to introduce himself to the commander of the Legion. The Legate was a man he'd met briefly before and one he knew would be helpful.

"Welcome, Olsar," said the Legate. "Where are your companions? I was sent a message by the tribune in Bononia telling me there would be eight of you in your group."

"That's correct. I've left the others recovering in the town. They're weary after our long trek through northern Gaul and Germania. One of my party is a young boy and another is not as young or fit as she would like to be to make such a journey. But don't tell her I said that to you if you meet her."

"I know exactly how she must feel!"

The comment came from an elderly man who Olsar had noticed when he'd entered the Legate's reception room in his headquarters. He was relaxing on a couch with a beaker of wine in his hand.

"Excuse me for not introducing you gentlemen to each other sooner," the Legate said, quickly making amends.

Having introduced Olsar, he went on to describe his guest.

"This is Felix Pontius. What can I say that explains what you do, Felix? You're a trader in anything and everything. You're a citizen of this and many other towns and cities, including Rome. You supply the Army with anything we want, together with a lot we don't but you somehow persuade us we do."

"I think that sums me up very well for now," said Felix. "Where are you and your group headed, Olsar?"

"Our ultimate goal is Rome, but who knows what distractions we may meet on our way?"

"Rome is my favourite home town," Felix joked, winking at the Legate. "Have you been there before?"

"I lived in a villa just south of the city, for a while, with a friend of mine and his family."

"Is that so? Who was it? Perhaps I know them."

"It was Senator Agricola and his son, Julius."

"By the Gods! I've known the Senator for many years. He's a fine Roman. I don't know his son so well, but I have met him on occasions. He tried heroically to fight the great fire. He saved many lives in that catastrophe. He did his best to contain the destruction. I lost a great deal of property and goods, but without his efforts I'd have lost a lot more. I owe him a great deal."

"I know what happened. I was there with him."

"You said earlier you're from Britannia. I heard there was a Brit fighting the fire alongside Agricola. Was that you?"

"It was."

"Then I owe you a lot as well, young man. By the way, I hope you aren't offended by me calling you a Brit."

"Not when I sense no offence is intended."

"When you get to Rome you must come to see me."

"So, Olsar," said the Legate, "is there any help I can give you? Legate Camillus Pecius is a good friend of mine. He sent me a letter telling me of his regard for you and asking me to give you whatever help I can."

"Before he answers you, let me be on my way," interrupted Felix. "I'm leaving tomorrow morning for Massilia and I still have people to see."

When Felix had left, Olsar gave the Legate a list of supplies he needed.

"What about an escort?" the Legate asked. "There's still considerable resentment from some of the Gauls following their defeat in Vindex's revolt."

"We've had excellent support so far. However, the four auxiliary soldiers who've been with us until we reached here are due to report to you for reassignment. They assume they will probably be ordered to return to their base in the north. Nevertheless, I've spoken to all of them and they would like to continue with us until we reach the port of Massilia, if that can be arranged. From there we can board a ship to Rome and they could then be released."

"That isn't a problem. I shall send a message to Camillus informing him. When do you intend leaving?"

"We shall rest for two days and then be on our way."

"Come to see me again before you go. I'd like to hear first-hand what it was like fighting the great fire. We've heard so many rumours about what happened."

*

"How were you received?" Lucia asked, when Olsar returned.

"Everything is being taken care of. We have to thank Julius again and particularly Camillus for that."

"What about our four friends? Will they be leaving us?"

"No. They can continue with us. Incidentally, the meeting with the Legate proved to have an added advantage. I met a trader who appears to be a man of some standing in Rome. He says he knows Julius and is an old friend of his father. He's offered to help us when we get to Rome. He seems to be a man we can trust."

*

Two days later the group of eight left Lugundum in high spirits. In addition to providing all the supplies they'd requested, the Legate had exchanged all their horses and mules for fresh ones.

Marcus was particularly delighted with the one he'd been given, especially when he was told it was a horse that had been assigned to a cavalryman in the past. Lucia was a little concerned for him at first, but had finally accepted Olsar's view that her son was becoming a very capable young horseman.

They'd been told there was a village within reach on their first day if they made good progress. Having fresh horses meant they easily achieved that, arriving there by late afternoon. The headman of the village welcomed them, offering places to sleep for the night.

"What's your destination?" he asked.

"The southern port of Massilia, on our way to Rome," Lucia replied.

"I see you're well-armed. It's a very wise precaution in these parts. A smaller group that left here yesterday weren't so well prepared and have paid the price."

"Why? What happened?"

"A wealthy trader with a slave and a three-man escort was attacked not very far south of here. Two of our men found them by the side of the road. The three men escorting the trader were dead. The slave had been left for dead also. However, our men found him still alive, but badly injured. They brought him back here. He's being taken care of in one of our houses."

"What's happened to the trader?"

"The slave said he heard the thieves arguing amongst themselves. Most of them including their leader felt he could bring them more money if they ransomed him. One or two felt it was too dangerous and wanted to kill him there and then."

Olsar asked for a description of the trader.

"That's Felix!" Olsar cried, when the headman had finished describing him. "That's the man I met at the fort. Are you sending some of the men from the village to rescue him?"

"We know this group," the headman replied. "There are at least ten of them. We are only a small village. We don't have enough men to challenge them and in any case we are farmers, not fighting men."

"Then we will have to rescue him quickly in case their decision changes and they think he's not worth ransoming," Lucia stated without hesitation. "How far away did the attack take place?"

"You could easily be there before nightfall. But, I must warn you they're a savage and ruthless group of hardened outlaws."

"Could your men take us to where they were attacked?" Lucia asked, completely ignoring his last comment.

"More than that. We know where their camp is. It's in a small valley not too far from where the attack took place. My son could take you there. He's had dealings with this group in the past."

"Good," said Lucia. "Then we haven't a moment to lose. Can somebody take care of Marcus and Caris until we return?"

"Certainly."

*

Throughout the ride to the outlaws' camp, Lucia had been developing a plan to rescue Felix, assuming he was still alive. She'd asked their guide, the headman's son, to bring them to a halt well short of the valley. This would give her the opportunity to explain her thinking to the others. As expected it was early evening when her group came to a stop, following a signal from their guide.

"The valley and their camp is only a mile away," he advised. "If we go any further we are likely to be seen by a guard. The others would be warned."

Lucia thanked him before addressing Olsar and the other four.

"We have a choice to make. Do we attack now while there's still enough light, or do we wait until it's dark? Attacking now gives us the advantage that we can clearly see our enemy and hopefully identify where Felix is being held captive. If we find he's already dead they will all suffer the same fate. The disadvantage with this choice is that the element of surprise is greatly reduced. If we can see them, they can just as easily see us. The first to die would probably be Felix."

She paused to look for a reaction, particularly from Olsar. They were all nodding slightly, showing their understanding if not yet their acceptance of this alternative. She continued.

"However, we could wait until dark. This would greatly increase the surprise element, assuming we get past their outer guards without being discovered. The disadvantage for us is that we don't know the layout of the camp, where their leader and Felix are. In the dark their knowledge of the camp and where everyone is located gives them a great advantage. What do you all think we should do?"

"I don't like either choice," Olsar answered before the others. "With either we could succeed, but not without our own losses by the time we discovered where Felix was being held. I'm wondering if he's worth it if I lost any of you."

Lucia took it to mean her since his first thought was always her safety.

The other four were in favour of an immediate attack.

"I do have another idea which combines parts of both alternatives and reduces the risks to us and to Felix," she said.

"We're listening," said Olsar.

"It involves the help of our guide."

"I'm not a warrior," the young man gasped nervously. "My father told you we are just farmers."

"You don't have to fight. I only want to use the fact that you're known and acceptable to our enemy. You could get me and Olsar into their camp without causing them too much alarm."

"That doesn't sound like a good idea to me," Olsar protested, "just walking into the hands of our enemy."

"Hear me out. This young man is known to them. He can lead us openly and unthreateningly to the first guard we meet. He explains that with him are two Romans who want to do urgent and important business with their leader. We should then be taken into the camp where we will appear to want to negotiate Felix's release."

"And they fall for it and just let us walk out with him."

"No! They take me as another hostage and let the two of you go."

Their four companions burst out laughing. Olsar just glared at her.

"I know what you're suggesting can't be as simple or as stupid as it sounds. What dangerous little scheme have you in mind?"

"Thank you, Olsar. I shall present myself as Felix's timid, frightened daughter, only interested in rescuing my father, whatever the ransom price. You're my escort. It won't take them long to realise they have a second wealthy Roman to ransom. You will offer to go back to Lugundum where the ransom monies can be quickly raised but only if you can see Felix is still alive. You will then be shown where he's being held. They will place me with him to keep him company. I will tell Felix what is going to happen so he's prepared."

Olsar's expression began to lighten.

"Meaning that I will be released by them to arrange the ransom.

However, I would then know the layout of the camp and which huts the thieves are likely to be sleeping in, particularly their leader. Most important of all, we will know where you and Felix are for us to be able to get to you quickly."

"That describes my plan very well. I add only one thing to your summary. When you attack, you don't have to be concerned about me and Felix. You can concentrate on taking the others out. Once I hear you in the camp I will take care of our guard or guards."

"What with? We'll be searched as soon as we arrive in the camp. You won't have a weapon."

"You, my military escort, will be searched! They will see no reason to search a timid, tearful Roman gentlewoman for a sword or any other weapon. I shall have my small knife hidden deep in my clothing. You will be displaying your sword and a large knife to show you have the full responsibility to defend poor, helpless me."

"It could work," said Olsar.

"It will work! When you leave the camp our guide can return to his village, his work done. You, Olsar, will draw up your plan of attack based on what you've seen. I only ask you to leave it until well into the night, to allow those villains to be getting their last beauty asleep."

*

The camp was pretty much as Olsar had hoped for. There were twelve huts arranged in a circle around a large open area. There was a small entrance gap between the huts facing the narrow tree-lined lane which was the way into the camp. In the centre of the open area was a large fire. Olsar's first thought was that this would be built up to last the night. The light it provided to the whole camp could be of assistance, or it might cause problems if they were discovered too soon.

On further reflection he was pleased to note the dense forest came right up to the huts on all sides. It would provide them with cover when carrying out any approach. He took notice when the leader of the outlaws, a giant of a man, came out of his hut directly opposite the entrance on the far side of the circle. Olsar's confidence was increasing as they dismounted in front of the leader.

"Well! Well! What have we here?" the leader growled. "More filthy Romans."

The leader recognised the man from the village and looked to him for an answer. Olsar suddenly realised a flaw in Lucia's plan. They hadn't envisaged the villager playing any part other than leading them into the camp. If he lost his nerve they were dead. Before Olsar could decide what to do, the villager answered.

"These two travellers came into our village today looking for the trader who'd stayed with us the day before. Two of our men had found the rest of the trader's group on the roadside near your camp. We told them the trader wasn't with them. They were told that since he wasn't left with the others, it was likely you were holding him for ransom. We thought it would be a help if we brought them to you."

Olsar realised they could be about to be betrayed. He placed his hand on the hilt of his sword, wondering how quickly he could take the leader captive to give them any sort of a chance to survive.

"They have a proposal to make about your hostage that I think will interest you."

Lucia burst into tears, drawing the attention away from the young man, who was becoming very nervous. Olsar guessed she was having the same concerns about him as himself. It worked. The leader walked closer to Lucia.

"What a pretty little thing we have here then. Don't be frightened. We are all kind and gentle woodsmen."

There was widespread laughter from the men who were coming into the square. Olsar had counted six so far in addition to the leader and the guard who had brought them in. The leader turned to the guard.

"Why have you allowed this woman's military escort to get so close to me? Can't you see he's a fighting man, no doubt paid to protect her at all costs? He's armed to the teeth. Search him and remove all his weapons."

Lucia let out a wail of anguish at the sight of her only protector being disarmed.

"I told you not to be concerned, you'll come to no harm. What can I do for you?"

Olsar was beginning to think the plan was working. Lucia started to explain she was Felix's adopted daughter. She'd been delayed for a day in Lugundum and was trying to catch up with her father. Olsar was her father's trusted security guard who'd been delegated to wait behind for her. She paused between each sentence to sob desperately.

"Why take the risk to come here if you think we are bandits and murdering thieves?"

"Because, if he's here, I can arrange the ransom quickly so I can have my father back without any delay."

"Is she speaking the truth about her ability to raise the money quickly?" The leader had turned to address Olsar.

"Felix is a wealthy man. He has friends in Lugundum who will help him out by meeting a ransom demand very quickly. If they're sure he's still alive, that is. We need to see him before we can come to any arrangement."

Lucia let out another helpless cry. Olsar was standing his tallest in a defiant posture. Any sign of weakness on his part could be fatal.

"And what is to stop me slitting both your throats right now? We can always send a ransom message to his friends with this villager."

Olsar didn't reply. He was letting this oaf have the time to work out the answer for himself. It worked.

"On the other hand. I now have two hostages. I can send this man with a demand for two ransoms. I think I'll just run you through with this sword of yours. I can then have my fun with this beauty while I wait for the ransoms to be paid."

The trap is closing on him, Olsar told himself. *It just needs a little further push and we're there.*

"Do you think those friends are just going to find a large amount of money on the word of a poor, unknown villager? I don't think so. However, if it's me, Felix's personal guard, bringing your demand to them, someone who they know and trust, then that is a different matter. But I must be able to tell them I've seen that Felix is still alive. On that assurance from me, the money will be found without delay."

There was a long agonising pause while the leader paced back and forth. In turn, he looked at Lucia, Olsar, the villager, even his own men. Olsar noted their number had grown to ten.

"I agree! You can go with the message. I want one hundred thousand sesterces for the pair of them."

His men interrupted him with loud astonished gasps.

"I want to see Felix before I leave," Olsar demanded forcefully.

"When you bring the money back we won't be here. So get rid of any idea of betraying me by bringing legionaries back with you. Come back alone with the money to the village where I will contact you."

"Show Felix to us," Olsar insisted, glaring fiercely at the smirking leader. Lucia let out a timely wail in despair.

"Follow me."

They were taken to a hut halfway between the entrance and the leader's. Olsar looked inside and was greeted by a sorry-looking Felix.

"Olsar! Praise be to the Gods. You've come for me."

That should convince the leader of my value to him if he was having any lingering doubts, Olsar thought. However, his anxiety was soon increased again. Instead of putting Lucia in the hut with Felix, the leader grabbed her arm and dragged her to him. Lucia managed to signal caution to Olsar with a stern expression and an almost imperceptible shake of her head.

"Remember I have this little beauty. Don't fail me. You'd better be on your way if you want to be back in time to save her. You have two days."

"If she's hurt in any way," Olsar snarled, "I will find you."

The leader just grinned and waved farewell, pointing to the gap in the huts.

*

Olsar took his time returning to his four allies to brief them. He knew he had to rethink the plan of attack which had been forming earlier in his mind. Lucia may still end up in the same hut as Felix. However, she could be in any one of twelve. The worst possibility was that she would be in the leader's hut. By the lustful look on his face it was very possible he was contemplating taking action that would bring to light Lucia's hidden knife in her clothing. He consoled himself a little with the thought that it was debatable who would be in greater danger if the weapon was discovered.

*

"We can assume the huts containing captives will have guards outside," Olsar suggested to his men. "There was one already guarding Felix. Therefore, if we find only one hut is guarded we can assume they've been put together."

"Not if she's in the leader's hut," argued one of his men.

"I've thought of that. That's why we approach Felix's hut first to find out if she's there. I had already agreed a signal with her to tell her the attack is about to start. We knock twice on the wall of Felix's hut. If we receive an identical reply it will tell us she's in there. If there's no reply and no other guarded hut she will be with the leader. I shall head straight for there."

"How are we to be allocated to the huts?"

"Two of you will take the huts on the left-hand side of the leader's hut, two to the right-hand side. But we need to be flexible. Purely based on numbers, we have to take out two of them each, wherever we find them. Once we've disposed of their outlying guards, we start the attack by spreading around the circle, hidden by the trees. We enter the huts quietly and strike while they sleep. Sooner or later we shall be discovered. If we take out the leader quickly the others will falter. Any questions or comments?"

"It won't be the first time we've been outnumbered," one of them said. "Only two-to-one against us, when they aren't expecting an attack, sounds good to me."

It summed up the confidence and camaraderie which had built up amongst the five men.

*

"Do you think it will happen soon, Lucia?"

"That's the third time you've asked me, Felix. Olsar will choose the moment that's the best for whatever he has planned."

"I still can't believe you're all risking your lives to save me. I only met Olsar two days ago. True, we learnt we're both friends of Julius

Agricola, but that hardly explains it."

"We happened to be passing at the right time for you. We couldn't just ignore you when we heard what had happened. I told you we were attacked like you at the start of our journey. Perhaps it was the raw memory of that which made us act instinctively."

"But you've put yourself in great personal danger. You are a remarkable woman."

"It's far from the first time I've faced death. I'll tell you all about it when we get out of here."

"You sound so confident."

"Of course. Olsar would go to Hades and back for me, as I would for him. It applies to Julius Agricola also, but that's something else to tell you about later."

"You've got me wondering—"

"Quiet! I think I hear something."

The tapping noise she thought she heard coming from the back of the hut was repeated. It was the signal she'd hoped for. She tapped her reply.

"Guard!" she shouted. "I need help urgently. My father is having difficulty in breathing. If he dies there will be no ransom money."

Almost immediately, the door swung open and the guard rushed in. The thrust of her small knife slowed him down but didn't immediately kill him. It allowed him to shout in alarm just before the knife struck a second fatal blow.

"We stay here, Felix. This shouldn't take long."

She was correct. Looking out of the hut to her left she saw the leader's door fling open. He rushed out, roaring for his men to fight off the unknown attackers. He ran straight onto Olsar's sword, causing him to collapse onto Olsar. The impact of the big man forced them both off balance and backwards onto the ground, driving Olsar's sword completely through his opponent's body. He cast the leader to one side to get to his feet.

"Your leader is dead!" he shouted above the noise of sword fights taking place in front of him.

It was sufficient reason to cause two of the bandits to end their resistance and escape into the forest. The rest were disposed of quickly. Olsar looked across to see Lucia standing guard over Felix. She waved to show she was unhurt.

"It appears that two of your captors have escaped," Olsar explained as Lucia brought Felix to join him and the four others.

"They're probably halfway to the next Province by now," one of them joked.

"I was afraid that giant oaf had taken you into his hut for the night," Olsar admitted.

"I could see he had it in mind. However, he finally tired of my hysterical wails and shrieking. He thought better of it."

Olsar chuckled in delight at the thought of it.

"You've saved my life," Felix managed to say, his voice breaking with emotion. "I'd resigned myself to death. I overheard them say even if a ransom sum was paid I would still be killed. I shall never forget what you've done for me."

"It will soon be dawn," Lucia pointed out. "I suggest we spend some time searching for your stolen property, Felix, and anything extra we can give to the villagers for the important help they gave us. There are quite a few spare horses here. They will prove useful to farmers."

"We can stop to rest at the village while we decide what we do next," said Olsar. "Before then though, we have one rather large camp to destroy."

*

Early the following morning, the delighted farmers gave them a warm welcome when they brought their horses to a halt in the middle of their village. They could tell the mission had been a success when they saw Felix amongst them.

"Are they all dead?" the headman asked.

"All but two, though they will never be seen again in these parts," Olsar replied.

"You can't imagine how that will change the lives of all who live in this village and the surrounding area. Those thieves and murderers have plagued us for years. You must break your journey to stay with us for at least one day. We shall feast together tonight in celebration."

Olsar looked at Lucia who looked at Felix. They all smiled their acceptance.

*

Later that night, at the request of Felix, the three of them broke away from the festivities to discuss their immediate plans. Felix began the discussion.

"I may have been a little emotional last night when the fighting was over and I realised I had my life back. But I still meant what I said. I shall never forget what you did for me."

Lucia took his hand to give it a slight squeeze.

"You remind me of my father, old Quintus."

"Having spent the rest of today thinking about what you did, I don't want you to go your separate way tomorrow only on the off chance our paths might cross again in Rome."

"But you have your trading organisation to run," Olsar countered. "Lucia wishes to seek a new life for herself, Marcus and Caris, wherever that may be. At the moment it's likely to be Rome, but who can tell? The Gods will decide what is to happen to each of us."

"In a sense that's what I'm trying to say. Last night I saw this beautiful Goddess enter my hut to tell me she'd decided to come to save me."

He looked at the slightly embarrassed Lucia, who gave him a comforting smile.

"Amongst all the homes I need and use as I travel the Empire the one I always return to is a villa I have in Antium. You will know of Antium, Olsar. Nero had a villa there. The town is known for its temple to the Goddess of fate, of luck both good and bad. She is Fortuna. She is the Goddess I pray to watch over me. When I'm staying in my villa I go to worship and pray to her in the temple. I repeat what I said. Last night she, in the form of you, Lucia, came to me and saved me. Forever more you will be Fortuna to me. I feel that as long as you are part of my life in some way, fate will always be on my side."

"I don't know what to say," Lucia replied, looking confused.

"At this time I only ask that we can tread the same path for the foreseeable future. Let's travel together for a while. Like you, I'm heading south to the main port of Massilia and the area around there to look for horses to trade in."

"You deal in horses?" Lucia asked, suddenly excited at what she was hearing. "I know a young boy who would be delighted to hear that. What kind of horses?"

"All sorts, mostly to supply the army. Cavalry officers are always willing to pay well for a special mount. I even supply the best horses to the teams at the Circus Maximus."

"What are you suggesting we do tomorrow?" Olsar asked.

"We go back to Lugundum for me to re-provision. While we're there we can talk some more about the future. At the very least we can travel together down to Massilia. You can board one of my ships there to take you directly to Rome if that's what you still want. Or you can stay with me in my large villa experiencing life in the southern part of Gaul for a time."

Olsar looked at Lucia with questioning, raised eyebrows. She smiled back, nodding her head excitedly.

"Back to Lugundum it is then," Olsar stated. "It's a town I would like to see more of rather than just pass through. I'm not sure what Caris will have to say about having to ride back to where we've already been."

Chapter 52

Governor Cerialis hadn't gone on to disappoint Julius since the first meeting after his arrival. He seemed to Julius to have grown in his new role. The pompous, arrogant soldier had become the measured, enthusiastic statesman. In addition, his desire to begin an early campaign against the Brigantes hadn't been reduced by his other tasks, those of dealing with the administrative and political challenges he faced in the Province. Therefore, it was with considerable optimism that Julius had approached a meeting with him to agree the final details of the strategy to invade the Brigantes' territory.

"I was pleased to find the Army in such a healthy condition, Julius. It's a credit to you considering the short time you've had to restore discipline here."

"Thank you, Governor. I'm confident the Legions will perform well in the coming battles and skirmishes with the rebels."

"What about our auxiliary forces?"

"We've successfully levied the tribes throughout the Province. The total number at our disposal is at least equivalent to the number of men we're taking with us in our four Legions. Not only that, I've insisted we were supplied with the best warriors available. We've been giving them training in recent weeks."

"What about the attitudes of those tribes which are in closest contact with the rebels?"

"I've recently visited the two main tribes to the south of the Brigantes. They've both had their own problems with Venutius in recent times. They won't cause us any trouble as we pass through their lands. They've committed to helping us by providing supplies and keeping our supply lines open from the south."

"Then we're ready to begin our campaign. What's your assessment of our enemy?"

"As you know, the Brigantes are made up of a collection of a number of smaller tribes. I've been having discussions about them with their deposed Queen, Cartimandua."

"Remind me again what the background story is concerning her husband. I remember some parts but not all of it."

"While we were fighting the civil war Venutius took advantage of the instability being caused. He and Cartimandua had divorced. She'd been the overall ruler of the Brigantes. He seems to have gained a majority of support among their tribes for a rebellion, against her wishes. He deposed her and she sought refuge with us at Viroconium. She still hopes she'll be able to reclaim her throne once we've put down the rebellion."

"Why has the rebellion lasted so long? I'm led to believe it's been going on unchecked for nearly two years."

"Governor Bolanus was unwilling and incapable of doing anything about it."

"Has the Queen been helpful to you in return for our protection?"

"She has indeed. Venutius only has a majority of the tribes supporting him. Those who were against his adventure have taken no part in it so far. She's told me which tribes will tend to be sympathetic to us and where they're based. That will give us considerable advantage in deciding which territory to concentrate on capturing."

"Now it's my turn to brief you. My plan is quite simple and it's helped by what you've just said about Cartimandua's assessment of Venutius's weak support amongst some of his tribes. Simultaneously, we shall attack from two fronts. You will head north and then east from your base at Viroconium, I shall strike north and west from a base I know very well at Lindum. The key will be speed of attack. The quicker we absorb his territory the weaker he'll become. He will have to defend on two fronts, a difficult task for any military leader. Our main goal is to capture or kill Venutius. Cut off the head of the snake."

"I agree," said Julius. "Hopefully, Cartimandua's view of what could happen will prove to be correct. She believes that in the end Venutius will face a rebellion of his own. She thinks that if our demonstration of power is impressive enough he will eventually be deposed by their own people."

"Not too soon, I hope. Let us each have the glory from at least one thrilling battle."

Julius continued with his consideration of the task ahead.

"The territory as a whole is divided into two by a range of hills running north to south. Do you want us to concentrate our efforts entirely on our own side of the range?"

"Initially yes, but I believe the hills don't reach to any great height. At this time of year, they shouldn't cause us any significant difficulty if we choose for strategic reasons to cross them to join our forces together. For instance we might combine our total forces to provide the show of power Cartimandua thinks would hasten the end of Venutius. Which brings me to my last point. It's vital the lines of communication between us are vigorous and safe. Put someone in charge who you can trust.

"So! What about timing?" Julius asked. "The Army is ready and eager to begin."

"Then we both move out at dawn four days from today."

*

The spectacle of the mass of legionaries marching proudly past him caused Julius to recall the day when he'd watched a Legion march through these gates at the fort of Viroconium once before. Then he'd been a young eager tribune, envious of Governor Paulinus, sitting proudly astride his horse taking the salute from his magnificent men departing in formation. He was now more than ten years older. He wondered if the battle-experienced General had thought then as he did now. His main objective was for a quick and easy end to this war.

He waited until he'd spent enough time accepting the salute to satisfy his staff officer, then he returned to his headquarters in the fort. He would leave two days later to join his Legions when they had established their first major temporary fort in enemy territory. He decided to speak to Cartimandua and asked his staff officer to bring her to him.

"Have you considered my suggestion that you accompany me on my campaign? I still think it would prove very useful to both of us."

"I'm still not sure," Cartimandua replied. "I will need to reunite my people when that treacherous former husband of mine is defeated. Riding into our territory at the head of the all-conquering Roman Army would be seen as treachery by those who support him."

"And if you aren't seen to be involved in ridding your people of a false leader you will be viewed as a weak puppet of Rome placed over them when the Army leaves. You'll be a target for some other tribal chief to depose you again. We might not want to intervene again then, as long as there's peace."

They stared at each other, both knowing the decision was not an easy one for her.

"What part will I play if I go with you?"

"Queen of the Brigantes, coming to save her people from disaster. You will take a full part in any negotiations we may have with tribal leaders, either opposing us or thinking of welcoming us. You could certainly help with interpreting some of the stranger accents we encounter the further north we go."

"I don't think I would impress many of my people if I'm seen to be a mere interpreter on the staff of a Roman General," the Queen countered with a show of annoyance.

"I'm sorry if I misled you. You'll be treated with the obvious respect and dignity deserving of a queen. That will be by myself and the whole of the Army at all times. When I mentioned the need for an interpreter I meant one or more members of the small staff you brought with you would play that role directed by you. You will have the best facilities we can provide bearing in mind we shall be continually on the move. Of course, you will dine with me and my officers at all times. I will be seeking your help and advice constantly."

Julius waited for a question or comment from her. None came. She stared intently at the floor.

"Is there anything else I can say to help you with your decision?"

"Nothing! I have made it."

"And it is?"

"I shall come with you, but I shall hold you to account for the promises you've made today."

Chapter 53

The beautiful Province of Lusitania could have been considered a paradise, apart from one thing. The summers were full of endless days of unbearable heat. Even cooling breezes sometimes coming inland from the mighty ocean to the west brought little relief. The rich citizens of the main town and port of Olisipo had a partial answer. In fact it was copied by many of the wealthy land owners throughout the Province. They were able to seek some respite by spending as much time in the summer months as they could in the cooler hills and mountains to the north. One such citizen was Catus Decianus, otherwise known as Alcimus Leonius, since his arrival in the Province a few years previously.

The sudden appearance of a new estate owner from elsewhere in the Empire had caused a considerable if only temporary excitement in the fashionable, gossipy circles of Olisipo. The interest in Decianus, Alcimus to them, had been heightened by the fact he'd been able to buy one of the largest and normally one of the most productive estates in the Province. It was generally agreed that he must be very rich.

The interest began to wane after a short while, mainly because the man led a reclusive life. He showed no interest in becoming involved in any way in the social or administrative activities of the Lusitanians. Some had tried to find out his background. The best that could be identified was the he'd become very rich in some far-off Province. Where precisely that had been had never come to light. Some thought that it was Thracia, while others were sure it was Dacia. After a while people had given up trying to get to know him. That was how Decianus had planned it from the start.

What Decianus hadn't anticipated was the other problem life in

Lusitania presented. It was so ridiculously boring for a man like him. There wasn't an Amphitheatre to speak of. He'd taken a look at it when he first arrived, only to burst out laughing at the pathetic size of it. Even if he decided to give it a try he would stand out amongst the small number of provincials attending. That was not what he wanted. Worse was when it came to chariot racing. There was no sign of any track where it could be held, not even a 'circus minimus'.

Because of his need to be reclusive he was denied the other main interest in his life. Drunken orgies had been an acceptable and popular entertainment in Rome, albeit if mainly for the rich and important citizens. Some of the best such occasions he'd attended had been organised by some of the most influential and respected members of the Senate. However, his favourite memory was of the one occasion he'd managed to get himself invited to an orgy at Nero's villa in Antium. It was on the occasion of the festival of the God Bacchus. Sadly, all he had now were those memories.

Nevertheless, he'd managed to distract himself so far by concentrating on restoring and expanding his estate. As expected, he'd found he owned a large number of slaves who on the whole were of the normally unremarkable type. Whether it was the heat or the recent lack of an owner making demands on them, they had become extraordinarily lazy. He soon rectified that. The worst were quickly sold for nominal prices while the rest were flogged into action.

There were two main products from the estate, an excellent deep red wine and olives. The wine was in demand throughout the Empire. At first he couldn't produce enough of it. He'd been able to buy extra vineyards from neighbours. Lately, he accepted he'd expanded this asset as far as he could for the time being. Frustratingly, that was also the case with the unglamorous production of olives.

Fortunately, he'd hit upon a new venture mostly by accident. The horses owned by him had to be treated in the same way as his other neglected asset, the slaves. However, while he quickly sold the worst, flogging proved not to be the permanent answer with the rest. Therefore, he sold them all. It meant he had to look at purchasing replacements. What he'd found surprised him.

He could buy the work horses quite cheaply, whereas personal steeds were extremely expensive. He soon realised why. The horses bred here were war horses, famous throughout the Empire, coveted by the Army and civilians alike. He remembered Nero having one. The horse Caligula had intended to make a Consul, when he'd become completely insane, was white and could well have come from here. Realising their commercial potential, Decianus had used every trick at his disposal in acquiring several stud farms. He'd even started one on his own estate.

This had presented him with a difficult problem. The lines of distribution for both his wine and olives were well established. However, he needed to develop his own contacts if this new venture was to give him the returns he knew it was capable of. Unfortunately, this came with a lot of risk. He would have to leave the Province to establish links with the main dealers in this exclusive trade.

He eventually decided it was worth the risk. In the two years since he left Rome his appearance had changed considerably. He'd grown a full beard, something he'd never done before. He'd cut his hair very close to his scalp to cope with the heat. His skin had turned very brown through constant exposure to the sun and his more active life had reduced his weight considerably. Perhaps most important of all, he'd worked at speaking with a very pronounced Lusitanian accent as the key part of his disguise.

So, he was boarding a ship in Olisipo bound for Massilia. He'd learnt that the main distribution point for his horses throughout the Empire would be from that port. He needed a contact there who he could trust, one who would give him a fair price for his horses. One slight worry he still had was that he might be recognised when he went there.

The very slim chance of this happening was increased because the main trader recommended to him was a man called Felix Pontius. He'd met him briefly once or twice when he was in the Treasury. If he recognised him, he would have to be quickly disposed of before any harm could be done. This thought reminded him of the need to prepare another escape plan to a similarly remote Province if he was going to risk exposure in the future.

Looking at four of his best horses being loaded onto his ship, his mood was lifted. This man Felix was unlikely to pay any attention to him when he saw these magnificent beasts.

*

"I would like to stay here forever, Mama!" Marcus shouted as he galloped past Lucia and Caris.

He was helping Olsar to move Felix's horses from the grazing fields lying close to the bank of the large river that flowed south into the town of Massilia. It lay just a short distance away. They'd almost finished their task of herding them into their corals for the night.

"He would be happy living anywhere that included horses," Caris suggested, smiling broadly. "What about you, though? Is this where you would like to live?"

Lucia didn't reply.

"You know Julius will come looking for you eventually. He'll find out from his friends in the Legions that you're here. I know he wouldn't be happy living on this farm."

"He may never come. He's off fighting another war by now. Where will he be sent to next?"

"You know very well he won't rest until he finds you, don't you?"

"He's married. He has a wife. Let's not talk about this anymore. I just have to decide what's best for Marcus, myself and you. Indeed! What about you? I've seen the way Felix looks at you," Lucia teased.

"Don't be silly, and don't change the subject. I know you too well, Lucia. You couldn't be happy here with or without Julius. In just a few years Marcus will be a cavalryman fighting on some far frontier of the Empire. I will say no more to annoy you. However, Felix will want to know your intentions soon. What does Olsar want to do?"

"He's returning to Rome, or to be more precise to Julius's home. He needs to be with his child. I can see him living there for a while. They're the nearest thing to a family other than us."

"That means you could go your separate ways. That will happen for certain if you stay here."

Olsar came riding over, closely followed by Marcus.

"These horses are all in wonderful condition. No wonder Felix trades successfully in them."

"Can I ask him if he will sell this one to me, Mama?"

"Let's not discuss that now," Lucia replied. "We need to get back to the farmhouse. Felix is back and he'll want us to share a meal with him."

*

Soon after the meal had ended Caris received a quick glance from Felix who used his eyes to suggest he wanted her to leave with Marcus. She made the obvious excuse that Marcus had had a tiring day and needed his rest. She left with him.

"I'm glad we're alone," Felix began. "You've lived and worked here with me for a while now. What's your answer? Will you accept my offer to make this your home? You can continue to help me with the horses as you're doing now. You're the best horseman or woman I've ever seen. We can talk later about all the other things I can offer you all."

Lucia looked at Olsar. They both had known this moment was coming and had agreed he would answer first.

"I feel I've found a friend for life in you, Felix. Your offer is something I could never have dreamt of a few years ago. But I must turn it down."

"But why? I know you've been happy here."

"For me, the timing is wrong. I have a little girl in Rome who I barely know. I've hardly shared any time with her since she was born. I want to go to her, to see what life she's made with Julius's family before I make any decisions about the future. I owe her that at least."

"I understand. In that case, I realise there's something I should mention to you if you're going to see the Agricola family. I was in Rome recently and heard some sad news. Julius's wife died recently."

Olsar stared at Lucia, who shared his look of complete amazement.

"I thought you must be unaware of it. If you're to visit them it's important you know."

"What happened?" Olsar managed to whisper. His eyes continuing to search Lucia's face. She just stared ahead of her, hiding any emotional reaction she may be having.

"All I know is that she died of a fever. It was a double tragedy for her family. Her father died of the same disease."

Felix turned his attention to Lucia.

"What about you, Lucia?"

She continued to stare, giving no indication that she'd heard him.

"Lucia! Are you listening?"

"What! I'm sorry, Felix. What did you say?"

"I asked you for your future plans."

"For me it's the timing that's a problem also. But there's something additional to that. I left Britannia for a new life. We've told you we are Iceni, and about us being warriors in that rebellion. You know we became slaves, gaining our freedom later. I fought in the Arena in Londinium to be able to make a new life. The problem is I haven't had the chance to find it yet. It may well be here or somewhere like this in the future. I just need to continue on to Rome to carry on searching for the time being."

"That sounds to me like my own Goddess Fortuna is putting her faith in the real one."

They all laughed and it broke the emotional tension that had been building.

"When do you plan to leave for Rome?"

"As soon as possible now we've come to a decision. We shall sail directly there. The hardest part will be persuading Caris to climb on board a ship again!"

"You realise we're not really parting," Felix insisted. "If you're going to Rome I shall arrange for one of my properties in the city to be made available to you for as long as you want. I shall give you a document to take with you to my people there, instructing them to take good care of you until I arrive. Then there's my villa in Antium, my trading businesses in the city, my dealings with the Circus Maximus, and many other things. Somewhere in there we'll find something that will allow us to continue working together."

"I certainly hope so," Lucia added reassuringly.

Olsar nodded enthusiastically to show that would be his wish also.

"Mentioning the Circus Maximus and horses reminds me of

something," Felix continued. "I'm expecting a ship in tomorrow from the Province of Lusitania. It's long overdue. It will be bringing a new horse breeder from there, wishing to establish contact with me. I've asked him to bring some of his horses for me to sample. While I'm dealing with him you can talk to some of the ships' captains down on the wharfs to choose the best ship and make some arrangements for your voyage straight to Rome. Be sure to pick one of my captains."

"Are you sure you can't come to Rome with us, Felix?"

"In a short time, when I've found horses I can bring back for the Circus Maximus. I will come to find you all then."

*

Decianus wasn't surprised no one was there to meet him when the ship docked. It was early morning and, according to the captain, unfavourable winds had meant they were several days overdue. Once his horses had been off-loaded, and secured on land to await the arrival of Felix Pontius, he'd left the crowded dockside to arrange a place to stay for the following few days.

The inn which the captain had suggested was barely acceptable, but it was as good as he could expect, being so close to the busy waterfront. Having deposited his personal effects in his grubby little room, he went downstairs to wait for one of the ship's crew to come for him. He didn't have to wait long. A crewman appeared in the doorway.

"The captain says Felix Pontius has arrived with two others and they're inspecting your horses," he shouted angrily. "You should come immediately. Those beasts are attracting a lot of attention and getting in the way of unloading the rest of our cargo."

In different circumstances, Decianus would have had the man flogged for daring to focus his anger on him. Instead he just signalled his acceptance of the message and rose from his stool. Soon after he left the inn, he became aware of the crowd surrounding his precious cargo. He could just about see three well-dressed people, two men and a woman in the centre. Presumably one of them was this trader, Felix. The rest of the throng, by their appearance, were obviously either crewmen from the many ships moored in the harbour or slave dockworkers.

Having got to within shouting distance, Decianus suddenly stopped in his tracks. It was because he recognised Agricola's Brit, Olsar with the trader. *How could that possibly be?* he asked himself. Whatever the answer to it was, his concern about being recognised had suddenly reached near panic proportions. Olsar had met him too often in Rome for him to take a chance he wouldn't recognise him now.

His alarm was immediately replaced by a state of shock and disbelief. Standing next to Olsar, gently stroking and calming one of the horses, was Boudica's daughter. It couldn't possibly be, he told himself. She undoubtedly died in the war the same as her mother. She would have been in the thick of the battle, slaughtered like the rest of those scum. He must be mistaken. He edged a little closer to get a better view. He hadn't made a mistake.

Now he had a real problem. She had good reason to recognise him whatever his disguise. He was thinking he would have to walk away, leaving behind those beautiful animals. There must be other traders he could find at a later date to start again. He took one last look. It was her for sure. Even dressed as a high-class Roman lady, ten years older than the last time he saw her, she still had that unique savage beauty.

His withdrawal was momentarily delayed when he noticed a change in what was happening. Boudica's daughter had just given the older man a kiss on his cheek. With a wave of farewell she'd dragged Olsar by his arm, moving away down the docks. Decianus changed his mind. He joined the back of the crowd, keeping his eye on the two of them. They were continuing to stroll along the docks gazing at the ships moored there.

Eventually, he came alongside the trader.

"So, you like my horses!" he cried above the noise. "There are plenty more where they came from."

"Ah! There you are," Felix replied. "As good as these?"

"I can guarantee it."

"You'll have to if we're to do business together on a permanent basis."

"We can't talk here with this noise," Decianus shouted. "We need

319

to be alone. I have a room at an inn close by. Please follow me?"

*

It didn't take them very long to come to a preliminary agreement.

"If I'm to pay the high price you're asking I need to have them for a few days first. I need to take a closer look and to test them."

"I understand. That's perfectly reasonable."

"Now we have an understanding, I have to go to find my two companions. I would like you to come to meet them. I'm sure you'll like them. We all share a love of horses."

"Perhaps another time," Decianus replied, hoping he hadn't given away his concern by answering too quickly. "I have to meet other traders in the short time I'm here. They aren't horse traders, I hasten to add. Perhaps another time. Who are they, these companions of yours?"

"They're new friends. They bravely intervened to save my life recently when I was attacked by bandits on my way here from Lugundum."

"Do they live here?"

"Oh, no. In fact they're looking for a ship at this very moment to take them to Rome tomorrow."

"Why Rome?"

"Olsar has family there. Are you familiar with Rome?"

"Not really, I've been there once or twice."

"Then you probably won't know Senator Agricola and his son Julius. Olsar is a close friend of Julius."

"I'm afraid those names don't mean anything to me."

"Rome is a big city!"

"You said there were two."

"Lucia is going there to find a new life for herself and her young son. She's a truly remarkable young woman."

"In what way?"

"She's a former slave who is now a Roman citizen like you or I. She fought as a gladiator in the Arena in Londinium before setting out on this journey of discovery. I understand she's also a close friend of Julius."

"She sounds like a very challenging woman."

"You really should meet them both."

"I'm sure I will one day. Perhaps when I next go to Rome I shall pay them both a visit. If you'll excuse me I would like to retire to my room. I've had a long journey."

"Of course!" I'll contact you here in a few days when my examination of your horses is complete."

*

In the quiet of his room, Decianus was reflecting on what had happened and what he'd learnt. He couldn't help but come to the conclusion that Julius Agricola would have met this Lucia originally when she was with her mother. He finally remembered what her name was at that time. She was called Linona, not Lucia.

To be close friends he must have known her for some time. Amazingly, he mustn't have disclosed her true identity or she would be dead by now for her wicked treachery. Why hasn't he? He began to realise this information was a weapon he could use to get his revenge on his deadly enemy. Not only that, it could well be the means by which he could get back into Roman society. He would have to think hard and long about this. Whilst it was extremely useful information to him, it could place him at great risk if he used it too hastily.

Chapter 54

Queen Cartimandua proved to be a much more important ally to Julius than even he'd imagined she would be. As soon as they'd entered the western lands of the Brigantes she immediately began to re-establish contacts with her own tribal supporters to gain information on rebel numbers and locations to give to Julius.

Cartimandua accepted that Venutius's support for his rebellion, after he'd overthrown her, had come from most of their tribes. However, the majority of the warriors answering his call were from the more numerous and aggressive tribes across the hills in the east. This was a weakness in the enemy that Julius and the Queen had discussed and both wished to exploit.

The effect of this on the military situation had been that there were only a small number of limited skirmishes in the west. As Julius's Legions made their confident way both northwards and towards the rising lands to the east, there wasn't any sign of large forces of warriors eager to do battle with them.

However, this absence of any significant opposition meeting him didn't come as a total surprise. Very early on Cartimandua had informed him that Venutius had reacted to the invasion of Roman Legions as she would have expected. He'd first learnt of Cerialis's forces approaching northwards in the east. Not realising it was part of a two-pronged attack either side of the hills, he hastily gathered the main bulk of his followers from both the east and the west to go to meet Cerialis. Hence the lack of any significant numbers of the enemy here in the west.

The dilemma Julius faced was whether to go to join his forces with the other two Legions. He would still have to leave most of one of his Legions behind to contain the enemy here. He didn't particularly favour splitting his forces at this early stage until he was sure what kind of enemy threat he faced. An urgent message to Cerialis, asking for a description of the military threat from Venutius's advance, hadn't yet received a reply. He decided to trust Cartimandua even further than he'd already done. He explained his concerns to her.

"I'm afraid I can't help you with your decision," she advised him. "I can see the problem you face. But, Venutius has a strong hold on some of the tribes even here in the west. If you were to take a large proportion of your army away, they could seize the opportunity to try to inflict a serious defeat on your remaining legionaries. I won't mislead you with foolish optimism, Julius. Our futures are too closely bound together."

"From your estimates of the number of followers he could have brought together at such short notice, he should still have double the numbers Cerialis has in any first battle. However, our seasoned legionaries and auxiliaries will be able to resist him. What I choose to do will depend on what sort of defeat is inflicted on him. I've decided to wait for a reply."

"And I shall send out instructions for me to be told of any news of fighting that takes place over there," the Queen added.

*

Two days later the two of them met again, as planned, to review the situation.

"I have what I think you will regard as good news from the east," Julius said excitedly.

"So have I. If it's the same as mine, then I have mixed feelings about it. Seeing my people suffer gives me no pleasure. But ridding them of this traitor is essential. Please tell me what you've heard."

"There's been a battle. As I predicted, Venutius was defeated and with heavy losses. Cerialis doesn't give me very much detail of what took place. However, he does tell me the rebels have dispersed in two main directions. He will pursue those heading north and east. That leaves those heading west for me to deal with. He doesn't know which way Venutius has fled."

"I know," replied the Queen bluntly. "He's heading our way with some of his surviving warriors hoping to regroup and rebuild. He will be a little wiser, but not enough to discontinue his rebellion. His next attack will be against you. This time he will be a little more cautious."

"Then I will make my preparations. If I can attack him first, I will do so. If you can find his whereabouts it would make that possible."

"I shall see what I can find out. I still have many supporters in these tribes here, maybe more so now. Even those who gave their support to him at the outset of this rebellion may be beginning to realise the mistake they've made. We shall soon find out."

*

Early the following evening Julius received a request from Cartimandua to meet him in her campaign tent. He was a little surprised since they were due to have their routine briefing session early the following morning.

"I've nothing to tell you of any significance that's different from what I was aware of yesterday," Julius stated as soon as he joined her. "However, I hope you're going to say you've received a message telling you where Venutius's hiding place is to be found?"

"I've got more than that for you. I've received this."

Cartimandua bent down to unwrap a bundle of cloth at her feet.

"You've never met my former husband, but I can assure you this is the head of the ex-king and traitor to us both, Venutius."

"Who's sent this?" Julius asked with a puzzled expression lingering on his face.

"It's just arrived with a message to me from three of our senior tribal leaders. Two of them will admit to you they've given Venutius their reluctant support in the past. Nevertheless, they are waiting a short distance from here, wishing to surrender to you on behalf of all the tribes in the west. They will come here to submit only to you. They require your commitment to negotiating a peaceful end to this war. I've given them an assurance that you are an honourable warrior, as indeed they are. My future, my life depends on me not being mistaken about that assurance."

"Send for them. You have a long life ahead of you."

Cartimandua's face showed her relief.

"Both of us need to get to those fighting in the east, to finally end this rebellion," she added.

"Once I've received the surrender of these tribes, and I'm confident we have peace here, I shall ride to Cerialis to help him bring the rest of the fighting to an end. I shall need at least one of those tribal leaders to come with me, one who is known to any retreating warriors we may meet on the way. I don't want to have to fight my way through to him."

"I understand. There's one of the three who is as well-known and equally regarded as Venutius was by those in the east. I'm sure he'll go with you."

*

"Well, Julius. I appear to have gained a famous victory at the start of my period as Governor of this interesting, if very demanding Province."

"It's your victory, but you've given Vespasian the triumph he desired to go with a defeat of the Judaeans by Titus. You'll be well rewarded."

"As will you, I shall see to that."

"I don't need a reward for merely having done my duty here. However, there's one thing I would ask from you."

"Name it."

"The swift crushing of this rebellion will be an example to all the other tribes in this Province. It delivers a message similar to that when we put down Boudica's revolt ten years ago. We can now enter a period of stability in this Province."

"I agree! You haven't said what it is you're asking for."

"The Army is well trained and disciplined. It has just proved its total loyalty to you. I'm no longer needed in the way I was when Vespasian sent me here. The Legates will give you all the support you need. I would like to be released from my position to allow me to return to Rome."

"You surprise me, Julius. Is there still a lingering problem between us?"

"I think you already know that isn't the case. I have two reasons. Firstly, I would like to continue to work more closely with Vespasian. Secondly, the news you brought me about their mother has made me realise I wish to see my children. I accept this isn't what a military commander wishes to hear from his young subordinate."

"Maybe not, but I understand the reasons for your request. The problem we both have with what you're asking for is that Vespasian appointed you to this important position himself. We know that I'm his brother-in-law but that wouldn't excuse me removing you without his agreement. I have an answer though. I will send you to Rome to describe for him in detail the nature of our victory. I will also send him a message giving my full support for your request for a permanent recall. It will tell of my gratitude for the vital part you played, particularly getting our loyal ally Queen Cartimandua reinstated. You can argue your own case with him. Knowing you as I do, you'll persuade him to grant your wish."

"I'm grateful to you."

"Give me a day or two to make arrangements to cover your loss and then you can be on the road to Rome."

Chapter 55

"This reminds me of the town house in Londinium," Caris shouted. "Except that it wasn't built on two levels like this one. Can you hear me clearly down there?"

"Of course," Lucia answered. "When you've finished come down straight away. I think Olsar will be leaving shortly."

She looked at him for confirmation. His raised eyebrows and forced smile showed he was.

"Are you sure you don't want to come with me?" he asked. "Lucius and Procilla will make you very welcome, and I want you to meet my Sarah."

"So, who would I say I am? Julius's old enemy, then his friend and then for a while something much more. Maybe there will come a time to explain all that, but it isn't now. I hope you can bring Sarah here to meet us. It's time Marcus had a friend who is more or less his age."

"I'll bring her with me to visit when I come back in two days. I could possibly return with more than Sarah. Julius's children are of a similar age. Three friends are better than one. Marcus would welcome that, I'm sure."

"Welcome what exactly?" Marcus wanted to know. He'd just entered the house from the street outside.

"Do you remember the General in Londinium?" Lucia asked.

"Of course!"

"Well, his family live in a villa and farm not very far away. His children are there. So is Olsar's daughter."

"Can we go to live there with her, Olsar?"

"I'm afraid it's not that simple."

"Why do you ask?" Lucia asked defensively. "We've only just arrived in Felix's house. Don't you like it?"

"I don't! We're crowded next to lots of other houses. The streets are full of people and there's nowhere to ride. To add to that, the stable for my horse is a long way away."

"I agree with Marcus," said Caris, arriving at the bottom of the stairs. "It's very generous and helpful of Felix but we need space, open fields."

"And we'll have them," Lucia declared. "However, for now we begin our life in Rome here in this house. In the meantime, Olsar is leaving."

*

Olsar was surprised by his emotions when he approached the villa. He had an overwhelming feeling of returning home. His last turbulent ten years had made him wonder many times if he would ever find a peace to compare with that which he'd experienced in his family's tribal lands before the rebellion. With the earlier brief life with Selima and the rest of Julius's family he'd almost achieved it. He wondered how he would be received after his latest spell of time away.

His heart missed a beat when he saw the woman standing with Procilla and his daughter, Sarah, on the villa's steps. For that one brief moment he wanted to believe it was Selima. It wasn't, but she looked so much like her. His eyes then concentrated on Sarah. She was clinging to Procilla, while staring at him. He knew she recognised him.

Dismounting, he walked slowly to stand in front of them, his eyes fixed on his little girl. It was a gesture that resulted in no one appearing to want to speak immediately. He held out his hand to Sarah. Hesitantly, she let go of Procilla, creeping forward to grasp it. Olsar brought her to him, pressing her close to his chest. Procilla moved to join and caress them both. Olsar knew he was home.

Procilla drew away slightly to welcome him back. She introduced the other woman as Miriam, Selima's older sister. Then, taking hold of his hand, she led him into the villa. Miriam and Sarah followed closely behind.

"I'm sure you've lots to say to us," Procilla began when they were all seated, "especially to Sarah. However, before you begin, let me tell you more about this remarkable young woman. Did you think you recognised Miriam, although you've never met her?"

"If I'm honest, my initial unguarded reaction was to think you were someone else," he replied, speaking to her directly.

"You mean my Selima, don't you?" Procilla replied with the sort of broad smile he'd become very familiar with over the years.

"I do. You look so much like her, Miriam."

"Weren't you expecting to see me here?"

"Not as I rode up the drive to the villa. That's why I was startled."

"But you knew of me?"

"Yes! Julius had written to me about you when I was serving in Gaul."

"Did he explain how I came to be here?"

"Only very briefly. I'd like to hear more."

"In a moment perhaps. There's one thing I'd like to add before that. Although I'm told there's a strong resemblance between us, I am in fact ten years older than Selima."

Olsar felt a sharp pang of regret at her way of referring to his wife as if she were still alive.

"Perhaps part of the reason I was surprised to see you was that it hadn't registered you were permanently living in the villa. That's now very obvious. I noticed Sarah grab hold of your hand when we walked up the steps."

"Now let me tell you of my past."

Miriam took a while to describe what had happened in her life. She concluded by explaining why she'd decided to live and play a full part in the life of the villa.

"We now have three young children to control between the two of us," said Procilla. "I don't know what I would do without the help of Miriam."

Olsar noticed what he took to be a rather shy, slightly embarrassed look on Miriam's face. Sarah unwittingly changed the subject.

"Will you be going back to fight a war again?"

"I'm no longer a soldier, Sarah. I will be spending my life with you now."

"Will you be living here with us?"

"That will depend on a lot of things. First of all I want to talk to you, for us to get to know each other better."

This time it was Procilla who changed the subject.

"Where was Julius when you last saw him?"

"He was in Londinium preparing to deal with unrest in the north. He told me he hopes he'll be able to return to Rome when that's been dealt with."

"Let's hope that's soon. Did you hear of Domitia's death?"

"Only very recently. How are Julius's children?"

"They're fine. They and Sarah have become inseparable."

"I would like to see them again. And there's also Lucius and Fausto."

"They're all somewhere in the grounds of the villa or the other farm buildings. Let's all go to find them."

*

Alone in his room later that night, Olsar felt that the day had gone better than he could have hoped for. Lucius and Fausto had been as happy as Procilla to see him. He'd spent a lot of time with Sarah but none of it alone. That would come later. However, he could already see she was growing into a happy carefree chid. She appeared to have established a close bond with Miriam. That could be a problem in the future if he wanted to take Sarah to live elsewhere.

Spending the rest of the day in the company of Miriam, he'd soon realised that, although she bore a strong resemblance to Selima, she was a very different woman. He was confident he wouldn't fall into the trap of treating her as a second Selima. The start of a new day couldn't come soon enough.

Chapter 56

Olsar broke his promise to return to Lucia and the others in two days. His stay away had stretched into four days. Not only that, his intention to return with Sarah hadn't proved possible. He entered their new house a little sheepishly, wary of the reception he thought he was very likely to receive from both Lucia and Caris. He guessed correctly.

"Lucia!" Caris cried. "We have a stranger come to visit us. I can't say I like the look of him."

"What's his name?" Lucia shouted from the upper floor.

Caris looked down her nose at him.

"Well?" she demanded.

"Tell her I'm called Olsar by my friends."

"He says he's referred to as Olsar by his friends. He looks to me to be the type who would have difficulty maintaining them for any length of time."

Olsar began to laugh and Caris gave way to a slight chuckle. Lucia came down the stairs to join them, smiling broadly.

"You deserved that," Lucia chided. "We are still mistrustful of this overwhelming city. We began to think you may have come to some harm. By the look of you we worried unnecessarily."

"I apologise. I can explain."

"Then sit down and tell us what you found."

"Sarah was understandably a little cautious of me. But we very quickly found each other. We've been talking non-stop all the time I've been there."

"How did Julius's parents behave towards you?"

"The same as before, very welcoming. However, they did present me with one big surprise."

"Which was?"

"I told you both some time ago that the wife I lost was their adopted daughter, Selima. I discovered that her older sister has been living at the villa."

Lucia looked surprised, Caris unmoved.

"We know she exists, but you've never told us anything about her," Lucia reminded him.

"That was because I didn't know any detail about her past myself until three days ago. I knew Julius had met her, but we'd never really discussed her."

"Well at least you're here now. Caris and I have some news of our own for you. Felix suddenly appeared yesterday."

"And he quickly began trying to organise our lives again."

Lucia laughed at Caris's false display of indignation.

"We told him you were late returning to us, and hoped it would be today. He's waiting for us to join him at the Circus Maximus."

"Why there?"

"He's brought those four horses from Massilia. He's taken them there. He wants to show us the stables and racetrack."

"That won't be new to me. I've been there before. I once saw Nero almost kill himself on the track."

"Well I haven't! Caris, please take care of Marcus until we return."

*

Lucia had prepared herself to be surprised by the Circus Maximus but not in the way it happened when the two of them arrived. Expecting Felix to be waiting for them, they were in fact greeted by four heavily armed guards when they attempted to enter the stable area from the street. An explanation that they'd been invited by Felix was no help to them. They were told to stand against the wall just inside the entrance. When they'd been secured there by the drawn swords of three of the guards, the fourth strode off into the depths of the stadium.

"What will happen if Felix can't be found?" Lucia demanded of the guard closest to her.

She got no reply, only fierce stares from all her captors.

"This is humiliating," she whispered to Olsar. "What do you suggest we do?"

"Considering we didn't bring any weapons with us, there's not a great deal we can do at the moment."

Lucia's growing frustration and alarm disappeared immediately with the sight of Felix approaching at speed out of the gloomy interior. He was roaring with laughter.

"It's my turn to free you two from ruthless bandits," he cried. "Watch closely and you'll see them put away their swords and withdraw at the terrifying sight of me."

Felix, slightly breathless, eased down to a slow walk to cover the last few paces to join them. He gave a wave of dismissal to the guards.

"You may think this is funny, but I don't," Lucia muttered.

"I can see from your grin that you at least have been enjoying yourself, Olsar. Being a military man, you understand the need for perimeter security."

Lucia glared at both of them in turn.

"I apologise, my angry Goddess. I shall try to be a little more serious. I should have told the guards to expect you. At the same time I could have warned you how closely the horses of the Circus are protected. Each of these animals is worth the price of many slaves. The next races will be taking place in a few days' time. Fanatical enthusiasts exist in all the factions. That's what we call the teams and their supporters here in Rome. Those enthusiasts are very capable of doing harm to their competitors' horses or chariots, given the opportunity. It's happened here in the past and will happen again unless we take the precautions which you've just experienced. Am I forgiven?"

Her gentle, playful punch aimed at his chest gave him her answer.

"Good! Follow me. I want to re-introduce you to my four new friends."

They were taken to the stables used by the White faction. Each faction had its own area set apart under the terraces of the vast stadium for them to maintain and prepare their horses and chariots.

"They are the same four white stallions you were inspecting in Massilia when we left, aren't they?" Lucia asked excitedly.

"They are indeed."

"Have you sold them to the owners of the White faction?" Olsar asked.

"I am the owner."

"Is there anything in the Empire you don't own?" Lucia teased.

"Yes! My heart since I met Caris, but don't tell her," he joked. "So! What do you think of my Lusitanos? That's what I've decided to call them and all the others I intend buying from this new breeder from Lusitania. That's the one I met in Massilia. Unfortunately, you didn't get the chance to meet him before you left."

"They are magnificent!" Olsar replied. "I've seen others like them elsewhere in the Empire. They're sought after by many Legates and tribunes, but more so by cavalry officers. They are strong, fearless, disciplined and obedient. They make the perfect warhorses."

"Those qualities are just as important in a chariot horse. When I win races with these four, all the other factions will want to buy the same from me."

"Will you sell to them?" Lucia asked. "Wouldn't it be unwise to let them use the same horses to compete with you?"

"Of course I will let them have some at the right price, but they won't be quite as good as the ones I keep for my faction," he replied with a grin.

"Trained carefully these beauties will make a chariot fly round this track despite its length," Olsar suggested.

"That's why I've brought you two here today. I want you to take control of all the horses and charioteers in the White faction."

"Why us? You already have your existing charioteers and horse trainers."

"True. But I've seen the way you two work with horses to bring the best out of them. I know you will do that with my Lusitanos, better than anyone else. In addition to that, from what you've told me of your past, both of you were virtually born and raised in a chariot. Which brings me to my often drunken charioteers. They cause me more problems than my horses, particularly when I'm not here. You're both fearless leaders. You'll bring much-needed discipline to them. And finally, the presence of you, Lucia, my personal Goddess Fortuna, will continue to bring me good luck. That is no bad thing when running a chariot racing faction. What do you both say?"

Lucia spoke her concerns before Olsar had a chance to speak.

"That sounds wonderful, but I'm not sure if this is what I want to do with my new life. I don't know if I want to be party to providing entertainment before a vast audience in an Arena again. I thought I'd left all that behind in Londinium."

"My first reaction is to say yes," Olsar added. "I've seen enough of war and brutal death in battle. On the other hand I don't think I could be happy with the quiet life of a farmer either."

"Don't give me your answers just yet. I have a further surprise for you. A chariot and horses are waiting on the track so you can get up close to what you would be taking control of. In addition to that, I still like to take a ride in a chariot around the track, despite my age. I want you to come to watch me enjoy myself."

*

Breaking out from the dark interior under the terraces into the hot white light of the open stadium momentarily partially blinded all three of them. When her full sight returned, Lucia was met with the awesome view of the race track stretching away into the distance in front of her. Felix had led them out at one end of the track where the chariots would normally enter on a race day. Waiting patiently for them was a swarthy charioteer who was standing quietly whispering into the pricked-up ears of two horses hitched to his chariot.

"The chariots are drawn either by two or four horses on a normal race day," Felix explained. "Sometimes, on very rare occasions thankfully, it can be rather unwisely as many as ten. I may be brave at my age, but I'm not stupid. I'm using only two to go around the track today. And they're the calmest and most easily controlled of all my horses."

He took a quick glance looking for reassurance from the charioteer, who gave it to him by gently double-tapping each horse's neck.

"This is way beyond anything I imagined," Lucia admitted. "For some reason I expected the track to be oval in shape, something like the Amphitheatre I fought in. Instead, it consists of just one very long, very wide straight running area there and back with a tight, complete turn at each end."

"It's designed to allow for speeding chariots to compete aggressively side by side over a long distance," Olsar explained. "However, the tight turns at either end demand the ultimate in skill and temperament from both horses and charioteer."

"I like that description, Olsar," said Felix. "Stamina is also an important characteristic required in both man and horses if they are to win races together. The track is nearly half a mile long, making it almost a mile to complete a lap. A race normally consists of five laps."

"How wide is the stadium, and how many chariots does that allow for in each race?" Lucia enquired.

"It's approximately one hundred and thirty paces wide. The thin island running down the middle is so the track is clearly divided into two separate racing areas. The answer to your other question is it varies. There are four factions and each faction can enter up to three chariots per race. However, as the owner of this precious asset, I have to be mindful of the fact that there can be many races in one day. Careful management of horses and charioteers, so that they can last the full day, is therefore all part of the challenge and thrill of race-day."

"Remember to add that this can be a brutal spectacle," Olsar suggested.

"Indeed!" Felix continued. "To be a winning charioteer it's often necessary to obstruct and even damage your opponents' chariots as much as it is to outrun them. As a result, there are many crashes into each other and the central island. Injuries are an all too frequent occurrence. Even deaths happen from time to time. Nevertheless, let's hope that I survive today. It's time for me to do a circuit."

Felix climbed onto the back of the chariot, taking hold of the reins. He returned Lucia's look of concern with a broad grin before moving off at a gentle pace. His one full circuit was completed at a decent pace without ever fully extending the horses. He drew up alongside them, more than a little breathless.

"I really should accept how old I am. Who's next? I see two eager faces looking at me."

"I'll let you go first," Lucia offered. "That way the horses will really be warmed up when it's my turn."

Olsar chuckled and, bowing to her, took hold of the reins from Felix. He took the first of his two laps carefully to get used to the feel of his horses. The second was at full pace, easing off as little as possible around the turns. His only comment before handing over the reins to Lucia was to admit it had brought back so many thoughts and memories of his youth.

Lucia's first thoughts could well have been sad memories of her past, especially her mother, as she urged the horses away. If that was the case, they would have been quickly swamped by the sheer joy of the feelings of power and speed, the thrill that risking her life again provided for her. After three laps she could see the other two getting restless, so she came to a halt in front of them.

"What do you think of that experience?" Felix asked. "It probably doesn't compare with gladiatorial combat, but it certainly makes you very aware of your surroundings."

"I know what you are up to, Felix. This is all part of a clever plan to get me to accept your offer. You can't fool me."

She stood still for a long, uncomfortable silent period, staring at him with apparent anger. She broke the silence, a wide smile spreading over her face.

"But you've persuaded me. I accept. Let the three of us talk details."

Chapter 57

One of the practices that had been established during the years when Nero ruled by fear was that observed by returning Generals and Governors to Rome. The first point of call was at the Royal Palace to see the Emperor. To go to see family, friends or members of the Senate, even to go to pay grateful homage at the temple of a favourite God or Goddess was taken as a personal insult by Nero. He saw it as a demonstration that he was considered less worthy, less important to the Empire than he considered himself to be. He judged it to be a treasonable act.

No such requirement was insisted upon by Vespasian. Nevertheless, it was understandable that someone like Julius would continue behaving in this manner. It was why he'd made straight for the Palace to give his report. As it was still only late morning, it gave him every chance he could reach his father's villa by early evening at the latest. Vespasian, already in a good mood, was cheered by the sight of Julius being shown into his private rooms.

"Welcome back, Julius. I was very surprised when a member of my staff told me you'd asked to see me. I only received the first communication from Cerialis a few days ago telling me of your great victory together over the Brigantes. He said you were on your way to give me a much fuller verbal report of the campaign."

"That's what we agreed was the best way to get an early, detailed account to you describing what happened."

"Even so, I suspect that there's more to this than that. Cerialis mysteriously added a short comment in his letter, supporting a proposal you have to put to me. What is it you have to say?"

"That's correct. When the rebellion was over and the Brigantes had our ally their Queen back to rule over them, I considered that I'd completed the task you set me in Britannia. I asked Cerialis to release me so I could return to Rome. Quite rightly, he pointed out that since you had appointed me before he became Governor he didn't really have the authority to grant my request. He suggested I make it directly to you. His message is to let you know that he's in agreement with my request. Before you ask, there's no animosity between us. In fact we worked very well together in the time we had."

"I understand all that. What I haven't heard is why the urgency in your request."

"No doubt you've heard that my wife died recently."

"I have. However, in the past you confided in me that she'd been your wife only in name for years. Why should her death be a factor in your request?"

"My children are being cared for by my mother. During the Nero years I saw little of them. I would like to change that in the future. In addition, I would like to concentrate on the non-military aspects of my career. I think I can bring my wide range of experiences from these last ten years and use them in your service by being a loyal member of the Senate."

Vespasian didn't reply immediately. When he did he stared straight at Julius.

"Your request is unusual, not for the reasons behind it but in the timing of it. I have to consider what is best for Britannia. Cerialis has promised me a further, much fuller assessment of the future state of his Province since this latest rebellion has been defeated. I'll decide on your future when I've received that."

"Thank you, Sir. Do you want me to go on to give you my report?"

"I have other things planned for today. Come back in the morning. We shall have plenty of time available then. At the moment, I've someone to introduce to you."

He summoned his private slave across the room to whisper in his ear. He left, returning almost immediately with Titus.

"Meet the new Commander of my Praetorian Guard!"

Taking hold of Titus's outstretched hand, Julius gave his friend a puzzled shake of his head.

"It's true," admitted Titus.

"But why?"

"Think about it!" Vespasian answered. "Recent years have shown that the second most powerful man in the Empire has been the Commander of the Guard. Caligula was assassinated by the Guard. Claudius was then appointed by them. Nero had a selection of Commanders who betrayed him. I needed somebody I could trust completely. It was either my son or you, Julius. Titus returned from the rebellion in Judaea before you came back from Britannia so he got the position."

All three of them laughed at Vespasian's exaggeration, but they all knew it told of the bond that existed between them.

"I hope we can get together soon to catch up with what's been happening to us at either end of the Empire," Titus suggested.

"I'm here tomorrow to give my report. Perhaps we could meet after that."

"In the meantime you have a family to surprise with your unexpected return," said Vespasian.

*

The welcome that Julius got was very similar to the one Olsar had received. Procilla, Miriam and his two children greeted him at first. He then had a quiet talk alone with Alexus and Livia. He had a quick chat with his father, promising him a full description later of his time in Britannia. Later he sat down just with Procilla to talk in detail about the death of Domitia and how the children were coping without a mother.

"The news of her death came as a great shock to all of us, particularly those two. They suffered at first as any child would, but they've come to terms with it. Miriam has played her part in helping me to take care of them."

"What is she like?"

"She looks like Selima, but is different in some important ways. Though she's also strong and energetic, she does things with a quiet determination. She's patient and has a persuasive manner rather than an inclination to overwhelm you as Selima did when she wanted you to do something. The result is that the children have come to adore her. That's especially true of Sarah, something that is a comfort to Olsar."

"Is Olsar here?" Julius blurted out in amazement.

"But of course, you won't know he's come back, and I haven't had an opportunity to tell you in the turmoil of your sudden arrival. He's only just returned himself."

"Did he bring anybody with him?" Julius asked guardedly.

"Not here to the villa, although he told me he's brought friends with him to Rome.

"Did he say where they were staying?"

"No. Why do you ask?"

"I may know them. I'd like to see them."

"You can ask him yourself. He should be returning home shortly."

She proved to be correct.

*

"It's good to see you, old friend," said Julius, reaching out his welcoming arm.

Olsar took a firm grip of it.

"I'm pleased to see you home safe too, Julius."

"Forgive me. Where is she? Please tell me she's well and here in Rome."

"The answer is yes to both."

"You must take me to her now!"

"I understand. We shall be there quicker if I take a fresh horse."

*

Caris was downstairs with Marcus preparing the evening meal when Olsar led Julius into the house. Hearing someone enter, she came out of the kitchen. Her short, sharp shriek at the sight of Julius brought Lucia rushing down the stairs. She froze when she reached the bottom. No one spoke a word for a long while. It was Julius who spoke first.

"I knew I would find you again. You've never been out of my

thoughts."

Lucia didn't reply.

"I came to look for you as soon as I could. You must believe me."

"I do," Lucia replied finally, her voice breaking with emotion.

"Olsar and Marcus," said Caris quietly, "there's something in the kitchen that you can both help me with."

When they were alone again it was Julius who spoke first.

"I have experienced fear many times, but it has never been the sort of fear that I'm feeling at this moment. It's a dread that you've changed, that you no longer have feelings for me."

He got no immediate response from her, only the appearance of a few tears moving down her cheeks. Eventually, swallowing hard to gain some control, she spoke.

"Nothing has changed. I've been waiting and hoping you would come to me."

Julius closed the gap between them in three urgent strides. They clung to each other, kissing with a passion and desperation caused by their time of separation.

"I have so much to say to you," he murmured in her ear.

"And so have I, but only when we're completely alone."

"This type of house has the bedrooms upstairs, I believe. I can't imagine what that looks like. Would you like to show me one of them?"

Lucia kissed him hard before she took hold of his hand, leading him to the stairs.

*

In the middle of the night Julius whispered onto the top of her head, which she was resting peacefully on his chest.

"I have to report to the Palace in the morning. I'll return as soon as I can."

"I may not be here myself until late in the afternoon. I shall explain why tomorrow. We both need to get some sleep."

"We've got the rest of our lives to sleep," he replied, lifting her head to kiss her lips tenderly once more.

Chapter 58

"What was your reaction when my father told you of his insistence that you are to be escorted into the Senate by the Commander of his Guard?" Titus asked.

He was talking to Julius, who was accompanying him on the short stroll from the Palace to the Senate House.

"My father was a little surprised, and I suspect disappointed, that he couldn't introduce me himself. Lucius has always had ambitions for me, chief of which was that I eventually joined him in the Senate. I think he's always dreamt of proudly presenting me there to his old friends. However, his mood soon lifted when I told him that the Emperor had insisted that he would be given a seat next to him today."

"My father is keen to impress upon the Senators that he rewards loyalty like yours. There are some amongst them who were supporters of Galba and Vitellus during our year of civil war. He still has to win over some of those old nobles who look down on a previously insignificant family like ours. He also wants us to appear side by side, his Generals who put down rebellions in Judaea and Britannia. It heralds the new power he's bringing with him as Emperor."

"Will Domitian be there?"

"Of course! My younger brother never misses an opportunity to suggest he's a candidate to be the next Emperor, a rival to myself."

"You know he and I are not the best of friends."

"My loving brother does mention from time to time that you upset him when he was enjoying his time as Nero's guest."

Julius smiled at Titus's sarcasm. Their conversation ended just as they entered the Senate House. Everyone except Vespasian and Domitian rose to greet Julius and Titus when they came into the debating chamber. However, not everybody cheered enthusiastically. Searching the rows of Senators, Julius's gaze paused at his father's beaming smile before moving on to spot the scowling face of Bolanus. He couldn't resist the urge to respond with a puffing out of his chest in a gesture of pride and satisfaction.

Once the formal speeches welcoming and honouring Julius had been completed there followed two short debates before the session came to an end. That gave Senators the opportunity to mingle informally. That included Bolanus.

"So you finally got round to taking some of our legionaries north into rebel territory. I stay in contact with my friends and their families in Londinium, don't you know. They keep me informed. I understand it was Cerialis who fought the only battle before the enemy surrendered to him, and that your contribution was minimal."

"Believe what you want," Julius replied. "Now, please excuse me. I'm having lunch with the Emperor and Titus."

Julius walked away with Bolanus's next remark ringing in his ears.

"Your father tells me your Brit has also returned to Rome."

*

In far off Britannia a very much smaller meeting was taking place in Londinium.

"Thank you for coming to see me so quickly, Paulus," said Tullius Marellus. "I've received some good news from Bolanus."

"I hope it's what I've been waiting so long for."

"It is! He tells me that Julius Agricola and his Brit are in Rome."

"What about that woman? Remind me what she was called," Paulus demanded.

"Her name is Lucia. He doesn't mention her. However, wherever those two are she won't be far away."

"I need to leave without delay."

"That's what Bolanus has ordered. There are instructions in his letter telling how you can find him. He insists that you keep your identity secret when you get there. He doesn't wish to become openly associated with your task. His own position in the Senate is still precarious."

Chapter 59

Life to Miriam seemed to be a series of almost impossible challenges. Each one started with pain and suffering of one kind or another. When the challenge was finally met and the hurting was at an end there followed a period of calm, sometimes even happiness, before the next trial came along. At a very early age she had faced the realisation that she was a slave, and that she might never be free. Soon afterwards she'd watched her parents die together.

That was quickly followed by separation from her baby sister when they'd been sold to different families. She had conquered slavery, liberating her spirit. She'd used her joyous freedom to search for her long-lost sister, only to experience the distress of discovering where she'd lived and died before she could ask for her forgiveness.

Once more, pain had been driven away by the friendship of Procilla and her family, but more especially by the love that she and Sarah had found. Olsar had returned to threaten this newfound happiness. The next challenge had arrived.

Her anxiety was increasing each day as she saw the bond between father and daughter, neglected for so long, growing ever stronger. It wasn't the growing love between them that threatened her. It was the strong possibility that he would leave on his next adventure, taking Sarah with him, and out of her life forever. Somehow, she had to confront this latest test. Sharing her feelings of anguish with Procilla was a good start.

"Can I talk to you, Procilla?" Miriam asked nervously.

"Of course. What's the matter? You look dreadful. Where has your happy smile gone?"

Taking a while to explain her dilemma, Miriam reminded her of her past before opening up her heart and bursting into tears.

"I don't know what I would do if I lost her. I know she loves me in return."

"This may surprise you, but I've been having similar thoughts and concerns," Procilla added. "When Selima died the Gods gave me Sarah to replace the enormous loss in my life. I have the same dread about what Olsar might do to take her away. But I recognise he's suffered throughout his life and has found real happiness with her. For once I'm at a loss as to what to do."

"He spends a lot of time with those two women in the city," Miriam noted. "Do you think he might go to one of them?"

"Not from what Julius has hinted at. He described the younger one as Olsar's close friend but nothing more. The other one is my age. So I don't think we should have any concern there."

Miriam allowed herself a quick smile.

"I've heard Julius tell you that Olsar is having a wonderful time training the charioteers and horses. So I try to convince myself that he won't have any immediate thoughts of leaving us."

This caused Procilla to move the conversation in a slightly different direction.

"What do you think of Olsar?"

"What do you mean?"

"I think you know what I'm asking. He's a very handsome man, and is roughly your age."

Miriam's face turned a bright red.

"I was beginning to think as much! Another woman can recognise the signs long before a man gets a first inkling."

"Please stop! He was married to my sister. It would be wrong for me to have feelings for him."

"It doesn't work that way. Feelings are feelings. You can't just wish them away as you appear to be trying to do. I ask you again but with a slight difference. What do you feel for Olsar?"

"When I saw and spoke to him on that first day on the villa steps he excited me in a way that I've never experienced before. Since then

I've seen nothing but a wonderful, kind, caring man in him."

"I agree with everything you say about him and I've known him for a few years not a few months. If I was half my age and free of my Lucius, Olsar would be in great danger."

This time Miriam allowed herself a chuckle.

"Please don't say anything to him."

"I won't. But let me remind you that you've spent your life fighting with all your strength for what you've wanted. Don't you dare give up now."

*

"Will you be staying tonight?" Lucia asked.

"Yes, of course. But it doesn't have to be like this."

"As you've told me many times in these past few weeks. My reply is just the same. I'm not ready yet."

"For what? To surrender your independence. To commit to the future. To have to put up with me all of the time."

"For the moment I wouldn't be comfortable moving into your villa where your wife lived until recently."

"Then we will get a villa of our own."

"That would be an even bigger step for me. I want to share the rest of my life with you. You just have to be patient with me."

"Our family villa is very much like the one where you lived near Londinium. Will you at least come with me to see it and to meet my family? You're spoken of frequently there."

"Who by?"

"Olsar talks about you all the time. He can hardly avoid it since he chatters on about what the pair of you are involved in at the Circus."

"Who do they think I am?"

"Olsar describes you as a friend of us both from Britannia."

"That will do for the time being."

"My mother is no fool. She'll be thinking already that either Olsar or I am involved with you."

"She sounds like an interesting woman."

"She is. Come and meet her!"

"Ask me again in a week or two. I may be ready then."

Julius grinned and pulled her to him.

*

"What have you been doing today, Sarah?" Olsar asked.

"Miriam has been teaching me how to sew. She can do anything."

"What do you think of her?"

"What do you mean?"

"Do you think of her as just a teacher?"

"Oh no! I think she's just like Grandma except that I've known Grandma since I was born."

"What else does she do for you?"

"Everything that Grandma does, especially when she's not around or too busy. She does the same for Alexus and Livia. She's very kind and patient for all of us."

"So I've noticed. You know she's your mother's sister, don't you?"

"Yes. Grandma told me a long time ago. Does she look like my mother did?"

"Very much so. Are you happy living here, Sarah?"

"Of course! This is my home. I'm even happier now that you've come back to me."

Chapter 60

Bolanus didn't enjoy being in this poor district of the city. If he was recognised as a wealthy man he could expect to be robbed and otherwise poorly treated. For that reason he'd dressed in clothes more of the type a slave might wear rather than his toga. As a result he was able to move quite freely and unnoticed to reach Paulus's rented rooms on the second floor of an apartment building. He had also chosen a time when it was dark, reducing further the possibility that he would be recognised.

"I didn't expect to be treated like this in Rome," Paulus moaned. "We look after pigs better than this in Britannia."

"I've explained to you why you have to stay here. Julius is a favourite of the Emperor. If things go wrong, you will be able to disappear back to Londinium without any difficulty. I couldn't. Agricola would want to blame me, to have Vespasian crucify me. I wouldn't be able to melt into the background as you would."

"I shall make sure things don't go wrong."

"So tell me what's happening. You've been here a week. What have you discovered?"

"I'll remind you that I'm interested in dealing with Olsar and Lucia first for what they did to my father and brother. Agricola comes third after those two."

"I've accepted that reluctantly."

"Therefore, I've concentrated on those two all week."

"What have you decided?"

"She dies first."

"Why is that? Olsar killed your father."

"Olsar is either working at the Circus Maximus or he's at the Agricola villa. It would be difficult for me to ambush him. I'm not stupid enough to go up against him in the open. I will have to give more thought to how I get my revenge with him."

"What about her?"

"She's different. She lives in a small house. She returns there every evening to an elderly woman and a young boy. That makes her very vulnerable. My plan is to take those two hostage during the late afternoon. With those two at my mercy she will have to surrender to me. When I've tortured and killed her I will kill the other two and make it look like a robbery. Then I will give more thought to Olsar and Agricola."

"When will you be ready?"

"I'm ready now."

*

"Caris! There's somebody at the door," Marcus cried. "He says Mama has sent him from the Circus."

"Tell him to come in and close the door," she shouted from the kitchen. "I need to clean my hands. I won't be a moment."

Paulus put his hand over Marcus's mouth, dragging him further into the room to wait for Caris. She only took two steps into the room before she could see what had happened.

"Don't make a sound or do anything silly. If you do, I will slit this boy's throat."

"What do you want? Is it money?" Caris murmured.

"You will soon see when Lucia arrives. I want you both to sit down."

Taking out a length of rope from his clothing, he instructed Marcus to tie Caris to her chair. When Marcus finished he inspected what he'd done.

"That is very good. I want you to do the same with your mother when she comes home. If you fail to tie her properly, boy, you will be the first to die. Do you understand?"

Marcus nodded and began to cry.

"Quiet!" Paulus ordered.

Marcus reacted by crying even louder.

"I said be quiet!

"I can't help myself. Can I go upstairs to get my toy cavalryman and horse from my bedroom? They will help me."

Paulus took a moment or two to think, during which Marcus's wailing got louder.

"I shall count to twenty. If you get back after that, I shall slice off one of your ears to present to your mother."

Marcus had returned by the count of nineteen. His crying had ceased.

"Now we all wait quietly," Paulus ordered.

*

"I'm home! Where are yo…?"

"Don't do anything hasty. Close the door and take a seat next to her," Paulus shouted, pointing at Caris. "This knife I'm holding against your son's throat is very sharp and I'm very clumsy."

"I will do exactly as you want," Lucia replied coldly. "Who are you and what do you want?"

"I shall tell you when you are secured to that chair. Boy! Tie her up."

Paulus satisfied himself that Marcus had done a good job, then told him to sit to one side, out of the way.

"You asked who I am and what I want. The answers to both questions are simple and ones you will understand immediately. My name is Paulus Marellus, brother of Gaius Marellus, who you butchered. As to why I'm here, it must be obvious. I'm seeking justice and revenge for your crime against my family. When I've dealt with you I will go looking for your friend and fellow murderer, Olsar. Finally, it will be the turn of your lover, Julius Agricola."

"You must be mad," Lucia growled. "If that is your reason for being here, your hatred can only be aimed at me. Let Caris and Marcus go."

He ignored her plea.

"I've rehearsed this moment so often, imagined how I would prolong your agony. Now it has arrived I want only to see you dead."

He moved to stand over her.

"Don't attempt to kick me or put up any resistance. I'm on my guard for any tricks you might be tempted to try."

He moved his face close up to hers to whisper.

"Prepare to leave this life. You are on your way to Hades."

The knife thrust was placed skilfully, penetrating deeply into the neck, bringing death almost instantly.

Chapter 61

"Come and join us, Julius," said Titus. "You remember Josephus, don't you?"

The two men were relaxing in Titus's private room in the Royal Palace. He may have been appointed the Commander of the Guard but Titus still enjoyed the luxury and privilege of being the Emperor's son.

"Indeed I do," Julius replied, "although when I last saw you your name was Joseph."

"That's correct. The Emperor thought this Roman version was more suitable if I was going to appear at his court on a regular basis."

"When was the last time you saw him, Julius?"

"It was just before Nero called me back from Judaea," Julius replied, directing his answer at Josephus. "You'd been taken prisoner. General Vespasian was interrogating you. If I remember correctly you'd just made the astonishing prediction that Vespasian would become Emperor. It was all the more fanciful because we all knew that Vespasian at that time had no ambitions of that sort whatever. He was a soldier doing his duty for Nero."

"And my prediction came true as I knew it would. Most of you thought I was mad, although there were those who thought I was just trying to save my skin with flattery."

"Some of those are in this room," Titus teased.

"But it came true. I insist I was just divulging what our scriptures were foretelling. It was all a matter of interpretation."

"Maybe so," Julius commented. "I also remember that Vespasian was so intrigued by your audacity that you were spared the execution you deserved. Instead, you became his personal slave. By your appearance and what you say that's no longer the case."

"The new Emperor was so surprised that I was obviously in close contact with my God that he decided to play safe," Josephus joked. "He freed me and made me a citizen of Rome."

"And my father gives him an allowance," Titus murmured, shaking his head in pretend disbelief.

Josephus used his goblet of wine to give a mock gesture of respect to Titus. Julius moved the conversation on to a more serious matter.

"Your people were finally defeated and Jerusalem sacked. How have you come to terms with that?"

"I also predicted that. During the siege of Jerusalem I tried to negotiate with my people on behalf of Titus. I couldn't save them no matter how much I tried."

Julius glanced over to see Titus nodding his head in agreement with him.

"At first, my sorrow at what happened was overwhelming, particularly when the enslaved survivors and the treasures from our destroyed holy Temple were paraded through these streets. I've recovered but the trauma of it has prompted me to begin to write a complete history of my people, culminating in this latest catastrophe. Hopefully, that will bring me some comfort, and understanding to those generations who follow us, yours and mine."

Titus and Agricola remained silent.

"That reminds me," Josephus continued. "I should really get back to my studying and writing. Will you excuse me, gentlemen?"

When they were alone, Titus was the first to speak.

"He's an interesting and clever man. I wouldn't be surprised if he does just what he says he wants to do, even if he's chosen a daunting task for himself."

"I'm sure the part we played will make interesting reading," Julius added.

"So, my friend, you wanted to see me."

Julius told him about his friends who'd recently arrived from

Britannia. He briefly explained how they'd become enemies of Bolanus, who now might seek to harm them, given the opportunity.

"I know of Olsar and the service he's given to Rome," Titus commented. "However, I have yet to meet this Lucia and learn more about her. She obviously means something to you."

"I hope to make her my wife one day."

"Really! You must tell me more, later. What about Bolanus? What would you have me do? Already my father doesn't trust him because of his previous loyalty to Vitellius. I don't trust him because it appears he's becoming a favourite of my scheming, ambitious little brother. I fear Domitian could be a serious threat to me in the future. However, my father doesn't want to hear of any bad feeling between the two of us."

"My problem with Bolanus is that he wishes to see me dead eventually. In the meantime, the harming of those close to me will help to partially quench his thirst for revenge. However, I don't think it would be possible for me to take action against him in the Senate at this present time. Nor am I asking for anything in particular from you except that you keep in mind what I've told you today. I'm on my way to let him know that I'm aware of what he has in mind. I shall threaten him about taking any actions he may be considering."

"I've noted what you've said. Now! How about some wine?"

Chapter 62

"Where did you get the knife from, and how did you know how to use it?"

"Getting the knife was easy, Mama. I know you always keep one under your bed. I just needed to find a way of getting to it. He fell for my sobs and a silly story about my toy."

"That was very clever for a young boy. I can understand you working that out even though you must have been terrified. But how did you know how to place the knife so that it would kill this assassin before he could retaliate?"

"Don't you remember that night when we first got to Gaul? You crept up from behind on that thief who was holding Olsar prisoner. You killed him instantly. I just copied what you did. Nobody threatens my mother's life and lives while I'm around."

Lucia and Caris looked at each other and shook their heads.

"What do we do now?" Caris asked.

"There's not a lot we can do until morning. The three of us just can't carry a bloody, dead body through the streets of Rome at night, even if we knew what to do with it. Tomorrow we go to the Circus stables. When Olsar arrives, he will tell us where Julius is and ask him to join us. Together we shall all decide what we do."

*

Walking side by side, Olsar and Julius marched at pace through the entrance into the Circus. Julius was wearing his newly acquired Senator's toga bearing the broad red stripes. The guards, recognising this, stood to one side giving him the customary salute. A stern-faced Julius didn't respond, his angry eyes staring determinedly ahead of him.

Olsar guided him to the stables where Lucia, watched by Caris and Marcus, was inspecting one of the horses. Being the first one to see them approaching, Marcus ran excitedly towards Julius.

"You should have seen me deal with Mama's enemy, General. You'd have been proud of me."

"I've told you before that Julius is no longer a General, Marcus," Caris cried.

Ignoring the boy, Julius walked straight to Lucia to take her in his arms.

"Olsar tells me it was a member of the Marellus family."

"He said his name was Paulus."

"That was the youngest son. I thought they might send someone to try to kill you out of a need for revenge, but not this soon."

"It wasn't only me that he intended to kill. You and Olsar were on his list also."

"I'm so sorry for not anticipating this attack."

"We were all guilty of that, not just you."

"How could they have discovered where you were living this quickly?" Olsar asked.

Julius pulled away from Lucia to pace to and fro in front of the horses' enclosure. He paused only briefly to ruffle Marcus's hair.

"You did very well, young soldier. It seems as if you not only saved your mama, you probably saved the lives of Olsar and your General also. I'm more than proud of you. I shall ask General Titus to make you an honorary member of the Praetorian Guard as a reward for your bravery."

He continued his pacing until Lucia could stand it no longer.

"What shall we do with the body?" she asked.

"The Commander of the Watch served with Olsar and me during the fire. He's already dealing with it. I can see Bolanus's hand behind this. Unfortunately, with Paulus dead we have no way of directly linking him with a plot to assassinate us all."

"If that's the case," Caris asked fearfully, "what's to stop him trying again with any one of you or even me and Marcus?"

"That's what I've been thinking about. As far as the Marellus family's future involvement is concerned we need have no fear. They are down to two, Paulus's older brother and uncle. When they hear of Paulus's death they won't be too enthusiastic to follow him here. However, just in case I'm wrong about that I shall write to Tribune Livius in Londinium. You may remember him. He was my young staff officer there. He joined Cerialis when I left. It was Livius who informed me that Bolanus was likely to be scheming against us at the time you all left for Rome."

"What can he do?" Lucia asked.

"I will ask him to give Cerialis details of how you and Olsar came to end the lives of Tarquinius and Gaius Marellus. I shall also send an account of what's just happened here. Cerialis will think of a sufficiently painful warning to ensure they forget all about us."

"That still leaves Bolanus."

"True! He's a Senator and I have no evidence against him to enable me to denounce him before the full Senate, which I would have to do. However, I shall let him know that his plot has failed. He will be told that Titus is to be informed of what's happened. Titus will accept my firmly held belief that he's behind it. If anything should happen to any one of you I will hold him responsible through Titus. That will be sufficient for him to rethink his dream of doing any harm to us."

"I'm beginning to feel slightly better about our future already," Lucia confessed.

"To make sure the three of you are absolutely safe in the future, you are all coming to live at the villa with Olsar and the rest of my family."

Caris and Marcus both let out cries of delight.

"We shall have to see about that!" Lucia replied defiantly. However, she was unable to hide the slightest hint of a smile easing into the corners of her mouth.

Chapter 63

74 AD

The large villa garden brought back warm memories to Lucia. Mostly, they were treasured moments that she'd shared with her sister, Flavia, in the very similar garden of Quintus's villa. Flavia had found peace and time to think there in that haven. Recently Lucia had begun to use this garden for the same reasons. On this occasion though the quiet solitude of the warm evening was broken by the arrival of Procilla.

"I thought I'd find you here, Lucia. Do you mind if I join you?"

"Please do!"

"I hope I'm not disturbing you. You seem to like being alone out here."

"I was just thinking of happy times I shared with my sister in surroundings similar to this in Britannia. I still miss her so much."

"I can understand that. Wherever I go in our villa it brings back memories of my dear Selima."

"I wish I'd met her. From what I've been told she was a very special young woman. Olsar has told me of the deep love he had for her."

"It was an extraordinary passion that they shared. That's the problem!"

"What is?"

"It's why I came to talk to you. You've lived with me now for nearly a year. In that time I've learnt a great deal about your past.

One thing that stands out is your enduring love for Olsar."

"If that's your problem let me reassure you that it's the love for a dear friend, or to be more accurate an older protective brother. What I share with your son is the same as what Olsar and Selima had together."

"I know all of that is true. Please don't misunderstand me. My concern is for Miriam. In lots of ways your sister sounds just like her. She is a shy, caring, loveable woman who wouldn't impose herself on anyone. As you know, all the children adore her."

"That's a very good description of Flavia. Marcus worshiped her."

"Unfortunately, that tendency to put others before herself is the problem I referred to."

Lucia gave her a puzzled look.

"Miriam is hopelessly in love with Olsar."

"You saying that doesn't come as a surprise to me. You can see it in her eyes whenever she's in his presence."

"You and I might notice it. Olsar doesn't. Miriam is so different from her sister. Selima wanted Olsar from the start and she let him know it. The poor man didn't stand a chance. You had to have known her to fully appreciate what I'm saying. She became his life."

"Olsar has told me the same thing."

"Therein lies the dilemma. I think Olsar cares for Miriam. I'm not sure how much, but I've noticed how happy he is when they're together. But something is holding him back. Is there something from your Iceni cultural background that can be lingering in his memory? Something that would be inhibiting him?"

"There are no taboos of the sort that you're hinting at."

"Then I suspect it's either a persistent guilt he has for Selima's death, or it's because the man needs Miriam to initiate things as her sister did. You know him. What do you think?"

"Maybe it's either, or perhaps both. Then again, it may be that he just doesn't love her in the way she would want him to, or for that matter, the way a concerned mother or friend would wish for."

The point wasn't missed.

"I know what you are saying, Lucia. However, I'm sure their future is together, I just wish they would realise it and get on with it."

"I suspect you're having thoughts about the future of Julius and myself. Are you?"

"Since you mention it!"

"I thought so. Since we came here to live together, we often talk about what the future holds for us. Please don't let Julius know yet that I've told you this. We're considering getting married when the time is right."

"I knew it! Praise be to the Gods! You deserve each other after all you've been through. Now! How do we make it a double wedding?"

*

Sarah dashed into the villa, tears flowing down her face.

"Miriam! Please come outside. Marcus and Alexus are fighting. Hurry! They aren't playing a game like they normally do. This is for real."

Miriam took hold of her hand, wiping her wet face to calm her down. "Let's go to see what those silly boys are fighting over."

By the time Miriam got to the two brawlers the contest was over. They stood a few paces apart, breathing heavily and glaring furiously at each other.

"Have you finished or are you just pausing for breath?" Miriam asked. "I don't mind which it is. If you want to carry on, Sarah and I can wait until you've finished this ridiculous behaviour, can't we, Sarah?"

The boys remained silent. Their fight had apparently evolved into a contest to see who could outstare the other. Miriam ended that by moving to stand between them, blocking their view of each other.

"How did this silliness start then?" she demanded to know.

"It was him! He started it," shouted Marcus. "He called me a savage Brit."

"That was because of what you called Sarah," Alexus cried back, with just as much force.

"And what was that, exactly?" Miriam asked in a calm whisper, contrasting with their loud protestations.

"He said that, because she is Judaean, she's no better than all the rest of her treacherous, evil people."

"Is that what happened, Sarah?"

"Marcus was wanting us to talk about the recent victories by Julius and Titus. They began to disagree and then they just became angry and started to fight."

"Where is Livia?"

"She's in the garden reading as usual," Marcus replied scathingly.

"Listen to me, all of you," Miriam ordered so sternly that she got their full attention.

"We are all Romans. We may come from different parts of the Empire, and for different reasons, but we are all Roman citizens. I was once a slave and a Judaean. Does Grandma Procilla think she is better than me or Sarah just because she comes from a family of nobles, Marcus?"

There was no reply.

"Answer me!"

"No, Miriam. I didn't mean that."

"Does Julius treat Olsar any differently than he does Felix or his Senator friends because he was once his captive slave, Alexus?"

"No, Miriam."

"No! And that's the last time either of you will speak to each other in that way. Now go to join Livia. A little more reading won't do you two any harm."

*

"Sarah tells me you had to stop the boys fighting today."

Olsar was standing in the doorway to Miriam's room.

"They were just being boys," Miriam answered. "I was just about to retire for the night. Was there something you needed?"

"She also tells me they came to apologise to you later."

"That put an end to it."

"Sarah thought I should come to thank you myself."

"And so you have. Was there anything else?"

"You sound tired."

"I am. It's been a hot, busy day. I've just been to the bathhouse to recover."

"There was something else that my discussion with Sarah has prompted me to mention."

"Which is?"

"I've been happy working at the Circus. However, it won't satisfy me for much longer."

"Why are you telling me this?"

"Felix says he's getting old. He's asked me if I'd like to run his villa and estate in Massilia, even take over some of his trading for him. He wants to retire to Antium."

"That seems like an offer that's too good to refuse."

"It would mean taking Sarah with me. How do you think she would react?"

Miriam took a short while to control her raging emotions before answering.

"She would be devastated. She would be losing her grandmother and grandfather. Then there are the three other children, and Fausto. And finally, there is Caris. She's begun to treat her like another grandmother. She would lose all those who she's learnt to love and depend on."

"Including you."

"Yes."

Miriam could hold back the tears no longer. Olsar moved forward hesitantly. He brought her gently into his arms, her head resting lightly on his chest.

"That's why I told Felix I couldn't accept his offer. I shall be staying here."

Miriam lifted her head fighting back her sobs.

"Do you really mean that?"

"Of course. There was another reason for saying no."

"What was it?"

"I realised that I would run the risk of you not wanting to leave the home and the happiness that you've found here, just to come with me."

"What are you saying?"

"The more I thought about it, the more I realised that I need to have you as part of my life. Just as much as Sarah does, but for a different reason. I think I've felt like this about you for a long time. I just didn't want to recognise those sorts of feelings again."

"What feelings?"

"I can't concentrate when I'm training the horses for thinking about you. I feel a rush of excitement and happiness whenever you're near me. There's so much more, but I'll stop. I'm sorry if I've embarrassed you."

"Please don't stop, you idiot. I've loved you from the moment I first saw you. I just never thought you could love me."

No more words were spoken for a long while afterwards, except for those whispered in passionate reassurance.

*

Lying in the semi-darkness of Miriam's room, Olsar was staring at the dying flame of the small oil lamp on the corner table.

"There's still that problem I have to face," he murmured with a yawn. "I don't want to train charioteers for the rest of my life!"

"That's a problem that you, I, and Sarah will discuss and face together," Miriam said, placing one last gentle kiss on his lips before she rolled over onto her side.

Chapter 64

Travellers on horseback normally remained mounted when they turned off the road to pass through the gates of the villa. A rider would then guide his horse down the centre of the track at a gentle walking pace. This was not only an obviously non-threatening gesture, it also gave slaves the time to warn their master of the arrival of a stranger. In this case, and rather unusually, the rider had dismounted at the gate to walk very slowly the remaining distance up to the villa steps. This had given plenty of time for the master to heed the warnings and be waiting there to welcome his visitor.

This particular stranger's decision to approach on foot would appear all the more intriguing to the villa's owner since he walked with a very pronounced limp. The clothes he wore were very simple and drab. The small horse looked as if it had seen many better days. On its back, immediately behind the saddle, the horseman had strapped a large well-used travelling bag. All of this suggested that horse and rider had spent many days travelling the road.

"Greetings stranger. You're welcome to stay the night if it's shelter you're seeking."

"I intend staying longer than one night," he replied aggressively, speaking with a thick accent.

"I don't recognise you or your accent, Sir. More significantly, I think your behaviour is rather strange and aggressive. So, I'm withdrawing my offer. Leave before I have you chased off my estate."

"You really don't recognise me, do you?"

The change of accent caused the villa owner to halt his hurried withdrawal into his villa. He turned to stare quizzically at the stranger, who continued to challenge him.

"Is it the full beard and long, greying hair that did it? Perhaps it was the accent, or the clothes and the poor old nag. Then there was the limp. Whatever it was, the full disguise was sufficient to deceive my own father."

"Decianus! Is that really you? The voice without the accent sounds like yours, but the rest of you suggests it isn't."

"You've given me the feeling of security that I needed. If my own father couldn't see through this disguise, then I can continue preparing my plan to get back to Rome."

"It really is you, son. Come in, come in. You look as if you need a visit to the bathhouse. While you're at it you should have a shave. I shall have new clothes prepared by the time you've finished."

"I will say no to all three of those suggestions. I want to continue my disguise for the time being. However, I would say yes to a full hot meal and a stable for my horse."

*

"Your disguise fooled me completely at first. It may well have continued to do so for a while longer, but sooner or later I would have realised who you were. You couldn't hope to get away with it at court for very long."

"That won't be a problem. It isn't what I intend doing."

"That's just as well. It's true that many new faces have been added to the Senate and elsewhere since the coming of Vespasian. Nevertheless, there are still many longer serving Senators who won't have forgotten you, even after all this time. They will want to do you harm. As you can imagine, as a former trusted tutor and advisor of Nero I had an uncomfortable period after his death. Fortunately, I had long since retired from his service and wasn't around him when he committed his worst atrocities. That saved me. You on the other hand were by his side almost until the end. I strongly suggest that you return to Lusitania and forget about returning for another ten years."

"Thank you for the lecture, but it really isn't needed. I agree with almost all that you've said. This disguise only has to last until I'm ready to strike."

"At what?"

"Not at what, at whom! I've come to destroy Julius Agricola and maybe one or two others in the process."

"Then you're a fool! Julius Agricola and his whole family have become the favourites of Vespasian and Titus. To make things worse for you, Titus is the Commander of the Guard."

"They won't be the favourites for very long after I disclose what I've discovered."

"It will have to be something of outstanding significance if you're to have any chance of success."

"Significant, it certainly is. Let's see if you agree."

Decianus then proceeded to tell Septimus what he'd discovered in Massilia, when he was horse trading with Felix Pontius. He went on to spend a lot of time describing in detail his experience in Britannia with Lucia when he'd known her as Linona.

"So, you're trying to tell me that the daughter of one of Rome's most hated traitors and enemies has been living undetected as a Roman citizen for years," Septimus exclaimed in disbelief.

"It's worse than that for Agricola. He knew her as I did when she supported her mother both before and during their rebellion. I don't yet know precisely how or when he met her after the war, but he can't have disclosed her true identity to Vespasian. That is treason."

"What is the first thing you intend doing about it?"

"According to Felix, it appears that Julius has not only been close friends with this Brit, Olsar, for some time, but that applies to that witch also. I know through talking to Felix that those other two have moved to somewhere in Rome. I have to find out where they are living before I can begin to put my plan into action."

"Then I have news for you. A while ago, Julius Agricola married a Brit called Lucia. The other one, Olsar, lives with them both on the Agricola estate."

"This is the best news I could have received," said Decianus, almost choking in his excitement. "This means that I only have to concentrate on how to deliver my disclosure to Vespasian."

"Why can't you just reveal who you are and tell him?"

"To get anywhere near him I would have to declare who I am and what I have to divulge. That would have to be to his Guard Commander, Titus. He knows of my past and would not believe one of Nero and Poppaea's henchmen. He would tell Agricola and I would be dead before the day was out. I need to find an ally at court who could guide me through to the Emperor."

"That won't be easy."

"Even so, I have to do it that way or I will have to disappear again. If I succeed I shall be welcomed back, the hero who brought Boudica's daughter to justice."

*

"I've been thinking about our conversation last night," said Septimus. "I have a suggestion to make."

He and Decianus had risen early and were taking breakfast together.

"I've been revisiting our conversation of yesterday also," Decianus added. "I can't believe my good fortune in finding out so quickly where she's to be found. It's even better than that. Marrying her, knowing who she is, compounds Agricola's treason. I must find a way to get to Vespasian."

"That's what I wanted to suggest to you. I think I know just the right person who's likely to be interested in supporting you. From what I hear, he's a Senator who tends to enjoy being an opponent of Julius Agricola in the Senate."

"What's his name? Do I know him?"

"His name is Vettius Bolanus. You'll have come across him years ago. He was a Senator during Nero's time."

"I do remember him. He was a rather insignificant little man, very ineffective at that time."

"That still describes him very well. However, he does have one great advantage for you. It is well known that in recent years he and Agricola have developed an intense dislike of each other. It borders on hatred."

"That's a good start. What's caused it?"

"Apparently, it began just after Vespasian became Emperor.

Bolanus, who had been appointed by the deposed Emperor Vitellius, was failing as Governor of Britannia. Vespasian sent Agricola to shore him up. Despite that, Bolanus still failed. He was called back with great loss of face to Rome, but surprisingly restored to the Senate. His friends say that he believes Agricola used his influence to have him replaced."

"This gets better the more I hear. This Bolanus will understand these treacherous Brits. Is there more? You said their dislike of each other has grown in recent years."

"They constantly oppose each other in the Senate, exchanging insults at every opportunity. There's something else, but so far the gossip hasn't produced any details. Something happened here in Rome a while back that made things a lot worse. They were furious with each other but neither has said why."

"I want to meet him as soon as possible. Can you arrange it?"

"That won't be a problem."

"I want to maintain my disguise until I'm sure he's the man I will use."

"I will arrange a meeting at the villa of a mutual friend. It will be better if I don't attend. Appearing together might increase the chance of you being recognised as my son. Talking of your disguise, let me give you some advice. Drop the limp. It will only draw closer attention to you, something you don't need."

"I agree. It was a last moment addition just to confuse you. I did enjoy it, though."

*

Decianus's arrival at the small villa of Senator Albus, in one of the better districts of the city, was less of an event than the one at Septimus's home. For one thing, the Senator had been warned in advance to expect a rather unusual-looking visitor. It was only because he owed Septimus several favours that he'd agreed to his strange request. The hardest part of doing what was asked of him was persuading Bolanus to attend.

Bolanus, like Albus, hadn't been given any details by Septimus of the purpose of the hastily arranged meeting. However, he was made aware that this stranger had some important confidential, damaging information concerning Julius Agricola. The man had asked that the meeting be kept secret.

"Where is this fellow?" Bolanus enquired.

"He's waiting in my guest room."

"Has he said what he wants?"

"Not a word. However, what he has to say is for your ears only. He says he's grateful to myself and Septimus for setting up this meeting, but he doesn't want me to be present when he talks to you."

"I see. Has he said where he comes from?"

"He didn't reply when I asked him. He speaks with a rather strange accent, and his manner of dress gives nothing away."

"I take it you've had him searched for weapons."

"There weren't any. He may be odd, but he doesn't appear at all threatening. He doesn't have an assassin's physical bearing, whatever that may be. His wide girth and fat jowls suggest he's lived a life of some wealth and leisure."

"Even so, I shall keep my knife close to hand. I think it's time you had him brought in."

*

Decianus took Bolanus's hand, offered to him in greeting. He immediately seated himself on the nearest couch without waiting to be invited. Bolanus, who as a Senator could expect a more obvious show of respect from a mere citizen, looked slightly affronted. Albus excused himself and left, closing the door to his reception room behind him.

"You've asked for this meeting," Bolanus began. "I should at least know your name."

"I will tell you in due course if we can come to an arrangement."

"Then it's money that you're hoping to get out of me."

"Don't insult me!"

"I hardly wish to insult someone I don't know. I have friends for that light relief. If you won't tell me who you are, will you tell me who you represent?"

"Myself!"

"Where are you from?"

"All in due course."

"That had better be soon because I'm beginning to lose my patience."

"I can assure you that it is in your interest to hear me out."

"Then why don't you give me something to listen to? I was told that it concerns Julius Agricola. Is that so?"

"Yes! I'm led to believe that you and he are sworn enemies."

"You don't expect me to admit to that sort of allegation to a complete stranger, do you?"

"What if we are in fact known to each other?"

"Are we? I don't recognise you."

"All in due course."

Bolanus sighed deeply with frustration. Decianus took the initiative.

"Stop me if anything I say is untrue. You were Governor of Britannia when Agricola was in command of the Army there. You were recalled by Vespasian with some loss of face. You've always thought that Agricola was the cause of that. There must have been previous animosity between you for you to think that. The gossip doesn't identify what precisely."

"Is that all you have to pass on to me, gossip? If so, our meeting is over."

"What if I tell you I have information that will bring down Agricola, possibly lead to his execution?"

"Then you should bring it to the attention of Vespasian or Titus."

"You think I'm trying to trap you, don't you? A trick being played on you by Agricola."

"I wouldn't put it past that villain."

"Thank you! Your hatred for him has begun to show. I think it's time for me to reveal myself. I am Catus Decianus."

"Really! And I am Emperor Caligula."

"We didn't meet very often, but look closely. See beyond the beard. Listen how my accent has disappeared. My father set up this meeting today. I have a letter here bearing his seal, confirming what I'm saying."

Decianus threw the document to Bolanus, who read it with a smile.

"From what I recall of your time in Rome when you were working for Nero and Poppaea, there was considerable gossip about your activities, particularly when you were in control of the vast wealth of the Treasury. There was also much mention of the animosity, even hatred, between yourself and Agricola."

"I'm prepared to admit that last part. I would like to see the end of him. If you're prepared to do the same, I shall carry on. If not, then you aren't the man I'm looking for. I shall disappear once again."

"You may carry on. You're beginning to gain my interest."

"I take it that you're aware that he has recently married a Brit. She calls herself Lucia."

"I am indeed. And I would just as soon see her hanging from a cross for the harm she did me in the past."

He went on to describe at length the incidents that occurred in Londinium.

"So, she went from being a gladiator, the favourite of the Arena crowds, to become an assassin of my invaluable clerk and friend, Gaius Marellus. It was only the protection of Julius that saved her from execution."

"Did you ever wonder why he did that?"

"Pure lust. He fell for her the first time he saw her in the Arena. I know I witnessed it."

"What if I were to tell you he knew her years before then."

"What are you saying?"

"He knew her ten years earlier, as I did."

Bolanus was silent, his face frowning in confusion. His expression slowly changed from one of puzzlement to one of growing understanding."

"That was the time of Boudica's rebellion. Did she take part in it?"

"Very much so. She fought alongside the Queen throughout the war."

"How do you know that for sure?"

"She could hardly do anything else. She was her daughter."

"But that means…"

"That he knew who she was when he recognised her in your Arena and said nothing."

Decianus then described the contact that both he and Julius had with Lucia during the build up to the rebellion and their own personal conflict over the handling of the Queen and her daughter.

"So you can see that my hatred for him goes back much further than yours."

"By failing to disclose her, he's guilty of treason."

"Precisely!"

"We mustn't go directly to Titus with this," said Bolanus. "He might just silence us to protect his favourite."

"That's why I sought you out."

"I will have to use the Senate. You must maintain your disguise for the time being. Who else knows your secret, and that you've returned?"

"Only my father."

"We must keep it that way. In future, we shall meet at his villa until such time we decide that we are ready."

Chapter 65

The items to be raised and debated on this damp, cool morning were even less inspiring than the weather. Either could possibly explain the poor attendance of Senators. The Senate Leader carried out a quick count to be sure that there were enough members present for proceedings to commence. Even though that was the case, he delayed the start to allow those usual latecomers, who were still strolling in, to take their seats. It gave time for those already in the debating chamber to circulate, catching up on the latest gossip.

Lucius Agricola was amongst them. His usual smile disappeared when Senator Bolanus crept up alongside him.

"Ah! Senator Agricola. How good it is to see you this morning."

"I wish I could say the same about you," Lucius muttered.

"Dear, dear! We are in a bad mood. Let's hope nothing happens today to make it worse."

"I know what would make it a lot better, but you appear to be staying."

"How unkind of you. Perhaps your son will treat me better when he arrives."

"He won't be coming. He has other things to occupy him."

"What a pity. I wanted to hear his opinion on a matter of interest to me. Nevertheless, you're here. That will have to do for now."

"Thankfully, the Leader is calling us to order," Lucius sighed. "Your friends, for want of a better word, sitting on the far benches, are trying to get your attention."

*

The Senate Leader brought the last debate of the day to an end, and was about to declare that the formal proceedings were over when he noticed out of the corner of his eye that a Senator had risen from his seat with his hand held high.

"You seem to have something extra to say, Senator Bolanus? I'm not sure I shall allow it this late in the day. Is it an important matter?"

"I can't think of one more so! It involves an act of treason against the people of Rome, and in particular our Emperor."

A barrage of questions from the benches caused Bolanus to pause briefly before continuing.

"It is extremely serious since it involves a member of this Senate."

The Leader struggled to maintain control but eventually restored order.

"You must name the Senator and the nature of his offence immediately or withdraw your statement."

Bolanus took a deep breath, searching for Lucius's face amongst the turmoil on the benches.

"His name is Julius Agricola. His monstrous crime is that for years he has been harbouring amongst us one of Rome's worst enemies. In failing to inform the Emperor of this he has betrayed him. I demand that he be tried before the Emperor sitting in this Senate."

He sat down with a broad smirk of satisfaction covering his face. Eventually the Leader was able to have the last word above the noise.

"I need to report this to Emperor Vespasian and the Commander of the Praetorian Guard immediately. You must accompany me, Bolanus."

*

"Thank you both for bringing this to my attention," said Vespasian. "I've listened to your allegations, Bolanus. I want to speak to Julius and his wife before I decide on whether a trial is necessary. The two of you can leave us so that we can consider what you've said."

"What do you think?" he asked Titus when the two of them were alone.

"I'm confused," he replied. "I don't want to say anything until I've spoken to Julius. I'll leave immediately."

*

Nothing was said either by Titus or Lucius as they met on the villa steps. The four guards in the escort remained mounted, letting everyone know their stay would be a short one. Titus made his way into the reception room to join Procilla, Julius, Lucia and Olsar. Titus spoke immediately.

"Lucius will have told you what happened in the Senate today, Julius."

"We've been expecting you," Procilla replied before Julius had the chance to speak.

Titus moved closer to Julius.

"You understand what I have to do, my friend."

"Yes. We are ready. Lucia and I will just need to collect a few things before we go."

"You can take your hand off the hilt of that sword, Olsar," Titus warned. "I'm just as concerned for these two as you are. There's nothing you can do for them at this time."

Olsar did as he was ordered.

"What is to happen to us?" Lucia asked.

"My father and I want to talk to you both first. However, because of the allegations about Julius, and because of who Bolanus says you are, I think there has to be a trial."

"I was Boudica's daughter, as Bolanus claims. However, I am now Lucia, wife of Senator Agricola. I've been a Roman citizen for years."

"I understand."

"Are we under arrest?"

"There's no need for that. I just want you both to be on hand in the city for when the trial takes place."

"Then we shall stay with Felix Pontius. He lives very close to the Senate building."

"We give you our assurance that we won't try to escape," Julius added.

"That's enough for me. We should leave. Go to collect what you need to take with you."

*

When they were ready, but before they left their room to re-join Titus, Lucia clung to Julius as if it was for the last time.

"I suppose I always knew this would happen one day. I just imagined if I was about to die I would be in a position to put up a fight."

"And we are going to do just that, except in this case we shall be fighting for our lives with words. Don't forget that together we are a formidable team."

"How could my identity have been revealed?"

"Maybe it was information that the Marellus family discovered and passed on to Bolanus, a last attempt at gaining their revenge. Whatever is his source, we're about to find out. Are you ready?"

A sad smile and a gentle lowering of her head told him she was.

Chapter 66

The Senate debating chamber was full to capacity as expected. The marble benches, providing seating for the Senators were built in parallel rows, forming a wide semi-circle five rows deep. They were staggered in height, each row higher than the one in front. This allowed an unrestricted view of the debating floor below for all Senators. At the mid-point of the arc, a large marble throne was built into the structure for use by the Emperor whenever he took part in proceedings.

To the right of this, a second much smaller throne was provided for the Leader of the Senate. Even when the Emperor was in attendance, as today, the Leader would still have control of the proceedings. For an occasion such as this, two of Titus's guardsmen were positioned either side of the two large entrance doors. Several others were stationed elsewhere around the inner walls of the chamber.

Since Bolanus had made the request for the trial, he would be making the case against Julius. Therefore, he'd taken up the last seat on the front row at the far-left end of the arc. At the opposite end of the arc the identical seat was occupied by Julius. Lucia, seated beside him, was receiving the wide-eyed attention of virtually everyone in the chamber.

The scene was set and the chamber resounded with the noise of excited chattering. A short sharp fanfare from beyond the entrance doors signalled the imminent arrival of the Emperor. Everyone stood in silence just as the doors swung open. Vespasian entered, moving slowly and directly towards his thrown. His solemn face gave nothing away, his gaze firmly fixed ahead of him. Behind, walking side by side, came Titus and the Leader.

Vespasian was the first to take his seat, followed by Titus. Everybody else sat down, with the exception of the Leader. He waited until all the murmurings had died down before he began.

"Senators! The Emperor reminds us that only Senator Julius Agricola is on trial today. The considerations and decisions regarding his wife will be a matter of Royal decree. Failure to observe that by anyone will not be tolerated."

He waited for his warning to be received and understood before continuing his short address.

"You all know the procedure to be adopted, but it is worth reminding you of it. Senator Bolanus has made a general accusation of treason against Senator Agricola. He will speak first, enlarging on why he has done so. The onus is upon him to make his case using witnesses if he desires. Senator Agricola will then defend himself. When they've finished, the rest of the time will be available to us all for questions and comment before a decision is made. Senator Bolanus, the floor of the Senate is yours."

"More than fourteen years ago," Bolanus began, "in the Province of Britannia, Boudica led a rebellion that caused the death of thousands of Romans. In defeat, she escaped and disappeared. She has never been found. Since then, Emperors and the people of Rome have been denied their revenge against her. Boudica didn't lead that rebellion on her own. She had the help of others. Chief among them was her daughter."

The leader rose to his feet.

"Senator Bolanus! I remind you that only Julius Agricola is on trial today."

"Agricola could have brought her daughter to face the justice of our Emperor," Bolanus continued regardless. "In deciding not to, he's guilty of treason. I have a witness to explain when and why he became a traitor."

He gave a sign to the guard at the door. In strode a clean-shaven, toga-clad Catus Decianus, instantly recognised by many in the chamber. He was greeted by thunderous cries of derision. It took a while for the Leader to regain control. He ordered Decianus to make his statement.

"I was the Imperial Procurator for Britannia before Boudica started her war. Julius Agricola had dealings with her, her tribal chiefs, and her daughter now seated over there. He did so on behalf of the reckless Governor Paulinus, who was away on an adventure leaving most of the Province unprotected. Boudica was determined to use his absence to start her rebellion. I went to her settlement and taught her a lesson. I also took that woman seated over there and her sister hostage to put an end to that Queen's ambition. It would have worked if Julius Agricola had not released them. As a consequence, without anything to restrain her, she destroyed the town of Camulodunum containing the Temple of the God Claudius."

"Why do you think he so disastrously released her?" Bolanus asked.

"His lust for her had already started before the war ever began. That was behind it. He betrayed those citizens of Camulodunum."

Julius shot to his feet, triggering uproar throughout the chamber. The only person to remain seated was Vespasian. A sign from Titus brought a number of his guards onto the open floor. Order was restored with difficulty. Decianus, indicating that he'd finished, was directed to take a seat next to his own by Bolanus, who began his closing remarks.

"I was Governor of Britannia ten years later when Agricola discovered Lucia had survived the war. Because of his lustful desires he chose to keep her identity secret. He's had many opportunities in the last four years to tell the Emperor but didn't. Therefore, I declare that his treachery is twofold. Firstly, his release of the hostages led to the rebellion. Then, knowing her true identity and not disclosing it, he betrayed our Emperor."

He returned to his seat next to Decianus. Both were looking very pleased with themselves.

"Senator Agricola, you have the right to reply should you wish to do so."

"Thank you, Senate Leader. I begin my defence by declaring that, rather than cause that war, I did more than anybody to try to prevent it. I carried out my orders from General Paulinus to the full. I will answer any questions that you may wish to put to me about that.

"I admit that I've kept my wife's original identity secret for a number of years. I use the word original because she is now as much a loyal Roman citizen as any of you here today. I did so for a number of reasons. One is that I felt that to surrender her for possible execution would mean one more unnecessary Iceni death. I have enough of those on my conscience. Another reason was that I feel it is time for Romans to lay to rest this part of our past. Britannia has returned to becoming an important contributor to the Empire. I did fall in love with her, but not in the vulgar lustful way these liars describe it. For ten years I thought she must have died in the war. I recognised her as Bolanus describes. My decision not to expose Lucia was at worst a selfish act to protect the woman I wanted to make my wife. The Emperor knows I would never commit a treasonable act against him."

"You haven't dealt sufficiently with the accusation that you released Boudica's daughters," the Leader pointed out, "and that this action resulted in an unnecessary war."

"To do that, I want at this point to call my wife as a witness."

A number of Senators, particularly those sitting close to Bolanus, jumped to their feet demanding this be denied. The Leader took a sideward glance at Vespasian. He shook his head. It was the trigger that finally released the anger that had been building inside Lucia since the moment she saw the man she hated more than words could describe, re-enter her life.

"I won't be silenced, even by an Emperor. You are about to condemn a man who has spent his life loyally serving his people and Emperors without question. He saved part of this city from fire when the rest of you headed for your villas in the hills. And he helped you to become Emperor."

She glared at Vespasian so hard that she didn't notice Titus gently raising and lowering his hands in a gesture aimed at getting her to sit down.

"If I am doomed for once being a rebel, so be it. But I won't let you destroy this good man without a fight."

The furious Leader was halfway to getting to his feet before Vespasian grabbed his arm to force him down again.

"Let Titus speak," he whispered to him.

"Leader, members of the Senate," Titus shouted above the mayhem. "I have a suggestion. Like Julius Agricola I fought against Boudica. But I wasn't party to the events described by Decianus and disputed by Julius. However, I can suggest a witness who was. In fact he's come from his sick-bed to enlighten us. With your approval, Leader, I shall invite him in."

Quieter now, virtually every face in the chamber bore a puzzled expression, including Julius's.

A bent, old man shuffled through the doors, assisted by a guard. He halted when he got to the centre of the floor. Raising his head, he was greeted by loud gasps from a small number among the Senators who recognised him.

"My name is Suetonius Paulinus. I was Governor of Britannia. I defeated Boudica."

Decianus nearly fell off his seat.

"General!" Julius shouted. "Is it really you?"

"It is, Julius. My illness has eaten away half of me already, but there is still enough of me to denounce this liar."

He turned to face Decianus, who slunk back on the bench.

"I was listening to your lies from behind the doors."

He turned to face Vespasian.

"The truth really is that Julius worked tirelessly for me to try to prevent that war. He had in fact got Boudica to agree to wait to discuss her grievances until my return from defeating the druids. There wasn't going to be a war. She was wise enough to realise the great danger her people would face if she openly challenged Rome. Decianus was specifically warned by Julius on my behalf not to do anything to jeopardise that understanding. Because of his lust for money he sacked Boudica's settlement, first having Queen Boudica flogged and this woman and her sister raped by his soldiers. He did take the daughters hostage. However, it wasn't Julius but a tribune at Camulodunum who had the wisdom to release them in the hope that it wasn't too late. Unfortunately, it was. The irretrievable harm had already been done by this traitor."

He pointed a shaking finger at the devastated Decianus.

"Julius fought bravely in the war. Afterwards we disagreed on the punitive measures I took against the Iceni. He felt I was going too far. He was right and I was wrong."

He turned to face Lucia.

"I apologise for what I did to your tribe after the war. Too many died unnecessarily."

Lucia just stared in disbelief.

"Thank you, General. Please take a seat," said the Leader. "Is that all you have to say, Julius?"

Before he could reply, Titus made another request.

"My investigations produced another witness. He wants to give evidence on behalf of Julius."

The leader gave his approval.

"Felix!" Lucia cried when the witness entered waving at her.

"I think everyone here knows you, Felix," the Leader said with a smile. "You've said you wish to be a witness for Julius. Go ahead."

"I lied. Julius has already been defended. I'm here to talk about Lucia. I understand that you Senators aren't considering her situation today and I shall be in serious trouble."

He turned to face Vespasian.

"However, you will be judging her, Sir. I may not get another chance to say this. A short time ago this woman saved my life. I was taken hostage by a group of bandits demanding a ransom. Fearlessly, she came right into their camp to surrender herself as part of her plan to rescue me. By the way, she was successful."

Laughter broke out everywhere. It lowered the tension, making it easier for Felix to continue.

"I won't bore you all with the details of how she did it. I ask you all this question, though. Who amongst you distinguished Romans would have done that for me? She didn't know me. She only knew I was a Roman citizen in desperate need and she came for me. Is that an act of a traitor to Rome? One last thing before the guards take me away, Sir. I understand you recently had a personal slave, a Judaean. I believe he led a rebellion against Rome like Lucia, in his case even against you personally, before he was captured. You have since freed him and he's now a citizen. I have met Josephus. He will make a good contribution to the Empire. I have said my piece."

Vespasian rose slowly to his feet.

"Sit down somewhere, Felix. I shall deal with you later. Senators! I have heard enough. This has been an unusual case, so I shall bring it to an unusual conclusion. Treason is too serious an act to be ignored and it won't be on this occasion. Treason has been proved and I condemn the traitor to be executed. Guard! Take Decianus to the holding cells at the back of this building until I decide his fate."

A guard did as ordered. Vespasian then commanded Bolanus to stand before him.

"I have had enough of your scheming, Senator. It seems to me that you are a dangerous man to have around. You are to be exiled for life to a small island somewhere very far from Rome. Report to me tomorrow. Get out of my sight. As for Julius Agricola, there is no case to answer. You are free to go. Which leaves you, Lucia."

He raised his voice so that all were sure to hear.

"But for Decianus, you might well have been Queen of the Iceni by now, a trusted ally of mine. From now on I shall regard you as precisely that, treating you with the respect that your position demands. I will let the dust settle for a few days, then I shall see you and Julius to discuss your future."

He paused, searching the rows of seats until he found what he was looking for.

"As for you Felix, you scoundrel, I need a new white stallion. I believe you might be able to supply a really good one."

*

Lucia pulled Julius to one side as the chamber slowly emptied.

"I think you should return to the villa to let the children know that we are safe," she said quietly.

"What about you?"

"I shall stay here for one more night. I have some important matters about the forthcoming Races to discuss with Felix, amongst other things."

*

Lucia was pleased that there was enough light from the half-moon for her to see what was happening, but not too much that she couldn't hide in the shadows. She was standing in the narrow street at the rear of the Senate building wanting desperately for her instincts to be proved correct.

When the guard had come to take Decianus to the cells, she was enjoying the last sight she would ever have of him before he went to Hades. However, something had struck her as unusual in what had happened between him and the guard. They'd exchanged looks that two friends might share, rather than those between a jailer and condemned man. In the few moments that followed, she decided she had to do something about her growing suspicion. Hence, the excuse to Julius that had enabled her to be here, sword in hand, as if stalking a hidden animal.

It was halfway to dawn when yet another yawn was interrupted by the sight of the small back door opening very slowly. When the gap was large enough, Decianus moved his head out sufficiently for him to glance quickly both ways. Sure that the street was empty, he moved out closing the door silently behind him.

"I knew it!" she cried.

Decianus saw her close the distance to him before he had time to think. She placed the point of her sword against his throat.

"Of course you did. You were always cunning, like a she-wolf," he managed to say.

"Before I do the executioner's work for him, tell me how you did it."

"First, you tell me how you knew to be here."

"There was something about the looks you and the guard gave each other, as if you were close friends."

"Very clever! Friends is perhaps too strong a word for it. He's been a most trusted senior member of the Guard for many years. That was why he was there today. When I ran the Treasury he did lots of work for me. Let's say he was paid well to help me spirit away cash and jewellery. He knows I'm fabulously wealthy. I've promised him riches beyond his wildest meagre dreams. I've given him a small bruise on his head to make my escape look authentic."

"And when I kill you he will have gained a sore head for nothing."

"I have no weapon. You should arrest me again. You wouldn't kill an unarmed man."

"If the tables were turned you wouldn't hesitate. But you are correct about me."

She threw her sword to the ground, spreading her arms wide.

"I think I shall enjoy it more if I kill you with my bare hands."

In what seemed to her like not much more than the blink of an eye he brought a short knife out of his clothing to lunge at her with all his strength. Instinctively, she moved back, taking hold of his outstretched arm. Gripping it with both her hands, she crashed it down across her raised thigh, breaking the bones in his wrist.

Screaming in pain, he forgot all about defending himself. Lucia swept his legs from under him, sending him crashing onto his back. Dazed, he offered no resistance. Acting out of instinct, she picked up her sword. Then she reminded herself that it would be too swift a death for her to use that on him. She placed it back on the ground, leaving her hands free. Placing one knee on the ground with the other on his chest, she put her hands on his throat.

Her grip began to tighten slowly. Bending her head close to him, she whispered in his ear.

"This is for the whipping you gave my mother and for causing her death."

Her grip tightened. He tried to knock her away with his one good arm. She took hold of this hand, bending back a finger till it snapped. She returned her hands to his throat.

"This is for the rape and death of my beautiful sister."

The gurgling sounds increased, his legs thrashing wildly.

"This is for ordering my rape."

His eyes began to bulge.

"This is for slaughtering my Marac when he tried to save me from you."

His body jerked violently.

"And this is for all my people who you sent to their deaths."

She squeezed as hard as she could, keeping up the pressure. Gradually his pleading eyes, gazing terror-stricken into hers, glazed over. His body became still. A while later, she realised it was over. She stopped squeezing. She felt an overwhelming sense of relief, totally at peace for the first time since before the rebellion all those years ago. She had finally avenged all those thousands of deaths. Their spirits could rest peacefully.

Getting to her feet, she moved her eyes away from the pathetic body which no longer had a purpose, to the sword and knife on the ground. She turned and disappeared into the night, leaving them behind.

Chapter 67

"I didn't recognise that old man," Lucia admitted. "I only met him once when he came to our settlement."

"Titus became his Staff Officer after me," Julius said. "He got on with him better than I did. It meant he kept in touch with him after he retired. It was fortunate for me he did. Titus told me that Bolanus had said he wished to bring Decianus as his witness. So, he went to see Paulinus to find out more about him."

"That monster will cause no more deaths."

"I was too busy looking at Paulinus to notice what went on with Decianus. My only regret is that it wasn't my pair of hands that did it."

"Olsar will say the same thing, I'm sure. I must go to find him to give him the news."

"Did Decianus beg you to spare him?"

"He never got the chance. He did try to trick me, but I was expecting something from him, particularly when I put my sword down."

"Why did you take that risk?"

"I decided in that moment that I wanted to make the act of killing him after all this time more personal."

"It was certainly that."

"After it was over I made another decision. If the Gods allow it that will be the last life I shall take. All the hatred and anger deep inside me faded into nothing as his life ebbed away. Come, we need to find Olsar."

They eventually found Miriam and Olsar relaxing in the garden with Sarah.

"Lucia!" Olsar shouted when he saw her approaching. "Anything to tell me from your meeting with Felix?"

Lucia apologised to Olsar for her deception, giving him a full explanation of the events leading to the death of Decianus.

"You seem strangely unaffected by the news, my friend," Julius noted.

"If it wasn't to be me, then I'm satisfied it was Lucia and not an impersonal executioner that did it. I had thought he might even be given the right to take his own life because of the influence of his family. I really would have felt that the three of us had been cheated if that had happened. I suppose I feel relief now that it's over."

"Tell them about your news and how you feel about that," Miriam prompted.

"After the trial I was outside the doors waiting to come in to rescue you two if necessary," he joked. "Titus saw me and came over. I thought he was going to order me to take my hand off my sword again. Instead he told me it was time for me to end my work for Felix at the Circus."

"He can't just do that," Lucia declared indignantly.

"He wants me to become his second-in-command in the Praetorian Guard."

"Isn't that marvellous?" Miriam cried. "It means that our future here together is secure."

"That's no more than you both deserve," said Julius. "Lucia and I now need to know what Vespasian has in mind for us."

*

"No doubt you've heard about the death of Decianus two nights ago when he was trying to escape," Vespasian enquired.

"Most unusual set of circumstances," Julius replied with a straight face. Lucia said nothing.

"Titus thinks it must have been thieves."

"Most likely," Julius agreed.

"We can't understand why a sword and knife were left at the scene. Surely, thieves would have taken them. They are quite valuable. And why strangle him when it would be easier and quicker to use those weapons. Don't you agree, Lucia?"

Lucia nodded.

"The strangest thing of all is that the bruises on his neck were made by slender fingers, as if a woman had done it. What do you think, Lucia?"

Lucia just shrugged her shoulders.

"I suppose we shall never know for sure who did it," Vespasian said with a grin. "However, let's talk about you two. After recent events I've decided you'd probably benefit from a period away from Rome. I'm appointing you to the position of Governor of the Province of Aquitania, Julius."

"Thank you, Sir," Julius managed to reply, despite his astonishment. "It's a great honour." He looked to Lucia to see her reaction.

"And you, Lucia. Are you going to say anything at all today?" Vespasian teased.

"When do we have to leave?" she muttered.

"There's no pressing urgency, but soon."

"Then I have a request to make that's in your power to grant."

"Name it!"

"Since I'm going to leave Rome, I may never have another opportunity to do what I would like to request of you. I want to take part in the chariot races which are due to start the day after tomorrow."

"But women are banned from racing," Julius said, just as startled as Vespasian by her request.

"Which is why I'm asking the Emperor to make me an exception for just one race."

"You do realise that by then it will be known by all those on the terraces that you are Boudica's daughter," Vespasian explained. "Learning of that will have angered them to start with. Hearing they are to witness a woman charioteer will make them much worse.

Should I also mention that it's very dangerous?"

"If Felix can accept all that to allow me to race for him, so can I."

"It's just too dangerous," Julius warned. "We have just achieved the happiness that we've been searching for. Why put it at risk?"

"Perhaps riding the chariot in this way will finally put my past to rest. I have to do it."

"I shall make an announcement authorising it," said Vespasian.

Chapter 68

Olsar was giving his last instructions to Lucia.

"All the other three Charioteers resent you challenging them. They regard a woman competing against them as an insult."

"That doesn't surprise me," Lucia replied. "I can't decide whether to let them win to prevent them from being shamed," she quipped.

"They will try all sorts of tricks to take you out of the race."

"All of which I'm prepared for."

"Maybe, maybe not," Julius advised. "Just be content to take part. You really don't have to win."

Lucia frowned at him.

"Both of you, please go to join the others in the royal pavilion. You're making me nervous. And before you say anything about the horses, Olsar, I know them as well as you do."

"That is the signal for her race," Felix stated nervously from his position in the royal pavilion. "Look! Her White team is leading the four chariots onto the track."

The parade lap was greeted with derision. Vespasian was enjoying every moment of it. When Lucia's chariot drew level with him, he rose from his seat to give her an exaggerated wave of his arm in acknowledgement and support. He sat down again as the other three passed by. The terraces quietened as a result. The four chariots got into their places at the starting line. Lucia had been drawn on the outside, the worst position.

"I suspect that this is more than accidental," Julius commented.

"Of course it is," said Felix. "Fortuna has decided to give her the slowest but safest position. By the first bend she will be coming last and out of harm's way."

Felix was correct. At the first turn, Red was in the lead, followed by Green and then Blue. This was still the case after the first lap had been completed. Early in the second lap Lucia had drawn level on the outside of the Blue chariot. The charioteer concentrated so much on trying to force Lucia wide he failed to anticipate the arrival of the next turn. His team of horses galloped straight on past the turning point. It allowed Lucia to cut inside on the bend.

At the start of the third lap Lucia was close behind the Green team. Her previous overtaking manoeuvre had won her some support in the crowd. Completing the next turn, she noticed that the inner horse had led the Green team very sharply and hence very slowly round the tight bend. At the next turn Lucia drove her horses in a fast, wide arc outside and around Green. By the time her opponent realised that she hadn't run wide accidentally, it was too late for him. Lucia drove on past him into second place.

The Red charioteer glanced back at the start of the fourth lap. By now, there were as many in the crowd cheering for White as there were for him. He could see that, unhindered by chariots in front of her, Lucia with the fastest team was rapidly gaining on him. With just over one lap to go the two chariots were racing nose to tail. Lucia, close behind Red, was weaving from side to side desperately trying to pass.

Coming out of the next-to-last turn, Red moved more to the outside allowing a gap on the inside to develop. Lucia headed her horses in that direction without hesitation.

"Be careful!" Olsar screamed, even though he knew she couldn't hear him. "It's a trap."

Lucia was almost alongside the Red charioteer before she realised that the gap was closing. She tried to slow her team. The sudden narrowing of the space crated panic in her horses. Their frantic movements made the chariot move from side to side until the inner wheel was destroyed against the retaining wall. The chariot, still travelling at high speed, dipped sharply sideward. Unable to hang on, Lucia was thrust head first against the wall. The ruined, empty chariot moved on, leaving Lucia's body rolling along in the dust of the track.

"Get her to safety," Felix shouted to nobody in particular.

The two remaining charioteers had enough time to see what was happening. They managed to steer around her motionless body. Those in the Royal Pavilion stared in horror as attendants dashed onto the track to carry Lucia back under the terraces. Felix looked at Julius and Olsar, sadly shaking his head at them. All three dashed off to the treatment rooms.

*

Julius looked down on Lucia's unmoving dust-covered body. He could see a large gash on her forehead.

"She just had to do it. She had to face danger one last time."

"The fault is all mine," Felix moaned. "I should never have let her use my team. I thought she was invincible, that she couldn't die."

"Driving a small war chariot across the open fields of Britannia is one thing," said Olsar. "Racing against seasoned, ruthless charioteers in the Circus Maximus is something quite different. I should have made her realise that she lacked the necessary experience."

"What are you talking about? What happened?" Lucia asked weakly. Her eyes remained closed. "The last thing I remember is beginning the parade lap. My head hurts."

*

One week later, a few days before they were to begin the start of their journey to Aquitania, Julius and Lucia were lying in each other's arms reflecting on recent events.

"Was the race worth it?"

"Of course! Apart from the cuts and bruises. I think it's finally put my past behind me."

"Just as my mother and father are facing up to it."

"That's true! They were shocked at first when they discovered who I'd been and what I'd done. Although, Lucius really liked the gladiator bit."

"I think my mother secretly admires what you achieved despite all the obstacles you faced."

"What do you think of Miriam and Olsar's situation?"

"And Sarah! Olsar has finally found a family and a home. He will be successful in that role in the Guard for years to come. Vespasian will be Emperor for some years yet. Then he will be succeeded by Titus."

"That only leaves our children and Caris for us to think about," Lucia reminded him.

"Naturally, they will come with us."

"The children, yes, but not Caris."

"What are you saying?"

"She told me today that the she won't be joining us."

"Does she want to stay with Procilla?"

"No! Felix has asked her to live with him. She's accepted. She says he calls her Venus, his Goddess of Love. Sound familiar?"

When they stopped laughing, Julius remarked that he thought they suited each other and would be very happy.

"Then there are the two of us," said Lucia. "We have a great adventure ahead in the coming years starting in Aquitania. Do you think we shall ever see Britannia again?"

"Only the Gods could answer that."

Printed in Great Britain
by Amazon